THE DAY OF THE SPACE VOYAGER

James Parker Walker

Copyright © 2024 James Parker Walker

COVER ART

Carlyle Alan Walker

DEDICATION

This book is dedicated to my brother,
Brian, and my sister-in-law, Tanya.

Two beautiful, hard working treasures who opened their
home to me during a chapter of my life when I felt I had
lost everything, including my way. Most of this manuscript
was written, and my way rediscovered, under their snow
covered roof in the woods. Their love of family, nature, and
heroic canines embodies the themes herein.

ACKNOWLEDGEMENTS

This story, a parable about spiritual transformation, was born from my own journey of self-discovery. Trapped in a prison of institutional religion and a bizarre version of Christian nationalism, I thankfully managed to escape, find, and embody my true self. Putting this personal tale of emancipation into words has been an arduous process, but a trail that I did not walk alone. Thank you to all who have been on this space voyage with me—some I kept in touch with, some live on as characters in this book, and some have changed the trajectory of my life. I want to express gratitude to my family and close friends who encouraged and supported me along the way.

My sincere thanks to Vincent Isaac Page, who acted as my philosophical sherpa, helping me carry my heavy spiritual and emotional gear during this seemingly impossible trek. Our many thought-provoking conversations over beers at smoke-filled Sonny's, a dive bar in Pittsburgh, shaped much of this work.

Most of all I want to thank Heidi Duelfer, the best person I know, for her expert literary skills, incredible heart, and, in all things, invaluable support. Without her, this book would not exist, on paper or even as an idea. Thank you, Heidi, for your devotion, for the hours spent editing this manuscript, and for enthusiastically prodding this book towards completion.

CONTENTS

PROLOGUE

GALILEO'S MIDDLE FINGER

Galileo Galilee's middle finger was kept in a glass egg for centuries in a museum in Florence, Italy—an ancient city on the planet Earth. The finger was kept a few blocks from the Basilica di Santa Croce, a church where the rest of his body had been entombed, along with Michelangelo, Machiavelli, Rossini, and many other artists, craftsmen and historical figures of that age. The middle finger had been snapped off and saved by an antiquarian, Anton Francesco Gori, when Galileo's body was moved from a dark, forgotten corner into a place of light and prominence ninety-five years after his death. Why Anton saved the finger and why the museum held it under glass for so many years was a mystery.

Galileo, one of that planet's first stargazers, was not, at first, particularly interested in the stars, or the far-off worlds in the cosmos, more than anyone else in his time. He originally wanted to be a monk, a religious leader, rebelling against his father, who wanted him to go into medicine. But Galileo was born with a curse, the eye, as I would learn later it to be called: an inner understanding that causes the bearer to bring illumination to others, which usually leads to their own destruction. One who has the eye sees what others cannot. They never stop asking questions. They prod—question upon question. Questions that kick up anger and fear. That's why the eye is considered a curse. People who question things are not welcome, especially in wealthy and established institutions.

Those with the eye usually get themselves into

trouble, such as the Dominican friar, Giordano Bruno, one of the first in his civilization to propose that the stars were distant suns, surrounded by their own worlds, and that those worlds might foster life of their own, something we take as common knowledge now. But, in his world, in his day, this was not commonplace. In fact, it was more like heresy. He was tried by the Roman Inquisition and burned at the stake.

Even with the threat of death, Galileo insisted on thumbing his nose at all institutions. He was defrocked from the ministry for asking hard questions about God at church. He was marginalized as a professor in the universities where he taught, refusing to run with the herd, refusing to wear a robe when he taught and refusing to accept what others claimed as truth.

His motivation for designing and building spyglasses, or what later would be called telescopes, was purely financial. He just wanted to produce something that would make money. He first peddled his spyglass to investors and merchants in Venice for use in the harbor and on ships. But then, he took his telescope home and the questioner couldn't help himself. One night, he pointed his contraption toward the moon, and then the stars, and then the planets. He discovered mountains and valleys on a moon that he was told was a giant, flattened mirror in the sky. He discovered moving stars he had been told were fixed in the sky and operated by angels. He discovered satellites orbiting the planet earthlings called Jupiter, and then deduced that Earth's moon must be orbiting the Earth, and the Earth must be orbiting the sun. He was told that the Earth was the center of the universe, but it was false and he had proof.

What I discovered during my time spent with the

space voyager is that what we truly desire is that same eye: to see what others cannot, to see the truth underneath the deceptions.

However, the masses willingly seek out the shadows. They prefer answers over questions. Ignorance is bliss, as they say. Sometimes the eye opens and we see things we don't want to see. The knowledge turns our world upside down, questions violently rip from us everything we've known.

Galileo was brought to trial by the Roman Inquisition and found guilty of heresy. He was forced to kneel before the God of the masses, abandon his completely false opinion and recant his entire life's work. Which he did. He recanted, and as a result was not burned at the stake, but sentenced to house arrest for the rest of his life.

There was a famous painting by Bartolomé Esteban Murillo of Galileo sitting in prison. In the picture, he has a nail in his hand and he sits staring at a wall where he has etched the image of the sun and the earth and the moon. And under the picture he has written in Latin:

e pur si muove

"And yet it moves."

Galileo, Bruno, Copernicus—they were right, and the masses were wrong. The Earth does indeed revolve around its star, as all bodies do. But the church would never admit it; even when presented with irrefutable evidence. It wasn't until centuries later that they acknowledged they had erred in condemning Galileo for asserting that the Earth revolves around the sun. And in the 2008th year, the church announced the plans to celebrate the 400th anniversary of Galileo's discovery by erecting a statue of him inside the walls of the Vatican, the holy city. Two months later, however, after the celebration was over, the plans for the statue were scrapped.

But no matter. A statue of Galileo wasn't needed, and isn't needed, for us to see. What we needed, we found. We needed a constant reminder to question everything, always. The reminder was discovered in a tiny glass egg in Florence.

Galileo's middle finger, which, strangely enough, turned out to be the key.

I tell you all this, my most excellent Theophilus, to prepare you for the story I'm about to share. Perhaps this attempt to explain what happened will open the door to reconciliation and peace. Perhaps it will help us accept the realities in which we live, allowing us to enter this new existence without being burned at the stake. And once we've passed through this threshold, may we have the courage to step through the next one. For the universe we dwell in will not be anything like the one to come.

So, as you may have guessed already, this document you are holding is not my recantation. Oh no, I do not recant. I cannot recant what I've seen with my eye. For once it is seen, it cannot be denied. On the contrary, what you are holding is my manifesto. A documented journey that was both outward and inward, which is important to note. For the old saying is true: looking out, we dream, looking in, we awaken.

e pur si muove

CHAPTER ONE

THE HERMIT

I met the space voyager on my one hundred and second birthday. Or at least I thought I was a hundred and two. And I thought it was my birthday. And I thought he was the space voyager.

It was the second half of the 21st century, according to the archaic calendar used on Earth at that time. Of course, depending on when and where these pages are delivered to you, my most excellent Theophilus, these events may or may not have taken place yet.

But more about that paradox later.

I stood at the sink rinsing out the dishes—my one coffee cup, the dog bowl. It was that time of evening, just after the sun had gone down, getting dark, but not there yet. The wind caused the snow to fly thick in all directions, through the frigid air, across the meadow. As I watched the choreography out of the kitchen window, and my own weathered face reflected at me in the glass, a sudden icy breeze blew in under the cracks of the cabin door and lifted some of my pages off of the table onto the floor. I turned off the water, dried my hands, and noticed my face reflected in the window. I looked exhausted, a corpse, beaten down by the decades.

The cabin was one room: a bed, a table set, a sink, a hearth, a pair of electrical outlets and a light that hung from the ceiling. There was also an old, orange armchair in the corner, the kind that sits low, almost to the floor. It had a small footstool covered with a wool army blanket before it, acting as an ottoman. Most days, I could be found there, napping or staring at the ceiling. It was all I wanted or needed. And I was hoping it would all soon come to an end.

After experiencing one great loss after another, the burdens that an old soul carries when outliving everyone ever known to them, I thought getting away from the world and living like a hermit would be an appropriate final chapter to a life that didn't seem to have an ending. Sadly, the peaceful solitude was turning to cold isolation and loneliness, causing me to feel untethered.

I gathered the papers from the floor and returned them to the table and sat, looking over all the meaningless words and drawings and doodles, my tangled mind spilled out on paper. I picked up my pen and continued writing words, sentences, many of which are contained in the very pages you are reading now. How I was able to share events that had not yet occurred or where exactly these words had even come from, some of them not in this language, or any language I'd ever been aware of, was a mystery to me and caused me to wonder if I was suffering from dementia. The pages looked like the senseless markings of a madman. Whether events were actually occurring or merely movies in my mind, hallucinations, was always a question, which has yet to be answered and is something I wrestle with even now.

And what is *now*? In an infinite universe, full of infinite possibilities, infinite versions of you and infinite versions of me, what does it mean to experience *now*? I sat there, in the cabin, in the *now*, writing this. And you, it would seem, sit there, *now*, reading. Are these the same *now*? Or different *nows*, very far apart? Or is "far apart" just an illusion and there is only *now* and nothing else. Can you imagine this? A *now* where I am writing, and you are reading at once. That this message is coming to you instantaneously, from my mind to my pen, to your eyes and into your mind, as if we were gifted with telepathy? All is happening at once. I met the space voyager, I am meeting the space voyager, and I sat at the table writing, in that cold shack, waiting for the space voyager's arrival, *now*.

The concept of infinity is a strange thing, and it's perhaps impossible for us to fully conceive of that terrifying immensity. Infinity is not just the largest number you could ever count to, plus one; infinity is the notion that every possible thing that could exist, will exist, and will exist, in fact, an infinite number of times. This includes you and me. It's incredible to think about. Especially on a clear night, gazing into the starry sky that has no end, when the acknowledgment comes that we are so tiny compared to infinity. And yet, we, who are so insignificant, can reach up and touch something so expansively large.

I was contemplating this very thing while I wrote in the frigid shack. The pen sometimes seemed to move without me even thinking the words. At times, the words flowed like a fountain, and other times, it would require a few hours to produce a phrase. But, as I had nowhere to go and much time to spend, I was patient and deliberate. The pages piled up.

That evening, however, something different happened—something unexpectedly marvelous: I realized I had come to the end. The book was nearly finished. All that remained was the epilogue, a poetic signing off, and this manuscript would be complete. I paused, to enjoy the moment, to admire my work and my withered old hand, my fingers straining to grasp the pen—the wrinkled skin sunken in between the thin bones and purplish veins. My entire body ached. Every joint was searing with arthritis.

My eyes, nearly frosted over, caused the world around me to blur, as if looking out a window covered in ice. I could barely walk, eat, or breathe. Clearly, I was a finite being.

Or was I? Am I?

I had outlived every significant person in my life, had endured every loss. I was ready, and had been ready, for my own end to come for a long time. The daily physical pain, coupled with the emotional torture of loss, loneliness and isolation, had led me down into dark places more than once. The results had been some bumps and bruises, cuts, and limps. And yet, I lived on as if something was holding me prisoner, keeping me from escaping this life. I told myself that I was subconsciously waiting for Cooper, a black labrador retriever and roommate, to pass away first. What would he do, after all, if I was not there to care for him? But he most heroically held on with me. As a matter of fact, I sometimes wondered if Cooper was capable of aging at all.

Our days together were slow, quiet, and uneventful. Pulling some dried beans from the pantry in the cellar for dinner or watering the plants in the small greenhouse behind the shack were considered major tasks. Mostly, I would sleep, write, smoke my pipe, and sit in my orange chair, waiting to die. I had done everything there was to do in life. I had seen everything there was to see. And I felt that even if there was nothing more beyond death, then not existing would be better than existing. Or so I thought.

I sat at the table for what felt like a few hours, contemplating what the final words of this message should be, letting the fire in the hearth diminish to a few orange coals and then to almost complete dark. The temperature in the cabin dropped rapidly as the cold air poured through the gap under the door. Cooper pulled himself up from his bed near the hearth and ambled to where I was sitting to curl himself around my legs for warmth. And yet, I let the chill have its way. Usually, I would go to the stack next to the fire and add a stick, but the stack was gone, and my tired body refused to even begin the long trek to the woodpile outside against the shed. Maybe part of me thought of letting the cold take me. It was my birthday, after all. What better day to call the end than the beginning?

But really, I had hoped to be haunted by the ghosts. I called them ghosts, for there was no other way to describe the phenomena, which had appeared from time to time within the four planked walls of the shack, always late at night and always in the deep cold, the kind of cold that causes breath to turn into ice crystals. The crystals would drift through the air across the room, play with the light from the overhead bulb and reveal what I perceived to be ghosts. They were almost undetectable, but if I remained still, I could sense a presence and that presence would move about, soft and distant, as if they were children playing on the other side of a waterfall. During one such appearance, I convinced myself that there was more than one, that they were occupying the other three chairs at the table, carrying on and laughing, as if at a dinner party. I joined in the revelry, myself, for a moment, until I stopped laughing as a sudden jolt of fear ran through me. Not a fear of the ghosts, but of the thought that I may be descending into madness. The following morning, I shook it off as a trick of the mind.

But now I sat at the table, my manuscript before me nearly completed, and my old frail body frozen to the core. I allowed it to freeze, though I wasn't uncomfortable in the least; I watched the plumes jet out over the table. Soon, the vapor became an instant cloud of sparkling ice. The shimmering flakes danced in the air above the table before stopping and collecting on the something that was there, confirming my suspicions. My heart jumped to the ceiling, but I stayed, placing both hands, palms down, on the table to hold me in place, then I drew a breath and blew another swirling cloud of tiny diamonds across the table, which accumulated on the object like the first flakes of snow on the ground, to reveal the outline of a face.

At first, I did not know what I was looking at, whether it was the face of God or death, an apparition or my own image reflected to me somehow. But it was definitely a face: a faint outline, a ghostly wisp of a being, which seemed to be speaking to me, calling out for me perhaps, though I could not hear a thing. While much of the face was obscured, its eyelids blinked, and its lips were moving. Friend or foe, I could not tell. Then, the head shifted up to the ceiling and then to the door, eyes and mouth open wide as if shouting. The shack door blew open by a powerful gust of wind, which broke the stillness and sent the particles that revealed the phenomena scattering about. The ghost vanished and the light bulb above me went out.

Cooper jumped up and bolted out of the door and onto the front porch of the cabin, scanning the horizon. I grabbed my cane to pull myself out of the chair, and I followed, albeit much slower and more labored, every step taking all my strength and concentration. Outside, the wind threw the snow about and through the doorway. Cooper stood motionless, gazing into the sky.

"Coop. Get in here."

As I grabbed the knob to swing the door closed, something behind forcefully pushed me through the doorway. I stumbled down the porch steps and onto the snow-covered path, landing face first, smacking my head and chest onto the frozen ground. I saw the blanket of exploding stars that comes with a sharp hit to the head. My stomach turned into a knot, and I pulled my arm into my side to protect what was probably a few cracked ribs. The pain was paralyzing. Cooper came to my side, placing his nose in my thigh as I lay still in the snow, the wind pelting me with ice. I took what I thought was my last deep breath, which sent a stabbing pain from my ribs across my body. I imagined myself being turned to stone and my soul set free.

But then, to my surprise, there came another breath. And then another. I found the strength to turn onto my side just enough to be able to peek back toward the door to see who was there. What was it that pushed me? The doorway was clear, other than a stream of snow flooding into the dark room.

Rolling from my side onto my back, my face caught a flurry of flakes as they came down from the night sky. The never-ending stream of white specks fell like stars and the effect made me feel as if I were traveling time. I was reminded of my father, who had died of cancer when I was just thirty years old. For his last days, he was sent home to pass away, surrounded by friends and family. When they pulled him on a gurney from the ambulance to wheel him into the house, no one covered his face to protect him from the heavy rain that fell that day. When he was finally in a space that had been cleared in the living room, teary-eyed kin came to his side. The dog licked his hand. My mother fetched a towel and returned to dry his face. But he stopped her. Leave it there, he said. The rain was like kisses from heaven, a promise of the infinite.

I closed my eyes, let the snow dance the same way on my face, and holding onto the hope of that same promise, I tried to release my life. But, as usual, my life remained—fixed in time and space on the cold ground. Instead of a freeing release, I felt the all-too-familiar drag of the world beneath. Something was holding me down. My whole life I could sense a pull that not only affected my physical body, causing severe pain and discomfort, but my psyche as well, sinking my mind into dark, secluded places. I had always felt as if I were a pilgrim in a foreign land—a place that was alien to my mind and body.

I braced myself as something reached into me from underneath and seemed to pour into my body like poison. The images of a lifetime of loss and hurt filled my mind. Loved ones who had left, never to return. A wave of regret and anxiety practically washed me away as I lay paralyzed, half covered with the fresh dusting of cold snow and instead of death, which I would have gladly welcomed, pain—the pain that comes with loss—unbearable pain. I clinched my eyes shut and writhed on the ground, fighting some unseen power. Cooper curled his body into my side to protect me.

It was moments like this, when the darkness came, that I would turn to the practices of transcendentalism. I would sit at the table in the shack with my eyes closed and I would disconnect from my body and the pain. I envisioned myself gliding through the room like a spirit. I liked to think of myself as a comet, flying up through the chimney, and out into the night. In my mind, I'd fly up into the mountains, along the creeks and spills and cascades of mighty rivers. Up and out, above the wooded hills that had once belonged to my great grandfather, when he was alive. I would sometimes see him out there, perhaps as another ghost, cutting the trees and thinning out the brush. I'd wave, he'd grab and tilt his cap toward me. And then I'd see how far I could rise without stopping.

What is the capacity of the human mind? How far can it roam beyond our planet, soaring away from it until it is just a dot, past the red planet and through the floating fragments, the Graveyard, past Jupiter, and the rings of Saturn? Did I really travel there? Or was it all in my mind?

On my back, on the frozen ground, I had a strange, metaphysical moment—I saw, in my mind's eye, the space voyager, millions of miles away, approaching our solar system for the first time in eons. To this day, I'm still unsure why this vision would come to me while I was on my back in the snow that first night. Perhaps the space voyager was trying to communicate with me. Or perhaps, in some other reality, I was standing there next to him. Whatever the case, there he stood at the great window in the vessel's cockpit, his hand on his forehead, as if witnessing a tragic horror.

Can you imagine what that must have been like for him, to return home, only to find it in ruins?

There's no way I could have known that the years that I had spent in exile, the years in the wilderness, living in a shotgun shack, had been a time of great sorrow, horror, and heartache for the space voyager as well.

We had lost everything. Both of us.

In 1596 (by Earth's calendar), a stargazer named Johannes Kepler believed that the ratio between planetary masses would only conform to design with the addition of a planet between Jupiter and Mars. Later in the 18th century, Immanuel Kant and mathematician Johann Heinrich Lambert would ask: "Who knows whether an already planet is missing which has departed from the vast space between Mars and Jupiter?"

Already planet. What kind of cold way is that to refer to someone's home?

In my trance, I continued to watch the space voyager, as he walked on Ceres, the largest of the asteroids in the belt, searching for any remnant of anything, some clue to help him figure out what had happened, where they had all gone. He only found rocks, of course. Rocks, ice, mud, ammonia, and methane-spewing volcanoes. Can you imagine what that must have been like to walk on the world that you've known, beautiful, bountiful, and full of life, and now, a hellscape?

My meditative trance was broken by Cooper, who rose to his feet and began pulling on my shirtsleeve. He wanted me to get up.

"He is coming. You must live."

In my memory, the words came from my mind, but now I wonder if it was Cooper, trying somehow to communicate with me.

Fighting gravity, a numbing pain in my side and my skeleton, I followed the lab's lead—rolling, crawling, walking, and falling and crawling again, clamoring to the greenhouse behind the cabin, through the wind, snow and night. My hands and feet were numb from the cold. I reached the wrought iron and glass door and stumbled into the little conservatory, collapsing onto the dirt floor.

The old greenhouse was an eight-by-ten-foot, metal framed, old worn, coke bottle-like glass structure. It gathered enough sunlight during the day to keep its heat, but needed the wood-burning stove at night. Burlap bags of seeds were piled in the middle. The shelves and tables around the perimeter held various sized planters where vegetation of all kinds made root. Carrots, turnips, and beets. Chard, kale, and arugula. Wild roses, orchids, and fiddlehead ferns. Some were food. Some were medicine. Some were friends.

I'd spent many hours working in the greenhouse, to the point of becoming one of the vines myself. The perfect symmetry of all things in nature—flower petals, corn husks, maple leaves, had always fascinated me. The greenhouse was a place of balance and rootedness for me, like the sweet, earthy smell of the air when hiking in the mountains. But as I lay on the floor, defrosting, it was its warmth I valued most.

Once I could feel my hands and feet again, I pulled myself to standing with the help of Cooper's strong back and the stack of burlap sacks. The dull pain in my head combined with the sharp pain in my side caused my breath to stop when I tried to take a step—then I half-collapsed, doubling over, coughing blood into my hand and onto the floor. My vision blurred, and the room was spinning, but I tried to focus, scanning the long shelf above the iron stove, in search of relief. In mason jars, herbs and fungi I had gathered in the woods were stored, each one labeled with a stretch of masking tape. White willow bark, devil's claw, ginger, turmeric, lion's mane, and psilocybin cubensis, those small mushrooms with the golden caps.

I loaded a half dozen jars in my arms and limped my way back to the cabin, stopping at the woodpile by the shed on my way to resupply the hearth. Cooper and I cautiously reentered the shack through the dark threshold from where I had been thrown out of earlier, fully expecting to encounter whatever presence awaited us. But when I flipped on the dangling light bulb, I found the shack was empty. Relieved, I shut the door, set the jars on the table, put the sticks on the hearth, tended to my wounds, and made tea.

It was not long until the fire had regained its full strength. The tea brewed, and I sank like a defeated battleship into my orange arm chair, my broken body melting into its soft cushions. Cooper returned to his nest beside the hearth, and we both fell asleep. As my medicinal concoction did its work, my body went numb, and the pain subsided, I had a final vision of the space voyager, standing in the domed cockpit of his ship, watching as the third planet, blue, green, and bright, grew to fill the entire field of his vision.

"He is coming. You must live."

When I woke up, I could not tell if I had slept for a few hours, a few days, or a few millennia. I was popped awake by the rattling wooden planks of the shack. The ground beneath rumbled and shook. My first thought was that it was an earthquake, but then my teacup, which had been resting in its saucer on a small stack of books next to me, rose into the air. This was not an earthquake. I cleared my eyes and rose slightly in the chair to see what was happening. Cooper stirred as well, stumbling on his way, for the gravity in the cabin had changed; lighter objects in the room—paper, pens, forks, and socks—floated six inches above their resting spots.

My eyes ran from Cooper to the door and then up to the window. It was still dark, nothing to see outside but the night. But then, no—something was out there. Suddenly, large spotlights beamed down from above. I nearly jumped out of my skin. The shaking ground, the blinding light, the deep rumbling sound, the floating objects—what was happening? I scrambled to my feet and as I did; I experienced an intense rush to the head, activating my mind, as if it were turned on for the very first time.

Overwhelmed, I fell to the floor as the cabin filled with light. I was suddenly hyperaware of myself, my whole self, my surroundings: the wind, the snow, the heat in the hearth, the clicking of the metal pots hanging above the stove, every branch on every tree in the woods outside. It felt as if I were connected to it all. I surrendered, laying on my back, looking to the ceiling, processing the experience.

And that's when the lightbulb, hanging from the ceiling sprang to life. The hot glowing filaments within the bulb began to multiply and grow like the branches of a tree. The bright golden wires spread out even beyond the glass shell, reaching and winding and curling in all directions until it looked like a full-grown tree of hot, golden light with a trunk, limbs, branches, and leaves. It had leaves of gold that shimmered and waved and made the tree look as if it were on fire.

Waves of golden light, emanating from the tree's branches, splashed on the table, the walls, the sink, and the hearth, drowning every exposed inch of the room. The entire room seemed to be baptized in the eternal, lifting the veil of the temporal and revealed to me what I had only suspected to be near. At the table, the lavish light allowed the ghosts to be seen, all sharing in a meal, eating and drinking, unaware and undisturbed by the light or my presence. The light from the tree and the vision of the feasting ghosts—maybe I had died after all, I thought. And now I was entering the beyond.

When I put my hands to my face to see if I was still alive, the bones within my hand, under my skin seemed to glow with the same golden light that bathed the room—and the rest of me, skin, blood, and muscle, turned translucent. That's when the final word of my pages came to me. I heard a voice, speaking the final word for me to write.

Whether it was the tree, the table, or the ghosts, I did not know. But the word was clear and distinct.

I rolled onto my knees, and with the help of a chair, and my cane, was able to get to my feet, snatch the pen, which was still floating above the table, hold down an errant page and write the final phrases, completing the text. As I did, the ground stopped shaking, the bright light moved away, and the floating objects fell to the floor.

As fast as the tree had grown from the lightbulb, it shrank back down to the size of a seed. A seed of light, which fell from the lightbulb, landed on the pages stacked on the table, illuminated them for a moment, with a flicker, and then vanished.

"What the hell was that?"

Out the window, the bright light from above had moved away from the cabin and was rolling like a pool across the snow-covered meadow. I hobbled to the door, grabbed my coat from the hook, and slid my arms through. A green winter hat was jammed upon my head.

"Come on, boy. Let's go see."

I zipped up my coat, took the lantern off the hook and swung open the door. A brush of snow swept into the cabin as the black lab bolted out into the darkness. I stepped out onto the porch steps and looked up, scanning the skies. The light faded, moving up through the woods and into the mountains before disappearing completely.

The moment had passed. I stood on the porch in a daze, trying to understand what I had just witnessed. Was I finally losing it? The loneliness, isolation, the time spent ruminating; the time spent hallucinating—was it the tea?

But no, there must have been something—the dog was my proof—he kept barking as he ran into the woods.

The snow was subsiding and low-lying clouds, grey

and white, gave way to black sky and bright stars. Fueled by a sudden kick of adrenaline, which overrode all pain and ailments, I grabbed the snowshoes leaning against the side of the cabin, strapped them on, grabbed a pole and the lantern and hobbled towards the woods.

As I approached the tree line, I held the shaking lantern up to see what was there. The wind shifted, and a gust blew the hat off my head and my white beard flattened against my chest and neck. Even with the snowshoes, navigating the deep snow in the dark forest was difficult. I crutched each step with a limp, the right leg still affected by an accident years ago. This poor, old, worn-out body which struggled with stairs was now clamoring through the woods, through the thicket, looking for who knows what.

Cooper stopped barking, and the sound coming from between the trees was like nothing I'd ever heard before. It was a deep, rhythmic whirling, humming from above and underneath at the same time. I cautiously ventured on, lantern held high but swaying in my whitened grip, snow crunching under my feet. I must have trudged a few hundred yards when I came to a clearing where the trees gave way to the starry sky above. In the middle of the clearing sat the black lab, still as a statue, and oddly silent. He cocked his head backwards to look at me for a moment, before turning his gaze back toward the dark wood.

"What is it, Coop? What's out there?"

I had to breathe heavier now to keep up with my heart. I would have preferred it if the old dog had been barking or snarling or growling, then the appearance of a bear or a bobcat would have come as no surprise. But Cooper was right to sit in surrendered wonder, for what came out of the woods, through the dark trees, was no bear or bobcat. I fell back onto my butt in the snow, fighting to keep the lantern pointed toward the object. I thought it was an eye at first, a small round object the size of a golf ball that slowly grew to the size of a grapefruit as it neared. It was floating in the air as if a child had blown it from a bubble wand. It looked light and fragile, glowing slightly silver and blue. If I hadn't been so terrified, I would have taken more time to appreciate its beauty.

It approached me, traveling over Cooper's head. The dog's gaze remained fixed on the orb. Neither of us dared even move as the object slowly floated to the place where I sat in the snow. As it got closer, I could see inside of it. Stars. Thousands of them. Possibly millions.

The translucent ball seemed to contain the vastness of space. When it finally stopped before me, just a few feet from where I lay, I could see that the silver globe was spinning. Streaks of light and sudden flashes sped across its face, revealing the velocity of its rotation. In a matter of moments, the orb grew from the size of a grapefruit to the size of a basketball to the size of a car to the size of the cabin. I could feel its intensity, force, and gravity. It was pulling me in.

I scrambled to stand up and maybe get away, but as I did, the draw of the spinning ball increased. The lantern was pulled from my hand and sucked into the orb. On the inside of the bubble, it just floated there, as if in the eye of a hurricane. The branches of the surrounding trees bent and reached towards the dark spot. If they hadn't been rooted in the ground, I imagine they would have joined the lantern. I kicked at it. My snowshoes were ripped off my feet and sucked into the void, and then I joined them. It happened in an instant. One second, I was turning to run back toward the cabin and the next second; I was floating inside with the lantern and the snowshoes.

While floating in the orb, fresh air filled my lungs. I felt like I was breathing for the first time. The globe spun with rhythmic intensity as I floated within, around, sideways, and upside down. I squinted, trying to adjust my vision to see outside, but the world outside the ball seemed to have paused, as if time had stopped. The snowflakes hung still in the night. I reached for the inside edge of the orb, attempting to find some sort of grounding, some sort of help to control what was happening. And as I did, I looked at my hands. They were wrinkled and spotted from age, but now they were shedding skin. There was no pain. On the contrary, I could feel my whole body healing, my head and ribs. It felt as if the blood in my veins turned to gold—liquid gold—bright, warm, and flowing to every part of my body. My back straightened, every joint cracked as if being freed from rust and decay, and then my legs—they transformed, completely healed. The frost in my eyes cleared. The ringing in my ears stopped.

How is it possible? What is this thing? And where did it come from? And how did it transform my body, from the broken, tired 102-year-old rusted out pickup truck to a newly restored classic, the body of my young adult self, baby faced, with a full head of dark brown hair?

As the ball shrank with me inside of it, I panicked. I'll be crushed, I thought. But as the orb collapsed, it set me safely on the ground on both feet. My clothes were now too big. My coat hung on me like an old tarp. The ball shrank back down to the size of a grapefruit. The lantern and the snowshoes fell to the ground.

I held out my hand, and for a moment; the globe hovered just inches above it, still spinning violently. As it levitated energetically above my palm, I could hear a deep baritone voice singing in the distance. It was a soft hymn, which seemed to come from within the sphere and the far-off mountains at the same time. I could not make out the words, but the melody was hypnotic.

I grabbed the waistband of my pants as they fell toward my ankles. Cooper came to me and ducked behind my legs, still watching the marvel. As the orb pulled away from me and drifted back to where it came from, the music stopped, and I was jolted back to reality.

What is this? What is happening? Is this real?

The ball floated away in between a grove of trees and disappeared. In the distance, I could still hear the low, thick humming and I looked down at Cooper.

"Now what? Should we go back?"

I bent down to pick up my lantern and when I did, Cooper took it as a cue and darted ahead.

"Cooper. Hold on, boy. Wait up."

Thinking back on that moment, I don't think I truly appreciated the gift I had been given. I was jogging through the snow without snowshoes. The strength of my youth restored. What could be more precious? There is no way I would have been able to survive the events that followed with that old, tired body.

I must have hiked into the woods another two to three miles, and significantly up in elevation, giving my renewed heart and lungs a workout. All the while, the low humming noise continued. I would stop now and then to listen and make sure that I was getting closer. I remember clearly breathing in the crisp air and taking in the sacred beauty and stillness as I stood and listened. I was honing in on the source of the sound, but also giving thanks for every breath, for life, and for the mountain I was climbing, which was an experience I had forgotten.

When I got to the ridgeline, I saw the source of the

humming. At first glance, I thought my eyes were playing tricks on me. I thought perhaps what I saw was an optical illusion created by some high reaching tree branches. As I stepped into an opening in the tree covering above me, and my view became unobstructed, I saw the vessel for the first time. Slowly rotating just above the tree line was an enormous wheel. It looked as if someone had hung a gigantic ceiling fan in the sky. Resembling a big wagon wheel, it had a large cylinder-shaped middle piece with grand spokes equally fanned out to an outer rim.

You might wonder why I didn't turn and run back to the cabin in sheer terror. By the time I got to the wheel, having experienced the glowing tree, the orb, and the strange metamorphosis within my body, I wasn't as surprised to see the spacecraft—now I was intrigued.

When Cooper and I got to the clearing beneath the wheel, I could see the object's immensity. As it hovered and rotated above the mountain, I estimated it to be a couple of city blocks wide and a few stories tall. It looked ancient, with strange, indecipherable markings on all sides.

We waited a few minutes before a rush of courage bolstered me. I lifted the lantern and swung it back and forth as a welcome signal. At first, there was nothing, just more rotating of the giant wheel, and then I heard a loud crunch and a long, thin crack appeared at the bottom of the middle cylinder. Double doors at the bottom of the big wheel opened.

"He is coming. You must live."

CHAPTER TWO

THE THREE SISTERS

In the 1978th year, a group of Earth's geophysicists working for a Mexican oil company discovered something extraordinary. They were performing a magnetic survey of the Gulf of Mexico, north of the Yucatan Peninsula, when their instruments picked up a gravitational anomaly. They collected all the data and sat down at the table and mapped it out—the fit was perfect. A shallow, ninety miles in diameter, gravity magnetic bull's eye. The oil company, searching for a good place to drill, had found the impact crater that they would call Chicxulub. It had been created by an asteroid that hit the planet an estimated sixty-six-million years ago, which caused the most recent of the five known extinction events on Earth, until that point.

Sixty-six-million years was plenty of time for most of life on Earth to start all over again. Life finds a way—it always does. But sixty-six-million years. Five thousand years. Thirty days. Thirty seconds. These are measurements of time on Earth, regulated by gravity, but what time is it, really? Where is the universe clock, and how long has it been when you measure the time with that watch?

When the double doors of the big wheel opened up, I took a breath, and held it as if it would be my last one. The door opened completely with a clunk, and a dim, golden light pulsated from within. I did not dare remove my eyes from it, but with my hands, I reached down to find Cooper's head to draw him into my knee. And then it appeared—what looked like the same orb that I had encountered earlier in the evening slowly descended from the core of the wagon wheel.

Now the ball was the size of a Volkswagen Beetle, maybe about eight to ten feet in diameter, glowing silver and blue and spinning like a top. It came down through the trees like one of those big glass elevators they have in fancy hotels. When it was almost halfway to the ground, I could finally see that something or someone was inside. Every muscle in my body tensed to where I thought I'd collapse into myself.

What is this? From where? And what if it, whatever it is, is hostile?

I braced myself, my heart racing, as the rotating orb fell from just above my head to rest on the ground. I could see within. It was human, or appeared to be so anyway: arms, legs, torso, and head. Then, a hand reached for the outer edge of the globe and, holding open a hole in the skin of it, a person stepped out of the sphere and onto the snow-covered ground, the same spaceman from my vision.

Standing before me was a being about six to seven feet tall and completely naked, although he seemed somewhat unaffected by the frigid air that blew puffs of snow in all directions.

His skin was translucent with thin streaks of blue, green, purple, orange, and red emanating from his core, radiating out to every part of his body, including his head and face—a Van Gogh painting come to life. His soulful eyes, silver or baby blue like a Siberian wolf's, peered into my very being. His appearance was unexpectedly warm, welcoming and strangely familiar. He turned both hands open toward me, and I let out the breath that I'd been holding. I didn't think he'd kill me, at least for now. Cooper, as always, was braver than I and was led by his nose to the space voyager's hands. As he turned his hand over to caress the dog's head, the space voyager's eyes moved about, taking in the surrounding terrain: rocks, trees, snow, clouds, sky. And after a moment, he turned his sight toward me and whispered, "Ella."

At the time, I did not know what Ella meant, but I could tell, even at that moment, by the look on his face, that Ella was something very important. I shook my head, trying to show that I didn't understand. And then, he pointed to the sky, and said, "pay-ray-day-zay."

"Pay-ray-day…?" I tried to repeat.

"Pay-ray-day-zay," he said again, louder this time.

"What is pay-ray-day-zay?" I responded. "Sky? You come from the sky?" If I only knew how ridiculous I sounded.

"Payraydayzay," he repeated, his voice breaking. And then his face fell, his mouth dropped open, and he released the sob that he had been holding in. The bright ribbons of color underneath his skin slowed, reversed their motion, and dimmed to shades of grey. Then, he doubled over, his hands on his knees, and let out a cry.

"Payraydayzay," he whispered.

I just stood there watching, processing. I must admit that, in retrospect, most of my thoughts were selfish.

Good, I'm still alive.

Cooper instinctively did his best to console the newcomer. The space voyager, still in tears, went down to one knee and received the lab's gesture. Then he looked up at me once again with an expression on his face that pleaded for help. I was at a loss knowing how to respond, so we stared at each other for a few moments.

"I AM WILL," I shouted at a volume that was completely unnecessary. "WILLIAM HENRY," I pointed to my head with one hand and patted my chest with the other.

He nodded his head and slowly rose to his feet.

"Henry," he repeated.

"Yes," I said, feeling slightly victorious, "Henry. I am William Henry."

"Henry," he repeated once again, as if the word tasted terrible. He then shook his head and pointed at me as if he didn't agree. "Oakruum."

"No. Henry," I insisted. "William Henry."

The newcomer looked at me in disbelief and then looked at Cooper for help. Cooper, of course, was speechless, so the space voyager changed the topic.

He tapped his own chest. "Axzum," he said.

"Axzum? Your name is Axzum?" I responded, "Okay, good. Welcome, Axzum."

And then there was a pause, and in that pause, as the wind kicked up, swirling around, beating snow against our faces, we both pondered our next volley.

"Ella," he tried again with his hands open. "Payraydayzay." I shrugged and shook my head.

"No," I responded. "I don't know what that is."

"Where do you come from?" I followed. "Are you alone, or are there more?" I pointed up at the wagon wheel rotating slowly above us. He made the same gesture at me I had made at him. We were at a stalemate. The space voyager shivered, extraordinarily unprepared for the Colorado winter. Obviously ready to retreat, he motioned to me with his left hand out and his right hand pointed up toward the wheel. It was an obvious invitation.

I looked up at the rotating wheel, which at once looked out of this world and quite ordinary. I laughed.

"No, thanks."

He motioned again, insistent, but welcoming.

"No, please, there's no way I'm going up there."
And then I pointed with both hands in the other direction,
inviting him back to the cabin.

"Please, come, I have tea."

"Tea," he repeated.

"Yes, tea." I mimed a cup of tea to my mouth, as if
he knew what a teacup was.

"Oakruum. Tea."

He looked at me for a moment, debating, and then
he declined with the same motion I used in my refusal

"Please," I motioned, beckoning him again.

After a brief calculation, he accepted. The space
voyager turned and raised his arms in the air and the
translucent orb rose and returned to the ship. As the ball
ascended, the wheel stopped its rotation. The vessel
submerged into the treetops, nestling safely in the woods. It
didn't come entirely to the ground but didn't protrude above
the tops of the trees either, like a massive tree house hidden
in the forest. As Axzum turned back toward me, I removed
my coat and handed it to him.

He took it thankfully and wrapped it around his
body. It certainly wasn't enough, but it would have to do.

We walked back to the cabin, retracing the trail I
had made in the snow. As we hurried through the snow, I
was again made cognizant of my newly restored body. I felt
like I could run all the way back without even breathing
heavily. Even then, I contemplated the benefits of having
that kind of restorative power, the orb. I wondered exactly
how it worked and where it came from. With each step I
took, a new question was thrown onto the pile in my mind.
I can remember plotting my strategy for building some sort
of basis of communication with him.

Can you imagine? Here I was, walking back

through the woods with Axzum, trying to figure out how I'd summarize the entirety of human history. It's funny to think about. I did not know how ignorant I was—the things I was about to learn.

We had not gone very far when he halted in his tracks. I had taken a few more steps and then realized he had stopped behind me. I paused, and I looked back at him.

"What? What is it?"

"Oakruum," he said.

"I'm sorry. I don't know what that means."

"Henry."

"Yes."

What happened next nearly knocked me to the ground. He did not speak with his mouth, but I could hear his voice clearly in my head.

"Are you afraid of dying, William Henry?"

Perhaps I should have wondered if the origin of these words was in my own head, but I didn't. I somehow knew it was him. I somehow knew he was communicating with me.

"Are you afraid of dying?" he asked again, with words that I felt in my mind and my body. My instincts told me to run, and I stumbled a few steps away from him, holding up my hands.

"No. Please, don't hurt me."

Then he opened his hands, a gesture which I interpreted as, "I mean you no harm."

"Are you afraid of dying?" again, came from within me. Relieved but confused, I stopped retreating and considered the question.

Afraid of dying? What? Why is he asking me this? Am I afraid of dying? Looking back, I don't know if I've ever been asked a more important question.

It's strange. In my younger days, I would have instantly responded: No, of course, I'm not afraid. This would have been my courageous response, emboldened by my stalwart religious fervor. But now, on the other side of such blind faith, I looked at Axzum with confidence and after a moment responded,

"No, I am not afraid."

I wasn't afraid, and I'm still not afraid for other reasons—deeper, more profound reasons, which you will soon know.

An expression of relief came upon Axzum's face.

"You are not afraid of dying," he confirmed within me. "I am not afraid of dying as well. We can share in peace." The multi-colored ribbons floating beneath his skin sprang back to life, resuming their dance across his body.

I realize now why he asked me such a question. It's not exactly the first thing you ask someone after you meet them. We like to stick with "where are you from?" and "what team do you root for?" But in this case, looking back anyway, I can understand why it was important to him. It's not the death part that concerned him, but the fear. For, as we all now know, death is a friend and is not to be feared. But the fear of death is.

It was after this that Axzum could relax and the walk back to the cabin in the cold, star-filled winter night became a lighter affair. When we got to the creek, Axzum stopped before crossing, bent down for a moment, reached into the running water, and gathered a handful of pebbles from the creek bed. I tried to put myself into his shoes, to see our world, our planet, through his eyes, but how could I ever? I had no way of knowing where he had been and what wonders he had seen and experienced.

We reemerged from the woods after retrieving the snowshoes—the half-naked space voyager, the courageous black lab, and myself. Looking back, the memory makes me smile. I had entered the woods as an old, wizened, sickened and fearful man at the bitter end of a fractured narrative, and now, I came back out, still gripping the same shining lantern, but transformed, and in more ways than I was ready to take stock of.

Once we were safe and warm in the cabin, I set to work pulling a fresh set of clothes from a plastic tub for my new guest. Axzum stood awkwardly in the middle of the room, looking at everything at once. I handed him a pair of pants and he wrapped them around his neck like a scarf. The sweater he tied around his torso. I watched him with a smile, debating whether to explain how clothes worked.

I decided it could wait, and I moved on to other tasks. I filled up the dog bowl, fed the fire, and filled a kettle of water for boiling. As I ran the water, I saw my face reflected at me in the window over the sink.

I froze.

It was a face I had not seen for a very long time. I put my hand to my cheek to make sure it was real. I then noticed Axzum's movements out of the corner of my eye. He moved about the room, taking in every object, still holding the pebbles as if they were diamonds. Axzum was the only other being besides Cooper to set foot in my hobbit hole. His presence emphasized its scaled down size. The place was made for half a person.

Cooper laid waste to his bowl, hunted a chewed-up tennis ball, carried it to his new friend and dropped it at his feet. Axzum looked down at the ball, and then looked at Cooper, and then looked at me.

"He wants you to play. See?"

I went over to the ball, bent down, snagged it, and flung it across the room. Cooper jumped at it and recovered the ball and returned it to Axzum's feet. The space voyager picked up the tennis ball and flung it across the room, and the ritual repeated itself.

"Welcome to Earth," I mused, knowing full well that the alien couldn't understand me. "Unfortunately, not everyone here is as friendly or as easily entertained."

Axzum played along and tossed the ball for Cooper several times, but then he stopped. He picked up the tennis ball, and instead of throwing it, held it up, contemplating it, as if he had discovered some rare artifact. He walked to the light hanging from the ceiling in the center of the room, tennis ball in one hand, and the other hand filled with pebbles. He set the ball down on the table, along with the pebbles, creating a small pile, and motioned for my attention. I nodded and took a step toward him as he sifted through the pebbles with his fingers.

Axzum selected a dark grey pebble from the pile and spun it in the air. The pebble spun, but it did not fall to the ground. Instead, defying gravity, the rock spun in place in the middle of the room.

"Oh!" I exclaimed. "How did you"—and the space voyager interrupted me, pointing at the stone floating between us.

"Gaieos," he said.

"Gaieos? What's Gaieos?"

He pointed to the ground and then pointed to the spinning pebble. "Gaieos."

"Oh, Earth." I pinged back at him. I pointed to the ground and then pointed to the stone, mirroring his motions. He nodded.

"Earth. Gaieos."

"Okay. Got it, Gaieos."

The pebble continued to spin in the air as he pointed to the light hanging down from the ceiling.

"Breeva," he said.

"Light?" I responded. "Breeva means light?"

"Breeva," he repeated. Then he touched the spinning pebble, and it moved around the light bulb, like a planet traveling around its star.

"Oh, sun, that's the sun. Okay, I get it now. That's the sun, and that's the Earth."

"Breeva. Gaieos."

He then picked up another pebble, and spinning it in the air, caused it to move around the light, this one closer to the bulb.

"Mercury." I said, "We call that one Mercury."

"Doldol," he said.

Now, once we understood each other, the rest was easy. He added two more rocks. Now four stones were spinning and orbiting the light bulb in the middle of my shack—Venus and Mars.

"Sennja. Avesta." he said, pointing at the miniature planets. Axzum paused and slowly, as if I were in the first grade, repeated,

"Breeva, Doldol, Sennja, Gaieos, Avesta." Sun, Mercury, Venus, Earth, Mars—I understood.

And then he picked up the tennis ball, and spinning it, set it on its own path around the room. Cooper made a few attempts to grab it, but it was just too far out of reach.

"Dayjah," the space voyager said, pointing at the floating tennis ball that was obviously now representing Jupiter. And then he selected four more stones from the table and sent them spinning and floating around the room, pointing at each one and naming.

"Hemenal, Hemptal, Moodal, Saysaul."

"I understand—Saturn, Uranus, Neptune, Pluto. Except, Pluto's not a planet anymore."

Axzum looked at me quizzically.

"Don't blame me. It wasn't my call."

Eight pebbles from the stream bed and a tennis ball now spun around the light bulb, creating a diorama of the solar system which would have made any third-grade science teacher green with envy.

Two stones remained on the table.

Axzum pointed with emphasis to the two remaining stones on the table and gestured as if his point was about to be made. As Axzum would repeat to me many times:

"Every orchid has three petals, every wild rose has five, every star has eleven worlds at birth. Five inner, five outer, and one giant in between."

I looked down at the pebbles and back up at the rocks spinning around the light bulb, and for the first time I saw our solar system as it truly was: a puzzle with pieces missing. Axzum picked up one of the pebbles from the table, spun it, placing it in the air outside of the stone designated as Pluto.

"What? Are you telling me there's another planet out there?"

Axzum nodded.

"Geuld."

"No. Come on. How?"

And then he picked up the final pebble, held it up to me like a kid with a shiny new penny, and said,

"Payraydayzay."

He spun the rock and set it into orbit around the light bulb between the stone that was Mars and the tennis ball that was Jupiter. I stumbled around the room for a moment, analyzing the spinning stones. Axzum pointed to the Earth and then to Mars and then to his own planet.

"Gaieos, Avesta, Payraydayzay. Senn Agra Days."

He said, "Senn Agra Days," with his mouth, but inside of my mind and body I heard him speak to me again, communicating to me the way he had done in the woods.

"The Three Sisters."

Three sister planets: Earth, Mars, and Axzum's phantom planet, Payraydayzay.

Except it wasn't a phantom; the remains of the planet, the rocky debris that made up the asteroid belt between Mars and Jupiter, was still there. As I stood there, watching the pebbles journey around the room, orbiting the golden light, I became hypnotized by their rhythms.

The stones accelerated until they were whizzing around the room at an incredible speed. And then, suddenly, I, too, was drawn up into the spinning mobile, joining the rocks in my own dizzying orbit. My mind, my consciousness, joined the revolving pebbles, while my feet and body stayed fixed on the cabin floor. As my mind circled the room, I could see myself, Cooper and the space voyager looking back up at me from the ground.

"What the hell?"

Whether my consciousness was in flight, or the flight was in my consciousness, I could not decide. Whatever the case, I traveled through space, gliding by each stone as it was transformed into the world it represented. One rock grew rings and became Saturn. The tennis ball morphed into Jupiter, complete, with its telltale red spot moving across the surface. The lightbulb that had become a golden tree earlier in the evening was now the hot glowing sun and the walls of the cabin disappeared, replaced by the vast starry expanse of space. I was now rocketing through the cosmos, my heart and mind opened to its wonder.

And then, there before me, were The Three Sisters —Earth, Mars, and Payraydayzay—three almost identical worlds, each orbiting at its own speed and trajectory around the light. My head swung from one planet to the other as they went by, trying to figure out which one was which. Each sister had blue, green, and tan coloring with the white glow of a cloud filled atmosphere. The only way to tell them apart, I decided, was to mark each one's distance from the sun. The closest, Earth, then Mars, and finally between Mars and Jupiter—the space voyager's lost planet. As I flew toward this newly discovered world to get a better look, it suddenly crumbled into bits. The fragments, gigantic pieces of rock and debris, drifted weightlessly in every direction. As a handful of pieces shot past me, one echoed with the cries of a baby.

Nature has designed a baby's cry, its pitch, volume, and tone to draw attention. The rock's wail rang in my ears with such intensity that I had no choice but to follow it. Why would a meteorite be crying?

As I trailed close behind the errant stone, the Earth appeared from the other side of the sun, on its way to making another revolution and I could see the two were going to collide. In moments, they did, with a rain of fire that turned the sky orange. The fragment slammed into the planet with such force that its ocean turned into a fiery torrent that dashed across the world's surface, wiping out everything in its path. The rock, still howling like a hungry infant, burrowed deep into the earth. And I followed. Past miles of mud, water, dirt, and rock, I found the meteor where it had become lodged in the subterranean bedrock. It emanated an intense heat, thousands of degrees, yet it still cried. I wanted see within, but in a blink, I was back on the floor, standing next to the space voyager, watching the pebbles fly around the light bulb. The crying stopped.

"How? What was that? Did you do that?"

The space voyager looked back at me blankly. And then we both returned our gaze to the mysterious rock drifting around the lightbulb.

"That's Payraydayzay?"

I walked across the room to where it was and took it out of its place in the cosmic dance. I returned and offered the stone to my new friend, placing it carefully in his hand.

"Payraydayzay is gone. It's not there anymore."

"Gone," he repeated, with a crumpled face, his heart broken. Axzum held the stone with both of his hands, cupping it as if it were a dead baby bird, and he sat down in the chair at the table. The water was to the point of boiling now, and I went to the hearth for the kettle.

I thought: How is any of this possible? Even if I'm in my right mind and there's a visitor from beyond sitting at my table, even if there really was a planet where he says there was, it's been gone for eons upon eons. If it really was there, and it really is apparently gone, how is it he's just learning about it now?

I poured the hot water into the cups and added tea, which performed its own transformation.

Senn Agra Days, Three sister planets. What does that mean? If there were two other nearby planets like ours, what were they like? Was there life? What kind of life? And what happened?

I took a cup of tea and turned to offer it to Axzum. His face was in his hands, and the small stone lay on the table. I waited patiently, watching the stones spin around my trailer park chandelier. Finally, Axzum's face appeared from behind his hands, his cheeks wet with undulating lines of blue, purple and green. The colored ribbons beneath his skin seemed to shift and change with his emotions. Through the grief, he beckoned me.

"Ella," he whispered once again, and he offered me both hands, as if they held something that he wanted to share with me. Yet they were empty.

"Ella," he called to me again and emphasized his hands. I put the cup on the table and walked around to where he sat. He turned to me and offered me both hands, as if he wanted me to pray with him.

It had been a long time since I prayed with anyone. I had spent plenty of time meditating and losing myself in deep contemplative practices, but praying with another, especially someone from beyond, wasn't something that I was prepared for, nor necessarily enthusiastic about. I had lived long enough to know that I knew nothing of God.

Reluctantly, I got down on my knees, closed my eyes and I placed my hands in his.

And that's when he shared the vision with me. I'm still unsure exactly how it works, but the connection created a vision in my mind, a kind of scene in which I lived a moment of Axzum's life, a moment through his eyes. The vision, haunting and gut wrenching, took only a few minutes, but it was enough. When he had shown me what he needed to show me, the vision stopped. I opened my eyes, and I pulled my hands away from him.

I sat on the floor for a moment, exhausted and bewildered, as if I had experienced what he had experienced. Watching the swirling model still spinning around the room, it occurred to me I might know. I looked back at Axzum.

"Ella. I think I know where she is."

CHAPTER THREE

THE VISION

In the autumn of the 1975th year, when I was just six or seven years old, I saw an angel. At least, I thought I saw an angel, and that's what I told everyone, until my grandmother chastised me: "When we see angels, we don't brag about it, William."

This, in my memory, was the season of bicycles with banana seats, and collecting buckeyes in red Radio Flyer wagons. We lived in a small house in a small town in western Iowa. The basement was a land of adventure, matchbox cars, green army men, rubber band guns and Legos. A hatch, with an ancient wooden door, was on one wall. It no doubt led to an electrical conduit, but in my imagination, it became the place where the angel lived.

I believed this because whenever I would return to the basement the morning after an evening of childhood adventures, certain items would be missing, or inexplicably rearranged. It must be an angel; what other explanation could there be?

One evening, I put my theory to the test. Spreading my toys across the basement floor, I called out for the angel and told it that if it really was there, then it should return all my toys to the bins during the night.

The next morning, when I opened the basement door and made my way down the steps, I could see that the toys had been cleaned up. I was right; I thought to myself, and when I got all the way down the steps and fully into the basement, there she was—an angel.

An angel, right there in the basement.

After hearing this story, which I've told several times, people were always skeptical, and peppered me with questions. Honestly, I doubted myself for years, wondering if it was all a dream or just in my imagination.

But I had proof; I still had the marble.

The angel held out her hand. Hovering above her hand, spinning in the air, was a silver marble. The marble then moved, still spinning, slowly away from her hand and toward my face, until it stopped just inches away from my nose. I took the glass ball out of the air and examined it, putting my eye right up to it. I had never seen something so beautiful, an entire world of color within. For a few moments, I was enraptured by the marble and what it contained. When I looked back at the angel, she was gone.

People always ask me what she looked like, although I stopped telling the story years ago. "It's hard to say," I'd answer. "I can't really remember very well." And so, no one ever really believed me. And eventually, I didn't really believe me either.

The event, whatever happened, set me on a quest of faith, through a whole career in theology, and out the other end, to this point, kneeling on the floor of my hermit house, sharing in communion with a visitor from beyond, the glass marble still in my pocket.

As I sat on the floor, looking up at my new friend, the space voyager, I did not realize yet what new doors were about to be unlocked for me. I closed my eyes, put my hands into Axzum's and he shared his vision with me. Though the events must have taken place in my mind, I felt as if I were transported to another place and time.

I opened my eyes to find that I was no longer in the cabin. What rose before me was a rocky and sprig dotted expanse, a painted desert. The hills in the distance and the mountains beyond were lined brown, red, and dark purple. My first thought was that I was in Utah or maybe northern Arizona, but then, as I focused on the ground at my feet, I could see I was some place else.

The ground swirled, moving about slowly in round circular spiraling patterns—the way creamer mixes with coffee when it's first poured into the cup.

I braced myself, thinking I might sink into the flow, but not only could I safely stand upon the undulating ground, I realized I was not in control of my body. Or should I say, the body I somehow was now indwelling. I realized I was a spectator of events, rather than an activator.

Within my frame of vision were several small dwellings, homes perhaps, but unlike anything I'd ever seen before, obviously built with materials from the surrounding landscape, the domed brown, red, and purple houses blended into the world around them.

Then, the camera lens of my vision turned completely in the opposite direction. Looking over my shoulder now, I could see a whole town, a city, with buildings, streets and people—people like Axzum. The figures were of many sizes and shapes, but all had the same translucent multi-colored skin.

There was screaming and shouting as groups of beings rushed about, running this way and that. The body I inhabited was also shouting and running in a panic. I looked in the direction I was running, and I could see one of the dwellings before me had a door, which was opening.

"Ariance," I shouted.

A woman appeared in the doorway. Although she wore a black hooded cape wrapped around her body and over her head, I could still see her eyes, the same silver and blue as Axzum's. We embraced.

"Ari," I said, of course, I wasn't speaking, and it was not in English, but I said it and somehow, I understood it. I was Axzum.

"We have to go. Do you have everything?"

"I think so," she responded, adjusting her bags strapped over her back. In her arms was a heavy, cloth-wrapped package.

No, it was a baby. She had a baby.

"Ariance? Axzum, is this your wife? Is this your baby? Is this what you wanted to show me?"

But there was no answer. Axzum couldn't hear me. The woman, Ariance, grabbed my hand and held it tight. "Let's go," she said. I looked down at our hands intertwined together; blue, green, and red ribbon-like strands ran from my arm into hers and vice versa. The threads encircled one another, dancing, tying and untying together.

We ran together, away from the city, the dwellings, and into the desert, running as if being pursued.

It was not long until we had reached a grove of what looked like aspen trees, the trees they have up in the Colorado mountains with yellow leaves and white bark.

"What are you doing here? You must go. Flee." A voice came from everywhere at once.

The aspens created a small circle where the swirling on the ground collected and made one dark black dot. I approached the hole in the desert floor, with Ariance clinging to the child.

"Please, we need your help."

There was a pause as the cool morning wind rushed through the branches, shaking the leaves, and then one aspen, which appeared to be the tallest, moved. The tree walked from within a group of the others, its trunk-like legs moving like a human, but its roots were still tethered to the ground. It had three large main branches, with smaller limbs and branches creating three boughs of leaves, the smallest middle bough cocked slightly to the side, almost like a head without a face. The other two larger limbs swayed about like arms on both sides.

"There isn't any time left," said the trees. "Go."

As the trees spoke, the limbs moved about, and a flock of starlings dove out of each limb and then soared back into the branches. The family of trees in the grove all seemed to lean toward us, as if all the trees and the starlings were one being. The ground suddenly shook, and the large boulders and rocks tumbled down from the surrounding hills.

"It's too late," whispered the trees.

A shadow blanketed the desert as if something were descending upon us from above. I reached into the satchel I had slung around my shoulder and neck and pulled a black orb the size of a golf ball from within, like the one I had encountered in the snow earlier in the evening.

The mother, Ariance, uncovered the baby and kissed her gently on the forehead. The babe, although alien looking to me, still had the same vulnerability and lack of defenses that human babies possess. I spent a moment taking her in, her beauty, her dazzling light blue eyes, and added a kiss to the spot her mother had placed hers.

The spinning black orb grew to the size of a basketball in my hands, and Ariance carefully placed the naked infant into the void. The baby floated safely within.

And then the roots came—tree roots. They came out of the black hole in the ground before us. The tree roots reached out like wild arms and moved together to weave a kind of basket which was held out before us.

"Axzum, what is this? I don't understand. What are you doing? Are you giving—"

Before I could finish, Ariance placed both of her hands on the sphere and together we set it into the twisted basket. The orb spun in the basket for a moment, and Ariance spoke, saying a short prayer. And then, the roots pulled away with the baby within. Ariance wrapped both of her arms around me and buried her face in my chest, sobbing. The baby cried as well. The orb descended into the hole as the cavity melted into a tan and brown swirl, like the rest of the desert floor. She was gone, and the crying stopped.

"Promise us," whispered Axzum.

The trees shuddered.

"When this world comes apart, this seed we'll send to Gaieos."

Then, an entire flock of starlings flew out of the branches and encircled us, soaring in both directions at once, and then returned to the trees.

A ghostly voice saying "Run" came from the aspens, but I couldn't move.

"Axzum, what is this? What is happening?"

The wind sped up, blowing dust and sand into our faces. I pulled Ariance tight and looked up to see what was coming.

Darkness.

For a long moment there was nothing—an aching, hollow nothing. I was aware that I was still kneeling on the floor in my cabin, my hands bound to Axzum's, but I dared not move or open my eyes.

"I do not understand, Axzum. Show me more."

Again, there was no answer. And then, within me, he spoke. "I cannot," he said. "It is all of my Koinonae."

"Koinonae…What is Koinonae?"

"Koinonae is my longing, my deep desire, which I share."

I thought for a moment.

"You mean you have the ability to reveal your desires to others?"

"All beings have this ability."

"All beings? I cannot do this."

"You can."

"No," I said. "This is not an ability that human beings possess."

"Have you ever tried?"

This proposition seemed preposterous. Human beings, by our very nature, conceal our deepest desires from one another. It is the most vulnerable act. So vulnerable, in fact, that we have developed the capability to even hide our longings from ourselves. To speak aloud a true want is akin to running naked down the street, and to visualize it and to witness a vision of that desire, and then share that vision with another could be a shame or an embarrassment that could send a person completely adrift.

Do all beings possess this ability to reveal a vision of our deepest longing with another, as Axzum has just done with me? Who knows? The chances that any human being has ever even tried are extremely low.

Axzum's hands pressed into mine like a vise.

"Show me."

Then I opened my eyes to new scenery, a place I had known long ago, no longer an alien desert, but now rolling hills of corn, rows and rows of corn, not yet waist high. The woods, the creek, the old white barn and a farmhouse, a big oak tree where a tire swing hung. I knew this place very well. I loved this place. I was now running through the cornfield toward the house, a warm summer rain pelting my face.

I knew this memory. I was in school, maybe seventeen or eighteen years old, at the threshold of adulthood, but still holding on to childhood.

And then she grabbed my hand. Madeline. Laughing, she stopped me, and we just stood together in that field, letting the storm wash over us. Her long brown hair was flat and dripping wet, dark brown eyes a shade darker than mahogany. I stood captivated by those eyes. She smiled at me.

And then the vision was gone.

I sat silent for a moment, as if I'd been punched in the gut and needed a minute to catch my breath.

"It's a beautiful memory," I confessed to Axzum, "And one that I've kept like a treasure in my heart all my life. But my deepest longing? My God, Madeline? I haven't seen her in eighty-five years."

"Heiros gamos," Axzum responded within me. "Heiros gamos."

At the time, I didn't know what Axzum meant by heiros gamos. Maybe it wasn't Madeline specifically that was my deepest desire. Maybe it was that moment in time. Maybe it was a connection in that moment, not just with another, but with something deeper within me: a belonging, a knowing, a being known by everything, and all things. I thought maybe heiros gamos referred to a pure moment in the *now*, lived without corruption, without the layers of deceptions and masks we use to prop ourselves up with.

I slowly opened my eyes to see Axzum do the same, and I removed my hands from his and moved to a sitting position on the floor of the cabin. There was a new ache within me, a fresh wound. The visions had pried open my insides and exposed the longing. The Koinonae, as it is called—it's that ache that we so often avoid. We want to avoid it completely. That's why we keep these doors closed. But here it was, wide open and exposed.

"Your child. I can't even imagine that kind of ache."

"Ella," he responded. And the space voyager fell onto the floor and gathered himself into the fetal position. His skin stiffened and the multicolored ribbons froze and faded to grey as if he were turning into stone. The floating pebbles abruptly fell to the floor, and the tennis ball bounced toward the corner.

At the sink, I ran warm water over a rag and brought it to him, folding it and covering his forehead, my version of extra-terrestrial first aid. I clamored across the room to an old cardboard box next to the hearth. It was filled with newspapers and magazines which I had been using as fire starter. I rifled urgently through the bin until I found it—thank God it was still there—a tattered and abused atlas of the world. No doubt dated, having forgotten countries on it like Zaire and Yugoslavia, but it would work. I found the page, and I was walking back to Axzum to show him my discovery when I was stopped. A car or truck or something, someone, was coming up the road.

I hurried to Axzum, flopped the book of maps on the floor near his head. He rose slightly to see what was there, and I pointed to the middle of the page.

"Right there, The Gulf of Mexico, right off the shores of the Yucatan, I think. Scorpion reef."

I left the atlas with Axzum, then exited the house and stood on the front step. I couldn't see any lights yet, but I could hear something—two, possibly three vehicles speeding up the mountain road. Someone else must have seen the wheel, I thought, and now they're on the hunt.

The narrow dirt road was covered with more than a few inches of snow, which meant trucks. It had been so many years and I had eluded any trouble. My advantage was the fact that no one knew I was there.

I turned around and investigated the cabin; the table covered with books and notes, and all the messages in my handwriting. The old ham radio, the transmitter and all the recording equipment. And the manuscript. It was plenty of evidence to have me committed and all of this seized or destroyed. I was a questioner and I had spent many nights asking my questions to whoever was out there listening. This kind of activity had become outlawed in many places in the second half of that century on Earth.

And, on top of all that, I had him, the space voyager, almost paralyzed on the floor, half naked, with a pair of pants wrapped around his neck.

"We have to go." I burst back into the cabin, not even bothering to shut the door.

"Axzum, come on, get up."

As Axzum rose to his feet, studying the map I'd given him, I grabbed a pack and began filling it with any items that were in reach, both necessary and not—there was no time to debate: an old shirt, pair of pants, a handful of socks, a knife, a pen, paper, and my manuscript. I zipped up the pack and made a final circle around the room with my eyes. What else? I patted my leg, which was my compulsive habit to make sure my marble was still there, and then I grabbed a blanket from the cot and threw it over the recording equipment. Much good that would do, I thought. I made for the door, grabbing Axzum by the arm.

"Cooper, let's go, boy."

The alien and the dog bounded out of the house, down the steps and into the snow. I followed, grabbing the lantern, cutting the power, and locking the door.

I pointed toward the woods, the path we had made earlier in the evening, and the mountains beyond. As we ran across the clearing, the lights from the coming vehicles hit the trees ahead of us, and no doubt, our backs. Cooper and I galloped through the snow toward the forest, my new legs moving me faster than I had moved in a very long time. Axzum, however, oblivious to the threat, shuffled at half speed behind us, still leafing through the book.

For a moment, I returned in my mind to the aspens and the sparrows from the vision, the shaking ground, the tumbling boulders, and the darkness from above. But it wasn't just any darkness. In the vision, it came from a threat, much bigger than a pickup truck. What was it?

When we got to the tree line, we kept running another twenty yards further into the woods to ensure our invisibility, and then I turned to watch the vehicles through the trees. Two pickup trucks pulled up in front of the cabin and stopped. Dark shadows of men tumbled out of the trucks, shouting to one another and approaching my home as if it were prey. It wouldn't take them long; they would try the door and when they found it locked, they certainly would break it down. And once inside, they'd piece things together in short order. We had to keep moving, but when I tried to coax Axzum deeper into the woods, he wouldn't budge, engrossed in the maps. As predicted, the men pillaged through the cabin and reemerged with the new objective. Finding our tracks, they waded through the snow toward us, flashlights fixed on our position.

"They're coming. We need to move."

Axzum moved his silver eyes from the pages and into what I felt like was my soul.

"Are you afraid of dying?" came from within me

once more. The men were halfway across the clearing, and now I could see they were armed.

"No," I lied. "I am not afraid. But right now, would be terrible timing."

The flashlights were closing in fast, and there was no time left for discussion. I grabbed Axzum's arm and turned to run, but he stopped me. He bent down and casually picked up a pinecone.

"What are you doing?" I blurted out. It was like trying to catch a departing train with a five-year-old child.

But just as he had done with the pebbles and the tennis ball in the cabin, he sent the pinecone spinning in the air and orbiting around us. Moments later, a stone joined it, spinning and floating but orbiting around us in a different direction. Then a twig, a decaying leaf, a shard of ice and another pebble rose off the forest floor and joined the dance, each fragment set spinning and orbiting in all directions at once, some pieces floating around our waist, and other pieces traveling over our shoulder and down around our knees and back up. Before I knew it, we were standing in the nucleus of a giant atom whose electrons were made of debris and scat found on the forest floor— pinecones, rocks, dirt, and pebbles careening about to create a makeshift globe. Flashlight beams, shouting, and the metal clicking of guns and rifles from just outside the tree line told me we'd been found. By the time a single shot was fired in the air, we were too far away for anything to hit its mark, for the globe suddenly rose out of the woods above the tree line and took us with it.

Defying gravity, Axzum, Cooper and I flew out of our hiding spot between the trees and over the hills and mountains and into the star filled sky. Before I even had time to react, we were 200 to 300 feet above the ground.

Through the low-lying whiffs of clouds and mist, I saw the men running, and then, to my surprise, they seemed to melt into dark shadows; they slithered across the snow like snakes, returning to their truck and to the cabin, where they seemed to swirl like ghosts around both. I looked up at Axzum, confused about what I was witnessing.

"Nuul," he grunted.

I continued to watch them, horrified, and wondered if this was what pushed me out of the cabin door and onto the ground.

I looked down to check on Cooper, in the orb with us, his four legs kicking out in all directions, as if he were trying to walk on ice. And then I realized my stance, nearly upside down with one leg at nine o'clock and the other at noon. Axzum grabbed my shoulder and helped me back to an upright position. As I regained my balance, Axzum handed me the atlas and pointed to the page. In the delirium of soaring helplessly across the sky within a giant dirty snowball, I could process the place on the map that the space voyager wanted me to see.

"No," I said, pointing at the map. "Ella is in Mexico. That is not Mexico. That is Africa."

Axzum pointed again to a spot in the book. He was tapping the country of Ethiopia with his finger. "Lalibela," I read the name of the village that he was pointing out loud. Axzum stared at me and then nodded. I laughed.

By now we had travelled above the hills almost two to three miles, and I took in the scene below, contemplating my situation. The dark wintery landscape, snow covered pines and naked deciduous trees, long dark lines of a frozen world. In the distance, a growing orange and yellow flicker appeared. My cabin, going up in flames.

I looked back at Axzum. "What's in Lalibela?"

CHAPTER FOUR

THE ANGEL

The people of that age were addicted to straight lines, it seemed, their entire world built on level planes and right angles. Jagged city skylines of boxes and triangles had replaced the original natural topography of sloping hills and valleys. Perhaps straight lines and angles gave them a sense of security and control in this chaotic whirling dervish of a universe.

The truth is, they are all an illusion. After what I have witnessed, I'd be willing to wager that there is no such thing as a straight line anywhere. Everything that exists has an orbit, and itself orbited by something else: every atom in your body, electrons around neutrons, our moon around our planet, our planet around the Sun, our system around the galaxy and the galaxy around the center of the universe, the singularity.

And what does that revolve around?

Who knows?

But whatever it is, I imagine it revolves around something else, and on and on, all of it moving in circles and spiraling like a corkscrew as it travels through space.

Just like everything else, we orbit and are orbited by one another, spinning, moving in a dizzying rotation, making our revolutions. Some trips occur in a blink of an eye, and others require eons. Then it's all flipped, and the ones that take a blink of an eye are stretched out to eons, and the ones that take an eon are condensed to a blink of an eye.

We are made of neutrons and electrons. This isn't

magic, or witchcraft, or religion—it's what there is. These orbits help to bind the universe together. Gravity, or the Oolah, as I would soon learn it to be called, the foundational law of the universe, can be harnessed to the mutual benefit of all or it can be abused, used for power, corruption and self-preservation, used for the benefit of the self alone. As Axzum says, to serve the self is to serve nothing, the great separation or what is called the Nuul. It is not death that we should fear; it is the Nuul, the fragmentation. You need to know this, my most excellent Theophilus, to understand what I am about to tell you. Perhaps when you learn some of this, you will at once welcome them as new concepts and things you seem to have always known.

At least, this was my experience as Axzum, Cooper, and I rose in the spinning orb, out of the forest, passing tree limbs three stories tall as we ascended into the giant wheel above.

Once we had arrived at the landing spot underneath the wheel and the dirty snowball had been scattered to the wind, it did not take me long to decide to go with Axzum. With the cabin burned, the only belongings I had left in the world were the worthless yard sale items I had jammed into my pack.

I had Cooper, of course, who, as usual, lived life in the moment, undaunted. I always heard nightmare stories of family pets being terrified of their own shadow, or perhaps some mundane, inanimate object. Not Cooper. Even on the Fourth of July, he was unflinching with the self-assurance that always made me jealous. I was grateful to have my friend with me as we passed through the alien hatch and into the ship.

Growing up in the twentieth century, with so many sci-fi movies, books and TV shows, I was ready for some otherworldly experience—blinking lights and mysterious, futuristic, high-tech modules covered with switches and buttons. It wasn't like that at all. If anything, it felt like walking into an ancient relic, like a sixteenth century galleon, or an old wine cellar in some long-lived chateau in France. The floor was made of stones of different shapes and sizes, worn shiny to a brass color, marking the path most travelled.

As we stepped into the Great Room, the globe that we had been traveling in shrank down to the size of a golf ball and floated to a hole twice its size dug into the side of the wall. The orb rested there, still spinning.

I looked around the room and found seven more holes that were similar, like little shrines built into the side of the wall, one containing another spinning orb, and the rest empty. I could see from the empty shrines that each one was a piece of art within itself, no doubt crafted a long time ago. Between each shrine was a large circular porthole, each porthole leading down each spoke of the wagon wheel.

Dead vines, as thick as tree limbs, ran in every direction on the floor, walls, and ceiling. The old, veiny branches, long dead, were imbedded in the rock and ran through every tube and chamber of the vessel. In the middle of the Great Room, a tall spiral staircase wrapped with dead vines led to the floor above.

It couldn't have been more simple, more logical, and somehow familiar. Cooper explored the room with his nose and disappeared into one of the round portals. "That must be the way to the galley," I joked to myself, and began moving in the same direction. But Axzum stopped me, with his hand on my shoulder, and motioned to the spiral staircase. I followed Axzum up the stairs, grabbing the solid wooden banister, inlaid with intricately carved designs all the way up the spine.

When we got to the top of the staircase, I found myself in what I guessed was the cockpit, with enormous windows all around us. The windows rose to a huge glass dome ceiling above with a glass hatch at the very top. Old, dead vines clung to the inside of the glass and spread in every direction, making the cockpit feel like a big, domed greenhouse.

In the center of the room was a round pedestal the size and height one would find in a tavern. In the middle of the pedestal was a metal sphere with lines cut into it to create a grid around its surface. A few inches above the floor and circling the pedestal, was a hula-hoop-like metal bar, and that was it. No computer screens, no displays, no buttons, no gizmos, no wires, or chaos, just a waist high round table, a metal ball and a hoop. Not futuristic at all. If anything, the worn edges of it all revealed its past. Part of me was disappointed, wanting to encounter some astonishing alien technology, but deep down I felt a sense of comfort that comes from the marriage of simplicity, logic and balance.

Axzum touched the edge of the pedestal and rotated it a few degrees counterclockwise. Above the table, hovering over our heads, appeared a shining, burning, spinning ball. I recognized quickly that it was a projection of our sun, but much smaller. Around the sun, suddenly filling the entire cockpit, inches above our heads, our entire solar system in miniature appeared, each planet ranging in size from a dime, Mercury, to a softball, Jupiter. Each orbited the center of the room at its own speed, creating a beautifully choreographed celestial dance. Now I was in awe.

"My god. It's a map."

Even as a kid, I loved maps, and I would pour over any map I could find like an investor with a ticker tape. Spreading out a map on the living room floor on Sunday mornings in my pajamas transformed me into an explorer, learning about unknown places and wondering what it would be like to live there. Something within me always sought my place.

Now I was roaming around the cockpit, being romanced by what was no doubt the most tantalizing map I'd ever seen. Eleven maps, actually. Where do I even begin? I thought to myself, as if I'd just won a shopping spree. Jupiter's red dot moved quietly across its surface, while Uranus was light blue-grey, spinning on its side, its pole facing towards the sun. Then there was Saturn. As Saturn slowly floated above my head, I reached out to take it, but Axzum stopped me in motion, grabbing my arm, indicating not to touch.

He walked over to the place where the Three Sisters were in orbit together. There it was, sure enough, orbiting between Jupiter and Mars—Axzum's planet.

"Payraydayzay," Axzum said, pointing to the brown, tan and blue planet. Then, the space voyager returned to the table and turned it slightly. When he did, the projection of Payraydayzay grew five times its size, almost taking up the entire cockpit. Now I could see this sister planet close up. The topography was like Earth, with mountain ranges and deserts, oceans, rivers and lakes, but it also had features that drew my curiosity: vast yellow jungles and deep cut purple and grey canyons. The world I was looking at was obviously populated; even in miniature, evidence of large cities and towns covered the globe. Then Axzum touched the metal ball in the middle of the pedestal, and red-orange dots appeared across the planet, hundreds of them, perhaps thousands.

"Destinations," I deduced. Axzum nodded. I stood in silence for a long time, trying to process what I was witnessing. Payraydayzay. A long-lost populated world. But populated by whom? And how was it lost?

He rotated the table again, and while Payraydayzay shrank back down to the size of an apple, the next planet grew to take the former's spot.

"Avesta," Axzum indicated.

"Mars," I said, but it wasn't the Mars I knew. This sister looked like the others, with mountains, plains, vegetation, and my god, water—vast oceans, rivers, and lakes. Not dead, dusty and red. Rather blue, green, lush and alive.

Axzum touched the metal ball again, and the red destination markers appeared on the planet's surface. This time, the red dots numbered in the dozens, maybe forty or fifty. What does this mean? I thought. Were there once truly Martians? Was the Red Planet populated as well? How was it all ruined?

Axzum went to the table again, and I almost stopped him. This was going too fast. I needed at least a few days to explore each surface.

But I was also eager to see Earth.

The alien turned the table, and Mars and Earth switched sizes. This sister, of course, was recognizable: the mountain range from Alaska down to Mexico, another in South America. But no ice in Greenland, no desert in northern Africa, and no sign of civilization. No towns, no cities, just a wild jungle planet.

Axzum's touch exposed the destination dots on Earth. Three, just three. Three red dots and one light blue blinking dot. The red dots, one in the British Isles, one on the boot that forms Italy, and one in eastern Africa. The light blue dot in our present location, the Rocky Mountains of Colorado.

Axzum walked to the earth and put his finger on the red dot marked in Africa. The dot turned white and the wheel that we were standing in moved.

Then I understood why I wasn't permitted to touch.

Looking out of the windows, I watched the tree tops descend out of view as the ship rose into the sky. It was almost morning now, and as we ascended, the sun came into view and pierced the glass dome of the cockpit.

Once we had cleared the trees and nearly penetrated the clouds, Axzum moved to the pedestal and set the metal ball at the center into a slow spin. Although the spokes of the wheel followed the same spin as the ball on the table, the cockpit remain fixed. Then, Axzum casually pressed the metal hula hoop that encircled the pedestal at his feet, at which point, two things happened at once.

First, I was released from gravity, my body floating just inches off the floor. Second, the wheel accelerated to a speed which I could not fathom. I tried to find something to hold on to, but it was unnecessary. Somehow, I was safely hemmed into place on all sides. I wondered how Cooper was fairing as I looked up at the miniature earth spinning slowly above me. The light blue dot on the projection of Earth was now moving across the surface of the globe, above the Atlantic Ocean and toward the red dot in East Africa. The blinking light blue dot was obviously the location of the ship.

The light from the sun flashed across the floor of

the spacecraft, so that by the time we reached the continent of Africa, it was setting in the west, although we had only travelled for thirty seconds. By the time we reached our destination, the sky was almost dark.

For a moment, I wondered if the wheel had been spotted or picked up on some radar somewhere. But how? At the speed we were traveling, all anyone could have seen was a dart across the sky, maybe even too fast for the eye to detect.

The wheel stopped moving and my feet were set on the floor once again. I rushed to the window to see where we were. Slowly, the ship descended into a rocky bowl surrounded by brownish-red rock formations, evidently somewhere in northern Ethiopia. The ship rested in a circular nest, almost the exact size of the wheel, as if the ship and the landing spot were designed for each other. We hid safely, out of reach from anyone or anything.

I exhaled the breath I had been holding for what felt like an hour, and I turned back toward Axzum in time to see Cooper emerge from the chamber below. The black lab made a beeline to me with a reticent tail wag. I'm sure if he was able to talk, there would have been more than a few expletives. Cooper gathered around my legs for reassurance and then returned to the top of the staircase; the confident lab, being a better leader than I'll ever be, looked back at me and beckoned me to follow him. Being a compliant dog owner, I obeyed cheerfully.

Cooper pattered down the stairs, and I followed, wondering what he had found. Axzum followed me. From the bottom of the stairs, we followed Coop down one of the wagon spokes to what appeared to be the galley. It was not just any galley. A gorgeous banquet hall fit for royalty, with dozens of round stone tables, glass chandeliers and

The Day of the Space Voyager

windows etched with alien designs that stretched twenty or thirty feet up to the ceiling, where dead vines hung like tree branches.

"You could feed an entire army in here," I quipped. As I took in the grand dining room, an avalanche of questions tumbled through my mind.

How old is this ship? Where is it from? Who built it? It's obviously designed for a large crew. But where are they?

Cooper moved across the dining room and through the double doors that no doubt led to the kitchen. Axzum and I followed. In the kitchen, there were even more tables and countertops, pots, pans and every imaginable tool and utensil. The pantry was stocked.

The hours that followed involved preparing and sharing a meal, cleaning up, and preparing to rest. It was as ordinary as any meal I've eaten, except now I was dining in an alien spacecraft.

But there was a moment, a beautiful moment, when we sat down at a table and ate together. I daresay that there is nothing more binding in this universe than sitting down and sharing a meal together. Two people that live across the street from each other become friends, and so it was for the two of us, or three, if you include the lab, who lived light years apart. We just sat, ate and shared in the most spiritual of practices. The language barrier created long moments of silence, but that only made the experience even more sacred.

After we had eaten, Axzum led us to the sleeping quarters, a huge, two-story atrium with dozens of wooden doors around the perimeter, each opening into a bunkroom. Axzum showed me to a room he selected, which was equipped with a bed and all the amenities you'd find in a

64

luxury hotel. Although it all seemed uniquely alien, it was comfortable, strangely familiar, and in mere moments, I was laid out on the bed and sound asleep.

Lalibela, Ethiopia, was famous for its rock cut monolithic churches. There were eleven different churches cut out of the rock that were sometimes two or three stories down into the earth. It was one of Ethiopia's holiest cities and a center of pilgrimage. Every year, thousands would travel to Lalibela from across the world to visit these sacred sites.

Invisible to everyone except a few locals, there was a twelfth church, a twelfth temple, carved deep into the earth, or at least this was what I discovered the next morning. We rose to the welcome scent of burning wood and coffee. Emerging from my bunk, I would have enjoyed exploring the rest of the ship, but Cooper's nose trumped all other senses, and he led the way down one of the long spokes and back to the vessel's core. Axzum grabbed the rail of the spiral staircase. The bottom hatch of the wheel opened up, and the staircase lowered to the ground outside, rotating as it descended. Stepping off the final step and on to the rust-colored Earth, I scanned the surroundings to gather my bearings.

The wheel had inexplicably landed perfectly upon eight similarly sized rock formations, an ancient landing pad which would have gone unrecognized and probably did, had the wheel not been resting upon it. One pillar had cracked under the weight of the ship, and a rocky piece had separated and fell to the ground to expose white marble underneath.

Axzum, standing at the base of the staircase underneath the center of the wheel, bent down, put his hand into a hole in the ground and pulled. A round door, a hatch in the ground, opened up, spreading a pile of dirt that had accumulated upon it. The air filled with a cloud of dust, smoke, and the same scent of coffee, but stronger now. Cooper ran to the hatch to investigate. Axzum opened the door and beckoned me to join him. I walked over and peered into the hole. Another spiral staircase cut into the rock led down into the darkness. I looked at Axzum.

He handed me my old, faithful lantern, which I held for a moment, considering, and then gave it a click. As much as my common sense told me I could be in danger, my curiosity drove me down the steps.

The stairs led down to a large, rounded cavern carved into the rock. This was not a natural cave, as evidenced by the ornate and intricate carvings on the walls. Carvings of owls and beetles, turtles and lizards, along with etchings of plants, flowers, vines and leaves. We ventured across the room, lantern held up to reveal an entryway on the far side; the opening led into a long, curving passageway, which felt like a labyrinth with smaller caverns cut out extending in all directions. We entered another larger cave with dozens of Afghan rugs covering the stone floor and a pit with hot coals burning in the middle of the room.

An old Ethiopian woman dressed in a long, white garb bordered at the hem with a gold, red, and green design, sat at the coals preparing coffee. She wore a light gold and white scarf as a head covering. Without looking at us, she gestured for us to join her at the coals. As Axzum and I slowly approached the fire and found a place on the floor to sit, Cooper trotted over to the old woman confidently and greeted her. She removed her ancient hands from the hot pan to pat the lab's head. Cooper returned beside me as the woman continued her work. She was roasting coffee beans in a pan and boiling water in a pot. We watched her silently as she moved the beans around the pan with a wooden spoon.

When the beans roasted, she held the pan toward my face so I could smell. She did the same for Axzum. Then, using an old wooden mortar and pestle, she ground the coffee down to almost dust; then, she mixed the coffee with the water in a tall pot with a big round bottom. It had a tall neck and a spout, like a teapot, with a long, thin neck. The coffee was poured into small cups without handles.

"Welcome, Oakruum," she said to me as she handed me a cup. "Welcome, Axzum," as she gave one to him as well.

"You speak English?" I asked.

"Of course," she answered, smiling, and looking me in the eye for the first time. Looking back at her, I froze— those light blue eyes felt too familiar…Wait a minute, hers was a face burned into my memory from, so long ago, from an event I knew as just a dream.

"I know you."

"You remember," she said, "Good. I am Mira."

"Mira. That's beautiful."

"And you are Oakruum."

"Oakruum? What's Oakruum?"

"Well, that is your name. It's who you are."

I laughed.

"I'm sorry, but you must be confused. My name is Will. William Henry."

"I know it will take some time for you to reorient, but you are Oakruum, son of Renstruum. And this is your brother, Axzum."

I looked at Axzum, and he looked at me with a

shrug.

"My brother? How?"

The room seemed to rotate on one side as my mind processed what was said. I closed my eyes tightly, convinced that when I reopened them, I would be home in my bed, but when I did, I was in the same cave, by the same coals grappling with the same bombshell.

Axzum spoke to the woman in his own language, and then the woman conveyed this to me.

"Axzum says he's full of joy to be with you again, although he still aches for his Ella."

"Wait, hold on. I don't understand."

The woman continued, "He's been held in captivity and finally could escape and make his way back home. Of course, our home was destroyed long ago."

I laughed in disbelief.

She stopped and looked at me. Then from inside of me I heard the voice again.

"You are Oakruum; your home is Payraydayzay."

This is the moment that I began to doubt that any of this was real. I stared into the hot coals, trying to tether myself, trying to will myself awake or into consciousness. What was really happening here? Was I truly there? Or was I somewhere else entirely? Perhaps I was lost in the woods or losing my mind, or in a hospital somewhere, sedated. Perhaps this was a hallucination.

"You are Oakruum; your home is Payraydayzay."

"How is any of this possible?" I whispered, acknowledging that I was still there. "I am William. I can remember…my life… I don't remember…anything but."

The woman interrupted me. "You've been here much longer than that, in Earth time measurement anyway."

"Earth time?"

"Oolah," Axzum chimed in, looking at me as if I understood.

"Oolah. What's Oolah?"

"Gravity," Mira answered.

"Gravity? How does gravity explain any of this?"

The angel smiled at me. "Oolah." She held out a stone that rose and hovered just over her hand. "It can hold us in place and move us around. It can be weakened, loosened, strengthened and tightened. It can affect space and time, bending it, shaping it."

My eyes followed the stone as it moved about.

"And, this place, Payraydayzay?"

"Yes," she answered. "Senn Agra Days. There were Three Sister planets. This one, Gaieos, Avesta, and Payraydayzay." As she spoke, the other stones joined the first in the air above the coals. "When Payraydayzay was destroyed, fragments of it spread out across the solar system." As she spoke, she gestured at one of the floating stones, and it broke into pieces, which sprayed about.

"These pieces impacted the rest of the system. Larger worlds absorbed the chunks, but molten rock rained down on Avesta and Gaieos, leaving them both in ruin."

"You mean Earth and Mars?"

"Since then, Gaieos has recovered; Avesta has not."

"This makes little sense. All of what you're describing, if it's even true, happened long ago."

She looked at me, more serious now.

"Do you still have it?"

"Do I still have what?"

"I think you know."

I realized what she meant, and I shifted my body in order to put my hand into my pocket.

"Not now. Keep it there."

I looked back at her, and as I did, the memory of encountering the angel in the basement returned to me and I heard the voice within me that accompanied a lifetime of wrestling with the event.

"This isn't real," the inner saboteur warned. "This isn't really happening. It's all in your head."

My face began to warm and pulse with every heartbeat, as if I'd been working out in the sun all day. I looked at my hands, shaking, which was nothing new. I had developed a tremor years before, accompanied by night sweats and anxious thoughts. My mind would play tricks on me, showing me things that weren't really there. I learned to doubt my mind.

"You are Oakruum; your home is Payraydayzay."

"Would you excuse me? I need to let my dog out."

I dragged myself to my feet.

"Come on, boy."

I picked up the lantern, looked over at the angel and the space voyager one last time, and turned to walk out.

As I started for the doorway, from over my shoulder, the woman's voice followed me out of the cave.

"Your feelings are understandable, Oakruum. You've been here for a long time, through thousands of lifetimes, and the body you indwell now is but temporary, just a vehicle for your true self."

Her disturbing words spurred me to run, hurrying

up through the passageway so quickly that she had to shout her final words.

"You've always had the eye, Oakruum; just ask the questions. They will lead you to solid ground."

Questions? Maybe we don't ask them because we'd rather not know the answers. We can be so much more content with an illusion. But how do you know? How can you know what is real and what is a deception?

By the time I returned to the spiral staircase and raced up to the surface, I had talked myself into doubting my mind. I decided that once I reached sunlight, I'd keep on running.

"Come on Coop. Let's go. Run."

Which we did, up and over the rocky formation where the ship was hidden, and down a hill covered with big boulders and desert shrubs. I convinced myself that if I ran far enough, I would shed this illusion; like emerging out of water. This arid landscape would change back into forest and I'd awaken from this dream and be back in my cabin.

I ran with Cooper for quite a distance down a dirt hill scarred by spring rains, with undulating chasms and troughs. I'm not sure if I knew exactly where I was going or what my plan was. My mind was trying to come to grips with potentially identity shifting information. I had spent my life as a questioner, batting around the mysteries of life like a kitten with a ball of twine, and I'd had the gall to stand up as a faith leader, so convinced of the truth and coax others into a fenced corral of shared beliefs. That fence had already been knocked down, but now, everything I ever knew about the universe and myself was being turned on its head.

My emotions jumped from embarrassment to shame

to humiliation and back around again. In my youth, I'd gazed into the night sky and whispered prayers, to whom exactly I wasn't sure, but I never let on, play acting for years a passionate religiosity, gobbling up all kinds of strange fiction as fact. When finally, in my later years, I came to my senses and let go of such delusions; I felt liberated. However, letting go of certain dogmas is one thing, being told that everything you have ever known is wrong is another.

My run slowed to a walk as I reached into my pocket and found the silver marble. I stopped at the crest of the hill where a family of trees gathered, and I sat down, resting my back on a trunk. I sat under the tree for a long time considering the marble and wishing I didn't have to keep going. If only my life would end.

I watched Cooper survey the neighborhood, sniffing at every rock, tree, and thistle. I was envious. Is it better to come to realize that everything you ever believed was wrong? Or is it better to know nothing at all? Or is it better to embrace a myth so that you can sleep better at night? What is it we desire most? Is it joy, contentment, happiness, peace? Or is it the truth? And how could that ever be found?

The sun cast long shadows on the ground, and finally disappeared behind a far-off hill, making the sky red, purple and dark blue, and the rock of the landscape the color of rust. Then it all gave way to night.

I gave way to sleep.

As I slept at the base of that tree, I had a dream. I was again standing in the rain in a cornfield with my Madeline and her dark brown eyes. She smiled at me, and then she spoke.

"Oakruum. Come find me."

When I woke up, I didn't even realize that I'd fallen asleep. I reached beside me to find that Cooper had settled down next to me. I gave him a pat, and I scratched under his chin as I rose to my feet. Walking from the trees to the crest of the hill, I looked out on the dark valley. A few lights shone from a distant village beyond and above the star filled vastness of space radiated. I put my hands forward, surrendering.

"You are Oakruum; your home is Payraydayzay."

I had wandered across the field and gathered up Cooper and was ready to walk back to the wheel when it appeared, rotating over my head. The craft stopped just above me, maybe fifty feet, and the hatch opened up as the spinning orb descended to the ground. When it got to the ground, the angel stepped out of the ball and stood before me once again. We looked at each other for a long time.

She held out her hand to beckon me onward. I took her hand, and we climbed into the swirling orb, Cooper jumping in after us. As we ascended, I looked down at the now sacred tree where I had found rest.

"How did you know where I was?" I asked the old woman. She looked at me with a smile.

"I imagine this vessel will always be able to find you wherever you go. After all, she is yours."

CHAPTER FIVE

THE CHILD

Questions. Doubts and questions.

Mira, the Ethiopian woman, the angel, was patient in helping me to understand, or at least she tried.

"What part of you is you? If I cut off your finger and hold it in my hand, is that you?"

"No, of course not. I would be watching you hold my finger in your hand."

"Then how about your hand? Or your arm? What if I cut them off and held those? I suppose you would still be there watching, right? So, what part of you do I need to take so that I'm holding you in my hand?"

I did not have an answer.

"Your heart? Your eyes? Your brain? Tell me what part of you is you?"

I thought for a moment and then asked, "What are you talking about? My soul?"

"The infinite you," she said, as if correcting me. "That part of you that is connected to all things and everything, although I don't like to use the word 'part', that implies that it's not the whole you, for you, your person, isn't part of you, it is you. You are here and now, as you have always been and always will be. The body and the consciousness that you now indwell must gain illumination."

"Is that why you're here? To watch over me? To illuminate me?"

"Yes. You and many other refugees were forced to leave home and find shelter here on this planet. It has not been easy. But perhaps with Axzum's return, there is now hope."

"What do you mean?"

We had been rising slowly in the spinning orb, into the center of the wheel. The hatch had opened and closed and the ball had returned to its home in the wall, and now we were climbing the spiral staircase up into the cockpit.

"More on that later. For now, we have work to do."

When we took our last steps into the round cockpit of the flying wheel, we were met by Axzum, who was standing below the large hologram of Earth and holding the atlas that I had given him in the cabin. He looked up at me and, without a pause, crossed the room in a wisp and embraced me with his whole body, burying my face in his chest.

"Oakruum," he celebrated.

I had heard stories of people finding long-lost relatives, and I had been curious what that experience would be like. This had to be up there with the strangest of all. Understanding now that this alien had returned for his family, and that I was his first visit, shook me to my core.

Axzum pulled away and pointed at the atlas.

"Ella," he said, and he gestured toward the floating planet, spinning slowly in the middle of the room.

"Scorpion reef," I said as I took the atlas and walked around the globe in search of the Yucatan Peninsula and the Gulf of Mexico.

"Right here" and I touched the spot on the earth where I believed we would find what we were looking for. Pulling my hand away from the map, I looked around the cockpit and out the window curiously. Sure enough, the craft abruptly changed direction. Axzum pressed the metal hoop at the base of the pedestal, and we were off.

I glanced back at the globe to watch the light blue dot travel above the Sahara Desert and back toward the Atlantic Ocean. This time, however, the speed was not as dramatic and our feet remained fixed on the cobblestone floor. I looked over at Axzum, who was at the helm as it were, to understand why. Being a questioner is frustrating when the one who has the answers does not speak your language. This barrier was a problem.

The ship headed out over the coast, traveling above the waves. Axzum held up his hand toward me, and the wheel stopped moving. He paused for a moment and slowly lowered his hand. As he did, the ship descended into the water, and then beneath the waves.

"Oh." I exclaimed in complete surprise, and I ran to the window. Of course, there was nothing to see. It was dark and the water outside was near pitch-black, but it was quite clear by the way the water played on the glass windows of the cockpit dome we were traveling in the ocean.

Axzum spoke in his language to Mira and she translated to me.

"Traveling in the sea will take longer, but it will give us a chance to rest, and we can show you your library."

"Library? I have a library here?"

"You do," the old woman replied. "Follow me."

Moments later, we walked down a corridor to one chamber I had yet to explore. Traveling the long tube laced with thick, dead vines embedded in the rock, I felt like a blood vessel moving through an artery. We came to a round wooden door with a handle on a latch. Axzum opened the door; its hinges were in the middle so the door created a half circle when opened. Axzum went in first and held the door open for the rest of us, Mira, Cooper and I. When I stepped into the room and looked around, I was amazed. A large window, two stories tall, made up the far wall and the deep ocean current washed by outside. Below the window was a long, curved waistline table with drawers and shelves. The table was ornamented with bowls, statues, vases, goblets, and heads made of all kinds of pottery and stone. In the middle of the room was a large piece of black marble or granite. It had a flat top and looked like it weighed a ton, was surrounded by soft, welcoming, low bottom chairs covered with a type of plush white fur. I sat, sinking down into the luxurious fur.

"This is your library. Your books, notes and journals are all here. Perhaps some of these items will help you find illumination."

I looked around at the rest of the room. On one wall, there was a massive series of bookshelves, floor to ceiling, filled with thousands of books, small boxes and stacks of papers, and on the opposite wall, a line of wardrobes.

"Axzum and I have some things to discuss. So we'll leave you here to sort through it yourself."

I agreed, and the alien and the angel left me, closing the door until it latched. I sat for a long moment as Cooper explored the room with his nose. Finding very little of interest, he climbed up into one of the friendly chairs and nestled in, letting his chin rest on the seat of the chair, his nose sticking out. There are moments in life, some spectacular and some mundane, moments when you're traveling through the depths of the sea, incredibly, with schools of surprised fish passing by your window, and then you have silent, not incredible moments that you share with your best friend. Incredible and not incredible, both kinds of moments are to be anticipated and appreciated equally.

I closed my eyes and attempted to tunnel within, perhaps to connect with my ancient self to find illumination, but after about forty minutes, the only thing I achieved was a quick nap. Afterwards, I got up, bleary-eyed, and explored the room. I went to the bookshelf, pulled a book, and carefully flipped through it. It was fragile to where I felt like it might disintegrate in my hands. Page after brittle page, I saw indecipherable text, letters, symbols and drawings, along with painted pictures of alien plants and animals. Although I could not read the text nor understand the pictures and symbols, I recognized some of them from the nonsense doodles I had drawn all my life. This served as confirmation that I was not going senile or losing my mind. Rather, there was a part of me, somewhere deep within, that understood and communicated in this foreign language. If I could only tap into it.

I put the book back into its place and eyed the wardrobes across the room. Opening one of the wooden doors revealed a top shelf with helmets, goggles, headgear, and gloves. Draped over a hanging rod in the middle was a long row of multi-colored pieces of long fabric. I pulled one from the bar and held it out before me to discover that it was some sort of garment, perhaps a shawl or vestment. It was dark blue with golden stars patterned across it. When I draped the stole over my neck, the two parallel ends fell almost to the floor.

In the back of the wardrobe, I found a wooden chest. It opened with a creak, revealing its contents: a stack of papers, some maps and documents, a set of old skeleton keys, a cloth sack containing a handful of rocks, some precious looking diamonds, emeralds, and gold nuggets.

Below all of that was a pancake-sized dish made of sandstone with pictographs elaborately engraved into it. Around the dial, like a clock, were eight carved pictures: a farmer ploughing a field, planting seed, watering, pruning, reaping, grinding grain, baking bread and then feasting. I went around the dial, studying each picture, and then I went around again.

The dial clearly told a story. A progression. For what, I wondered. A piece of artwork maybe? Something about it seemed familiar.

There was a tap on the door—Mira.

"So, how did it go? Did you find anything?"

"Not really. Except this." I held up the sandstone dish. "What is this?"

"Oh, you have found your Aion Plate."

"My what?"

"It's an Aion Plate."

"Are we farmers?"

"No, Oakruum. Your brother, Axzum, and you yourself were, and still are, Esregg."

"Esregg?"

"It is a kind of guide. You are protectors."

"Protectors? Protectors of what?"

"Well, protectors of those who can't protect themselves, and above all, Senn Agra Days."

"So, Axzum and I, we are protectors of the Three Sisters?"

She nodded.

"Protectors of something that no longer exists. Sounds like we weren't very good."

"Failures are deaths that allow the gift of rebirth."

"And the plates?"

"They are ancient relics that tell a story."

She took the plate and held it up so I could watch her rotate it.

"A seed, for example, goes into the ground; it sprouts, grows, bears fruit, and dies, and releases a new seed. Round and round it goes. It's a circle."

I nodded.

"But then take a being, like yourself, you are born, you grow, you bear fruit, you die and are born anew. You, yourself, are like the seed. You are a circle. And the entire universe is a circle, too."

"I'm sorry. I don't understand."

"Oakruum, listen to the most important part. The story of the seed takes a season. The story of a being takes a lifetime. And the story of the universe takes eons, billions of years."

"Of course."

"What if I were to tell you that each one of these takes the same amount of time? A breath. You breathe in, you breathe out. You breathe in and are born, you breathe out and die. You breathe in and a universe is born, breathe out and the universe dies."

I looked at her for a long moment, and said, "I'm going to have to sit with this for a while."

"Well, exactly. Thus the plate. It's like an existential map. It helps us to understand the nature of the universe and our place within the circle. Where do you think you would be found?"

I looked at the plate for a long time. I knew the answer. I was utterly lost, but I was too embarrassed to say.

"So Axzum and I, we were...What did you call us again?"

"You are Esregg—protectors. The stole you are wearing is one of the vestments."

"Are there more of us? Where are they? I want to know what happened. I want to know everything."

"Yes. I knew you would want everything. That's why I gave it to you. You never found it illuminating?"

I reached into my pocket and pulled out a worn leather pouch, and untied its strap.

"Yes, of course I still have it. It's right here."

I opened the pouch and dropped the silver blue marble into my open palm.

"It's been in this pocket every day of my life since you gave it to me. But how was it supposed to give me illumination? If anything, this thing has been the source of all the heartbreak I've experienced in the last ninety-five years."

The angel looked at me with pity, and then turned and walked out.

"Follow me."

I followed the mysterious woman down the corridor that led back to the center of the ship. We then walked through the big, round, doughnut room with the rotating orbs resting in their places in the wall, and into another portal I had not yet explored.

We traveled through another spoke of the wheel and into a chamber that I would end up calling the lightning room. The room was perfectly spherical with the walls made of some sort of shaded glass, except it couldn't have been made of glass. It had to have been able to conduct electricity, because a long rod stuck out of the bottom of the floor and came to a point in the center of the room, and electrical charges, lightning, continually shot from the walls to that central point and back again. Every second, four or five strikes of lightning shot out from some random direction; the space was alive, excited. I wondered if this was what it would be like to be reduced to the size of a molecule and given entry into the brain to witness the tiny receptors shooting data at one another.

Mira walked to the center of the room, unfazed by the high voltage strikes happening all around her. She motioned with her hand at a point in the room just above the metal rod and summoned me forth.

I approached and slowly placed the marble not on the rod, but a spot just above it, maybe two or three inches higher. When the marble found its home floating above the rod in the middle of the room, a lightning strike struck from the wall and hit the marble, maintaining the connection, and then another. In quick succession, twenty to thirty strikes hit the marble and held their beam upon it. The room suddenly filled with a whole other place, a whole other world, images, three dimensional and real. I can remember watching old slideshows of some boring relative's vacation once; if you could somehow step into one of those slides to live and dwell, this is what it would have been like.

Before and around me appeared images of strange places and people. At first, it was indecipherable, an odd-looking plant, a leg, an arm, a book, a bottle. Then a scene played out before me: a long table with people gathered, eating and drinking and laughing, talking. The people in the scene looked like Axzum, with the same telltale eyes and translucent skin, the multicolored ribbon-like streams running across their skin.

"That must be Axzum," I declared, pointing at a being in the projection.

The old woman nodded.

Then in the scene, Axzum held up the plate, the very Aion Plate I had found in the chest in the wardrobe.

Axzum handed it to another, who took it and was holding it up with pride. The being was wearing the very star covered mantle I had on.

"This is the evening of your call," Mira whispered, putting her arm around me. "It's a high honor. It is when a leader accepts a certain purpose."

"Who is this holding the plate?" I asked. The angel looked at me as if she might flick me in the nose.

"That is you, Oakruum. This is your anthology, after all."

I froze, staring at the strange looking alien holding the plate.

"You see, you spent years studying, training, persevering to a point where you finally received a call, just like your brother, Axzum. We were all so proud, so hopeful."

I couldn't speak. I had no memory of this. I watched this being to see if anything, anything at all about this person, resembled me as I now know myself—some look or hand gesture, some similarity. But there was nothing about this being that was like me at all.

"When did these events take place?"

"In Earth time," the woman whispered. "Millions of years ago. Tens of millions. Maybe a hundred million."

"What? How?"

"This flesh and bone you wear is but temporary. Your actual person is infinite—light and spirit and gravity."

I looked at her, trying to wrap my mind around her words. The angel went to the marble and turned it slightly and the scene disappeared.

"No, wait. I'm not done."

But a new scene now encompassed us. The room darkened, and I felt like running for shelter as the wind picked up and the rain filled the room. Except, it didn't. There was no wind, and we were completely dry. It was an illusion. A scene played out around us. As I oriented myself, I could see that we were on the water, on a lake or an ocean, in a small boat, rocked roughly by the waves. A dark figure caped in rain gear clung to both sides of the dinghy.

"And this is your failure," the old woman said, opening her hand toward the scene.

"Failure? What failure?" I responded, moving closer to the figure to understand what was happening.

"Remember I told you about your call and purpose? You refused your call and set out on your own, turning from your responsibilities."

"Running away? Sounds like I was a little selfish."

The angel nodded.

"More than a little, I'm afraid. A call is a difficult thing to accept. We always imagine glory and honor, but unfortunately it always requires suffering and sacrifice, two things which are easy to run from."

I watched the man, apparently myself, fight against the rain, wind, waves, and himself. Finally, I found the commonality I was looking for.

"Watch," the old woman whispered, and pointed to the horizon.

Something was coming. A large, dark nothing grew in the distance and moved menacingly toward the man and the boat at sea. It only took a few moments before the darkness had overtaken the boat, devouring it and its passenger entirely. Inside the dark blob, the wind and rain stopped and there was nothing—no light, sound, or air. I watched as the boat broke apart, disintegrate, and the sailor struggled to move, struggled to breathe.

"Is this how I die?" I asked the woman, keeping my focus on the scene, but she didn't respond. The man writhed in the belly of the dark glob, both hands around his neck as remnants of the broken boat floated off in all directions. The scene had almost gone completely black when a dim light appeared just outside of the nothingness. Then, the source of the light, a red lantern, cut through the bubble's membrane. It was Axzum, holding the lantern in one hand and grabbing the dying man with the other, pulling him out of the void and back into the storm, back into the water, and ultimately, onto the beach.

"Breathe. Oakruum, breathe."

He laid the man on the sand at the water's edge, rain and wind pounding his face. The man gasped and then pulled in a much-needed breath.

"Your brother saved you that day."

"So, I could have died." I murmured.

"There are much worse things than death, I'm afraid."

"Then what was that thing?"

"That is the Nuul. It preys on selfishness. You were fortunate to be pulled from the abyss that day."

The old woman went to the stand and removed the marble from its floating spot.

"Hold on. I want to see more. Isn't there more?"

"My dear friend, there's plenty more, but there's no time for that right now. This is your anthology, your history," she told me, handing me the tiny ball. "It contains everything. Keep it safe."

I looked at the jewel in my hand, tempted to place it back on the stand to see more.

"There will be plenty of time for more catching up later."

I took the marble and put it back into the leather pouch, and into my pocket. To think I'd been carrying this thing around all these years, all the answers closer to me than I ever imagined.

"For now, we must reinstate your call," Mira said, as she removed the stole from around my neck and walked out of the room with it.

Moments later, I found myself in the large round room in the center of the wagon wheel, where the small orbs sat spinning in their little nooks in the wall. The old woman had me stop in the middle of the room and stood before me, quite close, and spoke to me as if her words were the most important, the most serious.

"Do you know the four strongest forces in the universe?"

"There's four?"

"Fission, fusion, electromagnetism, and …"

"Gravity?" I guessed.

"The Oolah," she corrected me.

"Right, the Oolah. As I recall from high school science class, it is the weakest of the forces."

"It would appear to be for humans observing from their planet, but in actuality, the Oolah is by far the most powerful force in the universe. In most places, the Oolah is neutral, very weak, but it's like watching a river go by. On the surface, the water may appear calm, peaceful, and tranquil, but beneath, in the depths, the water creates a powerful force that can move mountains. So powerful, in fact, that a rather large river can create what is called an eddy, a place where the water swirls and even moves backwards. The current goes upstream, swirling, and it creates a vortex, a vortex street, a place on the river where you find a whole endless line of swirling Vortai."

"Vortai?" I looked at her skeptically. '

"Vortai," she replied, and she gestured to the swirling orbs in the wall.

"There are Vortai everywhere, powerful reversals of current. They are in the river, they are in the wind, they are in the ocean, and inside of you as well. These Vortai are weak. However, there are powerful Vortai, spinning, swirling in the aftermath that follows every star system. In the Wake. These Vortai are not made of water or wind. They are made of the Oolah."

"Wait—where? I don't understand."

Before she could answer, Axzum entered the room and spoke to Mira in his own tongue. The angel responded, and for a few minutes, the two seemed to have an argument, their voices strained and heightened. Mira turned back to me and said, "Axzum wants to tell you himself."

She took a necklace that she had around her neck and pulled out from underneath her white garment a spherical gold medallion. The medallion hung from the end of the gold chain carved with an ornate design. Mira undid a clasp and opened the medallion—within it, another spinning orb. She flicked her hand out like a magician, and the orb floated out of the medallion and into the center of the room. As it moved, it grew, as the others had done, so that by the time it reached the center of the room, it was almost large enough to step into.

Axzum gestured for us to gather around the spinning flickering orb, and when we were all in place, the blue, silver, and purple glow reflected on our faces. Axzum began to speak, words right out of his mouth this time, and this time, I understood him.

"Oakruum, you must not be selfish anymore. Accept your call and do not run away."

"I…I'm sorry, Axzum. I won't."

"Good. There is important work to do."

"I understand. But how is it I can understand you now?"

"As you see in this room, there are eight sacred shrines for eight sacred orbs." I looked around the room at the eight shrines as he spoke, some with glowing orbs, some empty.

"Eight kinds of Vortai are known to us. Each one manipulates the Oolah, providing us with tools that help us share in communion with one another."

Axzum put both arms out, referring to the orb before us. "This one can help us communicate with each other. It has been in Mira's possession until now. The other two in our possession you experienced: one can be used to transport, the other for healing and restoration."

"So where are the other Vortai?"

"This is why we're here, Oakruum."

"We know of one other, but the rest have been lost." Axzum spoke with words I heard not only with my ears, but within my being as well.

"There is still time for restoration, but you cannot be afraid to die."

I closed my eyes for a moment and absorbed the words. I suppose at that moment, I also accepted my call.

"As I told you before, Axzum. I am not afraid."

"We must find the Vortai and return them to this wall."

I nodded to Axzum. I did not know what this task would require, but there was a willingness within me I welcomed and enjoyed. Many times in life, when we stop and take an assessment of our value, our skills, and our abilities, I think we often overlook willingness. It's a small, simple thing, but very well could make the difference, and possibly, the only thing you really need.

I bowed my head slightly and Axzum placed the mantle around my neck.

Three loud metallic gong sounds came from the cockpit, and the vessel stopped.

"We've arrived," Axzum said, looking at me. "We must equip ourselves for our quest to find Ella, if she is indeed here, as you theorize. Come."

As Axzum moved toward one of the round portals, the orb that we had been using to communicate shrank down to the size of a golf ball again, and floated into one of the wall shrines. Looking around the room, I noted, now there are three present, five more to go.

We journeyed down the corridor, another arm of the vessel I had yet to explore, emptied into a large tool room. If this ship had a garage, this was it. It was the size of an airplane hangar with tools, machinery, and equipment of all kinds stored on shelves along the wall. Massive worktables lined the middle of the room holding a menagerie of odd-looking tools and devices, all other worldly in design, yet archaic: no electrical outlets, power cords, no sign of anything from an age of industry.

Axzum went to a rack coming out of the wall and grabbed two brown, leathery-looking suits and handed one to me. I held the suit out to see what exactly it was: a full bodysuit, not leather, but a lightweight, presumably waterproof, material with fins at the feet. We were about to go swimming. I looked from the suit to a round glass door that led to a smaller room that had a round window with dark blue water slapping against it from the outside. I looked at Axzum in disbelief, tempted to go back and get the magic conversation ball so that we could have some sort of discussion, but he just nodded and gestured for me to put on the suit. Seeing no other option, I wiggled my legs in. It fit like a glove, and in moments, I was completely outfitted for scuba diving. It fit over my head with big round goggles, and a pyramid shaped snout mask for the nose and mouth. Above the goggles, at the forehead, was a lamp.

I watched Axzum through the goggles. He grabbed what looked like a giant, six-foot-tall pair of pliers from another rack on the wall and carried them to the glass door. The glass portal slid open, and he stood in the doorway and looked back at me. I must have looked ridiculous, waddling across the floor with those flipper feet, through the round opening and into the smaller chamber. I stood in the airlock, staring out at the deep through the window. Axzum joined me and the glass door slid closed behind us.

I could feel my muscles tighten and my anxiety ratchet up within me. I was not a poor swimmer. I could hold my own. But this wasn't the pool at the YMCA. I hoped that my newly restored youth and strength would carry me places that my senior citizen mind did not want to go. The lock filled with water, hitting my feet and rising up my legs, then waist, chest, and chin high in just a few seconds. Somehow, our feet were locked to the floor, so while the water rose over our heads, we did not float. Once the room filled, the outside door slid open, our feet were released, and Axzum and I swam out of the side of the big wheel and into the warm waters of Scorpion Reef.

The reef was a beautiful, multicolored fantasy world with exploding plumes of purple, red, blue and pink coral. Small tropical fish, black and white, orange and red, swam away from us in all directions as we journeyed toward the ocean floor. Axzum turned on the light at his forehead and I followed his lead. Two bright beams of light shone down on the rocky ocean bed below.

When we got to the ocean floor, I stopped, treaded water for a moment, and looked back up from where we had come, at the schools of brightly colored fish, the coral, the big dark wagon wheel above, and the sunlight dancing on the surface beyond. Axzum swam to the base of a rock formation covered with coral and teeming with ocean life. The light from our foreheads searched over the jagged rocks until it met the dark void of a small cave.

At the bottom of the rock formation where the coral reef found its home, there was an opening just big enough for two people to swim through side by side.

The tunnel seemed to have a strong current, as water flowed against us and then with us, back and forth, as if the ocean were breathing. It felt like swimming into the belly of a dragon. As we swam into the darkness, every part of me wanted to go back. Part of me wishes we had gone back, and maybe if we had, things would have been different.

We swam further, down through a chasm in the ocean floor, deeper into the dragon's throat, to a place where the cavern was blocked by a rock the size of a compact car. As we approached, I remember thinking how much the rock looked like a big peach pit, covered with deep wrinkles, the way a peach pit has. As it turned out, this is exactly what it was.

This was no rock. This was a seed.

Axzum knocked on the seed and softly caressed it as if it were a priceless treasure. Then he opened the big pair of pliers so that the mouth was gripped tightly around the seed and let go. The alien pincers seemed to do all the work, squeezing the seed until it cracked open and dislodged from the side of the cavern.

The underwater current flowed against us, suddenly switched directions, and as the water surged away from us, it took a sizable piece of the seed's shell with it. For the first time, I could see inside the shell and confirmed that my intuition had been correct. Inside the shell was a swirling orb, and inside the orb, a baby. Ella.

Axzum pulled the pliers and threw them aside, which disappeared into the darkness, and put his hands into the shell and then the orb. It was a moment I will never forget. Axzum caressed his daughter's tender cheek, the baby still covered from the elements by the orb's mysterious protection. My heart breaks every time I think about it, for Axzum only got to touch his child for a brief moment before tragedy struck.

As the ocean current shifted again, the flow going against us now; the seed broke apart. Axzum pulled the orb with the baby inside out of the seed just seconds before it completely blew apart, sending pieces scattering in all directions and into our faces. One of the sharp rocky shards caught Axzum directly in the face, knocking him sideways and ripping the mask and goggles from his suit. His equipment was carried away with the current. We both held on to the side of the cavern as the water pressure intensified. With the seed out of the way, the ocean breathed with an even more powerful flow.

Without a mask, Axzum held his breath and handed me the baby, still safe within the orb. I held the baby tight and braced myself, jamming my body into a cleft in the cavern's wall. I yelled at Axzum to hold on, but as I did, the water flow switched back again and pulled Axzum off the rock and into the depths below.

"Axzum!"

But he was gone. His body flailing as he disappeared into the depths. Waves of panic washed over me. I looked into the abyss and then I looked at the baby in my arms. I'll search for Axzum, I thought, after I get her to safety.

When the current shifted again, I pushed away from the rock and swam as hard as I could out of the cave, over the ocean floor, above the coral, and back to the wheel.

When the water finally emptied from the airlock and the glass door slid open, Mira was there to meet me.

"Axzum? Where's Axzum?"

She took the baby from my arms.

"I'll find him. I promise."

The glass door closed again, the lock refilled with water, and I swam back into the sea searching for Axzum. For hours, I swam around the coral reef, hunting for my brother, but there was no sign of him. Heart stricken, I couldn't help but think of the memory I witnessed in the lightning room, Axzum pulling me from the abyss, saving me.

I failed him again.

I had promised the angel and myself not to return without him, but after an exhaustive search, I finally had to give up. After taking off the suit and re-hanging it on the wall, I found an old bench in the tool room and sat, the navy blue mantle in my lap.

My whole life, my entire existence, it seemed, had been slashed and cut and shredded with loss, every loss leaving a mark, a scar. This loss would someday be another scar, but at that moment, it was a gaping wound, making standing, walking, even breathing a chore. Consumed with this grief for what seemed like ages, Cooper came in, fresh off of his nap. He came to my feet, tended to me as if he understood what had happened, and comforted me.

Mira followed, carrying the baby, now wrapped in a blanket.

"He's gone. There was nothing I could do."

The angel approached me, still sitting on the bench with Cooper at my feet, and gently set the baby in my arms.

"Let me introduce you to your niece, Ella."

"Ella," I whispered, looking into the light blue eyes of an infant that was both newborn and apparently tens of millions of years old.

"She was sleeping safely in an orb that sustains prolonged hibernation. Now she needs her mother."

"She's beautiful."

Ella looked at me, her face exploding with bright ribbons of light—blue, purple, green and gold.

"There's still time to make things right," Mira whispered as she sat down next to me.

"I know. I see."

"But we can't do this alone. We are going to need help."

CHAPTER SIX

THE SHAMAN

Later that night, I dreamt I was a sheepdog, a border collie. One of those driven black and white streaks that you find on a farm, running with the sheep, between, over, under, and through the herd. They guide and move the vacant-faced bleating crowd down the dirt path, beside stone walls, broken fences, and rusty gates.

I can remember the feeling of urgency, like a parent taking their child to the hospital after a nasty fall. Also, there was an awareness of being one of the flock; I was at once the shepherd and the shepherded. I'm not sure why I would dream such a dream. Perhaps the loss of Axzum, coupled with the new responsibility of taking care of Ella, made me feel like a sheepdog. Afterwards, the dream felt more than just a projection of my unconscious; it felt real, as if I had been there before. The path, the stones, the rolling green hills, the granite outcroppings—it was all so familiar. It was a place I knew well, though I had not been to such a place, and I certainly had never been a sheepdog, not that I can remember.

The red eyes of the black wolf—this remains seared into my mind. Even now, after such a long time, I don't think I had ever seen something so terrifying. It came out of the dark, through the morning mist, not with a sudden pounce or a sneaking crawl, but with a confidence, a steady saunter that conveyed strength and power, like the leader of a world power that had no chance of losing, parading before his victims to feast on their fear.

The sheep huddled, sewing as a flock into one

another. The wolf raised its snout and sniffed the air with a grin. One more step, and then the entire herd exploded, and did what herds do in such a moment. They fled, stampeding as one down the dirt road. As they did, they expelled their weakest member, trampling the runt under foot, and kicking her out behind them, an offering of sorts. The half-broken outcast tried to scramble to its feet and get away, but the wolf was too big, fast, and ruthless to allow it.

I can remember, in the dream, attempting to defend the lamb, but was easily cast aside with a bolt of black jagged fur and claws. I rolled about helplessly as the wolf held me down with its hind leg and tore into its shrieking prey with its teeth. The bleating of the lambs caused me to awaken.

The baby was crying, or at least I thought she was. The crying was echoing through the tunnel-like passageways that fanned out to the perimeter of the spaceship. I stumbled out of my sleeping compartment and made my way down the tube toward the chamber where we had laid Ella the night before.

With the trauma of losing Axzum still fresh, we had gathered enough strength to find a safe place for the babe to rest. Mira had carried her, and I followed, to a room at the ends of a spoke I had not yet explored. This chamber was completely different from the others. I called it the cocoon room. As we entered, we breached a thin membrane made of who knows what. The room was soft and dimly lit, spherical. It was like standing inside of a golf ball if the dimples curved outward. The ceiling, wall, and floor were comprised of dozens of round, three-foot little dimples. Cocoons.

Mira led me to a platform in the middle of the room,

the only spot without a dimple. And then in one continuous motion, she pulled a ball from her pouch, held it in her hand, which grew to the same spinning globe I found the child in, and she gently placed the baby into the spinning orb and we watched as the orb nestled itself into a cocoon on the perimeter of the room. It was a perfect fit. The ball kept spinning, lodged halfway into the wall with the little girl inside. Mira assured me she would be safe, every need supplied, and we both retreated to our bunks for a much-needed night's sleep.

Now, I hurried down the corridor, through the membrane, and into the cocoon room. Cooper, who had heard me stir, was up as well and on my heels. We found the baby quietly sleeping in the spinning orb, just as we had left her. The crying in my ears stopped as I realized my mind was playing tricks on me. I stood on the round platform for a moment, watching the alien child sleep. Her translucent skin glistened, and the multicolored ribbons streaked across her face and body. She was definitely alive, and quite content.

Mira entered the room behind me. She heard me rise and clamor through the ship to check on Ella. Mira stood behind me for a moment in silence.

"I don't think I can do this," I whispered.

"I understand. This will not be easy."

"I want to go back."

"There is no back. All we have is now, this moment, and the next."

I turned to look at her. I knew what she was saying was true; I needed someone to say it out loud.

"The past is gone. You can't go back there. The past dwells within us now. In the present moment, we stand upon the past and use it as a resource."

"I had a dream. I think I was a dog."

"It is the past."

"I was a sheepdog?"

"At one point or another, I'm sure you were. Our being connects the dotted experience of our past lives through dreams."

"This dream seemed more real than ever. I thought I heard the baby crying."

"I'd imagine since meeting Axzum, your true being has begun to awaken. Don't be surprised if you experience more dreams and visions. Hold on to them. They have something to teach you."

Mira walked to the place where Ella was cocooned in the wall and placed her hand on the spinning orb Ella slept within.

"Our job now is to deliver this child safely to her mother."

"And where's that? Is she here, on earth?"

"No, I'm afraid not. She's not even in this system."

I looked at her, trying to process the old woman's words. Not in this system...

"We will have to go to Geuld."

I remember the orientation Axzum had given me in the cabin, and remembered the planet he claimed was in orbit at the edge of our solar system, far beyond Pluto. Geuld, he had called it. Since then, I had wondered about its existence and how it could go undetected.

I must have failed at hiding my doubt, for the old woman held out both her hands to me as Axzum had done in the shack. "Do you know what this is?" Mira whispered to me.

"Koinonae. Axzum showed me."

"It is how we share in intimacy, desire and, ultimately, truth," the angel instructed. "When we are bound in Koinonae, it is impossible to deceive. There are no lies. So here, let me extinguish your doubts."

The woman closed her eyes and stood still before me, hands out and open. The soft white light that shone from the spinning orb that held the infant danced on the angel's face. I slowly placed my hands in hers and closed my eyes. In an instant, I became her, sharing a precious experience which she had held on to for ages as if it were a priceless artifact.

I was now standing as Mira before a great throng, hundreds or thousands, seated in an immense gathering space or temple. An aisle ran up the middle, dividing the masses. The vaulted ceiling rose hundreds of feet above to a dome covered with round windows. Light streamed through tall windows, which caught particles of dust and made the air seem alive. I looked around, and I found I stood at the center of an elevated stage made of marble or stone, surrounded by finely clothed attendants, royalty perhaps.

"We must be on Payraydayzay. Were you the leader? The queen?"

"Hush. Just watch."

At the far end of the aisle appeared a tiny figure, a little girl of maybe six or seven, if she were human. She walked ceremonially up the aisle, trying her best not to make a mistake. The eyes of the entire room were upon her. She held both hands just below her heart, and in her hands, she carried a small red bag made of cloth. When, smiling brightly, she got to the stairs; she stopped and held out the bag toward me, toward Mira. I descended within Mira down the stairs, and when I got to the girl, took the red bag and softly ran my hand over her head for a moment and then turned and climbed back to the top. As I rose, bag in hand, I noticed two beings standing together at the very top, the place I had been standing a moment before. The two held each other's hands.

"Oh, this is a wedding."

And then I recognized the alien being from the vision in the lightning room.

"Is this my wedding?"

As Mira, I opened the red bag and poured its contents into my left hand. It was like sand, golden and bright, yet lighter, and powdery, like pollen. I raised the pile of pollen in my hand up to my mouth and blew. The yellow dust exploded out in all directions, covering the bride and groom. The couple cheered and laughed, which was echoed by the gathered crowd. And then the pollen, which seemed to multiply exponentially, like magic pixie dust, spread to every corner of the temple, filling the room with sparkling light and falling upon every head that had gathered. The people laughed, kissed, hugged, and blew gold dust at each other. The groom kissed the bride as gold flickering pollen showered past their locked faces. I laughed out of sheer amazement.

"I know this! I've seen this before!"

"Of course you have. In a dream, I'd imagine."

Mira, in the vision, raised her hands in the air and invited all those gathered to look up. The dome, the lid of the temple, opened up and pollen swirled out of the room as the air carried it away. At once, the congregation took a deep breath, and then, as one, blew the dust toward the opening. The pollen puffed up and out of the temple and into the early evening air.

Once outside, almost in an instant, we became that

dust and then the dust became light. I was no longer indwelling Mira, rather I floated as one particle of dust out above the alien temple and into the sky. The green and blue Payraydayzian landscape below me. In that moment, the dust became light, and I too was light and shot out into space, traveling at a ridiculous speed away from the planet and away from the sun, whizzing toward the outer edges of the solar system. Mira showed me, from the perspective of a particle of pure light, the world on the edge of the solar system, the eleventh planet.

Geuld.

The dark planet spun with the speed and intensity of a spinning top on a glass table, making a complete revolution in less than a minute. Across its surface, black holes opened up and collapsed back down to nothing in mere seconds.

"My god," I said, still gripping Mira's hands with all my might. "How is this possible? I don't understand what I am seeing."

"All systems have eleven worlds at birth. Some are solid, some are gaseous, but one is always made of gravity. Along with its star, the far planet gives balance to its system." She continued, "And it becomes a gateway to other systems in the galaxy."

I watched as I quickly approached the mysterious world. A handful of black eyes opened and closed across the planet's surface.

"Are those wormholes?"

Mira didn't answer. Instead, as we crashed into the planet's atmosphere as a particle of light plummeted towards its surface, a hole opened up. I shot into it, and it closed behind me.

I took my hands away from Mira's and opened my

eyes. The old woman opened hers, and we looked at each other.

"I thought during Koinonae we share our deepest desires?" I pressed her, remembering what Axzum had shared with me.

"We do. And I just showed you mine. I desire for my people, my community, to be reunited, and for that light in which it births to spread through the entire universe."

"The woman in the vision?" I asked, "The bride."

"Heiros Gamos."

"Heiros Gamos? Axzum said this too."

"Her name is Juulez."

"Juulez. What happened to her? Where is she?"

"That remains a mystery. We escaped together when Payraydayzay was destroyed, but since then, she's been lost to us."

"It's strange—I have no memory of her at all, but I had a familiar feeling when I saw her, a feeling that I've had for one I knew a long time ago." I held out my hands to Mira, inviting her to share in Koinonae, to see my deepest desire. She closed her eyes and put her hands in mine.

Moments later, when she had witnessed my heart and the scene with Madeline in the field, in the rainstorm, she pulled her hands away and looked at me, astonished.

"Juulez."

"Her name is Madeline. I only knew her for a short time many, many years ago, but..."

"You have thought of her every day of your life since."

"She is always in my dreams."

"She is not truly Madeline, just as you are not truly William Henry."

"What are you saying?"

"I'm telling you what you've always known, but have been too afraid to embrace."

"No, it's impossible."

"Let me ask you, how long did you know this Madeline?"

"I don't know…Maybe a few months. We had a class together in school."

"How long ago?"

"This was well over eighty-five years ago."

"And where do you suppose she is now? We need to find her."

"This was back in Iowa."

Without another word, Mira turned and left the chamber.

"Oakruum. Come find me."

Cooper and I found Mira moments later in the cockpit, standing beneath the enlarged hologram of the planet in the vision. Geuld. The mysterious dark globe spun wildly as the old woman examined it. Hundreds of black holes opened and closed like mouths across the surface, without pattern or symmetry.

Mira acknowledged my presence and gestured toward the dark planet.

"This is Geuld," she said, "Where we need to go. Each of these openings is a gate, a kind of doorway that opens to another similar planet at the edge of another solar system in our galaxy."

"There are so many gates."

"There are many systems."

"And Ella's mother? Through which gate will we find her?"

As we talked, what must have been another hundred

mouths opened and closed in their own unique timing. Some holes seemed to remain open for a few seconds, and others appeared and disappeared in the blink of an eye.

"This is our dilemma: I don't know. But I know of one who has studied such things."

"And you know where that person is?"

"No, but I may know of one who would. The Shaman."

"The Shaman?"

"Yes, he's a kind of guide. One who sees."

The angel moved to the wheel in the middle of the room and switched illuminated planets with a flick of a wrist. Geuld shrank and returned to its orbit at the far side of the room. Earth became magnified. A light blue dot marked our position in the Gulf of Mexico on the map. The three other points marked by red dots still appeared on the globe, one in Africa, Italy, and southern England.

Mira positioned the earth so that the red dot in England was within reach, and she touched it with her palm. Moments later, the ship ascended slowly out of the sea; the sun beaming through the windows as it emerged. Once it was above the water, it flew off.

Mira, Cooper, and I floated safely above the floor of the cockpit, once again locked in place by gravity. As we zipped across the ocean just above the water at lightning speed, I fit some pieces together.

I was now on a preposterous scavenger hunt sixty-five million years in the making. Earth years, of course. By other measurements, much shorter. Just before Payraydayzay was destroyed, sending fractured pieces of the planet across the system, causing extinction events on Earth, Mars, and possibly beyond, a group of survivors escaped and scattered across the cosmos as refugees. I, apparently, was one of them, as well as some long-lost love who may have not been so long lost after all. Who else was out there? How on earth could we ever find them?

The wheel came to a stop moments later and descended into a lonely field in the English countryside. It was early evening on this side of the planet, and dark, cold, foggy, and rainy outside, a stark contrast to the sunny blue skies of the Gulf of Mexico we viewed from the cockpit just a few minutes before. The fog was thick, making visibility beyond a few feet impossible.

I retreated to my library to change. I threw on jeans and a jacket I discovered in the wardrobe, and met Mira in the main chamber. She had already pulled the orb used to disembark from its place in the wall and was standing inside of it. I stepped into the orb and Cooper, who had been at my heels the whole morning, joined us.

The door in the ship's belly opened, and as we descended within the spinning orb into the foggy air, I could see that, again, the wheel had parked itself upon a gathering of boulders set in a circle. As we floated away from the ship, I knew where we were, and I had to laugh out loud.

"Are you kidding me?"

I had seen pictures of Stonehenge, but with the wheel resting perfectly on the ancient Celtic monument, partially obscured by the fog and the rain, I suddenly felt like a tourist on my own planet.

"We truly know nothing…" I said, still watching the scene as we floated by the park's visitor center.

"Moving forward," the angel responded. "It may be best if you simply forget everything you ever learned."

Moments later, the ball floated into a small hamlet, hovering just above the sidewalk, passing streetlights. The streets were empty, but the lights from homes and businesses gave signs of life. Mira stopped the orb in front of an old pub, and it shrank, dropping us safely onto the sidewalk. A wooden sign hung over the door: "The Old Stone Tavern." We quickly tumbled inside.

Inside the old pub, it felt more like a cave than a room, with a musty smell that reminded me of my grandmother's attic. Some scattered seats and stools were occupied by a dozen patrons. A small, slender man with a shiny bald head and a long beard braided to a point, stood behind the bar. He looked as if he were shouting at an upside-down kettle that sat on the counter.

"Okay," he laughed. "You're right. I would not have attempted such things, even in my younger days, but you wouldn't be in that wrinkled skin if you'd been a little more careful, eh?" The bald man laughed again, pointing at the upside-down kettle.

Mira approached the bar, and I followed. As we got to the bar, the man looked up from the kettle.

"Mira! My god, Mira. What are you doing here?"

The man took a step back, and the kettle suddenly moved. That's when I realized the kettle was not a kettle, but a tortoise. Yes—a huge tortoise. The tortoise pivoted its body and twisted its long neck to get a better look at us.

"Muurchia," Mira said. "It's time. Axzum has arrived, and this is his brother, Oakruum."

"My god, Oakruum," said the bald man.

"Oakruum. This is Muurchia Eliade."

I offered my hand, and the man grabbed it with both of his.

"My apologies. I'm very new to all this," I said. "Actually, part of me is convinced that this is all some sort of drug induced hallucination."

The man laughed again, the sound bellowing across the room.

"Were you just now talking with that tortoise?"

Muurchia Eliade looked at Mira and laughed again.

"I suppose you haven't told him."

"No."

"And Axzum? Where's Axzum?"

"We lost him," I answered.

Muurchia laughed again, to my surprise.

"Of course you have. That's the Axzum I know. Always getting himself blown up, crushed, or disintegrated. Not to worry, Oakruum, my boy, you will see your brother again. Axzum will turn up, he always does."

Muurchia hobbled to the end of the bar, holding the counter for balance until he got to his walking stick.

"You must be the Shaman?"

"Oh, no," Muurchia laughed again. "I'm no Shaman. I'm more of a bard. Dadka, Dadka is the Shaman."

"Dadka? Well, where is he? Can we see him?"

Muurchia motioned toward the tortoise. I looked at the tortoise and then I looked at Mira.

"The Shaman is a tortoise? Come on now."

Muurchia interrupted me, no longer laughing, now more pastoral.

"He says your person is fractured."

"Excuse me?" I replied. "He said what, exactly?"

"He can see your person, your true self," Muurchia replied. "He can tell that you have experienced much loss."

I looked from the bearded man down to the tortoise and back to the man. The man looked down at the tortoise and back at me, and then, smiling, said, "You've been in exile, alienated, isolated. This is not a peaceful existence."

Mira interrupted. "I believe he may have found

Juulez without even knowing it."

"Is that right?" Muurchia responded. "How wonderful."

Muurchia smiled and then shared in soft conversation with the tortoise on the counter.

"But our priority must always be the health of our person. We are absolutely no benefit to anyone else or any endeavor while our person is diminished, or in fragments."

"You really do not need to be so concerned about me," I retorted. "My person, or whatever you want to call it, is fine."

The angel, the magic genie, and the tortoise all looked at me without saying a word.

"No, really," I said, "This isn't even what we came here for. We came here because..."

Muurchia suddenly raised his walking stick that had a stone the size of a grapefruit at the end, and gently touched the center of my chest with the stone.

"Close your eyes and place your hand on the shell."

I hesitated, but when I saw that the bald man would probably hold the staff to my heart until I relented, I set my right hand upon the tortoise shell.

"Now, open," he instructed. I opened my eyes and looked down at my body, and I don't know how, but I could see beyond my flesh, my skin; I could see myself, my person, as they called it. I could see the same bright colored ribbons flashing through my body as Axzum's body had. What they were made of, I had no clue. Matter? Light? Spirit? All the above? Whatever it was, it was not alien to me. I knew it well, as if I'd always been able to see it.

At first, my body seemed fine, complete and whole, but as I gained courage to examine it more closely, there were indeed pieces missing. It looked wilted, tired, old and sick, with spaces, voids that I had conditioned myself to overlook. I was a dead leaf in February. Recognizing the fractures and tears caused me to feel them: the pain, a pain that is hard to describe and worse than any physical pain that I had ever endured. I felt weak and exhausted.

"My god, I had no idea."

For a moment, I thought I might crumble into a million pieces on the floor. I jerked my hand away from the shell and the old man slowly pulled the rock away from my chest.

"Come with me," he commanded, and he slowly hobbled with the help of his stick into the back room, and I followed. The swinging door with a round window made me think we would find ourselves in the back kitchen. This was nothing like a back kitchen; it was much more like a zoo or an aviary.

We entered an enormous cavern with a glass-windowed ceiling, almost two stories above. Around the perimeter of the room were dens cut into the rock wall, perches and branches protruding from the side. Perched on the branches, birds of all kinds—an owl, a dove, and a very large crow. In the ledges and dens, there were mice, cats, dogs, and other small mammals. A red fox slept on a ledge near the entrance, undisturbed by our presence. The room was lush with plant life, fronds, flowers, fruit trees and fiddlehead ferns. I felt like I had just walked into an enchanted forest.

A cobblestone walkway curved out to the right and to the left, surrounding a rather large rock the size of a Cadillac, protruding out of the ground.

"Our worlds—the Three Sisters, Payraydayzay, Avesta, Gaieos—they are living bodies, living beings that provide energy and gravity so that life can flourish. We are all bound to our worlds physically, mentally, socially, and spiritually. We find healing and wholeness by resting upon the rock and sharing in connection with our own planet. Those who belong to the earth understand this. It's an abundant resource, not too difficult to access—unless you don't belong to the earth."

Muurchia pointed to the large rock as the tortoise crept into the room.

"This rock will bring you healing, for it is not of the earth."

I looked at the large rock in the middle of the room.

"Oh, this must be a fragment of Payraydayzay."

"Precisely."

Like a man who has found an oasis after crawling across the desert, I slowly climbed up onto the piece of Payraydayzay and I sat on top of it with my legs crossed underneath me. As I did, the crow, high on its perch, dropped onto the rock and stood before me. My heart almost jumped out of my chest. I had never been so close to any bird, much less this menacing looking crow. It was magnificent, beautiful, and terrifying all at once.

"He wants you to lie on your back," a voice chirped from the side of the cavern. It was a young, redheaded girl of maybe eleven or twelve. A muscular dump truck of a man, at least eight feet in height, stood quietly behind her.

"Just relax," she ordered. "Let the fragment do its work."

As I reclined onto my back and let my head rest upon the rock, I scanned the room, seeing that every eye of every person and creature was upon me. When I was flat on my back, the crow hopped up and perched on my knee. I didn't know whether to laugh or scream as I looked up at the crow's eye staring down and through me.

"You have to relax," the diminutive redhead continued her commands. "Just close your eyes. Let go of control. Surrender to its gravity."

I watched as the crow, sitting on my knee, closed his eyes, and feeling safe, I followed suit.

"Surrender to its gravity," the little girl said again.

Now, I don't know if it was simply my imagination or an actual vision, but I traveled inside the massive meteorite and could see its matter, its atoms spinning wildly, and creating the gravitational field that reached into my being. The gravity of the atoms, the gravity of the microscopic spinning orbs acted like crochet hooks, knitting within me, and mending those wounded places in my person.

Whether I fell asleep, I cannot remember, but when I finally felt the healing come to completion, I opened my eyes to see that Muurchia, Mira and the redheaded girl at my bedside.

"Is it finished?" I asked. "What happened?"

"You're never finished," the little girl replied. "And you won't be complete until we've restored our world. The rock's healing is temporary. The effects last only a short time, the reason so many refugees reside in this room."

I looked at the girl, surprised by her knowledge and assertiveness.

"And this is Jaan," Muurchia said.

"You seem to be rather bright for your age." I smiled.

"We are not our bodies." The little girl chided. "How long is it going to take for you to catch up?" I thought she might hit me. The large man behind her gave her a nudge, and she nudged back.

"Oakruum has found Juulez." Mira interrupted.

"He has?" Jaan exclaimed, looking at Muurchia.

"I have?" I blurted.

"Yes, Madeline," Mira reminded me.

"But this was well over eighty-five years ago."

Jaan rolled her eyes and sighed.

"Would you please stop telling time with the spins and orbit of this planet?"

"I'm sorry, but that's all I know."

"Well, maybe until you know more," the little girl chided, "You should keep your mouth shut."

Muurchia chimed in. "Do we have any idea where she is now? Does she still dwell in the same flesh?"

They all looked at me.

"I don't know," I said, "But I have this strange feeling that she's waiting for us."

"We must find her," Muurchia replied. "And then return the baby to her mother."

They all shifted their focus to a point over my shoulder. When I turned to see what they were looking at, it was the tortoise resting on a stone ledge. I think it may have slightly nodded its head in approval.

"We'll need to get through the gate," Jaan chirped to the ceiling.

"Yes," Muurchia replied.

"The *correct* gate," Jaan said.

"Agreed," Muurchia replied again.

"If we pick the wrong one, all is lost."

"Then we pick the right one," Muurchia replied.

"Which means I need my journal," Jaan reminded.

Mira looked at me to explain, "Jaan has spent our time in exile studying Geuld, the gateways, and creating a kind of map or instruction manual. It was completed many

Earth lifetimes ago."

"And at some point, it was stolen," Jaan added. "I don't know why someone would steal it or how they'd benefit from it; it was written in Payraydayzian script, but if we're going to make the jump, I need that book."

"Don't worry, Jaan," Mira said, "We know where it is. We'll pick it up on our way."

Mira pulled the spinning orb, which we arrived in from her bag, and released it into the center of the room. It rose above the alien rock, growing from golf ball size to a size large enough to carry us all. The crow, who had been perched on my knee, took off with the flap of both wings, flew around the cavern a few times and then into the sphere. Jaan bounced up onto the asteroid and into the orb, followed by Teum, the eight-foot giant whose legs seemed to need only two steps. Muurchia picked up the tortoise, Dadka, and rose effortlessly into the globe next. I whistled to Cooper, and we stepped in, followed by Mira.

I looked out into the room from inside the spinning ball, and then I looked at Muurchia, who as if he could read my thoughts said, "Don't worry, those we leave here will be cared for, and if we succeed, we can return for them."

The orb rose out of the cavern, carrying us into the night air, rising through an opening in the pane glass window on its way out. The rain had stopped now, and we traveled back to the wheel through the night, soaring over rooftops and the hills outside of the town. Returning to the ancient ruins on which the wheel was parked, we zipped underneath to the center porthole and into the belly of the spaceship.

Once we were safely on the ship, the spinning transport went back to its home in the wall, followed by a motley parade down the corridor to the cocoon room, to see the baby floating securely in her nest.

"An absolute miracle," Muurchia exclaimed.

After bowing in reverence toward the infant, everyone dispersed into different chambers of the wheel. The big crow found a home perched in the cockpit, with Jaan and Teum taking the helm. Mira and Cooper wandered into the galley, presumably to gather a meal for the new crew. Muurchia and Dadka retreated to the library. Bewildered and not knowing what to do with myself, I followed them.

Once in the library, Muurchia carried the tortoise to the large stone slab in the middle of the room and let him rest there. He sat down in one of the plush chairs. I walked to the window and looked out onto the grassy hills that surrounded us. The sky in the east was now showing signs that the sun would soon rise.

As the wheel started to turn and rise off of its landing, Muurchia spoke from over my shoulder.

"Something troubles you."

"This is a troubling situation."

"But I mean in you, beyond this situation, something is tangled up inside you."

I turned and walked toward them and relaxed into an adjacent chair.

"I do not understand. All of you know yourselves, your persons, so well, and mine is only now being revealed to me for the first time."

Muurchia paused for a moment, stroking his long, slender beard, his forehead folding in wrinkles as he thought. And then he spoke.

"First, it is an eternal journey we undertake, getting to know the person we are. It is not a destination; one never arrives. I'm on one place on the path, and you are on another. Second, you have been isolated, in exile, alone, adrift in an inhospitable ocean. We have had each other." Muurchia looked at Dadka. "We've been here to remind each other always of who we really are. And last, we have the fragment. This planet is not your own, and just as the rock from Payraydayzay can bring wholeness, this world we're on works to scramble, tangle and confuse us. Before long, we forget who we are all together and cling to fables and mythology for enlightenment. We are part of the world of our birth, not just residents of it. When we connect to others from the same world, we become aligned, like puzzle pieces joined to make a complete picture. For you, this began when you first met Axzum, and since then, I imagine you've experienced a kind of rebirth, as you've come to learn more about who you really are."

"I want to know more."

"All in good time, but here, come, lay your hands on the shell and see."

I pulled myself from the reclined position and stood before the stone slab. Then I closed my eyes and I placed both hands on the tortoise. I felt Muurchia place the rock on my chest, just as he had done earlier.

"And now, open your eyes."

I opened my eyes, and I saw my person, my true self, still fragmented, but much healthier than before. The brightly colored strands exploded brilliantly across my core.

"You see," the Shaman said, "You are returning to us."

He smiled. "Welcome back."

CHAPTER SEVEN

THE RETIRED SCHOOLTEACHER

Before I continue my story, my most excellent Theophilus, I must tell you that until this point, I had stolen nothing in my one hundred and two years in the flesh. I had grown up in a home where stealing and cheating were frowned upon. I lived most of my later years as a minimalist with very few possessions, so stealing anything never entered my mind.

Now, there was no choice.

The coveted object, Jaan's journal, was under glass in a secret second basement display room in the Beinecke Rare Book Library at Yale University in New Haven, Connecticut. The book had been kept there for researchers to study since the 1969th year. Many tried to decipher the manuscript, but all had failed since the notebook was written in a Payraydayzian language. Every word comprising of alien characters. Jaan had also drawn many pictures of Payraydayzian plant life, trees and flowers unique to the lost planet. Jaan's notebook had been stolen while she was living as a farmer in Italy in the fifteenth century, Earth time. For centuries, its whereabouts were unknown.

A man named William Voynich had come into possession of the book in the twentieth century, and now it was kept under lock and key at the Ivy League school in Connecticut.

It was crucial for us to possess it if we hoped to complete our mission. Jaan needed it, she insisted, to navigate us safely through the gateway, Geuld, at the far end of the solar system.

There was no other way. I had become a thief.

The Beinecke Library was an architectural wonder —a five-story granite building sitting on four granite piers. At first glance, it looked extremely secure, the doors wired with cameras and alarms. The library had been called a jewel box because of its gridded treasure chest appearance. Instead of windows, thin octagon shaped pieces of veiled marble had been fitted into each grid. I'm sure the building's designers never expected an alien craft landing on its roof, and the occupants breaking through one of the marble slabs to gain entrance.

Without detection, we tumbled out into the building from the orb that spun partially inside and outside the building, in the marble window frame. Jaan, Teum, Cooper, and I stepped down out of the transport and into the large room.

The library's interior was one great hall. The floor was marble. The ceiling, five stories above, was dotted with dim golden lights that made large pools on the floor. I stopped for a moment and took in the stacks; there was a glass encased tower in the middle of the hall, five stories of bookshelves, each lined with rare books. The effect was spiritual, like an altar in a sacred temple. As I scanned the stacks, wondering how we'd be able to find what we were looking for, the books were speaking all at once, at different volumes and languages. It reminded me of standing at the clock tower in the middle of Grand Central Station, the echo of a million voices. The sound, whether real or in my mind, normally would have been one of harmony for me, like listening to a choir, but underneath the ancient conversation, was a vibratory grind, a deep growl. Something was not right. From the off, I sensed we were in danger.

"Come on. We need to move," Jaan barked. "Get it and get out."

The young redhead's chirpy voice didn't match the grit of a drill sergeant she carried. She was Pippi Longstockings on the outside, but Sergeant Rock on the inside.

"Do you know which one?" I asked, gesturing toward the huge monolith of books.

"It's not up there," she responded, holding up the old lantern that she had grabbed from the ship. "It's down below. Come on."

Jaan moved across the hall to the stairway. Teum and I followed.

"Come on, boy," I motioned to Cooper, who remained seated in the middle of the hall, his eyes, nose, and ears on alert. He didn't move, the same sort of behavior he displayed in the woods when we first encountered the space voyager.

"Cooper, come on." The lab remained stock still. "Something's wrong," I called to Jaan, who was almost halfway down the marble staircase that led below.

"Of course there is," Jaan barked back. "They know we need this. There is no better place to cut us off. Stay alert."

Jaan and Teum disappeared down the stairs, into the darkness, the lantern's bouncing glow their only marker.

"They? Who is *they*?" I called back down, but there was no answer.

When I reached the top of the stairs, I looked back at Cooper and beckoned him to me. Hesitantly, he crept across the floor to the stairs, ready at any second to tear off in the other direction. As I descended, Cooper came to the top of the stairs and stopped. He wasn't going any further. That chaotic choir of voices from the stack had gone silent, but the deep, almost imperceptible ghostly growl continued.

Quickening my pace, I made it to the bottom floor two stories below, where Jaan and Teum searched for the book, holding the lantern up over a row of waist-high, glass display tables. The entire floor was dark, except for the glow from the lantern and a handful of small lights emanating from smoke detectors and electronic devices throughout the floor.

I joined the girl and the giant at a group of glass display tables in the middle of the room. Each contained an ancient book sitting on a stand, open to a random middle page. A placard beneath each book gave a description.

Gutenberg Bible, 1454 AD
Plato fragment parchment, 357 BC
Beowulf, 1063 AD
Voynich Manuscript, origin and date unknown

"Here it is." Jaan declared, holding the lantern over the display containing the book we sought. It was on a stand like all the others, under glass, open to a page on which there was an elaborate drawing of a strange, flowery plant, and alien text.

Jaan's face beamed with joy.

"Finally," she said, and pulled a hammer from a bag on her hip. She slammed the head of it onto the display, shattering the glass, setting off the alarm. She cleared the broken pieces from the open pages and as I reached in to help her, I saw something move out of the corner of my eye. The darkness in the room's corner looked as if it became a body, no, two or three bodies, and they stepped out towards us. They were not human—they were shadows formed to look like bodies.

"Jaan—"

But it was too late; the shadows grabbed each of us from behind, holding our arms behind our backs. I looked down at my arms to see not a pair of hands or claws, but felt a cold darkness, like being gripped by ice. I tried to jerk myself free, but the more I pulled, the tighter the hold became.

"I told you," cried Jaan, struggling to break free.

"What is this? What is happening?"

The shadow reached down, and grabbed both of my legs, covered over my torso, and I remembered the vision of being swallowed by the blob. I pushed with all of my strength to avoid the pull of the darkness, my heart racing.

"Help!"—but both Jaan and Teum were fighting their own shadows.

"There is no escape." A voice snarled in the darkness.

A colossal figure stepped out and stood between us and the stairs, illumined by the lantern now upended on the floor and the flashing strobe lights of the screaming alarm. I could see it was a man, heavyset, with a salt and pepper goatee and a security guard hat and jacket. Standing beside him was the source of the deep growl I'd heard—a wolf, large, black as pitch, teeth snapping at us, back arched, ready to strike.

"Teum—" Jaan cried as she was almost engulfed by the shadow wrapped around her. "The book."

I gasped my last breath as the dark blanket covered my mouth, reaching toward my eyes to take me completely under. I saw Teum pull his arms free momentarily from the blob's grip, reach into the display and grab the book. As the shadow recovered and began another attack, Teum flipped a few pages of the book, put his finger on an exact place on the page and read the words.

ꟾꟾꟾꟾꟾ ꟾꟾꟾꟾꟾ ꟾꟾꟾꟾꟾ

A Payraydayzian language. I had heard the language before, spoken by Axzum and Mira, but somehow, this was different. These words read from the book had some sort of power. A kind of shockwave knocked us all off our feet. Jaan and I were thrown to the floor. The security guard and the wolf blown over like bowling pins, and the shadows withdrew, retreating and disappearing into the corner. Teum remained standing, continuing to read the phrase over and over, and then stopped. Freed from the shadows, Jaan scrambled to her feet and pulled me up to mine.

"Let's go."

Teum, Jaan and I made it to the stairs and halfway up the first flight before the guard and the wolf regained their footing. Once they did, they were on our heels. Leaping stairs two or three at a time, we exploded onto the main floor and joined Cooper, who was already halfway to the orb spinning in the granite frame. Cooper leapt into the orb, followed by Jaan and me. When we were safely in the ball, I turned to see the blurred image of Teum, outside of the orb in the hall, fall to the ground. The wolf had tackled him, and through the silver and blue streaks of the transport, we could see the struggle, Teum versus the wolf, and then the security guard.

Jaan moved as if to jump back into the hall to help, but Teum immediately interrupted her, crashing into the orb upon us.

"Go." Jaan cried, and the ball floated out of the building and up toward the belly of the wheel. From outside, we could see the warped images of the guard and the wolf come to the opening and watch us flee. They both melted into shadows, forming two dark stains on the marble floor.

Moments later, dark wisps of movement, ghost-like, flew out of the building and climbed the air toward us. The shadows were chasing us.

"They're coming."

But before the shadows could reach us, we were engulfed by the ship, the circular door closing behind us. For the moment, we were safe. The ball shrank and returned to its place in the wall, and we stood looking at each other in the large, round room.

Within seconds, we were hurtling through the night sky in the wagon wheel, miles above the ground. We all took a moment to catch our breath and to regain our senses.

Jaan nodded to Teum, "You have it?"

Teum held up his fist, clenching a shredded clump of pages. He handed the remnants to Jaan.

"Oh, no," Jaan whispered in disappointment. She examined the ripped pages, front and back of each, reading what she could.

"Did we get it?" I asked. "Will it be enough?"

"It's going to have to be. We can't go back." She took another moment, scanning what little she had.

"What was that?" I finally asked.

"What was what?" Jaan replied.

"What was it that attacked us?"

"The Nuul. Vacant, empty, nothing set upon ripping everything apart." She held up the pages.

"I don't understand,"

"For everything that exists, there is the reverse nature. The Nuul's nature is the reverse of ours. Our nature is birth, growth, death, and rebirth. A shadow's nature is the reverse."

"But why here? Why now?"

"They will not let us escape—not escape this world —without a fight."

"Escape?"

"Yes. They are most likely close behind us, even now at this very moment."

Mira and Muurchia had joined us, coming down from the cockpit. Jaan handed Muurchia the fragments from the book. Muurchia held the pages in both hands as if he was holding a dead bird and looked at Jaan with concern.

"We have to go," Mira said, looking at me. "You said you might know where we can find Juulez. Come, show us."

"There is no time for that, Mira," Jaan barked. "If we don't get off this world right now, we may never leave."

"We need Juulez."

"No, it's too risky. We can come back for her."

"I would agree with you if she were still hidden from us. But if Oakruum is right, then we need to try."

Mira returned to the cockpit with Muurchia. I followed. Jaan, obviously frustrated, returned with Teum to their work in the tool room.

In the cockpit, Mira and Muurchia stood beneath the projection of the earth. Mira motioned to me to point out the location on the slowly rotating globe. I stepped forward, trying to find it. But this globe, this map, had been created long before towns or roads, long before civilization.

Even the continents had a peculiar shape and placement. I found a placc where I thought a small farm in Iowa would be and set my finger on it. Immediately, the ship changed course, and we bolted toward the spot my finger had touched.

"We will arrive in a few moments. Remember, we have little time. Jaan is right. If they catch us, all is lost."

I looked at Mira blankly. I did not completely understand what was being asked of me.

"Oakruum," Muurchia added, "You must go."

"Wait, me?"

"Yes, you must be the one to retrieve her."

"Okay, but..." It was then that I realized what was about to happen, and I imagined myself knocking on Madeline's door, her answering, and then what? Would she recognize me? How would I explain all this? And then, convince her to join us in a very short amount of time?

"Heiros gamos," Mira whispered.

"Excuse me?"

"When two persons who are bound to one another through all of time connect, then there is heiros gamos. Show her heiros gamos and she will see what she needs to see, and then she will come."

In mere moments, we were soaring above the cornfields of the Great Plains. I went to the part of the window that faced northwest and tried my best to help navigate, with one eye on the horizon and another on the hologram globe in the middle of the cockpit. But it was dark, and likely midnight on that side of the world. Locating the county, much less the farm, seemed daunting. This was the land of farms, after all.

Then I spotted a familiar marker, a water tower with "Spencer" in big letters on the side of it.

"This is it," I said, "Spencer. And there's the farm, way out there." I guided Muurchia to put the wheel down in the field near the old farmhouse, the very field from my vision, my desire.

As the wheel descended, coming to rest just two stories above the ground, I scanned the old white farmhouse and the adjacent barn for signs of life.

Does she still live there? Is she still alive even? If she was, she would have been my age, over a hundred years old. Would I even recognize her if I found her?

Seeing the farm—the old tire swing hanging from the tree, the wraparound porch encircling the white shingle house—caused long lost memories to come flooding back into my mind. I remembered playing cards around the table, husking corn, running together through a downpour. She was there. Somehow, I knew it; somehow, we had never parted ways. I felt my stomach tie into a knot as a wave of anxiety washed over me. I laughed at my own stupidity and looked down at Cooper.

"Let's go, boy. I need a wingman."

Cooper and I met Mira and the rest of the crew in the main chamber. The orb that would deliver us safely to the ground was already spinning in the middle of the room.

"There's no time for this," Jaan barked at us. "You have five earth minutes, tops."

I hopped into the ball, which was now not as alien to me, and Cooper joined me. The center hatch opened, and the spinning elevator slowly lowered us to the ground. Just a few days before, I had watched Axzum arrive for the first time by the same means and now I was doing it as if completely naturally.

Once on the ground, we tumbled out of the ball and onto the frozen field. A light dusting of snow crunched under our feet as we hurried to the farmhouse across the gravel driveway and onto the back porch.

All was quiet inside. A single dim lamp was aglow on the second floor. I was certainly about to awaken all inhabitants and cause more than just a crisis. I held my breath, opened the screen door, and knocked forcefully on the wooden door, peeking into the door's pane glass window to see if anyone stirred.

There was a pause, just silence.

I was about to knock again when I could see through the window curtains a light come on in a downstairs room. A few moments later, the porch light flickered on above us and a woman appeared in the door's window. It was a young woman in her early twenties with dark hair and dark eyes. Was it...?

"Madeline?"

"I'm calling the police right now," she shouted from the other side of the door, holding up her phone to prove it.

"Wait, please. I'm not here to hurt you. I'm here to see Madeline Zimmerman. Is that you?"

"What do you want?"

"My name is William. William Henry. I'm searching for Madeline Zimmerman. She used to live here."

The woman looked at me skeptically, but something must have eased her anxiety, for she touched the red dot on her phone, ending the 911 call.

"Step off our property and come back tomorrow. Everyone here is asleep."

She looked up at the ceiling. That look was all I needed.

"You mean she's here? Madeline Zimmerman, she still lives here?"

"I need you to step off the porch and come back

126

tomorrow."

"Please. I don't have time. Can you please tell her that Will is here and I need to talk to her? It's extremely important."

The woman just looked at me.

"Tell her, and if she wants me to go away, I'll go peacefully."

The woman looked me over one last time and then down at Cooper, who was looking up at her with his big, dumb mouth open.

"Wait there," she instructed, and disappeared from view.

While Cooper and I waited on the back porch, I took a moment to look up into the night sky. Cold, but clear. The Big Dipper, Orion's Belt, the Pleiades. Then, the kitchen light came on inside the house. The door unlocked and the young woman opened it for us.

"Okay, come in."

Cooper led the way and began exploring. The woman shut the door behind me and stood in the middle of the kitchen with her arms crossed. In the doorway leading to the dining room and beyond, stood a frail, old, white-haired woman in a pink bathrobe, holding herself up with a walker.

"Madeline?" I whispered. "Madeline Zimmerman, is that you?"

"Will?" she gasped with a crackling voice. "What? How?"

She let out a kind of half scream, which she tried to stop from coming out with both hands. Then she looked over at the young woman and fell backwards.

"Grammy." She dashed behind, caught the old woman and led her to a chair at the end of the dining room table.

Once she recovered from the initial shock and found support in the oak chair, she looked back up at me as I stepped into the room.

"Will, my god, how? You look like you haven't aged a day."

I opened my mouth to explain, but the young woman interrupted.

"You know this man, Grammy?"

"Of course, dear. Of course. But it's been so long, a lifetime."

"Five lifetimes," I joked.

"Yes, many," Madeline agreed.

"This is Will. We went to the junior prom together."

The young woman looked at me and then looked back at her, confused.

"This is one of my great granddaughters, Eliza."

"Eliza. How wonderful."

"Oh, Will, how I always wished we had stayed in touch. You know there hasn't been a day that's gone by that I haven't thought…"

Eliza looked down at her great grandmother and Madeline stopped speaking as she realized what she was saying, and reached for Eliza's hand for reassurance.

"I know," I responded. "I've had the same experience. Every day, I have the same memory pop into my head out of nowhere…"

"The rainstorm," she whispered.

My heart rose to my throat and my eyes teared up.

"Yes. Exactly. The rainstorm. I think you and I are..."

I didn't know just how to end the sentence, and so I just stood there for a moment looking out the window, trying to hold back my emotions.

"You are what, exactly?" Eliza probed.

"I wonder if I could show you something," I said, and moved to the chair to help Madeline to her feet, but they both recoiled.

"It's right outside. It'll just take a second."

"No." Eliza jabbed, pushing my hand away. "What are you doing? Are you crazy?"

"Please. It's just outside on the back porch. It'll explain everything."

I scratched the back of my neck in frustration. Madeline looked at me and softly whispered, "You think you and I are what, William?"

"This skin and bones we dwell in, it isn't who we truly are. We are something else entirely, from another place entirely."

They both looked back at me blankly.

"I know it sounds impossible. But if you just come with me to the porch…"

I stepped toward Madeline again and offered her my hand. She looked at me for a moment and then transferred her hand from Eliza's to mine. I pulled her to her feet, and for the first time in almost a century, we embraced.

"Oh, William…"

"Madeline…I always wondered whatever happened to you."

I guided her across the dining room floor and into the kitchen toward the back door, Eliza at our heels.

"I taught third grade for almost forty years. I loved every minute."

I opened the back doors, holding both the wooden door and the screen door so that she could navigate through.

"I met Larry in college and we got married. Forty-eight years until he passed. Three children, eight grandchildren, ten great grandchildren…"

The three of us stepped out onto the back porch, and I gestured toward the field.

"And one more great grandchild on the…Oh my word!"

"Oh, my god," Eliza echoed.

The wheel slowly rotated out above the frozen cornfield, the glowing, spinning orb resting on the ground below it. Madeline and Eliza turned to stone as their eyes and minds adjusted to the scene.

"Have you ever had a dream? A dream where you weren't you but someone or even something else entirely, in a place and time somewhere else entirely?"

"All the time," Madeline whispered, still watching the wheel. "When I was a child, I thought it was normal, a common thing, but as I got older…"

"She has nightmares," Eliza interrupted, "Terrible nightmares."

"Yes," Madeline confirmed.

"Let's get back inside Grammy," Eliza commanded, opening the screen door.

"I think you need to go now." She flicked her hand toward me, but Madeline didn't move.

"I've seen this before," she whispered. "Yes, I most definitely have seen this before."

I gripped her hand tight and turned to look her in the eyes, and she did the same.

"I've been called to go on a journey. I believe you're supposed to come with me."

"What? No. Grammy." Eliza shouted. "She's not going anywhere."

Suddenly, there was a deep rumbling, a growl that echoed across the night and through our bodies. Looking up, a dark blob floated over the farmhouse, followed by another over the big tree with the tire swing. Then a dozen more moved menacingly over the entire farm, covering the sky and surrounding the wheel. They looked like black teardrops.

Eliza screamed and lunged at her great grandmother to take her inside, and I pulled Madeline to me at the same time.

"Grammy." Eliza shouted.

"We need to go right now." I blasted.

"No." Eliza shot back and shoved me away from Madeline, guiding her back into the house. I still had Madeline by the hand as I looked up to see the shadows melt from the teardrops and seep ominously to the ground. They were the same sort of shadow creatures that attacked us at the library. Dark, bulbous drips and black ghosts littered the sky above the farm. The shadows looked like black pantyhose legs falling from the sky.

"Madeline, please, listen to me. I don't have time to explain, but we have to go, and I wish you would come."

Madeline, awestruck, looked from me to the ship, to the sky, to the shadows, to Eliza, and around again. Eliza pried my hand from Madeline's, pushed me away and pulled her grandmother inside in one quick move, slamming the door shut. The streamer-like shadows hit the ground, like liquid poured onto a tabletop, and crawled along the ground toward us. I froze in terror. "What the hell are they?" I stepped down the back steps, looking back to watch Madeline and Eliza argue through the back door window. Cooper ran toward the ship. I turned to run as well, but was stopped halfway across the driveway by

Madeline, who exploded out the back door and onto the porch.

"Will." she cried, taking two steps and then stumbling onto the porch floor, bracing herself against the top banister post. Eliza chased and crouched to her aid. I glanced at the approaching shadows closing in from several directions as I ran back to the porch to help her up.

"Will." she said to me as I helped her to her feet and down the back porch steps. "I can't, I don't..."

"Grammy!" Eliza cried. "Stop, please. What are you doing?"

Madeline looked back at Eliza standing on the porch, and then at the wheel, and then out and around as the shadows drew close.

"Am I dying?" She gasped. "Is this what happens?"

The shadows were nearly upon us. Running to the ship or even to the porch was no longer an option.

"Perhaps we are," I said to her softly to reassure her, "But this will not be the end, not this time. This time, I will follow you."

I kissed her, at the very place, the very ground on which I had kissed her every day of my life. I'm not sure what heiros gamos is, but what happened next awakened us to each other and gave us some sort of protection from the darkness.

As we kissed, a small flicker of light appeared between our foreheads. As I pulled away from the kiss, the light grew, a glowing ball of flickering light, fire with two very distinct points. For a brief moment, our souls were exposed to one another. The bride and groom from Mira's vision, weathered and distressed but still very much alive, appeared—the bright flicks of multicolored lights shot across our translucent skin. While our bodies beamed and the fire burned between us, the ghosts-like shadows, just a few feet away, were stilled, as if the light kept them from coming any closer.

"Will, what is this? What is happening?"

"I don't know, Madeline, but I think it's an invitation."

She looked into me for a moment, with her chestnut eyes, now slightly frosted from age, but the eyes that I'd gotten lost in too many times. And then she turned, still holding my hand, the flame still burning between us, the shadows still held at bay. Calmly, she said, "Eliza, I am going."

"Grammy, no." Eliza shouted.

"Eliza, it's okay. I'll be okay, but I need Nigel."

Eliza stood on the porch in disbelief, staring at us for a moment, and then went back into the farmhouse. Madeline turned back to me.

"I know this sounds strange, but since Larry passed, I felt like I've been waiting for something. I thought I was waiting to die. But now I think I've been waiting for you, Will."

"You've been waiting for something far more important than me. Wait and see."

Moments later, Eliza emerged from the old farmhouse, ran down the back steps and across the gravel driveway toward us, shrieking at the surrounding specters, carrying a grey cat.

"There he is. Thank you, Eliza, thank you," Madeline said, taking her pet.

"Grammy please." Eliza begged again, and Madeline hugged her great granddaughter, who put her hand over her mouth to stifle a sob.

"We have to go. Run back into the house and lock

the door."

As Eliza bolted back to the farmhouse, Madeline said, "Please don't cry, my dear. Everything's going to be fine. Just tell everyone that I've gone on a little trip."

Eliza looked back at us one last time, looked around at the encircling shadows, and ran into the house, her eyes big as saucers. I picked Madeline up in my arms, her arms around her cat, and carried her across the field toward the wheel. I looked back as I ran; the ghosts freed from their trance, renewed their pursuit, slithering like snakes over the frosty cornfield toward us. I looked ahead at our destination, the spinning orb, and back again at the pursuing shadows. It was going to be close. A few feet away, I threw Madeline and her cat with all my strength into the globe, and followed, jumping like an Olympian seconds before the shadows reached us. The headless apparitions swarmed the ball as it rose into the awaiting vessel. The center hatch closed behind us, leaving us safely in the main cavernous chamber of the ship. As the orb receded back to its place in the wall, Mira greeted us and Muurchia called up to the cockpit.

"They're in."

Madeline took a step back, clutching her cat tightly in her arms. The frail old woman looked as if she might collapse.

"Juulez," Mira said with an edge of reverence in her voice, "At last."

Madeline looked completely bewildered for a moment, her eyes bouncing back and forth, to and from all the new faces in the room, the glowing spinning orbs that encircled us, and then to my surprise, she regained her footing, straightened herself up and gasped.

"Mira? I know you," she said. "How do I know

you? And Muurchia." She stepped forward, and Mira and Muurchia both greeted her with a hug.

"Welcome back," Mira said softly. Madeline turned to me and spoke to the amazement of us both.

"And you are... your name is... Oakruum, your real name is Oakruum. How do I know that? Why do I know that?"

I embraced her.

"Juulez."

The flicker of light that had hovered between us earlier reappeared, and we kissed, this time long, passionate, and unhurried. The flame between us grew to the point of engulfing us both, ablaze without burning.

When we disengaged, the fire retreated, and then flickered out completely.

"This all feels like a dream," Madeline posed, scanning the room.

"It's no dream, Juulez," Muurchia countered. "As a matter of fact, you're just beginning to wake up."

In the cockpit, Jaan and Teum were at the helm, and the wheel had travelled many miles above the Earth into the outer atmosphere. We clamored to the window to watch the entire earth come into vision, the glowing white, blue, green and tan marble in space.

"My gosh," Madeline said, "Look how beautiful. This is incredible."

I looked over at Madeline, gazing out of the window with childlike amazement. I was at once impressed by her resilience and embarrassed by my lack of it. I looked back out at the world, shrinking as we rocketed away. I made a quiet promise to myself at that moment to enter this new adventure with the same playful spirit that Madeline carried. The appearance of more dark blobs instantly broke that promise.

"See them? Right there." Jaan pointed out the window at the group of ominous teardrops that had descended upon us at the farm. They were still in pursuit.

"Oh, my. What in heaven's name?" Madeline said.

"They have held us here for a very long time," Muurchia said.

"Make no mistake," Jaan interrupted. "This is a jailbreak. We just need to make it over the wall. We're going to have to make a jump to another world. But which one?"

Jaan pulled up a large hologram globe of the planet I always knew as Mars.

"Or," Jaan said, and then she switched planets. Mars shrank back and Payraydayzay took up the room. "We could try for home, or what's left of it. What do you say, Captain, Avesta or Payraydayzay?" Jaan asked.

And I thought Jaan had gestured to me.

"Me? Captain?"

"No," Jaan responded. "Not you, her." and she pointed to Madeline.

"Me?" Madeline shrank. "I'm not the captain."

"You were the last time I checked," Jaan stabbed. Madeline and I looked at Mira.

"It's true," Mira said. "Juulez, you are our leader. You have been for a very long time."

"Oh no," Madeline stammered. "I could never."

"You have before," barked Jaan, "and you will again."

"Jaan," Mira said, "She's going to need more time."

Jaan pulled up Mars; the projection of the red planet wasn't red at all, but green, blue and white, as lush and alive as the planet presently in our rearview. She pulled up

Payraydayzay, again, another sister planet, looking fit and fruitful.

"I have an idea," Jaan finally announced, and she touched a red dot on the planet's surface, causing the ship's gravity to activate, lifting us all slightly off the floor. The craft instantly accelerated in a blink of an eye to an incredible speed. The moon flashed by us like a race car, and the earth behind us shrank to the size of a pea and then to a grain of sand.

"Is this...is this light speed?" I asked.

"No, sorry," Jaan said, "That's quite impossible, but it's pretty fast. Nonetheless, Payraydayzay is far. This may take a few hours."

Teum grunted and left the cockpit for the galley, followed by Jaan. It seemed to be the signal that, for now at least, we were safe and could relax. I took Madeline down into the chamber where the alien baby, Ella, was sleeping. I told her about Axzum, my brother, how he had found me, discovering the baby and how I had lost Axzum in the sea.

Despite the sudden interruption to her life, she seemed to do a better job of awakening than I had. As Mira took her under her wing, giving her some clean clothes and a place to rest. I retreated to the library to change.

In the library, the tortoise rested motionless in the corner. I went to the wardrobe and opened its doors to see what was there to wear. As I stood there, the tortoise spoke to me, not with its mouth, and I didn't hear it with my ears, but the Shaman spoke to my being as Axzum had done in the woods when we'd hiked back to the cabin.

"We do not heal in isolation. We heal in the circle."

I looked down at the tortoise and my thoughts went back to my lonely shack in the woods—the place I had gone to find refuge, but ended up being a place of great sorrow. I took a deep breath to stifle a sob.

"The role of the shepherd is to open the great well so that all may drink and be satisfied."

The tortoise went silent. I stood there waiting for more, but what else was there to be said? I changed my clothes and walked over to the large window as I buttoned my shirt, looking out into the vastness of space, distant stars and galaxies beamed from billions of light years away, but presently, just inches away, my reflection in the glass.

Another reflection emerged from behind and joined mine. I blinked from the reflection to the person next to me who projected it.

It was Madeline, no longer old, no longer frail, but renewed and strong, with the body and face of her young adult self. The Madeline that I had known so many years ago—bright and beautiful.

"Madeline," I said, "My god."

"I know," she replied, smiling and spinning. "Aren't these new clothes lovely?"

That evening, we all gathered in the galley to share in a meal with the entire crew, a motley crew, to say the least. As we ate, I took an inventory of my new flock, all the faces gathered around the table: a tortoise, a giant, a redhead, a lab, a crow, a genie, an Ethiopian angel, a grey cat, and a retired schoolteacher.

That was the last time our old names were spoken. After that, we were Juulez and Oakruum.

CHAPTER EIGHT

THE MADMAN

By the time we rose the next morning, we had traveled one hundred and fifty million miles. Jaan reported to us at breakfast. We would arrive at our destination in just a few hours. We were traveling at an incredible speed. I imagine if it were not for the artificial gravity on the ship, the g-forces would have killed us all.

In the galley, Mira asked the entire crew to gather in the revelation chamber after breakfast. This was the room that I called the lightning room, where Mira used the marble to show me the vision of Axzum rescuing me from the blob.

Every person on board gathered around in the dark circular chamber. I watched as the faces of my new friends lit up a bright pale blue when the lightning flashed from the wall to the rod in the middle of the room. Every few seconds, the flash would appear, conjuring a new vision.

Mira stood in the center of the room beside the rod jutting out of the floor. She took a moment to make eye contact with each voyager, emphasizing the importance of what we were about to witness. As she held up a marble, I instinctively checked to find my marble safely in its place. The marble she used was her own.

She turned and silently placed the marble onto the rod, or rather, in a spot hovering just inches above it. We all took a step back as bolts of lightning struck the marble from all directions and then the simulation, the living memory, unfolded.

As we were transported to another place and time,

the room provided us a 360-degree projection of what I assumed was Payraydayzay, the beautiful, tiered landscape I had witnessed in the previous vision with Axzum on the alien planet.

I looked over at Juulez to watch her experience such a vision for the first time. She had the face of a child watching fireworks on the Fourth of July. She took in the scene, glanced in my direction, and took my hand. The act was significant to me. I was no longer experiencing this journey alone. I had a partner, the most precious thing in the universe. You can go through hell with a partner and experience pure joy. Likewise, you can spend a lifetime in paradise alone, and only know despair.

"This is our home," Mira said, "Payraydayzay, just a few moments before it was destroyed. Or at least, this is my memory of the event."

We were now watching as if we were miles above the planet's surface and able to take in its entirety.

"The Nuul," Mira pointed out. We watched as the vast shadow descended upon the planet. The shroud covered the world, like maple syrup pouring over a basketball. We all looked on in horror as the glob covered the entire globe and seeped into its soil, disappearing under its surface.

"Our world wasn't destroyed with bombs or weapons," Mira explained. "It was eaten away from the inside out. The darkness seeped into its core. It was torn apart from the center."

The surface of the once beautiful world turned into what looked to me to be like brownie mix swirling under a beater. The ground rumbled, convulsed, and crumbled. The planet stopped spinning, was stripped of its gravity, and chunks, large and small, detached from each other and floated away. Some pieces tumbled off and spun away with force and speed, but others dropped off like a dead body, motionless. I had remembered watching sci-fi movies as a kid, the ones where the entire planet would explode with fire and light. This wasn't that. This was horrific, watching a world gutted, its insides disintegrated, its shell, mountains, rivers, fields, and cities torn apart. Payraydayzay, a once natural globe, was gone, its body shattered and strewn flat.

I looked around the room at all of our devastated faces. It's one thing to learn about a death, it's another thing to witness it. Tears fell from every face, including mine, including Juulez. How she could process all of this, I will never know, but in the few short days since we left Earth, Juulez had undergone a wonderful metamorphosis from befuddled and weak centenarian to the fit and commanding leader that was resting just below the surface the whole time. When it seemed like the moment would be brushed aside as insignificant, Juulez took action. As Mira's memory continued to pull away from the debris field that was Payraydayzay, now a rocky, gravelly spray, a bell rang in the cockpit.

"We're almost there," Jaan said, swallowing her pain. "We should get ready." She turned with Teum to leave the room.

"Hold on, Jaan," Juulez stopped her. "I don't think we're quite finished here yet."

"No," replied Jaan. "We are. I was finished with this eons ago. It's time to move on."

"It doesn't matter how long ago the loss occurred. We need to deal with it now, as a group."

Jaan grunted and continued walking out of the chamber, so Juulez raised her voice slightly to catch her.

"Jaan, I thought you said I was the leader?"

Every eye in the room widened in surprise at Juulez's assertive expression. Both Jaan and Teum stopped in their tracks and turned back toward Juulez.

"Whenever a student in my class experienced loss, whether it was an important ballgame, or loved pet, I always took time to give the children a moment to be sad, to grieve. Yes, this may be a long-lost memory, but it still hurts. They say time heals all wounds, but that's just not true. Acceptance heals all wounds, but you don't get to acceptance by ignoring the pain."

Jaan and Teum nodded and rejoined the circle.

The vision had almost gone black and the asteroid belt faded to a faint whisper. Then Mira spoke. "Over time, fragments of our broken planet scattered across the system, some falling to Earth, some slamming into Avesta, that is Mars, causing destruction and extinction. Our people became refugees, traveling to Gaieos. Your person survived and dwelt in earthen skin."

"And Axzum?" I asked "And his wife, Ariance?"

"My guess is they were taken away, along with this ship. How Axzum was able to escape and find us remains a mystery."

"So, we are the remnants," Juulez whispered. "The survivors."

"Yes," Mira whispered in response.

"Then there were others," Juulez continued. "Important people, lost to us."

There was a pause, and we took a moment to process her words.

Muurchia spoke up, "I have spent many long hours in meditation trying to remember, to conjure a face or a name, but I cannot."

"I don't remember anyone either," Jaan confessed, "But there had to have been family, friends, teammates."

Teum shook his head. Juulez and I looked at each other. We both knew there was something and someone that had been forgotten, but not sure what or who.

"I have some memories," Mira shared, "Perhaps if we connect," Mira was already standing in the middle of the room, so we all took a step toward her and connected.

For a moment, we were one, standing together with our eyes closed. I experienced something I can only describe as thankfulness—a deep connection to my true self and my memories. Those around the circle must have had the same experience, for each of us began speaking names

"Clairias," Muurchia started, "She was my wife."

"Grinnell," Teum stated. "My twin brother."

"I had a dear friend named Cassia," Mira shared. "I think we liked to wander together."

"My father," Jaan followed, her face crumpling, "I do not remember his name, but I can see him. He's calling for me to come home for dinner."

"My brother, Axzum," I said. I saw him in my mind's eye, in a memory I never knew I had.

"My mother." Juulez whispered. "I think her name was Miretta. She loved me. She tried to protect me."

Juulez opened her eyes and looked at me.

"She's gone," Juulez gasped with grief. There was a long, shared sadness.

The interlocking group became untangled, and we followed Jaan and Teum to the cockpit. When we got to the cockpit, the hologram image of Payraydayzay was rotating in the middle of the room. Where a red dot was on its surface, there was now a light blue one. We had arrived at our destination, our home planet, Payraydayzay. If it still existed, we would have landed on it. However, when we moved to the window to see, there was nothing but a few large rocks floating in a vast field of asteroids.

It was like walking on the concrete foundation of a home swept away by a forest fire. There was nothing left. Tens of millions of years later, the crumbs still wandered hopelessly adrift. For a long time, no one said a word, but walked around the cockpit to different vantage points of the 360-degree window, looking for any sign of anything.

"Look at this," Jaan snarled. "It's a graveyard."

And she was right—every rock was a tombstone. Everyone in the cockpit stood still, as if waiting in line at a funeral procession. Mira broke the silence.

"There's always hope. As long as we are here, we can rebuild. But if we are to keep going, we can't afford to forget who we are ever again."

Juulez approached Jaan, "You said you had an idea?"

"I do," she responded.

Jaan paused, looking out on the millions of tumbling bits and pieces of the lost world. She gestured out the window and looked at each of us. She had a habit of trying to communicate without words. We all stared back at her blankly. Jaan gave a deep sigh and explained,

"We need to get a fragment and bring it back to the ship." She opened her arms to indicate the size, about the size of a bed. "Bonding with each other, and a fragment, should be enough to keep us from falling back to sleep."

We all turned back to the foreboding and fractured scene outside. The asteroids, the dead, dark grey and charcoal rocks were small compared to a planet, but in relation to the wheel, they were massive.

"We can land on one of the larger ones and cut a

piece off."

"Right there." Juulez pointed. "We can take a piece of that one, like cutting a stem from a tree. Jaan, Teum, Oakruum and I will go."

I looked at Juulez with absolute wonder. How could this be the same person I met hobbling around with a walker and beckoning for her cat? She looked over at me for a brief second and gave me a wink, and then continued,

"What tools do we have?"

"I'll show you," Jaan replied.

Jaan and Teum headed to the tool room. Juulez and I followed. Once in the hangar, it was clear that Jaan and Teum had been preparing for such an endeavor. In the middle of the worktable, several pickaxes, shovels and pikes awaited assignment. Jaan went to a rack along the far wall and pulled down a large net made of wire.

"Each of us will have to pin a corner of this to the rock. Once we have it dislodged, we can haul the fragment back to the ship in the net."

From another rack, full body suits and helmets were distributed. They were like the suits Axzum and I had used in the Gulf of Mexico, but weightier, and without fins. Once outfitted, Jaan led us out of the tool room and into the airlock compartment.

My stomach turned as a crippling anxiety engulfed me. Juulez looked at me with an expression of trepidation and exhilaration. As we walked into the bay, she grabbed my hand and squeezed it hard. Jaan hit the button to close the airlock's door. We looked out into space, through the same round window I witnessed lapping water just a few days before. I remembered the feeling of terror I had when disembarking into the sea, the amount of courage summoned to take that leap. This was much more intense. I had been in the ocean before; I knew what to expect. Stepping into the vastness of space was a different matter.

Jaan showed us how to attach the life support cable to our suits. It was like an umbilical cord that fed from the ship to our suits, keeping us from floating away and providing oxygen and heat. Once the tethers were attached, Jaan handed the three of us each a corner of the net, a spike, and a hammer. The instructions were to spread the wire net over the rock formation, hammer a spike into the rock, and attach the net to the spike. We all nodded, and Jaan opened the hatch that led out into space.

Juulez and I continued to hold hands as we stepped into the void together. The sudden lack of gravity caused us both to flail in space for a moment, but once we were used to the sensation, we found our way. We floated away from the wheel. I gave thanks for the tether, let go of Juulez, and gripped the line for good measure.

The wheel was slowly turning high above, as we descended on to the asteroid below, the tethers snaking down behind us, the net unfurling between us. Walking in space felt like swimming in a bowl of Jello—everything moving in slow motion. When I hit the rock, I landed on all fours like a cat, and bounced right off. The others did the same. On the second or third bounce, I was able to get a handhold and pulled myself into the pockmarked rock. The wire net fit over the formation, even with a little slack. When we finally had the net in position, Jaan gave us all the thumbs up and held up his hammer, his way of telling us to drive in the spike.

As I went to position the spike against the rock with my left hand, I fumbled, and the nail floated away from me, head over heels over head again. I leapt and grabbed at it, but now I too was floating away from the rock. In order to return to my corner of the net, I had to go all the way back to the wheel using the tether and then descend into my place once more.

Once I was back in place, the others had completed the task and were waiting for me. My corner of the net was the only one yet to be secured. I positioned the point of the spike on the rock more carefully this time and swung the hammer into the head of the spike. Instead of embedding into the rock, the spike broke a chunk off, and the broken piece went spinning and floating away.

I positioned the spike once more, but as I pulled the hammer back to strike, I noticed something strange within the rock. It was not hard, jagged and grey, like the rest of the asteroid, but soft, bright and silverish. I brushed away some of the crumbs that remained from the first strike, to find that it was a finger.

I knocked off more of the rock using the hammer and spike like a chisel, exposing an entire hand. I looked up at the others, who were waiting for me to secure my corner.

"There's a person." I shouted.

There was no way they heard me, but my manic gestures were enough to beckon the other three to my corner. When they crawled across the rock and get to me, using the net like a ladder, they too were stunned, and joined me in chiseling the hand, the arm, and eventually the entire body out of the rock.

The silver toned, translucent skin, lanky arms and legs and the grey ribbons beneath the skin made it obvious that this person was Payraydayzian. It was completely frozen.

Once we freed the torso, we pulled the legs free. Teum grabbed the whole body, holding it like a baby, cradled it in his arms, and we used the tethers to pull ourselves back to the ship.

When we arrived at the airlock, we could see Mira and Muurchia waiting for us through the window. They had been watching us and scrambled to the bay to help with the discovery. Once the seal was tight, and it was safe to move into the tool room, a table was cleared, and Teum placed the body gently upon it. The frozen man lay with his hands and arms extended out and up as if to block something from above. Mira placed a silvery metallic blanket over the body, the kind they hand out to marathoners at the end of a long race.

Jaan positioned what looked like a heat lamp over the table, and then, without a word spoken, we all waited, standing around the table as if nothing else in the universe mattered. Extracting a chunk of the rock was completely forgotten. We waited for a few hours, while gradually, the body softened and limbs gave way to gravity, collapsing jelly-like onto the tabletop. Arms, legs, fingers and hands all relaxed into place. Whether the person was alive or dead, there was still no sign, until finally, Jaan spoke.

"Well, I guess that's it."

Suddenly, as if the person was responding to the voice, a leg twitched, and the right hand moved.

"My god. He's alive."

All at once, the room filled with chatter.

"Hello." Juulez cried. "Can you hear us?"

Teum, Mira and Muurchia spoke to the man in the Payraydayzian language.

"ϱſϱ ϱſϱ ϱϛϱϱϱ," Mira said.

The alien clearly could hear us, now trying to shift his body and move his head, struggling to see, but still half frozen. Then, he groaned as if he were in intense pain, softly at first, but then growing in volume.

Each of us, continuing to vocalize encouragements, took a few steps back.

"ᗞᶠᗞ ᗞᶠᗞ ᗞᔆᗞᗞᗞ" Mira shouted again.

The man's eyes shot open, and he curled himself into a ball, in the fetal position on his side, and started screaming. The sudden movement and the screaming caused us all to separate and back up further. Juulez and I were disconnected and pressed against the wall. The man continued screaming, body convulsing on the table, completely straightening in one motion and collapsing into itself the next. He turned on to his back, clutched his stomach with both hands and pushed his head straight up, straining his neck.

Mira stepped forward and tried to give the man aid, but he swatted her away, flipping off the table and onto the ground. On the floor, he flailed about like a rabid animal, and staggered to his feet. The man went wild with desperation, screaming, shouting, and grasping at the air for relief. He would reach out with both hands and grab at the air as if it were water or food, and tried to pull it into himself. When that didn't work, he moved to a shelf holding an array of tools and began doing the same thing with the objects he found there. He grabbed a coil of rope, tried to jam it into his core, and then threw it onto the ground in frustration. Object after object, he pulled from the shelf and tried to stuff into his gut, and then violently discarded each failure with a shout.

When the naked, possessed man had cleared the entire shelf, he went into an uncontrollable fit, his arms and legs kicking and fighting the air, his body convulsing and throwing itself in every direction. He finally slammed his front torso into the edge of the table and splayed his arms and head upon it, pausing for a moment. We all froze as the man, breathing heavily, scanned the room for help. His eyes caught a pile of tools on a nearby bench. He lunged at the bench, desperately grabbing a pike, and with a shriek, stabbed himself in the side. The spear fell to the ground, and the man followed with a thud, and was silent.

We rushed to the man, surrounding him, in time to see the dark shadow escape from the body. The specter, similar to the ones we encountered in the library and at the farm, spilled like liquid out of the hole in the man's side, and slithered onto the floor. We all watched in paralyzing terror. The ink stain gathered itself, formed the shape of a headless person, and stood.

The ghost draped before us like an oil-soaked rag, constantly shifting its shape. Juulez screamed, and each of us retreated in shock, searching our surroundings for some sort of weapon, while keeping both eyes fixed on the shadow. As quickly as it had emerged from the hole in the body, it projected itself out with six extending arms like an octopus, grabbing each of us by the neck and slamming us against the wall. I struggled to fight off its ice-cold grip as it spread down my chest and up over my face. I looked across the room to see Mira, Muurchia, Teum and Jaan bound the same way. Cooper had come to the chamber to help, but could only stand at the portal and bark. Juulez was next to me, flailing as the darkness overpowered her.

"Juulez. No."

She glanced frantically over at me as the shadow covered her mouth and nose, and she reached for me with her hand. Summoning my last bit of strength before I was completely taken under, I grabbed her hand.

When I touched Juulez, the shadow reacted. The ooze slowed its deadly pace and then stopped completely. Remembering the experience we had at the farm, I pulled

Juulez into me, and we embraced so that there was no space between us. The two arms of the shadow that held us by the jugular released us and shifted across the room to the others. By the time we were freed from the darkness and could move to help the others, they were all completely shrouded, engulfed by the blob, which coalesced itself around its victims and picked them up off the ground as it floated up above the table.

"Jaan. Mira." I shouted, but there was nothing, no sign of them. Then a leg, either Teum's or Muurchia's, briefly came into view within the floating shadow, and disappeared again.

I pulled Juulez toward the entrance of the room. "This way."

"No," she pulled away. "We can't leave them here."

"We are not leaving."

I took the lantern from the hook on the wall near the entrance. By now, the giant amoeba was standing upon the table in the middle of the room, its tentacles running down to the floor on all sides like a squid. I held out the lantern toward the shadow with one hand and held Juulez with the other. For a moment, the blob seemed to shy away from us. We looked at each other and then took a shaking step toward the table, lantern out. This time, the shadow definitely reacted, recoiling.

"Just don't let go," Juulez said, and we approached the table and climbed upon it, holding out the lantern and on to each other.

Once we were on the table, the big ink stain bobbing before us, I held tight to the lantern, and even tighter to Juulez. Juulez, with one arm around me and extending her free arm, quivering in fear, she reached into the mass of icy darkness. She felt around, grabbed and pulled. The Nuul fought back, and I thought Juulez would be dragged into the void as well, so I braced myself on the table as she strained with all of her strength to hold on to whatever she had. I stretched the lantern toward the darkness and Juulez yanked. But the blob would not let go. The shadow slithered onto the floor and toward the porthole that led to the rest of the ship.

As the shadow pulled away, Juulez had no choice but to let go. We stood on the table for a brief second, watching the dark ooze slink toward Cooper, who was still barking in the doorway, and then Juulez took two big steps and leapt from the table into the shadow, and I joined her.

I will never forget what it felt like to submerge into the cold emptiness of the Nuul. The overwhelming feelings of hopelessness and dread sank in, tempting me to surrender the will to live.

Our saving grace was the dim golden light from the lantern I still clenched in my hand. As I held tightly to Juulez, a small spark ran through our bodies and into the lantern, which sprang to life. The hot glowing filaments within grew like branches. The golden beams tangled out, reaching and winding in all directions until it looked like the lantern had a tree of light growing out of it. Its warmth lit the cold shadow, and it lost strength.

Juulez flailed about feverishly, trying to find our friends. A foot traveled into the light. Juulez grabbed it and pulled the body into her. It was Muurchia. His connection with us caused the tree to grow even bigger and brighter. In quick succession, we found the rest—Mira, Teum, and finally Jaan.

Once we reformed the whole group and were bound together, the bright golden tree branches filled the room and overpowered the shadow, which became a transparent mist. As the dark cloud vanished, we were dumped as one on to the floor near the porthole where Cooper stood.

For a moment, we remained on the ground, stunned. Then Juulez and I rose to our feet, bracing ourselves with the table. I placed the lantern on the table and the tree of light shrank back into the bulb.

"Are you alright?" I embraced her.

"Yes. I think so."

Turning toward the others, I knew immediately something was not right. The others had not spoken, nor did they scramble to help. Jaan crawled across the floor and sat on the bench, head in her hands. Muurchia stood leaning on the table, staring at the wall. Teum stood like a pillar, with his eyes shut, and Mira walked like a zombie toward the window to look out.

"What, what is this?" she asked, still looking out the window. "Where are we?"

Juulez and I shared looks of deep concern.

"You're in shock," Juulez answered, assisting her to a seat. "You need to rest."

As Juulez and I went from person to person, checking on their status, it was clear the shadow had affected our friends' minds. What exactly happened and whether this was temporary or permanent, we could not tell. After attending to each one, we stood together at the portal to the chamber, looking over the room and evaluating our situation. Our new friends were not gone, but they might as well have been.

"Now what?"

Without the knowledge, experience, and expertise of the rest of the crew, we were lost. And on top of it all, we ourselves were still processing the event. We were millions of miles from Earth, in a spaceship we didn't know how to operate, with a shellshocked crew, recovering from a violent attack. We both sat on the floor to regroup.

Once we had stared helplessly at the ceiling long enough, it was Cooper who sensed our distress and came to our aid. After taking one of his exploratory circuits around the room, he sat between us for a moment and then,

"Take them to their bunks."

I didn't hear these words with my ears, but echoing within my being. I looked at Juulez, and without speaking, we helped each other up and escorted our friends to their rooms. Not one of them said a word either, but by the way they looked around at every passing object with confusion, we knew their minds had somehow been scrambled.

Once everyone was safe, we returned to the tool room and picked up the alien body lying lifeless on the ground, placing the stranger on his back on the table. Clear, gelatinous liquid oozed from the man's side onto the tabletop. Juulez gingerly touched his forehead and cheeks with her palm. I went back to the Great Room where the orbs spun in the wall. I decided the most silvery ball was the one I needed, so I took it down from its place and returned to the tool room. I approached the table and placed the orb gently on the alien's chest. I took two steps back and watched.

The silver orb spun in place for a few moments, then rose above the body and grew. When the sphere achieved the right size, taking up most of the room above the table, it sucked the limp, lifeless body into its void, where it was held fast. We watched as the wound in the man's side was sewn shut, reduced to a scar, and then disappeared altogether.

Within just a few minutes, the man was sitting upright on the table, his legs hanging over the edge, eyes open. The orb diminished and floated out of the chamber to return to its place on the wall in the Great Room. The man looked both of us over, and I wondered if he had ever seen homosapiens before. As strange as he looked to us, we no doubt looked alien to him.

"ᗪᐟᐟᐟᗡ ᐟᐟᗡᐟᐟ ᗡᑉᗡᑉᗡ," he spoke.

We both shook our heads.

"Juulez," Juulez said, pointing into her chest.

"Oakruum," I said, following suit.

The man looked at us for a moment and then touched his own chest.

"Lejuun," he said. His first few steps away from the table made him look like a toddler learning how to walk for the first time, but once Lejuun had gained his balance and strength, we took him on a tour of the entire ship, making a stop to check in on the infant sleeping in her cocoon.

Lejuun had the same wandering amazement that both Juulez and I had exhibited when we first walked through the wheel, as if the vessel were as alien to him as it was to us. On the other hand, when he entered the cocoon room, he immediately approached the orb that held Ella, moved his hand over its surface, and whispered a prayer.

Juulez and I returned to the tool room, led by Cooper, donned the appropriate gear, selected the weapon of our choosing, a pair of pickaxes, and reentered the airlock. As we prepared, Lejuun followed and watched and was able to figure out our plan. He positioned himself at the lever which opened the outside door. As the airlock door opened and the air pressure shifted to allow our exit, I watched Lejuun through the window intently, hoping to God that he could be trusted. If he decided to cut our lifelines, send us adrift and make off with the ship, there would have been nothing we could have done to stop him. But in the end, the new addition to the crew turned out to not only be trustworthy, but extremely valuable.

Once we descended upon the rock, drive the final spike in, secure the net and break the rock free from the asteroid's surface, chopping away at it for almost an hour; it was Lejuun who helped us drag the huge boulder back into the airlock. Having watched our progress from the ship, he threw on a suit and helmet and stood in the open airlock, the tether in hand.

When the rock broke free and began drifting away from the hole, Juulez and I clamped our tethers to the wire net bound to the rock, and Lejuun pulled us back to the ship, all the way to the bay, me, Juulez, and the boulder the size of a single bed.

Once we were back on board, we moved the huge rock to the Great Room by shutting down the artificial gravity and floating it down the corridor. With the stone in place, we were ready for the recovery. One by one, we carried each of our friends from their bunk into the Great Room to rest upon the fragment of Payraydayzay and nurse themselves on its gravity.

Each one spent eight to ten hours recovering on the celestial rock, during which Juulez and I would retreat as well. Hours were spent in the galley, eating, drinking and sharing, the faithful lab sleeping under the table.

We also spent much time in the library, sitting with Dadka, the Shaman, meditating and getting to know our true selves. The more we connected with the fragment of Payraydayzay and with each other, the more our earthly selves faded and our bodies of light emerged.

When the crew was put back together, and there was life once again in the galley, we met in the cockpit to debrief and discuss the next step. Jaan and Teum took charge once again in the cockpit, and Mira returned to her motherly nature. Muurchia's laugh could be heard bellowing through the passageways and Lejuun was now clothed and in his right mind. Gathering at the 360-degree window, we took in the scene outside, the scattered ring of asteroids spanning millions of miles into the horizon.

"I was wrong," Jaan stated, looking from the window to Lejuun, who stood in the middle of the room looking out. "It's not a graveyard, it's a nursery."

"Perhaps, in time, life will spring forth." Mira said. "But for now, the baby needs her mother. On to Geuld."

With that, Lejuun opened up the navigational projections and flipped through the planets, finding one of the three sisters and enlarging it so that it almost took up the whole cockpit. Without a word and giving no one time to stop him, Lejuun approached the globe and touched one of the red dots glowing upon it. Instantly, the ship's gravity shifted, and we all floated just above the floor. Within a blink, the ship sped away from the asteroid we had been parked above. The entire asteroid belt was left behind and disappeared from view in a matter of seconds.

"No. What are you doing?" Jaan shouted at Lejuun. "Avesta. Why Avesta?"

"Avesta?" Juulez asked, looking from face to face.

"Mars," I said to her. "It looks like we're going to Mars now."

CHAPTER NINE

THE RED PLANET

I opened my eyes and jerked my head off the pillow, scanning the dark room. It was that blurry moment just after waking when the brain needs a minute to process and reassure the rest of the mind and body that everything was fine, all systems normal.

But all systems were not normal this time.

My eyes darted from the table to the hearth to the cabin door, and back down at the cot on which I lay.

The shack?

I swung my legs over so that my feet hit the cold, wooden plank floor, and sat on the edge of the bed, clearing my eyes with the palm of my hand.

How can this be? I thought. I had watched the shack burn. Or was that just a wild dream? Have I returned to reality after some spaced out trip?

I ventured out onto the front steps, where the ground was covered with fresh snow, which caught the moonlight spreading down upon it. The woods were quiet, the sky above filled with stars.

Where am I? Am I really here and I dreamt all of that? Or is this a dream and I'm actually somewhere else?

I stood at the doorway to the old shack, debating, ducking into and out of the room countless times.

"Cooper," I finally blurted. "Coop, here, boy."

But there was nothing. No sound, no Cooper, no Juulez, nothing. I was alone.

I went back into the shack, and I splashed water on my face at the sink. While drying myself with the kitchen towel, I glanced out the window, seeing both the snow-covered landscape beyond and my aged, weathered face looking back at me.

"No," I whispered into the glass, turning to look over the room again, searching for answers and trying to remember how I got there.

In my memory, there were chambers in the wheel, the baby in her sanctuary, the tortoise in the library, the lantern, the crow. Then the scene in the cockpit came into focus. The floating projection of Avesta slowly spinning in the middle of the room.

I stood in the cockpit beside Juulez, watching Jaan argue with our newest addition, Lejuun, who had caused the ship to navigate away from the debris field where we camped for days, toward an unplanned destination. It was clear that Jaan was offended that someone else would dare take the helm.

The door of the cabin suddenly flung open and slammed against the wall. My concentration was broken as I snapped around to see who was there. No one appeared. It was just the wind. As I ambled to the cabin door to close it, I saw a shadow move out of the corner of my eye.

It was at that point that I perceived the actual prison I was in and the specters that controlled it. The dark shadows in the corners of the room shifted again, and I realized I was not actually in the cabin—my mind was under attack. More determined now, I returned to my memories.

In my mind's eye, I saw the Great Room, the large slab of Payraydayzay resting in the middle, the orbs spinning in their temple-like alcoves in the wall. I saw the faces of the gathered crew encircled around the stone fragment. Above the rock, one orb was engaged and rotating before us.

"We have no time for this," Jaan started in. "We need to get to Geuld. There's no going backwards."

"Please, Jaan," Mira replied. "Let's give our new friend a chance to explain."

"Friend?" Jaan questioned. "How do we know if we can even trust this one?"

"You cannot know this," Lejuun responded. "Just as I cannot know if I can trust you, but I look around and I see only a few Vortai. We need them all."

Jaan barked, "Yes, we know this already. It's the reason we need to go to Geuld."

"First, we must go to Avesta."

"Avesta is in the other direction."

"There is Vortai on Avesta," Lejuun explained.

In the cabin, the wind whistled, the window over the sink smashed, and the long, wooden planks that made up the walls of the house rattled, but I held my mind fixed on what was real.

Juulez, who stood next to me in my memory, took my hand, and a new collage of memories sprayed across my mind—standing together in the temple in a marriage ceremony, the moment the fire appeared between us as we escaped the shadows on the farm, and the memory from our youth together, in the field during the rainstorm.

"Oakruum. Come find me."

Then, the illusion of the shack collapsed and disappeared altogether. As I suspected, I wasn't in the cabin, but somewhere else entirely. Whatever spell I was under was breaking down as the memories of Juulez gave my mind an anchor.

I closed my eyes and reopened them to find my actual position in time and space. Blurry at first, I could see rock, red and orange, illuminated by dim light coming in from an opening within arm's reach. A shallow layer of rock, dust, and debris covered me.

I was not hurt, from what I could tell, but I needed to free myself from the pile. Kicking my arms and my legs, wiggling free, I pushed away from the rocks and emerged from the ground to stand at the base of a large embankment in a dusty ravine on what I assumed was Avesta. I was standing on Mars, wearing the same suit I had worn in space a few days before.

I took a few steps away from the cliff, trying to get my bearings. The sky, the dusty air, was a dim greyish red. The gravity was weak, and each step caused me to launch into the air. I checked the horizon, but I saw no one, nothing.

I looked back toward the rocky outcropping from which I had come and scaled the slope. I noticed a hollow in the rock three-quarters up the embankment. I set about climbing the cliff toward the cave. The focused task of scaling the bluff gave my mind an opening to recall the events that led to this moment.

I saw in my mind's eye the same scene as before. The group gathered around the conversation orb, spinning above the stone slab in the Great Room. Lejuun walked away from the circle and went to the wall where one orb rested in its alcove. It was the very orb I had used to heal him. Without saying a word, Lejuun held up his left hand, making a fist, and with his other hand, took the orb from its place and set it into orbit around his clenched hand.

Then, he moved across the room, the sphere still orbiting his fist, and pulled another orb from its place. This one, he also sent rotating around his fist, but at a different angle. Finally, he returned to the conversation orb, which he added to the dance. Now, all three orbs were orbiting his hand like electrons around a neutron.

I remember watching this magic trick, thinking that, at any moment, two of the three would collide, but they never did, as if in sync with one another.

"There should be eight," Lejuun said.

"We have four," Muurchia responded. "Including Ella's."

"We need eight," Lejuun whispered, looking at the balls traveling around his fist. "Plus one."

He pulled his fist away and pointed to the space it had just occupied.

"The nucleus. The eye. The Ninth Orb."

"These orbs," Juulez chimed in. "What exactly are they for?"

"The Vortai," Lejuun explained. "Instruments used to help us commune with ourselves, to one another and the universe. Three aid the body in healing, protecting and transporting. Then three aid us in communing with our true selves. This one, he gestured, the conversing orb, and then two others, "ꭹꭹꭹꙩꙍ" and "ꙍꙍꙅꙅꙍ" which translate to Knowledge and the Shepherd. One teaches, the other guides. And then, there are two that connect us to the origins of everything, one to time and space, and the other to nature. Together, these eight orbit around a ninth, which draws and binds them to each other."

"Okay," Juulez answered. "But which of the orbs do

you know to be on Avesta?"

I paused my climb as I put all of my focus on the memory with a fear that if I did not, I may miss a crucial detail. This memory was important.

Lejuun put his fist back into the core of the spinning orbs and carried each one back to its place in the wall.

"The Vortai that rests here," Lejuun said, gesturing to an empty alcove in the wall. "The Shepherd."

"The Shepherd." I repeated out loud as the memory sprang back. Our quest was to find the Shepherd here on Avesta. But what happened after that and where was the rest of the crew?

Scaling the bluff was easy. The pitch and height of the mound would have been a challenge on Earth, requiring a rope and harness, but the lack of gravity to pull me down gave me superhuman strength and the confidence that even if I lost my grip or missed a foothold, I would have plenty of time to catch myself.

Half way up the wall, something caught my eye in the rock—creases and cuts in the stone that did not seem natural. With my gloved hand, I brushed the red dirt and dust from the spot to reveal characters, alien letters like the ones in Jaan's book. I examined the wall for a moment, staring at the markings, and then looked out. This isn't just an embankment, I thought to myself. This is a landing circle like the ones we landed on while we were on Earth.

I felt a renewed sense of self awareness and knowing. My mind was strengthening, and my memory returning. This became a key moment for me. I realized the Nuul's most terrifying power was to negate and remove one's sense of knowing and being known. To rob a person of their ability to know themselves, their past, present and potential future, is the power to do much more than take a life, but erase it, negate it, make it so it never happened at all. This leaves their victims separated, isolated, set adrift in the abyss.

In such a conflict, knowing thyself becomes the greatest defense of all.

I could remember standing at the window on the ship with the rest of the crew watching our approach to the red planet. The desolate, red-orange world had a kind of green-blue aura around it, perhaps an echo of its former self. I kept returning to the hologram globe of Avesta floating in the middle of the room, examining its topography, rivers, lakes, and oceans. I walked around the map several times, noting the vast variety of natural wonders. Then, I wandered back to the window to see none of it, just a lifeless wasteland before us.

The wheel traveled to a place just above where the red dot on the map showed. Certainly, this would have been a settlement, perhaps a city, but outside, it was just dust. The ship descended through the Martian atmosphere and down upon the rocky platform I was now climbing. I could remember the wheel rotating just above the round mesa.

That is when I found the cave in the cliff I was climbing. A small ledge jutted out from the entrance, providing me with enough space to peer into the void. It was dark, and the wind whistled as it spun about the opening.

The light from the lamp on my helmet beamed into the dark cavern, but not far enough to see anything beyond the red dust particles that seemed to fill the planet's atmosphere, and the cave walls, which at first glance looked to be natural. As I ran my hand across the wall a second time, I could see signs of design, black metal covered in layers of dirt and dust. I brushed my hand over the wall just inside the entrance and found more characters, writing, similar to what I had found on the side of the bluff.

This was no cave.

From where I stood, it was only twenty feet to the top, so I left the cave opening for a moment and climbed the rest of the way up to the top of the mesa.

From the top of the formation, I could scan the horizon in every direction. There were no signs of life, no sign of anything except red dirt, rock, and blown dust. Looking up into the pink and orange sky, the memory of our arrival returned to me.

The wagon wheel.

"The wheel was just above me, right there," I said to no one. "We all stood here."

I looked down to confirm the footprints.

But where did they go? What happened?

I followed the footprints. They led down the side of the sloping bluff to the mouth of the cave, twenty feet below the rim. I peered over the edge to the opening, out to the horizon, and back up to the sky.

Something was wrong. It felt like the air had changed. The dust particles floating about me began to stir and blow off in all directions. The wind was kicking up, and as I scanned the horizon once again, my eyes caught movement in the far distance. It was a red cloud glowing and moving toward me at an incredible rate of speed. The dust storm looked like a rolling wall of red-orange water.

I bounced down the side of the bluff, scrambling over the dirt and rocks, sometimes bouldering, sometimes sliding toward the dark opening on the hillside.

When I returned to the entrance of the cave, the storm was almost upon me. It hit with such force and fury that it knocked me off my feet and into the dark, cavernous hallway. I braced myself, using the floor and the wall as the pressure of the storm threatened to pull me into its belly.

The torrent whistled and roared across the mouth of the cave, filling the hall with rock and dust, shielding the outside light. Visibility was almost nil because layers of dust covered the face shield. The only thing I could do was wait for the storm to pass. It was there on the ice-cold ground in the cavern that I finally put things together.

With the dim light of my helmet shining down on a small patch of ground covered with rust-colored dirt, I drew in the dust using my gloved index finger. I found I could carve small lines into the crust, exposing the black metallic floor underneath. I drew the mesa first, then the ship, the wheel upon it, and then the crew, as figures below the ship. I watched my finger chip away at the red dirt until the entire image on the floor was a black teardrop.

I lay there for a moment, staring at my drawing.

The shadows had come and had taken the ship. The entire ship was gone, along with Cooper and Ella.

But where? Were they captive or dead? What about Juulez and those on the ground? Were they out there in the storm somewhere trying to survive?

A bright red light began blinking inside my helmet at the jawline and a screaming alarm sounded in my ear.

I sat up. The air tanks.

I looked around for a solution, but my options were few. The storm continued to rage outside. My only choice was to push deeper into the darkness, so I inched myself away from the entrance, fighting the suction that the windstorm created. I grabbed whatever I could find to serve as a foothold, and as I crawled deeper into the ancient chamber, I saw in my mind's eye the memory of the attack.

I remembered the look on Juulez's face as the shadow blanketed her, pulling her hand away from mine. I saw the shadows overcome the others as well. I saw the shadows surround the wheel and consume it from all sides. The teardrop enveloped them all and drifted away.

And then, the shadow came for me.

It hit me hard, sending me over the cliff, down to the jagged ground below, along with an avalanche of dirt and rock.

Why I was left behind, and where my ship was taken, I had no clue.

As I moved away from the portal, down the cavern, the pressure eased, and I got to my feet and stumble further into the darkness. The light on my helmet beamed out before me only a few feet, revealing a rockier cavern.

After a few more muscled steps, I came upon a metal rod jutting out from the wall. I grabbed the bar with both hands, flipped it downward and the outside door slammed shut, covering the entrance to the cavern and blocking out the storm, leaving me trapped in darkness except for the headlamp and the red, blinking light inside of the face shield.

The alarm continued to scream with growing intensity, and the air in the suit became thinner. I flailed about in the darkness, reaching for any kind of aid, when the air stopped flowing and I fell to my knees. My vision blurred, my stomach turned, head spinning.

It was there, on my hands and knees, taking what I thought were my last breaths, I expcrienced the strangest memory.

I remembered sitting as a young man in my early twenties in the office of a mentor of mine, Dr. John McCleister—maybe I was transported there. Who knows? Either way, Dr. McCleister sat before me in his office. He was a wise old sage that taught religious studies at the university and enjoyed sharing in friendly debates with his students. I had been struggling with some moral issues, trying to grapple with my understanding of good and evil, and find some satisfying release from the guilt I always seemed to carry with me.

Dr. McCleister looked at me with compassion from his chair on the other side of his big oak desk. He scrunched his nose and pushed his glasses to his eyes.

"Seems to me there is only one unforgivable sin."

He paused for a long, dramatic moment.

"It is to deny your true identity as not just another being dwelling within this universe, but to acknowledge that you are, in actuality, the universe eternal that dwells within this temporal skin. Your mortal body lasts just a short time. Think of it: even if it lasts a hundred years, it will only mark some 36,000 days, a mere speck in the yawning chasm of time."

"And this is the unforgivable sin?" I tried to follow. "Not to acknowledge this?"

"You are infinite, kept in this finite vessel. Not to acknowledge this truth is to deny your divinity. To deny this truth is to embrace a falsehood, a great deception. The shadows will descend upon you and keep you convinced of this lie. Salvation is found in the light, the truth that is deep down below it all. And there are many layers to strip away."

The professor leaned forward in his chair and gazed

at me intently.

"Atman is Brahman," he whispered to me finally.

"Atman is Brahman?"

"Atman is your true self, your essence, your person. Brahman is everything, the universe. Atman is Brahman. When you realize that, you find salvation."

Even as the alarm continued to flash, the lack of air weakening my mind and body, I scanned the large room to see that I wasn't in a cave. I was standing in the Great Room of a spaceship, another wheel.

Across the round chamber, in an alcove in the wall, was a lone orb glowing light gold and rotating in place. I bounded across the room and pulled the orb from its place in the wall. When I pulled the golf-ball-sized sphere from the wall, I expected it to grow in my hand as the other orbs had done, but this one behaved much differently than the others.

Instead of growing, it shot out of my hand as if fired from a gun. It moved at a speed that made it almost impossible to see, leaving a faint streak of gold in its wake. It flew around my body, whistling like a sparrow, weaving in and out, around and through; one moment, it was swirling around my head, the next, in and out of my chest, around my arms and legs, and back to my head again. As it danced around me, a high, almost imperceptible, female voice sang a cheerful melody. Even though the orb was near, sometimes within me, the hymn seemed to come from miles away.

The gold ball paused right in front of my nose for a moment and then it shot up the staircase into what I assumed was the cockpit, and then back to my nose again. At the speed of a hummingbird, it bounced from my nose up to the cockpit and back to my nose at least a dozen times in a matter of seconds. I struggled up the spiral staircase, dragging my exhausted legs up one step after another.

The cockpit replicated the exact design of the cockpit on the other wheel. Except, in the middle of the room where the control rod should have been, there was nothing. The windows were blanketed outside with the layers of red dirt and rock.

The golden streak shot around and through my body what felt like a thousand times. I stood with my arms out in complete surrender as it sewed into and out of me like a needle and thread. The cockpit flickered with golden light as some profound transformation seemed to take place in my body. The layers of skin and bone, flesh and muscle felt as if they were being stripped away. Yet there was no pain. I felt as if I was being dipped in a bath of healing balm. From the very top of my head to the heels of my feet, the little orb pulled me from my shell.

When its work was complete, the streak of light orbited me like a Hula Hoop while I bathed in its glow and a newfound feeling of pure bliss. The struggle for air was gone, along with all anxiety. Then the ball came to linger at my nose and floated to the middle of the room to hover above a metallic pedal rising from the floor.

I bounced forward and pressed the pedal with my foot. The ship's artificial gravity kicked in like a magnet, holding my feet to the floor. A band of light flickered on, encircling the room and the navigation equipment, bar, and hoop shot up into the room from below. The flashing red light and alarm in my helmet stopped, and I removed it. I took a deep breath to refill my lungs, but there was no need. I could still breathe, but now every breath seemed to enter and exit my body at every point of me, from my head to my toes. The sensation was transcendent.

As I walked around the cockpit, helmet in hand, assessing my situation, the golden ball returned to me and continued to streak like a whirling dervish around and through my body at every point. I held out my hand, palm up, and the orb settled upon it. This must be the Shepherd, I thought to myself, and I sat down on the floor of the cockpit, examining the golden ball.

My back was leaning against the big glass window, and I rubbed my free hand over the smooth glass, marveling at the color and texture of the layers of dirt and rock that accumulated on the outside of the ship, centuries, millennia of sediment. My thoughts moved to Juulez, Cooper, Mira, and Ella.

The golden orb rose from my hand as if it had a mind of its own, and it continued to do its work, swirling around my body, knitting in and out of my flesh, while it sang a joyous song.

While my body remained where it sat, my consciousness entered the golden orb, like a cowboy on horseback, jumping onto a speeding locomotive. I can remember floating above my body for a brief instant, and then up and out of the ship, above the Martian landscape, and through its atmosphere and into the vastness of space. This happened in what felt like the blink of an eye. Within seconds, I found myself in the presence of my friends. I was floating in the middle of the Great Room of my ship, surrounded by the crew, looking out from inside the small, spinning, golden orb. I could see Juulez, Jaan, Mira, and the crew; each one was bound hand and foot and suspended from the ceiling by a long, black tether which tied around their wrists and ankles.

"Hello. Can you hear me?"

"Oakruum." Juulez cried.

"Juulez. Where are you?"

I tried to scan the room to check on each person, but the view from the spinning orb was smeared and warped.

"Help us. Find us."

"Where? How?"

I wished I could jump immediately into the room and free them from their bonds.

"Through the gate. Geuld." Jaan strained to even speak. "Pageedra"

Suddenly, the room got darker and the black, rope-like tentacles that bound their limbs now snaked around their bodies, closing in around their chests and necks.

"Your suit." Jaan gasped through a strangled breath. "The pockets."

The room filled with desperate cries and I felt my heart freeze in my chest.

Moments later, I was back in my body. I stood up, removed my gloves, and searched my pockets. I pulled at the fasteners and the zippers at my thighs, but found nothing—my pockets were all empty.

But when I opened the pocket on my chest, I pulled out a folded piece of paper, and when I unfolded the parchment, I became paralyzed by two major revelations.

The first was the page I held in my hand, a page from the book we had stolen from the library, a page covered with alien words and a drawing of a star and its planets that were in its orbit, a solar system that was not our own.

And then, the second revelation struck. My hands, which were shaking as they held tight to the ancient document, were no longer made of human flesh. Both hands were the alien silver and gold translucent form that looked like all the other Payraydayzians I had encountered. Amazed, I undid my suit and disrobed, inspecting every inch of my frame.

Now naked, I turned to the window, which reflected to me a body and face that was frighteningly alien to me, and more familiar to me than the human flesh I had worn since birth. The green, blue and red ribbon-like threads wove a complex trail through my being, and maybe for the first time, I did not feel alone.

This exiled hermit was uncloaked and revealed to be at the center of a great web of existence. I walked to the window to get a closer look at my face, my hands exploring my cheeks, eyes, and mouth. My mind travelled back to the moment I saw Axzum for the first time on the mountaintop. Then it jumped to another memory I didn't realize I had, a long-forgotten image of Axzum and myself as young brothers, working together on Payraydayzay eons ago.

"You are Oakruum; your home is Payraydayzay."

I was blanketed by the comforting thought that Axzum was nearby, even sharing with me at this very moment. The feeling was so powerful that I turned around, expecting to see him behind me, but there was nothing there except the glowing ball that floated to the control bar in the center of the room. It stopped just above a small knob that I had not noticed before. It was almost the size of a quarter, so easily overlooked.

The orb rested above it and pulsed. I approached the control bar, engaged the navigation bar, and the same hologram model of our solar system appeared above my head. Payraydayzay, Gaieos, and Avesta floated slowly by. I looked back down at Jaan's page in my hand. In the middle of the page, surrounded by ancient alien text, was a drawing of a star system, a star with eleven planets in orbit.

"This must be Pageedra," I said to myself, tapping the drawing. I reached for the knob that the orb was resting above and turned it clockwise, beginning my search. At once, the hologram of our system disappeared and a different one took its place above my head.

This one had a star that flickered like a fluorescent light in a roadside rest stop. What's worse, the system's gas giants were gone, the rocky worlds destroyed. In their place were five concentric rings of asteroids surrounding the dying star; the dead rocks drifting around the ghost-like star gave the system an empty, hellish quality.

One in every ten to twelve systems that appeared above me as I scrolled through the array contained nothing but bits and pieces of lost worlds. When I came to those, I paused for a moment and wondered what happened. Were these systems always a wasteland, or did they at one time contain life and vitality? If so, what happened? How were they destroyed, and when?

I pulled my hand away from the knob, and when I did, inadvertently pulled it out, which instantly changed the hologram above me. Little lines of light, thousands, if not millions, jutted out in all directions from the middle of the room. It created a galactic Rolodex.

This wasn't a new system; this was all of them.

The thin lines of light formed together to make a disk around the center of the console, like a record on a record player, giving the disk an inner and an outer rim.

Around the inner rim, each beam of light originated from a dot, the system's sun. Each star was a different size and color, some bright white, yellow, orange, and red. I walked to the outer rim of the disk and found each beam's end, a dark world made up of small gates opening and closing, swirling about its surface. Above each outer planet floated a label with an alien word written on it.

That's how I found the system I was looking for: Pageedra. I simply walked the circumference of the outer rim of the massive hologram, holding up the word and comparing it until I finally met its match. Touching the label held the system in place as the rest of them disappeared. Then, the system amplified itself, and above me grew the star system called Pageedra.

Its worlds appeared alive, vital, populated and even the gas giants each had a few red dots indicating settlements. I flipped through each planet in the system as if shopping for a new tie. The bright colors and patterns on every world's surface made each planet look like a paradise. Which places were inhabited, I wondered, but more importantly, where were my friends?

This was definitely the Pageedra system, but to get there, I'd have to travel to Geuld, the gateway planet. I returned to the original system to find Geuld, and as I did, paused for a moment examining my silver and gold translucent hand, and glanced back to the window, seeing my alien reflection. My old flesh and bones were now completely gone, and all that remained was a strange being of light. I reached up, and I touched Geuld, now rotating above me.

As I had hoped, the wheel shuddered to life, and with a thundering roar, the rock outside the window cracked and crumbled into pieces. The red dirt slid down the windows, revealing the vast landscape of Avesta. The ship quickly gained speed and rocketed out of the dusty atmosphere and into the clear vastness of space.

"Oakruum. Come find me."

CHAPTER TEN

THE PROFESSOR

When he was alive in human flesh, Vincent Van Gogh painted forty-three self-portraits of himself in a three-year period. He used short, quick strokes of contrasting colors to create images that had power, life, and excitement. He himself admitted he was trying to convey an emotion that he could not put into words, a kind of extreme joy or awareness.

His many self-portraits were a vast harvest of small paint strokes emanating from the center of his face, as if some kind of light or energy was exploding out from within. The culmination of the strokes and colors created a picture of a man who was more than alive, perhaps eternal. Maybe this is how he perceived himself.

In the 1889th year, Van Gogh, who struggled with depression and mental illness, entered an asylum where he painted his now-famous Starry Night, a dazzling sky of celestial light. In 1890, the master painter took his own life.

I wonder if he struggled with something that he could not get his finger on, a truth that was so very close and present, but elusive and unattainable. Something that I had struggled with as well all my life, something which was now not a mystery at all, but fully realized.

I stood before the 360-degree window, my reflection looking back at me, the distant stars outside drifting silently by as I traveled through space. My face had the same explosive energy as one of those Van Gogh self-portraits; small, multicolored ribbons shot in all directions from the center of my face, or more accurately, from the very center of my head. The colored beams of energy and light radiated out of my head and face and traveled beyond my being, spinning, curling, and corkscrewing out like string and vanishing with a pop. I made a circuit once around the cockpit, watching my reflection, looking over my hands, arms, legs, and feet in utter amazement, and beyond myself to the rest of the room.

When I extended my attention out, my senses were expanded as well, and it felt as if many others were in the room with me. I felt a flame push to the center of my skull as if my head was on fire, and it worked its way down through my body. I felt like it was pulling stuff out of me, powerful emotions passing through like weather systems. I could perceive a presence, but more than one presence, the physical presence of particles, every particle of matter in the cockpit, the presence of light and sound as emanating waves all around me. I sensed echoes of other beings, other souls who perhaps stood in the very place where I was standing.

I stopped pacing and took a moment to process the waves of sensation. Through the window I watched the ship shoot past the world that earthlings had called Saturn, careening at a dazzling speed through the rings of gas and rock. I could feel everything, and I could see it; the air moved like water around me, and I had the awareness of a unity of all things, an interweaving. I wasn't just traveling through the rings, gazing upon the majestic planet, I was part of them.

But as much as I was hyper-aware of my outward surroundings, inwardly, I remained scrambled and confused. I felt my consciousness could reach out and stand upon one of the frozen shards that made up the giant's rings if I tried, but within I was lost—something stopped me from entering.

I watched the mammoth world go by as I strolled from one side of the cockpit to the other, and then the globe shrank to a dot as the ship shot deeper into space. When the massive ringed body had become the size of a pin's head, I turned and moved to the spiral staircase. Even at the speed I was traveling, I knew it would be many hours before I even came close to Geuld at the outer rim of our system. I decided to explore the ship, see what new treasures could be found, and perhaps find a place to rest.

Downstairs in the ship's belly, the layout was very similar to the first vessel, with a large central chamber and eight channels leading out like a wagon wheel. Exploring the first few legs, I found a galley, a bunk room, and a tool room, almost identical to the other ship. Objects such as tools and plates and ropes rested where they had been left eons ago. A thick layer of rust-colored dirt and dust covered just about everything. I felt as if I were exploring the ancient ruins of some extinct civilization.

I found a large study, like my library, and settled into a dust covered chair in the middle of the chamber. I closed my eyes once again, trying to tap into my unconscious. Why was it so easy for me to reach out with my mind—sometimes quite a distance—but any attempt to travel inward left me repelled to the surface? Here I was on this new grand expedition, the mysteries of the universe being unveiled, and I was still in the dark when it came to my own being. I must have spent hours meditating in that dirty old chair, with nothing gained except a nap.

For those alive in flesh and bone, the closest one ever gets to communicating with the unconscious is in dreams. Even then, the messages are encrypted with images and experiences that require interpretation. For many years, I had a recurring dream in which I stood before a dark stone citadel with high walls, towers, and a wooden drawbridge. The bridge had been pulled closed with a heavy iron chain, barring my entrance to the castle, which seemed to be cold and silent within. Despite my countless attempts to breach the wall, lower the bridge, or beckon something or someone forth, the dream always ended with the same cold stillness.

Now, as I slept on that dusty chair in the study, I found myself in that same dream, standing before that same fortress. The gate was still closed, the bridge drawn, but I had shed my skin now, my bones were gone and the citadel in my dream was no longer dark. White light beamed out through the thin gaps between the threshold and the door. Above the wall, the glow of a city or town radiated into the night. Something stirred within.

As I approached the drawn gate to see if I might peek through the crack and get a glimpse of what it was, I noticed something carved into the wooden bridge. Etched into the beams was an elaborate drawing, a maze, made up of all kinds of alien characters and symbols—flowers, leaves, stars, birds, fish—every imaginable shape. How did I not notice this before? Had this always been here? I could run my hands over the narrow ruts carved into the wood before it all disappeared.

Waking up, I went to the towering window where the cosmos sped by outside. My reflection glowed back at me in the glass. I felt as if I were at the threshold of some important discovery, a whole new unexplored continent within. I had found the door, but still needed the key.

When I returned to the cockpit hours later, the

hologram of the mystery world, Geuld, swirled with activity above my head. I went to the window to see if it existed. To my amazement, the wheel was rapidly approaching something, but its shape and its dimensions were hard to define. There before me, with the blackness of space as a backdrop, was a massive, swirling, planet-like object. If the sun were a fiery collection of gaseous explosions, this object, perhaps equally large, was the exact opposite: cold black holes opening and folding into the voids, each mouth would yawn open, pulling in light, energy, and then close again, as if swallowing its prey.

We were approaching at such an incredible rate of speed that the dark mass grew to an immense size, taking up the whole window in a matter of minutes.

I pulled the page from my pocket and opened it, knowing that I would have to figure out which black hole to navigate through to find Juulez. My eyes ran over the page, trying to translate the alien language, with little success. The bottom of the page had five drawings of Geuld, each one depicting the black eyes of the strange planet.

Clearly, each drawing represented a different phase of Geuld's openings and closings. Perhaps what looked like random chaos was a choreographed dance with logic and natural design. The fifth configuration on the page was circled, which I assumed was the gate I needed.

As I looked back up at the approaching sphere, two large holes opened at once, one in the northern hemisphere toward the west and another in the southern hemisphere toward the east. The configuration matched the second drawing in the series on the page. Three more, I thought, but we were approaching way too fast.

I looked over at the control bar, cussing at myself

that I had not learned how to stop or even slow the ship down. I glanced back at the holes, as massive as the red dot, the eternal storm, on Jupiter. They both closed, and an eye slowly grew at the equator, dead ahead of me. I held up the page confirming the match. This was definitely the third phase, not the fifth, in the series, and the ship was so close now and moving so fast that it was clear—I was headed toward the wrong gate.

I ran to the control bar to slow the ship down. But all the grabbing, pulling, turning, and pushing had no effect. Outside, the dark mouth yawned open, and it seemed to surround the ship, and then it was gone. All that lay before me now was the light from distant stars.

For a moment, I thought Geuld had disappeared, but then something caught my eye behind me. I turned and walked to the other side of the ship, and to my utter amazement, the massive world now took up the whole back window and was quickly shrinking in size as we sped away from it.

What I was looking at was no longer Geuld but another world, a sister world, at the far end of another star system somewhere else in the universe. I had traveled through a wormhole safely. Unfortunately, it was the wrong one.

I looked up at the departing world in awe and then back down at Jaan's page. Now what? I thought to myself. I turned from the window, back toward the controls, thinking for a moment that I might turn the ship around, but there before me, floating about the cockpit, a new array of animated planets had appeared. The holograms of the worlds floated by as they orbited the center console. It was the navigational map of the star system I had just entered.

I traveled about the room, examining each planet,

trying to will the model into aligning with the schematic on Jaan's page, but to no avail. A sense of panic and dread washed over me as I stared at the metal bar of the navigational system, contemplating my next steps. I looked down at my body and noticed for the first time the strands within seemed to respond to my emotions. The strings that had been emanating out now switched directions and were moving towards my core, to my heart.

As I walked across the cockpit, I passed underneath the projection of a small, dark green planet that caught my eye. I stopped, watched it rotate above me, and then moved to the console and had the hologram magnified.

The image was beautiful and teeming with life, forests, rivers, and lakes, and across its face were a few dozen red dots. Something about this curious planet was familiar.

"I know you. Why do I know you?" I reached up and touched one of its red dots with my hand. Instantly, the wheel changed direction and sped off toward a new destination. Looking back, I really didn't know why I reached for that red dot, but clearly my unconscious self was trying to communicate with my conscious self, for it was exactly where I needed to go. Later, I would learn the deeper connections my consciousness had, and has, to the places in this universe where I've been. The people we meet and the places we go create energetic marks in us, like ruts, that guide our being to return.

The night and the light streamed by the window for what seemed like hours. Others may have gotten bored and retreated below, but I embraced the wonder and the solitude of my place in the cosmos. I'm unsure how much time had passed before the dark green and blue dot came into view and grew in the window as I made my approach.

She looked like an emerald.

Once we were skimming the outer atmosphere, I could see the outline of the land masses, places where the ocean met the shore—green hills, mountains, vast forests, and a great white desert.

As I descended into the massive body's airspace, a black speck appeared in the distance, almost at the horizon, the place where the planet's face curved away from me. The speck grew rapidly; something was coming towards me. As I tracked it, its shape soon became distinct. It was another ship, another wheel, exactly like Axzum's and the vessel I was traveling in now. My eyes widened, and as it approached, I opened my arms wide to wave it down, but the craft shot by like an F-16. I ran across the cockpit, giving it chase, but within seconds, it was gone.

Awakened by the idea that there could be others, maybe many others, I made a half dozen hurried circuits around the cockpit, scanning the horizon in all directions for more activity. But I was descending quickly now, and the distant horizon gave way to a local landscape of green hills, fields and what looked like settlements. Before I could get a better assessment from a bird's-eye view, the ship came to an abrupt stop, just a few feet from the forest floor.

I can remember watching the Wizard of Oz as a kid, amazed by that moment when Dorothy stepped out of her house and into the land of Oz. My experience of stepping out of the wheel and onto Apotheon, as I would come to know it as, was very much like that. I wasn't sure if it was the air, the alien fauna, or my newfound senses, but I was keenly aware of every molecule, every vibrating particle of my surroundings. The air seemed to move and sparkle like water. The plants were a twisted brush of yellow, brown, purple, and green limbs, vines, and roots. A bright purple bird, or insect, fluttered by, and as it beat its pillow-shaped wings, I could see bright, sparkling dust particles spray about in its wake.

The wheel rested upon eight white, marble-like pillars that were set in a circle. Between two of the pillars was a well-maintained gravel path that rolled out into the woods. I paused for a moment, spotting a grove of yellow-leaved, aspen-like trees like the ones from Axzum's vision.

As I stood there gazing into the treetops, two beings came up the path, running toward me and waving their hands. They were shouting at me in some indiscernible language. When they got close enough to see my face, both froze, their eyes wide. I stared back, speechless. These beings were not human, nor were they Payraydayzian, but they were beings of light. Their skin had a silvery, dark-green sheen, with light green and blue ribbons moving across their bodies. By their dress, I assumed they were guards or civil servants of some sort. I took a step backwards and thought about retreating to the ship when one of them shouted,

"Oakruum." And then they both fell to their knees and bowed their heads.

Stunned, I stumbled toward them, holding out my hands to get them to rise.

"Oakruum. Yes, I'm Oakruum, but how? How could you know me?"

Both slowly looked up and I could tell by their expressions that they did not understand me.

"Oakruum," the other one whispered, and rose to meet me with an embrace.

The connections between us created a visceral

feeling that caused me to tear up as energy and light rushed to my face. All these reactions were involuntary and caught me by surprise; it felt as if I went from wanting to flee in fear to finding the welcome of a long-lost family within mere seconds. The two motioned for me to join them. I agreed, and they turned and walked back down the same path. I followed.

We hiked for roughly twenty minutes when we came to the crest of a hill. The path flowed like a ribbon to a small settlement set on the edge of a grand lake or sea. The homes and buildings seemed to be made with the same white stone as the pillars at the landing site. A huge, domed building rose above every other building in the town, and I wondered if I'd be welcomed as a friend or confronted as a foe. My answer came almost immediately, for as I started down the path, I noticed a group of beings coming out of the town and up the path toward me.

The scattered group grew into a massive crowd, and within minutes, I was walking slowly through a large mob, many cheering, waving, and shouting at me. I smiled and opened my arms to them. I was embraced for what felt like a thousand times over, each touch creating a palpable emotion within me. The crowd jammed around me, each one trying to share an embrace, some simply touching my shoulder, my back, or my side. Some children were squeezing in underneath the din, grabbing my arm for a moment, and then running off, laughing, and cheering.

When I was finally stopped completely by the crowd and it looked like I may even be trampled or crushed, a much taller, distinguished looking man with a long, thin face, pushed his way to where I was, chastising the gathered as he went. He was wearing a long stole with a fiery pattern, and he carried a book under his arm, red with gold letters. When he reached me, he grabbed me by my arm with one hand and cleared a path for me with the other, pushing three or four cheering fans out of the way at once.

"Oakruum, welcome back," he said calmly, despite the chaos whirling around him. "Come."

Then he shouted at the crowd in another language. The crowd parted, allowing us room to pass.

The throng now numbered in the thousands, lining the road on both sides, to the village and to the enormous, open double doors of the domed temple. As we navigated our way through the streets of the city, I held out my arms to those who wanted to connect as I passed.

Welcome back? I had no memory of ever leaving Earth, much less journeying to another world across the universe.

Entering through the wooden double doors of the temple and down a long corridor, I found myself in a rotunda, a domed ceiling high above. The floor was made of white stone, and two stories of balconies encircled above, which were populated by thousands of onlookers.

My guide, whose name I'd learn later to be Yuung, was a ranking citizen, a professor at the city's most prestigious school, an artist, and an ambassador for the high council. The council which governed the surrounding area was comprised of eleven elected servants. They stood before me now in a semi-circle, while Yuung stood at my side. As we eyed each other, an orb floated from its home in a nearby alcove, grew, and came to rest between the council people and myself.

Once it was in place, rotating in the center of the room, one of the council people stepped forward to speak.

"Oakruum, you've returned so soon. Please tell us how we can serve you."

There was a long pause, as I looked around, every eye in the room was upon me.

"You know me. You say I've returned, but I don't know you and I don't remember ever being here."

The room was silent for a moment as the council people looked at one another—they didn't know quite what to say.

"You were with us just three seasons ago, Oakruum," the leader said.

"I don't understand how that can be. Something has happened. Payraydayzay, my home, has been destroyed."

A loud gasp came from the crowd, and the chatter roared up again.

"Everyone, including myself, was driven into exile and our minds were twisted and confused." I continued to explain. The room went quiet again, and the members of the council looked at each other, perplexed.

I reached into my pocket and produced Jaan's page. I held it up to them and pleaded,

"I need your help. My friends are lost."

"Juulez?" one of the council people jumped in.

"Yes," I responded in surprise. "Juulez. She's lost."

I pointed to the drawing on the page.

The rotunda was once again abuzz, and a diminutive female councilwoman stepped forward, walking slowly through the orb rotating between us, her hair flowing wildly as she did, and she came to stand before me.

"You do not remember me, Oakruum?"

"No, ma'am, I don't remember any of you."

She embraced me and whispered, "Oh, Oakruum, what have they done to you?"

Another member of the council, an older gentleman, had followed Ito across the room and took the page from me and studied it for a moment. Then he held it up to the crowd surrounding us from above.

"Oakruum needs help. We will gather at the table."

Affirmations rained down as those gathered above slapped their chests in approval, after which, the crowd dissipated out of the building and back into the city streets.

Soon, only a handful of leaders remained, and once I had been greeted by every member of the council, Professor Yuung patted me on my shoulder and invited me to follow him.

"Don't worry, my boy. We'll get you reconnected. Come with me. I'll show you to your guest chamber."

"No. I can't stay. I have to go."

"Patience. There's time, Oakruum. There's always plenty of time."

The professor and I walked together across the rotunda floor to an exit on the far side. The woman who first embraced me, Ito, and the elder councilman, who seemed to be the leader, Velosi, followed close behind.

As we walked, I asked them about their planet, their system, and their experiences with the shadows.

"The Nuul," Velosi said. "Ravagers, they will gut a world from the inside out."

"We have been fortunate," Ito chimed in, "to have had such generous friends who have invested in and protected us."

"That is fortunate indeed," I encouraged. "Who are these friends you have?"

She looked at me like I was crazy.

"Why, you, of course. And your brother, Axzum."

We arrived at the chamber door, and Yuung opened it and held it open for the rest of us to enter. The chamber looked like any normal guest room, with a bed, wardrobe, and a desk. Iron and glass French doors led out onto a veranda covered with exotic plants of all shapes, sizes, and colors, overlooking the city. On the wall was a rather large painting, a piece of alien artwork: three beings, Payraydayzian, stood together at the gates of the city.

"You see here," Velosi said, pointing to the art. "This is you, with your father, Renstruum and your brother, Axzum."

"My father?" I said, gazing at the man in the painting. "He was here?"

"Of course," Ito crowed. "This is his room."

"I'm sorry," I said, turning and looking at my new allies. "I wish I could remember…"

"It's okay," Ito interrupted. "You're here now. That's all that matters. Professor Yuung, here, can show you the ropes, and in time, perhaps things will return to you."

I continued to stare at the painting, trying my best to retrieve some sort of memory, but nothing came.

"Let's get to work then," Velosi followed. "Professor Yuung will take you out to the Flats. Ito and I will put together the table preparations."

The two leaders swept off, giving their goodbyes as they left.

"The Flats?" I turned and looked at the professor. "What's in the Flats?"

"You'll see." He whispered, and he held out the red book with the gold letters for me to take.

The professor led me down a narrow staircase. It emptied onto a cobblestone alleyway, and then down the main road and out of town. We left the city and trekked out to the landing spot where the wheel still sat on the pillars, and then we ventured further into the woods. We hiked for another couple of hours, I estimated, until the sun was completely gone, and the dark of night settled in. I tried a few times, with various questions, to get some idea of where we were going, but the professor was silent and encouraged me to do the same. Rightly so, for the farther we traveled away from civilization, the more I realized that this was not a simple walk in the woods. This was a pilgrimage, a sacred journey.

The forest opened to a vast salt flat. We stood at the edge of what I guessed was an ancient lakebed. Thin wisps of vapor flew about like ghosts, just above the desert floor. The sand would have been a bright, blinding white by day, but now, in the dim light of the planet's two pale moons, the ground seemed to glow a beautiful shade of lavender.

I stepped out into this desert without hesitation, looking up into the night sky, taking in the wonder of the cosmos. The two moons and the stars, which were aligned in all new constellations for me, gave a mystical performance. When we got to a place in the dry lakebed where there was hard, flat sand in all directions, the professor stopped.

"The Flats." He said, setting his pack down on the desert floor. "This is a place that is thin, allowing a greater connection within."

"Is that why we're here?" I said, somewhat relieved. "I'm afraid you'll be disappointed."

"You need not worry about that." He answered.

"The way is sealed and has been for a long time." I countered, lowering my head.

"Show me." He whispered.

"I don't know what you mean. How?"

"Here, sit."

I sat down on the warm flat lakebed. The professor did the same so that we were face to face under the starlit night. Then he took the red book from me and placed it on the ground.

"Open it."

I opened the red book to a random page, and as I did, the fortress from my dream appeared as a hologram above it. The castle, bridge drawn, floated in the air between the professor and me as if it was being projected out by my mind. It was translucent so that I could see through it to the professor's face beyond. The maze that had been cut into the wooden door was more prominent than before.

"I know this from a dream."

"Of course, you do."

"What is it?"

"This is the gate to your most sacred place."

"It's locked."

"You've been in exile for a long time, Oakruum. You're locked outside of yourself. We need to set you free."

"I don't understand."

"Beings of flesh and bone are terrified of themselves, tragically, afraid that they are not worthy of entering such a place. Ashamed of what they might find within, what they might really be. So, they run to everyone and everything else but themselves. You are flesh and bone no more and the gate can now be reopened."

I looked down at the open book lying on the ground before me, the pearl white pages covered with every imaginable character and shape, each one glistening gold. I reached down and ran my hand over the pages to find that the letters and symbols weren't written in gold ink, rather every shape was made of solid gold and could be pulled from its place on the page. I pulled a five-petaled wild rose, gold and brilliant, from the page and held it up for examination. It was the size of a quarter, but heavier.

"My god—it's beautiful."

I looked from the flower to the professor and, as I did, noticed the same shape in the carved maze etched into the drawn bridge. I placed the golden rose into the cut in the wood—a perfect fit.

"This is your mandala," the professor whispered. "The map of your soul."

I reached into the book and pulled a golden ring, placing it carefully in the maze before me. And then an arrow. Then a leaf and a star. One by one, I fit the missing pieces, the golden shapes, and symbols, into the geometric design carved into the wooden beams of the bridge until the puzzle was complete and the mandala was no longer a dark cavity, but a dazzling jewel. The map that the shapes created had dozens of crooked passageways that all seemed to lead to the very center where a gazebo shaped piece sat majestically. It was the last piece to be placed and as I set it into the wood, the drawn bridge opened, and the professor raised his hand to me and nodded as if to bid me farewell.

"When we look outward, we dream. When we look inward, we awaken."

Then the floating castle, the professor and the desert faded to black, and I found myself back in my dream, standing at the grand citadel, its drawbridge yawning open before me, the chain rattling around the pulley wheel. I looked beyond the bridge, through the gate, and at first, saw nothing but white light. For as dark and cold as this fortress had been in my dreams for so many years, now it was just as bright and welcoming. As I shielded my eyes with my hands, I saw something tall moving toward me.

A white horse and its rider came into view, galloped onto the bridge, and stopped just at the edge before me. The horse was magnificent, colossal in muscle and stance. Its mane and tail both flowed together like a river, nearly sweeping the ground. And upon its broad back rode a naked woman, her skin translucent, long white hair contouring over her body and filled with white wild roses. It was the last thing I expected to see come out of the light and I took a few steps back as if I had knocked on the wrong door.

But the woman stopped me with a smile—not just any smile. The kind of smile that causes the eyes to fill with tears. A smile that says I love you more than anything else in the universe and I've waited so long to see you again. A smile you give someone who makes your life complete. I smiled back, and I thought that my heart might explode with the amount of energy and emotion that was pumping through me. She beckoned me to come to her as she pulled a wild rose from her hair and handed it to me.

As I approached, I thought about Juulez. What is the matter with me? How could I ever desire another woman? Then, as I reached up and took the white flower from the rider, I realized that this was not another woman. She was me and I was her. I instantly found myself upon the horse, still holding the rose, my feminine body bared, my long white hair caressing my skin. Within, I felt a sense of completion, as if that missing piece I'd been looking for was found. At the same time, shame caused me to shiver, and I understood the reasons this door had been locked.

"She is your feminine side, Oakruum," the professor's voice came, "Your anima. Embrace her. She knows the way."

I could feel my cheeks warm at the thought of someone else knowing this most intimate secret. Never had I felt more naked and exposed. But as I surrendered to my anima within, the horse turned and trotted back across the bridge and through the threshold of my unconscious.

Within the walled city, streets and alleys fanned off in every direction, creating an elaborate maze. This was the mandala, the same mandala, now in three dimensions. The maze led me to a garden where a gazebo shaped temple stood. As I approached, I could see a gleaming jewel glowing within. Its shape made me think it was a seashell. But when the horse's hooves clomped onto the marble floor of the temple, I could see clearly what it was.

I gasped, and it all disappeared.

The next moment, I was sitting on the floor of the desert with the professor, the floating castle before me. The golden shapes and letters were falling from the mandala back down into the book, still open on the ground.

"No. Wait. What happened?"

Professor Yuung shook his head. "You're no longer flesh and bone. You're free now. There's no need for religion. No need for such shame."

I reflected on the professor's words for a moment. It had been such shame that had locked me out to begin with and now drove me away once again.

"I just don't understand why this would be at the very core of me."

"The very core of you?" The professor laughed. "Son, you have a long way to go to get to the very core. Hell, you're barely standing in the foyer."

I began pulling the characters from the book and putting them back into the mandala.

"This is why so many live quite happily with the gates closed and locked, which really is the true function of religion. It teaches shame, which keeps the bridge shut and the self hidden away. Which becomes salvation for some. Encountering the true self isn't a pleasant experience. It's much more comfortable to cling to falsities and myths."

I didn't respond. Instead, I completed the puzzle once again, drifted back into the dream where I waited for the bridge to lower, and welcomed my anima with a smile. I rode horseback through the city to the garden and right up into the temple where the jeweled treasure lived. This time, I didn't stop. The stallion kept trotting between the open wings of the red, orange, and white petals of an orchid. I felt as if I were riding into a Georgia O'Keefe painting.

The orchid which had caused me to wilt in shame earlier was now my honor and pride. I was now riding through the most intimate of passageways, into a mother's uterus. The horse stopped once it had stepped into the womb and I gazed in awe across a great body of water—an ocean or a sea, its waves gently lapping on the shore. An embryo, a zygote, hung above me like the sun in the sky.

Then a soft, sweet voice of a child spoke to me:

"ܒܒܬܒܒ ܒܒܬܬܒ ܒܬܒܒܒ"

The words were in Payraydayzian, but now, somehow, I understood: "You are loved, and you are Love."

As I watched the small seed levitating above me, my horse stepped from the sandy shore into the shallow tide below, the water lapping around its legs. There were strange patterns in the sea—circular ripples on the surface originating from a thousand different points across the water. Concentric circles emanating out in all directions and overlapping each other, as if the water was communicating with itself. Amazed, I dismounted, stepped into the sea, and reached down to feel the cool water run over my hand—only it wasn't water. Instead of water, I pulled a whole handful of tiny orbs. The squid-like spheres were the size of a pea and spun wildly in my hand, each one a mystic combination of streaking darkness and light with a starry universe within.

I dropped the orbs back into the sea and gawked at the vast number of them spreading out into the horizon in every direction. Infinite. Then I waded into the deep. One step after another my naked female form was covered until I was submerged and then, I too, became one of the spinning orbs and I descended into the deep ocean of the unconscious—and not just my unconscious, but every unconscious everywhere together. All around me were voices, young and old, singing, talking, praying, and laughing. It was so loud that it was almost overwhelming until I heard through it all the voice of Juulez.

"Come find me, Oakruum."

I kept descending into the deep, Juulez's voice calling in my head. Down, down, down I went until, inexplicably, I found myself back in the cabin in the mountains, sitting at the table, working on my manuscript, writing the very words you're reading right now. The black lab was under the table, sleeping.

"What? How?"

Then I looked up to see Professor Yuung sitting across from me at the table, smoking a pipe and grinning ear to ear.

"You do realize that you're not really writing that book, my dear boy. Not really. This is a dialogue. You're speaking with your own soul. All this is just a conversation with the unconscious—yours and everyone else's."

I looked back down at the page, and it vanished. Then I looked back up to find myself sitting on the desert floor again, the professor sitting before me, the night sky above. As I slowly rose to my feet and took in a deep breath of the light, cool air, the desert sprang forth with life. Out of the salty flat, a whole meadow of blue and purple crocuses sprayed forth with a shiver. I looked back at the professor, who was rising to his feet, and we shared a knowing smile.

Then, I opened my own mouth and for the first time in a long time; I spoke.

"ᗡᗡᎱᎱᗡ ᗡᗡᎱᎱᎱᎱ ᗡᗡᎱᎱᗡ" (I remember now)

I remembered and could remember the things that had been hidden away from me for eons. I recognized the professor's face, the two moons hanging in the sky, and the blooming desert, all of which caused my eyes to fill with tears. This was The Flats of Apotheon. I had come here many times through the ages to refresh my soul.

"ᗡᗡᎱᎱ ᎱᗡᎱ ᎱᎱᎱᎱᗡ" (You know me)

"Of course I know you." The kindly professor replied in our common Payraydayzian tongue. "I've known you forever and ever."

And from that point on, I no longer needed a translator. I had been baptized in the waters, my conscious and unconscious were reconnected, my native language released. The memories would not all come back at once, but the gate had been unlocked and I was on my way toward a deeper understanding of myself, who I was and who I am.

We hiked back to the city, through the woods, under the star-lit sky; by the time we returned to the village, it was dawn. We both retreated to our rooms, and I collapsed with exhaustion onto the welcoming bed. Yet I could not rest. Thoughts and memories that had been locked away and repressed were now free to roam my mind. I had a fitful sleep as Juulez continued to enter my dreams.

"Oakruum," she pleaded. "Come find me."

Several times her voice would cause me to wake, sitting up in bed. But then, my weary body would overwhelm my stirring mind, and I would collapse back on to the pillow. The dreams grew with volume and intensity until finally Juulez's voice went silent. No longer did she cry out in my mind, no more whispers of "come find me," just a vision of her lifeless body. It was this haunting dream that not only sat me up, but brought me to my feet. I grabbed my things, left the room, and rushed down the hall.

It was in the hall that I met Ito, the councilwoman, coming from the other direction.

"Good morning, Oakruum. I was just coming to wake you."

"Please, it's Juulez. I have to go."

"Oakruum," she responded softly. "Calm down, son. Breathe."

"I have to get to my ship. I have to find her."

"Yes, yes, I know, I know. And you will. But first, the table. We must gather at the table."

"No. There's no time." I pushed past her, and I ran. "I have to go."

"Oakruum. Please."

I stopped in my tracks. I turned back to her and looked her in the eye, which caused a long-lost memory to emerge from deep within.

"Ito," I said, "I know you now. You were a friend of my father."

"Yes, we were good friends," she continued. "And I know he lives on somewhere in this universe."

Then, she walked to me and touched me on my arm.

"You're a lot like him. Passionate, determined,

sometimes intense. I know there's always a mission that needs completing, but your father always showed up at the feast. The table comes first, he would say. So come, join us, and see if he was right. Besides, you must be famished."

The white stone table was indeed grand. If it had been on earth, I thought, it would have certainly been one of the seven wonders of the world. It started in the back courtyard of the domed temple where village leaders would sit, and then it extended out of the gate, all the way down the middle of a long thoroughfare, and then branched out into every neighborhood of the city—a great tree. I tried, but I never saw the end of it. The street was lined with old buildings and homes, and in between the table and the buildings, hundreds, if not thousands, of revelers crammed together to share in the feast.

The white stone table had been set with ornate place settings and sculptural centerpieces made of ice or crystal. Lanterns hung from wires that ran from one building to the next, crisscrossing the corridor all the way to the horizon. Ito led me to my seat at the table, which seemed to be among the other leaders of the city. Ito sat down next to me with Velosi on my other side, and we shared in a meal together; the whole city, it seemed to me, was together as one: an endless sea of celebration, one block after the next, connected by the stone table and our shared existence.

At the end of the meal, I was more anxious than ever to leave, despite the heaven-like banquet, but Ito put her hand on my shoulder and said to me, "Just be patient."

Velosi got up and climbed on the table so that the massive crowd assembled could see him. The entire city came to a hush and all the attention was placed on the elder councilman. He waved to the throng and then beckoned me to join him. And so, I did; I climbed up onto the table and stood next to him. From this vantage point, my knees almost buckled by the breathtaking view. And it wasn't just the scenery: every face was pointed in my direction as Velosi started his speech

"Oakruum, your father, Renfruum, would always say the universe centers on this truth: in giving, we receive. Many times, we were in need, and he came to us with gifts. Those gifts made it possible for us to have all of this, so it is time for us to give back to you. We have three gifts."

Suddenly, a group of two dozen children ran up, carrying what looked like burlap sacks. They placed the sacks on the table at our feet and then ran off with laughter and commotion.

"The first gift," he announced, "Seeds of every kind of plant that grows in our world, so that when the soil is right on Payraydayzay, you can start again. The second…" and he paused for a moment as an attendant delivered a white stone chalice. He took the cup, and I thought he might drink and then share it with me, but there was no wine in this goblet. Instead, he reached into the cup and pulled out a green, glowing orb, similar to the many other orbs I had encountered since meeting Axzum. It was one of the missing Vortai.

"We would like to share this wisdom and knowledge with you. Never take for granted what the enemy seeks to rob from us, the truth."

Velosi set the spinning ball in my hand. "And finally, we present to you our most precious gift."

And with that, Professor Yuung stood up from his seat, shoulders back, head held high.

"Please bring him back to us in one piece."

CHAPTER ELEVEN

THE HEART OF DARKNESS

On the planet called Earth, that is Gaieos, those trapped in the flesh perpetuated the idea that the great battle to be fought was the one that pitted good versus evil. This is why so many of their epic myths and legends involved some sort of evil being: Hades, the Devil, Satan, Darth Vader, or the Wicked Witch.

Villains. They loved to hate villains there. It was someone who could be blamed, the personification of the darkness that is all around us and within. Every good story had an antagonist, a bad guy—all the forces of evil and adversity collected into one ugly being who deserved the destruction that those who were good sought out. These good souls were the heroes of the stories.

So, on Gaieos, anyway, most perceived themselves to be the hero of their own story, and those who got in the way, who caused adversity, were the enemy, the evil ones who had to be defeated. It was good versus evil, in their stories, belief systems, and religions. God versus the Devil, Heaven versus Hell, the Holy versus the sinful.

All of this, unfortunately, was and is an illusion, a trick of the mind. The real conflict is not between good and evil; the real conflict is between truth and myth. In truth, the darkness is not necessarily evil—it exists and will always exist, as light will always exist. Light and darkness, the Yin and the Yang, you can't have one without the other. Darkness cannot be eliminated—it always has been and always will be, dwelling within.

If only there were a villain in this story, a Dark Lord

or a Mother ship that could have been destroyed to make everything "happily ever after." But the fact is, the darkness is more like an infectious disease, turning every protagonist into the antagonist. The deceptions blanket, blind, and pull everything apart. The masses let it happen. They welcome, even worship it.

This is what happened on Gaieos.

The beings there had become so overcome by the shadows within that they would call darkness light, and that which was light they would call darkness: the ultimate deception. And so, Gaieos, because of its arrogance, had become so open to the shadows that its destruction was inevitable.

Gaieos was in danger.

After the feast on Apotheon, the entire village, led by the council, accompanied us up to the ship carrying our supplies: the seeds, the orb, and whatever provisions we might need for the journey. Professor Yuung and I loaded our gear on board and said our goodbyes to a throng of thousands, waving and cheering.

Once aboard and away, we set our course for the farthest body, called Dor, the system's wormhole planet connected to Geuld.

Professor Yuung studied Jaan's page, which had been edited with some notes by Apotheon scientists and engineers. If their math was correct, and our timing was right, we could jump to the marked system, Pageedra, and rescue Juulez and the crew.

Although we were speeding toward the gateway planet at an incredible rate of speed, I knew it would be several hours before we arrived, so I went down to the Great Room and tended to the orbs, placing the golden

Shepherd's orb, and the greenish knowledge orb into two alcoves in the wall. They both spun in their notches peacefully and sang a sweet duet. I sat down cross-legged on the cobblestone floor beneath them and settled in to meditate, indulging in a few moments of solitude.

As I shut my eyes and blocked out my surroundings to focus within, I made the same journey I had taken in the desert, over the drawbridge, through the gate, down the streets and alleys, to the orchid's shrine. And then, into the inner chamber and down further, into the deep sea. The professor had been right—this wasn't the core of me, not even close. I kept traveling below the ocean, into an abyss that opened up into a vast celestial field.

I descended into the multicolored universe of myself. I traveled past bright objects that looked like stars or galaxies and swirling, arching nebula. Ribbons and strings of all shapes and intensity drifted and whizzed past me. The inside of me was a vast and beautiful universe, as big as the one on the outside of me, it would seem.

Then I came to a bright little planet the size of a treehouse. The small world shone as bright as the brightest star. It had three minuscule volcanoes and a tiny red rose. I landed, stepping down on its surface like Neil Armstrong onto the moon. I flopped down on the tiny world within my soul, and just sat there for a long time, looking out and around at all the life and vitality, the order and the chaos, the calm and the turmoil that was me.

If the outside universe has a central point, a singularity, then this point was mine. There was no deception there, and I realized how crucial that was to my life and existence. This tiny world within me was noble and true. That led me to a deeper understanding of what deception was and what it had the power to do—blot out anything and everything real. And while we spend much energy guarding against the deceivers without, there's a bigger threat within.

For the first time, I saw the darkness within myself. It was not at my core, and not very large, so I did not feel alarmed or concerned. But amid the beautiful, an ugly darkness lurked. It was on one side of me, swimming like a microscopic ghost. It coiled up and sprang away and slithered like a snake, swimming between blue and red nebulas across to the other side, darting in every direction to avoid the many sources of light, especially the brightest one on which I stood. Therefore, I felt safe. I wanted to know more about this dark presence, what it was, and where it came from.

But then, the cockpit alarm interrupted, and my eyes sprang open. I got to my feet, clamored up the spiral staircase into the cockpit to watch our approach to the gateway world of Dor. I went to Professor Yuung's side, who was at the controls. I thought it would be wise to learn how to operate the ship, or at the very least, slow it down.

However, I soon realized that there was no need to slow down. Rather, once we were close enough to the massive collection of swirling openings, Yuung simply took two steps to the light blue dot that was hovering above us, marking our position in space and time, put it between his finger and his thumb, and set it into orbit around the planet. Now, the ship, traveling the same speed, locked into orbit around the dark gigantic sphere.

Putting the wheel into an orbital pattern would give us plenty of time to wait for the correct gate. Soon it became quite obvious that not only was this the way it was done, this was not an unusual event at all, as another wagon wheel, also in orbit, whizzed by us, and then another.

As I walked around the round space and recalibrated my eyes, I counted at least twenty other spacecraft, all made of the same wheel-like design, orbiting Dor at different speeds and distances.

Who are they, I wondered, and where did they all come from? Where are they going?

When we finally found the connecting gate, it was embarrassing how very simple the process was. When the openings aligned with Jaan's page, the professor warned, "Three more to go. Get ready." Our gate opened up like the eye of Cyclops, and Yuung reached for the light blue dot moving around the hologram world and placed it into the opening of the glowing model rotating above us in the cockpit.

Outside, in an instant, we shot into the wormhole and came out the other side. Just as before, the opening and the entire planet were no longer in front of us, but now behind us. We had entered the Pageedra system. Like clockwork, the hologram planets orbiting above us in the cockpit changed, revealing a new series of worlds spanning out from the blazing white star in the center.

With a quick survey of the floating worlds, I could see that this system was busy with life and settlements. The Earth-like worlds that orbited closer to the sun were blue, green, brown, and covered with red beacons. The huge gas giants, each multicolored gem, also had settlements.

My curiosity peaked, wondering how a civilization colonized what was likely an inhospitable place. The light blue beacon that marked our position was hurtling into the system, skirting by a planet which, according to the projection in the cockpit, had at least ten to twelve moons orbiting around it. It was an absolute wonder, and I walked across the cockpit to the window to see it as we traveled by.

However, what I saw wasn't a wonder at all, but something out of a nightmare, and the first clue that something was terribly wrong. There, in a field of space where the planet should have been, was a tangled mass of fractured pieces—asteroids of all sizes connected to one another, by what I can only describe as a dark, gelatinous ooze. The black, oily arms resembled the teardrops in texture, but extended from one asteroid to the other, draped over each rock, and then sagging in between.

The scene was horrific.

Not only had the shadows destroyed the planet, but they used the carcass, the remnants, to build its lair.

"They're parasites." I declared with indignation.

But then I looked closer at the professor, who had a dark spot on the side of his torso. It looked like a large ink spot, and it was slowly growing, enveloping his body.

"My god," I cried. "Look." I gestured to the professor's side.

"What is it?"

"It's—inside you," I pointed, and then I searched my body, and found a similar spot.

"Oh, no," I whispered in terror. The darkness that had been a harmless little worm was now mushrooming inside of me. I could now see what was almost invisible just a short time ago. It was not as large as the professor's, and not growing as fast, but something had to be done to stop it. I put pressure on my side with both hands, seeing no other immediate options.

"What is it?" Yuung pressed me.

"You don't see that?" I exclaimed, pointing at the grapefruit-sized ink spot floating inside his torso. Yuung searched his body and then back to me with an expression of skepticism on his face.

"We don't have time for this."

Yuung went to the array of hologram planets orbiting above us in the navigation system, and selected the closest planet to the star. The image was immediately magnified, revealing a white, yellow, and orange cloud-covered marble, with a handful of small moons. It was incredibly beautiful, even majestic. The entire world was covered with thousands of red dots.

Yuung selected a red dot on the planet's surface, and pressed it with his hand, and the wheel shifted course, shooting us towards the system star at the center of it all.

As I took a few steps toward the now front of the ship, I noticed something strange. The projected image of the star in the center of the cockpit was bright white, but the actual star, which was growing as we sped toward it, was hazy and dim and emitted a cold, blue purplish light.

I turned back to the professor.

"Are you sure we're in the right system?"

"Quite sure."

"Something's not right here," I muttered.

I peeked underneath my hands that were holding my side; the dark glob was still there and expanding rapidly. I rubbed my eyes and held my head, trying to give myself an anchor. I turned and went to the staircase and returned to the grand central chamber below. I stood before the two golf-ball-sized Vortai, floating in the notches in the wall, holding my side and debating my options. I pulled the golden ball, the Shepherd, from its place. I sat down with it on the opposite side of the room, my back leaning against the wall. I sat there for a few minutes with my palm facing up and the growing orb rotating just above it. I had hoped that the orb would somehow respond to the black tumor forming in my abdomen, but nothing happened. It didn't even move. Instead, my mind again became confused and clouded with images and moments from my life in the flesh on Gaieos, my human life on earth.

There was the light bulb, the table, and the hearth of the shack in which I hibernated in for years. But then I also experienced other painful episodes that I had long forgotten: the time when I was a child and got lost in the woods, a fight that I had with a close friend, and the tragedies and disappointments that come with life in the flesh. Traumas that I had processed and had gotten over appeared to me as if they had just happened.

Suddenly, I found myself in my son's bedroom in my old house in Iowa. I was back in my middle-aged skin, standing in front of Christian's bed where he lay motionless. I held a plastic bag full of pills that I had found on his bedside table. I looked toward the mirror above the dresser to see I was back in human form. This was not a memory or a dream - I was re-experiencing one of the most painful days of that existence.

I had found my child, Christian, dead from a drug overdose.

What happened after that—the tears, the pain, and the agony—had long since been a distant memory, but now I was in the midst of it, about to relive it all over again. I looked down at the clear plastic bag I was holding in my hand; the contents shaking as I grasped it. The human feelings of pain, grief and anger that come from experiencing such loss took control of my mind and body.

"What is happening?" I called out to no one.

The emotions flooded my entire head, leaving room for nothing else, and causing my eyes to water and my mouth to gape open. I screamed in pain and threw the bag of pills on the ground, and then I was back in the ship, sitting on the floor.

I rose to my feet and took stock of my surroundings, my body. The darkness had grown to encompass almost all of my torso and was reaching up toward my neck. My fist became clenched as a wave of bitterness and resentment washed over me.

"This isn't real," I whispered to myself to relieve the intensity.

But look at you, my thoughts answered back. You lost everything. You are crushed. Someone should pay for this.

I watched as the golden Vortai that had been at my side retreated to its place in the wall, in what seemed to be an expression of self-preservation.

Shouting reached me from the cockpit above. It was mixed with thuds and scrapes, the sounds of a scuffle. But with who? The professor and I were the only ones onboard. I scaled the stairs in an instant to find the usually orderly and reserved professor engaged in a chaotic and irrational melee with a stranger. Who this stranger was or where he came from, I did not know.

The professor's face was red with rage, his white hair bedraggled, and pummeled the mysterious intruder with wild blows. The stranger countered, grabbing the professor and throwing him across the cockpit, his back and head slamming against the window. The professor's body sank to the ground, and I stepped in front of the attacker to stop him.

And that's when I recognized the intruder—the human man who introduced my son to the pharmaceutical poisons that led to addiction and ultimately took his young life on earth so long ago. This is the one whom I had blamed for my loss. I was momentarily stunned, but then my body moved impulsively and aggressively at the man, grabbing him by his neck and knocking his head against the window, my fist beating into him repeatedly. Instead of struggling, the man just smiled at me, which caused me to explode inside.

"I'll kill you." I shrieked. And I might have if the professor had not grabbed me from behind and threw me on the floor. I slid across the stone floor and into the window. Stunned, I looked at the professor, who now had the same face of the human man whom I had blamed for my son's death, also smiling mockingly at me. Now, both men looked like my enemy. Now, I wanted to kill them both, and I rose up, ready to attack. Without pausing, I lunged toward the men and they at me. None showed restraint as we wildly punched, kicked, and wrestled each other to the ground. I pinned the professor on his back and squeezed his neck into the floor. A voice came from within.

"No. Oakruum. There are no enemies."

But the words had no effect. The shadow was in control now. With one last burst of energy, the professor pried my hands away long enough to cry out,

"ꟼꟼꟼꟼ ꟼꟼꟼꟼ ꟼꟼꟼꟼ"

And I was thrown across the cockpit again, into the window, and then onto the floor. The stranger disappeared like vapor and the professor rolled onto all fours, holding his neck, coughing, and trying to catch his breath. Once we both had recovered, we slowly got up and sheepishly approached each other.

"What is happening, professor? What was that?"

"It was a delusion," the professor responded. "A trick of the mind and the emotions."

"You, your face, his face… looked like the one who took my son from me. His face haunts my nightmares."

"You also appeared to me as one of my enemies of old," the professor confessed.

"I am not him." I responded.

"Of course not, and neither am I your enemy. It was a shadow, a deception."

"What were those words you spoke?"

"[illegible], It means the darkness cannot overcome. There are some Payraydayzian words and phrases that come from the Originals, which give them a certain power over the shadows."

"The shadows can take the form of our enemy?"

"It's their best trick." Professor Yuung gestured at the hologram planets still orbiting in the cockpit above us. "What we see here is not what is. This system has become a hive for the Nuul. We need to be careful."

I stood and joined Yuung, surveying the different multi-colored globes.

"Juulez?" I asked.

"She is here," Yuung said, causing the world closest to the sun to be magnified. "See?"

I examined the white, yellow, and orange world for a moment, and as I did, Yuung doubled over and put his hand on his knees, shouting in pain. Then he looked up at me and growled. He had the face of my enemy once again.

"Darkness cannot overcome," I said to him calmly, in Payraydayzian. His growl faded, his anger subsiding, and his true face returned.

"Darkness cannot overcome," he whispered, recovering from the attack.

Yuung seemed to swallow his anger as he stood straight again, but we were both battling the darkness within. We were now approaching the inner orbits of the Pageedra system, close enough that we should have been able to see at least two or three worlds in the far distance, but there was nothing. It became clear why as we approached another asteroid belt, this one the same as the first, each massive rock covered and connected to the others by some oil-like substance. From a distance, it looked like a mangled, disorganized spider web.

According to the hologram map above us, we should have been passing a brilliant blue and beige world covered with settlements, but out the window there was nothing but gurgling sludge. And this was the same condition in which we found the next three planets. Each had been destroyed, remnants scattered for hundreds of millions of miles across space, covered with black, greasy tentacles that draped between the fragments. We navigated close to one of the tangled masses, maybe a few thousand miles above, almost skimming the surface. The alien darkness that encased the asteroids looked like some sort of liquid, a black ocean with currents and waves. Finally, as we approached our target, planet number one in the system, we could see that it too was encased in a dark ocean, the blackness covering its entire surface.

From the window, I looked back at the hologram image of number one, a beautiful orange and yellow gem, and then back out at the ominous black sea.

"This has to be the only world in the system that hasn't been destroyed," I remarked to Yuung as we sped closer to the black liquid orb.

"We must go in," the professor said softly.

I looked at him for a moment, trying to process his words.

"Wait a minute. What do you mean?"

"We must go in," Yuung repeated, this time pointing at the dark ocean approaching.

My eyes widened, and I braced myself against the window. I remembered the experience of traveling in the ocean back in Gaieos, but back then I knew it was saltwater. There was no telling what kind of liquid we were about to be submerged into, if it was liquid at all. We moved like a shooting star across the surface of the sludge ocean, the black waves spraying across the window, and then in an instant we slipped underneath the surface and down into the depths.

There was nothing but darkness outside the window now in every direction, which caused the windows to become mirrors, and I could see the transformation that had taken place in my body: streams of light here and there, but the ink stain had spread to every part of my body. Images of hurt and pain and isolation flashed through my mind, but I was ready this time, and held my emotions in check.

The ship shook, and I wondered if we'd be torn apart and drowned in the abyss. The only way to tell where we were was by following the light blue dot on the navigational hologram above us.

Yuung and I watched it as we entered what would have been the planet's atmosphere and rocketed toward the surface. Suddenly, we emerged from the dark ocean on the other side and entered a grey and rancid space between the planet's surface and the dark blanket. The black sea was now above us and moved about like an ominous thunderstorm.

We went back to the window for a closer look. Across the brown and grey landscape, black funnels reached down from the ocean above onto the ground below. The funnels, much like tornadoes, moved about the planet, carving out big channels of rock and debris. The swirling tornadoes, maybe ten to twenty in our field of sight, weren't made of wind, but of liquid from the dark ocean.

The light from the sun did not reach the planet's surface. Everything was illuminated by the constant barrage of lightning that seemed to flash from all directions at once.

We navigated just above the planet's surface, darting in between the black water spouts, this way and that. The light blue dot that tracked our location on the globe moved across the map toward our destination, a red dot in the northern hemisphere of the planet.

Outside the grand window, the landscape was an apocalyptic mess of dreary grey and brown. The settlements approaching and passing in a blur underneath us were mangled ruins of debris and fractured pieces. Rusted metal shards pierced out of the ground in all directions like trees in a forest after a wildfire. The ground was charred and lifeless.

The wagon wheel abruptly stopped above the remnant of what looked like a once beautiful city and then descended onto a half-broken landing pad. The professor and I walked around the window, surveying the hellscape.

Several large funnels rolled across the landscape in the distance, illuminated by constant lightning flashes. In the immediate area, right outside the ship and spreading out for a few miles, was a field of thin dark pillars reaching from the ooze above all the way to the ground. From a distance, the pillars looked like the bars of a massive jail cell.

"Look there," Yuung pointed, "We found them."

At the very bottom of each dark pillar was a wagon wheel, a ship. The ooze covered over each one, pinning it to the ground as if the black ocean above us had legs and it was standing on its captives, holding them down, denying escape. The streets of the ruined city had become a kind of cage with rows and rows of pillars imprisoning its hostages.

"Let's go, we have to find them," and I turned from the window and raced to the staircase.

A few frantic moments later, Yuung and I cautiously traveled down the middle of a cracked and eroded street in the ruins of an alien city. The crumbled remains of buildings laid to our left and right, the golden shepherd's orb floating out before us, guiding us to our objective.

The world we now hiked through was inhospitable, to say the least. The planet's gravity was weak, and we bounced slightly as we walked. The black ocean of darkness hung ominously above us and may have had its own gravity or some kind of attraction, for some pieces of sedan-sized debris hung in the air, as if caught between falling to the ground and drifting into space.

As we approached the wagon-wheel that was closest to our landing spot, we could see its outline and prominent features peeking through the shroud of darkness that blanketed it.

Who was inside? I wondered. Where were they from? How long have they been here? My mind wandered to Axzum. Was this where he was taken? I decided he must have been held captive here, but how did he escape exactly? Where was his wife, Ariance?

The golden Vortai led the way, guiding us to the vessel we were looking for, and once we got to the black shroud that covered the wagon wheel, the orb enlarged itself and pushed into the darkness, creating a porthole for us to pass through. We were now in a space between the dark wall that ran down from above and the ship. It was pitch black, and the only light came from the orb and our lanterns. The warm yellow light flickered on the outside of the massive spacecraft. We stepped underneath the hatch at the belly of the ship. Professor Yuung pulled a pry bar from his pack and opened the hatch, allowing us to enter.

In the Great Room, I could see that the ship was indeed ours. There in the middle of the room was the large piece of Payraydayzay that we had carved from the asteroid. Along the wall in their alcoves, the orbs still rotated slowly. Scattered around the room, nine dark pillars stretched from the floor to the ceiling. They were similar to the massive pillars outside that stretched from the ground into the sky, but were smaller in scale.

I approached a pillar and held up my lantern to see inside. As the dim yellow light shone into the gelatinous ooze, I could see the faint outline of a body.

"They're inside," I said, surveying the room. "All of them."

Yuung joined me at the pillar. He looked at me with an expression that said, dare we? And then he reached into the pillar. I followed his lead and did the same. The substance was cold and oily, but thick like jelly, like frozen motor oil. We both grabbed a piece of whatever we could get our hands on and pulled, and a body fell out of the pillar and onto the floor. It was the angel, the Ethiopian woman, Mira. She lay on the floor, motionless.

"Is she alive?" I asked.

"I don't know," Yuung responded.

We had both gotten down on the floor to check on her when we heard a loud pounding sound and the ship rocked as if hit by something. We stood up and paused for a moment, but before we could even speak, it happened again with a bang and a jostle.

"It knows what we're doing," Yuung whispered.

"Then we have to move fast," I said, and we went from pillar to pillar, pulling the crew from their cocoons. Muurchia was next, then Teum, Jaan, Lejuun, Cooper, Nigel, the Crow, the Tortoise, and then finally, Juulez, who I held in my arms, kissed her forehead and carefully laid her on the floor. Her body was motionless, her eyes closed. I administered CPR, pushing down on her chest several times.

"Juulez." I shouted, "Juulez, wake up." I smacked her cheeks and shook her shoulders. Then, across the room, Muurchia suddenly coughed and moved his head to the side.

"They're still alive." Yuung said. The ship shook violently again, and I could hear the hatch slam open.

"It's coming," the professor warned. I pushed on Juulez's chest once more, and she gasped for breath and moved her legs.

"Juulez, can you hear me?"

Juulez nodded and squinted her eyes in recognition.

"You came," she whispered, and shakily placed her hand on my leg.

"We need to get you out of here."

"Okay," she whispered, her eyes now closed.

With that, three shadows came up through the hatch and made a violent circuit around the chamber. I stood up to fight, but it was too late. The shadow hit me hard, consuming my whole body. I struggled to fight it, but it was too strong. The specter dragged me to the hatch, and then out of the ship, throwing my helpless body into the massive pillar that reached down from the heavens, or in this case hell, and I was pulled up into the vast ocean.

The current was so strong, felt as if I was being

carried away by a fast-moving river. When my body reached the black waves of the ocean lording above, I was submerged within its depths. The suit that I was wearing, and all of my belongings, were torn away, and I felt as if every part of my body was detached from the whole. The pain was unbearable, and I writhed as I drifted into the deep.

I kicked and swam back to the surface momentarily, my head bobbing in the slate black surf. I looked down to the ground hundreds of feet below, and I reached for it, hoping to fall to my freedom, but I was yanked back under.

My last waking thoughts were of Juulez and the crew. Were they swept up as well? Were they here, drowning in the darkness with me?

I found myself back in the shack on Gaieos, the single light bulb swinging in the middle of the room. I had been here before—this trick of the mind. Nonetheless, the thought of being exiled again gave me intense anxiety, but I wasn't in the shack long enough for the impact to set in, for moments later I stood in Christian's old bedroom, holding the plastic baggy again.

The darkness wants to break me; I thought. It wants to own me. Killing me isn't good enough. It needs to enslave me forever.

The next moment, I was stepping up on an old wooden platform. A crowd was gathered, and I looked out onto the sea of angry faces. They were shouting, jeering at me, as I was led to the middle of the elevated stand and a noose was placed around my neck.

This wasn't the vision of someone else. This was something that had happened to me in another existence, in another life, in human form, on Gaieos. I was living it all over again. The rope tightened and terror flooded my being. Inexplicably and immediately, another trauma was heaped upon my soul. I found myself in a field of battle, in a war, bullets flying around me and a soldier with a bayonet shouting and thrusting a long blade into my chest. I felt the cold metal cut into me and the blood spill out.

And so it went.

One moment, I was the slave in shackles, beaten by my oppressor, and the next moment, I held the whip. I had no memory of these events until I relived them. I could not deny that these events were an actual part of my eternal experience.

The darkness had recreated traumas in every life I held, pulling me through a thousand faces, a thousand skins, and a thousand villages across the world, across time, of every race, and gender repeatedly. There were dual moments of insult, defeat, and public disgrace. Events where I was killed or the killer, raped or the rapist, betrayed or the betrayer.

We hold our pasts in our celestial bones, echoes of the good and the bad, the dawn and the night. It mattered not whether I was the victim or the assailant. The darkness grew within me—loss and suffering, spanning centuries.

As a result, I wanted revenge. As I seethed, small chunks of me disconnect from my body and float away into the abyss. I looked over my form as another segment detached from my side, disappearing into the Nuul.

I was coming apart, one piece of me at a time. Soon I wouldn't just be dead, I would dissolve into the cold, murky darkness to become part of it. I closed my eyes and set out to make the now familiar journey down into my unconscious. I descended through my own deteriorating existence, once a bright, limitless dance of color and light, now a cold, dead graveyard.

When I made it to the singularity at the core of my being, the light was all but extinguished, dying embers were all that remained. The red rose lay dead on the ground. I knelt down on my heart—now an empty shell and wept. Around me, my inner universe was collapsing as fragmented chucks of myself fell away. I wanted my last thought to be of beauty, of Juulez, of love. Using my last gasp of energy, I uttered a word.

"ᘯᔭᘒᒐᘒ"

I did not know what it meant when I said it. I had no memory of ever learning the word, but my heart did. It was all that my heart had left, but it was all that I needed. For not only did I speak the word, I experienced it; I felt it. The word came alive inside of me.

It is an old Payraydayzian word conceived by the Originals. It has no comparable translation. It means to accept, forgive, surrender, and prevail. All at the same time.

I whispered the word again, and the dying ember on which I stood flickered like a hot coal when blown upon, and a small, detached piece of me that had floated away returned and reabsorbed into my side.

I returned to my son's old bedroom, where I set the plastic bag on the bed, sat down next to Christian's lifeless body, placed my hand on his head, and gently stroked his hair.

"ᘯᔭᘒᒐᘒ"

CHAPTER TWELVE

THE BIG BANG

During my epic journey through existence, indwelling body after body, reliving forgotten lives, I found myself walking along the rocky coastline of the Pacific Northwest, centuries before the dawn of civilization. I was a young girl, maybe seven or eight years old, splashing my light brown feet in the ice-cold water, letting the waves cover over them with sand and small pebbles.

It was a crisp early morning, cold but not frigid, with the bright sun and blue sky trying to greet me behind the lines of white clouds. I looked down at my feet and watched as another foamy wave kissed my ankles and my shins.

The ocean keeps time like a clock. The waves crash in, and the water recedes, all day, all year, always. The waves that lap over our feet lapped over the very first feet, and they will lap on feet yet to be born. The same waves. There's a kind of assurance they bring, an agreement.

I put my hands down into the surf to explore for rocks and shells, when suddenly the ground rumbled and bounced, and I fell onto my backside with a chilly splash. I sprang to my feet with a shout and brushed the sand from the backs of my legs. I bent down once more to clean my hands in the next wave.

But the next wave didn't come. The waves stopped.

I looked up and down the shore, watching the water drain from the beach, navigating gracefully around boulders and rocks. And so, as most children would, I ran after the sea, splashing with laughter in the puddles and streams it left behind. I ran way out. I had never been so far from the shore.

And then the waves returned. Playfully at first, but then the water picked me up off my feet and swept me away. Before a tsunami, the sea will retreat. It will gather itself before it releases its torrent.

The nature of life is the beautiful circle—birth, death, and resurrection. The shadow's nature is the very opposite. Not a circle at all, but a shattered windshield of disconnected fragments. It guts an entire world from the inside, leaving fractured pieces scattered flat and lifeless in the void. It works to do the same to you and me.

This was the menace I faced, submerged deep in the black ocean over planet number one. Outside, my body had turned into an empty, grey shipping container. On the inside, my once fantastic cosmos was dying, collapsing in on itself. Like the waters on the shore before a tsunami, the ocean within was retreating.

The small core of me shrank even more. It was so tiny, in fact, that I could no longer stand upon it. It slipped away from under my feet and traveled up to my face, where I reached out and I held it. The fragile essence of me danced a joyous dance above my palm and then the singularity pulled everything into itself. All of me—beams of energy, quarks, and particles, vacuumed without resistance into my hand, which became brighter with every iota it devoured.

For a moment, I was dead, cold, and alone in the dark abyss.

"Are you afraid of dying, William Henry?"

"No. I am not afraid."

And then, blam.

The blinding inner star exploded, unleashing a spectacular torrent of light, heat, energy, and artistry. Curling, corkscrewing, spiraling, and spinning, it was a three-ring circus, both terrifying and breathtakingly beautiful at once. It was as if someone had thrown a thousand hot, spinning, multi-colored marbles on a glass table. The formation of the universe within me was nothing less than a sacred catastrophe. I looked out into this marvel, like a toddler gazing up into a sparkling Christmas tree. I wanted to be out there. I wanted to go exploring, to map its new features, and slay the dragons.

The exploding star had now grown too large for my hand to hold, and it settled back down beneath my feet again. Stepping out into the newly created vast expanse, a fresh set of experiences, ones without trauma, hurt, or pain, greeted me. Experiences rich with golden nostalgia and belonging.

I found myself on a stone bridge that hung gracefully over a small city pond. It was a winter night, and the stars and the lights from the city lamps and the lights from the nearby skyscrapers blended in the reflection on the water below, the hand of a loved one in mine.

And then I was soaring, skimming above the sea in a sailboat, the wind pulling the white sail into the sky, the ocean current pulling the keel into the depths, and I was caught in between, the water splashing up on the deck in rhythm with each wave that we hit. A loving hand on my back gave me chills, a smile, and a full heart.

Then I was in a flowery meadow, in a narrow valley, way up in the mountains. The high, green grass, the orange day lily, and the white-capped mountains made me wonder what season it was. The sound of the icy water racing down through the valley and the streams toward the river was intoxicating. I felt as if I had found what I had always been looking for, and there it was, within me. I laid down in the tall, green grass, bees and gnats buzzing by, and let the white clouds in the blue sky above become my parents. Another hand rested on my stomach, a nose pressed into my chest, and the long hair tickled my nose. I did not want to leave that place. I was not going to leave that place.

Rumi once said, "I looked in temples, churches, and mosques, but I found the divine within my heart."

I'm not sure how long I was there in that valley. The sun set, bathing the peaks above in gold, and the diamond rose again the next day. There was the hope of midday and the repeated command of midnight. Maybe I was there a thousand years, or maybe just a few moments, but I was awakened, pulled from my dream by a disturbance outside. My conscious self rose out of my core. For a moment, I tried to stay, not wanting to leave, grasping at anything around me to hold me there, but I rode the wave of light and energy that was now pulsating from my middle, out and up.

When I opened my eyes once again, I was still floating in the dark sea, but now the experience was different. The light from within me cast out around me into the murky water, so I could see ten feet in all directions.

The black water, now illuminated, revealed its own concealed beauty. Designs and shapes in the water danced around me, bouncing off each other, making me feel like I was looking into a kaleidoscope. In the end, it is not the trauma or the hurt or the pain that is unnatural. Indeed, all of it is part of the Everything, and so it has its own place, its own beauty even.

It is the deception that is not natural, and how it attempts to convince us we *are* the trauma, that we *are* the pain, that we *are* the hurt, that it's our identity, our very identity, and in doing so, the dark waters threaten to take everything from us, even our own soul. So, recall the traumas, if you must, and place them where they need to go, but don't call them by your own name.

The disturbance which brought me out of my deep slumber was now out before me. It was the wheel. I could make out its shape through the cloudy deep. I swam toward it, my arms reaching and pushing, my legs kicking furiously. As I got closer to the ship, I could see light coming from the cockpit window, shining out in all directions like a lighthouse on a foggy night.

The light was intense, even with the murky water diffusing its effects, and it guided me to the ship's side hatch, which was already open and awaiting my arrival. I swam into the airlock and shut the outside door, which caused the water to drain from the chamber. I placed my hands on the inside window and peered into the ship, wishing the water would drain faster and expecting to see the faces of my friends who had come to my aid. As the water cleared my head, neck and chest, no faces appeared.

What is happening? I wondered. Where is everyone? Why aren't they coming to get me?

The blackness drained to my legs and feet, reduced to a trickle and a puddle. I engaged the inside door, which slid open, and raced through the tool room, down the tunnel and into the central chamber.

I had hoped to find it as I had left it, with Juulez and the crew recovering from their imprisonment and Yuung attending to them, but the circular chamber was empty. Light beamed down the spiral staircase from the cockpit above, and then there was movement.

A body blocked the light momentarily and then the four familiar paws of Cooper pattered down the steps and the faithful lab greeted me with a tail wag and a nose to the leg. I knelt and embraced my old friend, scratching his head and checking his health. Cooper turned and looked toward the cockpit above.

"What is it, Coop? What's up there?"

Cooper climbed back up the stairs, and I followed.

The cockpit was filled with so much light that at first it was difficult to find the source. It was like standing inside of a blazing hot light bulb. Cooper paced excitedly around the perimeter of the room. I wondered if the navigational equipment had malfunctioned, overheated, or who knows what, but as I turned toward the brightest place in the cockpit, I shielded my eyes enough to see the light was emanating from a being floating inside of an orb in the middle of it all.

The hologram planets of the Pageedra system still orbiting around the room made the being appear as if it were a star that had gone supernova.

It was the baby, Ella.

How she was able to release herself from the cocoon where we had placed her, or how she was able to get to the cockpit, I will never know. But she was there now when apparently everyone else on board had vanished. I could see through the intense light that she sat naked within the orb, her eyes wide open and alert, and although there were incredible levels of energy emanating from her body, she looked quite calm and content, as if nothing out of the ordinary was happening at all. She surveyed the room with the innocence and wonder that only babies possess.

I took a few steps toward her, and as I did, her eyes met mine and her mouth opened to a precious smile, her legs kicked as she floated some three to four feet from the floor. She reached her arms out to me, inviting me close. She looked to be maybe six months old, with soft eyes, chubby cheeks, hands, and feet, and much like a human baby in size and strength, but with the otherworldly features that I had come to know that characterized beings of light, Ella now being the brightest of them all.

Cooper was close to my side, and we approached the orb, our eyes dancing with wonder, my hand held out to meet Ella's, already stretched out towards me. My hand breached the orb's outer membrane and our hands met. The light within me also became magnified, and I felt like I might explode.

I shut my eyes, trying to control what seemed like chaos within me, and in that moment of intimacy, Ella shared with me through Koinonae, her deepest desire. Just as I had become Axzum and Mira when they shared their visions of desire with me, now I became Ella.

I was the babe, cradled in the arms of her mother, Ariance. The woman was radiant and looked upon me with such adoration that I felt no need for anything else. I lay there as Ella, looking into her mother's eyes. All anxiety was gone, and I felt no need to work or shield myself ever again. The idea of earning my worth or defending what was mine became as strange as a foreign language. Ariance held me tight in her arms and whispered words to me I understood. The words came not from her mouth, but from her center to my center.

"Why fear when you are loved? Why fight when you *are* Love?"

I opened my eyes and pulled my hand away.

"You want your mama."

Ella looked at me, held her arms out in a V, and tapped her fingers to her chubby palms a few times.

"I don't know where she is. I don't know where anyone is."

A determined look came across the baby's face, and she pushed the bottom of her palms out as far as they could reach, and the spinning orb she was sitting in grew even bigger. I took a step back in surprise as the bubble moved toward me, and then, before I could react any further, the orb enveloped both Cooper and I.

Once we were encapsulated in the streaking orb with the babe, I assumed the globe would stop growing, but it did not. It kept going, developing to a point where it had eaten everything in the cockpit, expanding to the 360-degree window, and then pushed out of the ship.

Now, the whole wheel was inside of the blue and silver, streaking, spinning orb. The black water of the sea was pushed away from the vessel and lapped against the outside of the ball. The baby relaxed her arms, put her hands in her lap, and the orb stopped growing.

I looked at the radiant child for a moment, trying to understand, and then back out of the window. That's when a body breached the orb from the darkness beyond and floated toward the wheel. It was Juulez, her eyes shut, her body motionless, and contorted most unnaturally. The darkness had consumed her, the light within her extinguished, making her body look as if her insides had been drained and replaced with dirty dishwater.

I had to get out there, so I pushed off the window with my legs and shot toward the spiral staircase. I navigated down using the rail like a rope and then tumbled down the tunnel to the tool room like an astronaut, weightless on the International Space Station.

I opened the airlock hatch, both doors at once, and sprang from the ship towards Juulez with a tether in my hand. It only took a few seconds to rocket across space and collide with Juulez's body. I grabbed her, tackling her in midair. We spun a few dozen times in the weightlessness of space; the tether wrapping around us both and pulling us together. I embraced her.

"Juulez, wake up. Come back to me."

But there was no response.

And then I remembered perhaps I wasn't the only one who had endured trauma, that Juulez may be in her own hell of residual hurt and pain.

"ꝺꝵꝺꝻꝺ," I whispered in her ear.

If you've ever held past trauma, you know how challenging it is to rise above it, to prevail. And it's easy to embrace the deception that to prevail means to have revenge or to hurt back, but we only prevail with ꝺꝵꝺꝻꝺ. I whispered the Payraydayzian word once more. This time, it echoed. She didn't say it with her lips, but it came from her core, and it was received in mine.

The transformation began. First, small pieces were pulled violently into her center. An instant later, she collapsed into herself, and then she was gone, reduced to an undetectable speck. My arms were empty, the tether around me loose, drifting down like a loose-fitting pair of pants. There was a pause, and I almost let myself think the worst, but then, wham! Her singularity detonated, unleashing incomparable light, heat, and energy. Her body came alive as swirling stars, galaxies, and nebulas were born and spread out within her. Her eyes opened. Her hands moved up, light streaming down her arms to her fingers, and she held my head, searching to see if I was real.

"Oakruum, come find me."

"I did. I have. I found you."

"Come find me, always."

She kissed me, and the same fire that appeared above us on the farm appeared once more, but this time much hotter, and more intense. When I think about the real reason for life or existence, I think of that shared moment floating in space, the lit streaks of blue and silver light shooting by us as the orb held back the abyss.

And then I stood at the very core of a self, at the center of a being. But it was not mine.

I was standing next to Juulez, looking out into her universe within. We simply stood there together and shared the most intimate expression, bearing witness to the chaotic mess that was Juulez. Massive bodies crashed into one another, creating an infinite landscape of exploding particles and spiraling comets.

Exactly how long we stood there together remains a mystery to me. It felt like all of infinity. It was perfect, and I did not want to leave. But breathtaking as the chaos was within, it simultaneously reflected an external chaos that was also unfolding. Our conscious selves rose out of Juulez's core, our eyes opened, and we both turned to see another body wash out of the sea and into the orb.

It was Professor Yuung, this time, whose body was as dark and lifeless as Juulez's had been moments before. Using the tether, we could navigate across the inside of the orb to his body and tend to him. We grabbed the professor together, but before we could administer any kind of aid, two more bodies breached the orb's outer membrane and drifted in, tumbling toward the wheel—Jaan and Teum.

Jaan's body drifted close enough by me I could grab

her while still holding on to the professor. While I held on to the two forms, Juulez took the tether and spacewalked her way to Teum, collected him, and brought him back to our growing cluster of comatose bodies.

And so it went: every few minutes, a body would tumble out of the darkness and into the orb. Juulez and I would take turns fetching each one. As we gathered the cold bodies of Mira, Muurchia, and Lejuun, I was reminded of the dream I had had of the border collie and the wolf. I would have done anything and gone anywhere to find my friends and pull them from the darkness.

Finally, the last two returned to us, the Shaman, who no longer took the form of a tortoise but was now a Payraydayzian like the rest of us. It was the same for the Crow, whose true identity remained a mystery to me at that point. He was Payraydayzian for sure, but his role, at that point not yet revealed.

Once we had the group corralled, it was the Crow whose core sprang to life first, exploding with such energy that we could not hold on to him any longer. He slowly drifted into space as he was reborn. Like watching a baby being born or an elder taking their last breath, seeing a being's singularity bring forth a whole cosmos within is something you cannot take your eyes away from. The Crow's body gained strength and mass as the furious hurricanes of light buzzed through each other like wild beasts. He spread his arms wide, and his eyes came alive as curlicues of golden light leapt from his body. The rest underwent the same transformation as the inner explosions became contagious.

Each one had to disengage from the group to have enough space to undergo the metamorphosis, taking time to stand within and experience the wonder of themselves.

Meanwhile, Juulez and I remained at Professor Yuung's side, awaiting his detonation, but nothing happened. His body remained lifeless.

"ᑐᐟᑐᒡᑐ," Juulez whispered to him several times to awaken him, but the professor would not stir. It was the Crow who levitated to us first and placed his hand on the professor's chest, and then as others became aware, they drifted over to us until all of our glowing faces were in a tight circle around Professor Yuung's body.

To watch the light and energy flow through all of us and down our arms, into our hands, and into Yuung's chest, was something mythical to behold. Professor Yuung's own core ignited and sent a subatomic universe searing through his person. Once the transformation had fully taken place and the professor had the chance to behold his own unfolding, his eyes opened, and he took in each face around him.

"The darkness cannot overcome," he whispered in Payraydayzian, and we all celebrated. As the professor recovered and reconnected with his old friends, our new bodies exploding with heat and light.

Then something outside of the orb caught my eye. There was movement beyond the outer membrane, and a purplish light danced into the sphere.

"Something's happening," I said, and motioned toward the purple light, which was getting brighter.

"Back to the ship." Jaan commanded.

We scrambled up the tether, hand over hand, in a long chain of glowing persons, into the tool room. We shut both the airlock doors behind us and raced down the tunnel towards the cockpit. Cooper met us at the spiral staircase, greeting all who passed him with a wag of his tail. We reached the cockpit in time to watch Ella pull the orb back into the ship. The outer membrane traveled back to the windows and collapsed back down to the size of a beach ball, baby Ella still floating inside.

I would have predicted since the orb was no longer holding back the darkness that the black water would again be lapping against the outside of the window, but this was not the case. The sea parted, but not in one direction, in every direction. The black water broke into thousands of smaller teardrops. The light from the lavender sun stretched down in between the massive globs which filled the sky to every horizon. Down on the surface of the ravaged planet, the storms and lightning ceased and the light from the sun and the shadows cast by the teardrops made the world look diseased at the threshold of death.

"We have to leave." Lejuun shouted to the group.

He moved to the center control bar and brought the navigational field alive above us.

"Wait." Professor Yuung met Lejuun at the controls. "The other ships. They're still down there."

"There's no time." Lejuun barked back. And with that, a teardrop fell from the sky just outside the ship and hit the ground with a tremendous slosh and then seeped into the crust on which it lay.

Everyone froze as we watched a few dozen more. Teardrops splashed to the ground, detonating like bombs, two quite close to us, and another, miles away in opposite directions.

"There's nothing we can do." Jaan joined the debate. "All of this will soon be gone."

I placed my palms on the window and peered down at the ruined city below. The long pillars that had held the wheels captive were now gone.

"No." I turned to the rest. "We can't leave them. Our

233

people are down there. Our family."

And I gestured toward Ella, who was still sitting calmly in her floating egg. Outside, another dozen teardrops embedded themselves into the planet below with a wet thud that gave the effect of a bullet hitting flesh.

"What do you suggest we do?" Mira asked me with all sincerity in her voice.

"I don't know, but there has to be something."

Then, two unpredictable things happened at once.

The baby, Ella, put her hands and feet straight down on an invisible floor inside her orb and pushed herself up to a standing position, as if this were her first time standing without help. The ship took off. It navigated closer to the planet's surface, zig-zagging to avoid the falling teardrops that splashed into our path.

"What's going on?" Lejuun grunted. "Who's doing that?"

"I think she is," Mira answered, drawing closer to the child, who had her hands out, fingers grabbing, like babies do when they want a cookie. As we skimmed along the surface of the planet, giant drops of sludge raining down around us, we could see activity around some of the captive ships on the ground, now free from the pillars.

"Look." Professor Yuung pointed to a grounded wheel some distance away. The side hatch was open and illuminated beings were climbing out. They jumped to the ground and ran toward another nearby ship.

"They're freeing themselves," Muurchia noted.

"They have each other," Mira remarked. "As we have each other."

"Yeah," Jaan quipped. "And they'll all be frozen in rock for eons together, as we're going to be frozen together if we don't get out of here."

"That will not happen," the professor inserted. And with that, there were three loud crashes as three teardrops slammed down in quick succession, just a few feet away from the ship. The windows were sprayed with black goo. "I hope," he added.

The ship stopped and descended to the ground. Everyone in the cockpit looked at Ella, who still had her hands out grasping even more urgently.

"This must be it," I said. "Let's go." I clambered down the staircase to the chamber below.

Professor Yuung, Jaan, and Teum followed closely behind. The rest of the crew stayed in the cockpit with Ella.

Opening the bottom hatch, we found we were parked just above another wheel. We stepped onto the top of the ship and made our way down its body to its own bottom hatch, which the professor pried open, gaining us access. We each climbed inside the ancient vessel.

Outside, the intensity and frequency of falling teardrops was escalating. Inside, we stepped into the ship's main central chamber, the only light flickering from a lantern that Teum held up and out with his long arms. The cavernous room was completely empty except for one lonely thin pillar that ran from floor to ceiling. Teum approached the pillar, holding the glowing lantern up to the oily surface, exposing the outline of a body within. Jaan and Yuung both reached in and wrenched a body out, which collapsed onto the cobblestone floor. Her body was dark, and her black hair wet with gunk, but it was definitely the mother from Axzum's vision.

"Ariance." I gasped, and Jaan and I knelt to revive her. As I put my hands together on her chest and pushed, there was a cluster of loud crashes outside.

Professor Yuung stopped me. "We have to go."

Teum bent down and picked up the mother, carried her over his shoulder, and made his way to the hatch. It would be a quick trip from one wheel hatch to the other, but there was nothing easy about it.

When we had poured out of the bottom of the derelict ship and onto the alien surface, two more drops hit the ground like shelling in a war zone. All four of us were knocked to the ground by the power of the impact. I slowly got back to my feet and watched the black ooze sink into the dirt.

The oily sludge seemed to burrow a hole into the planet like a toxic chemical, seeping into the rock below, taking with it whatever got in its way. Large pieces of rubble and ruin were carried into the sinkhole as if they were toys. The sinkholes surrounding us were widening and threatened to drag us down too. Teum led us up the side of the ship like a mountain climber. Ariance slumped over his shoulder, using protruding pipes, utility boxes and whatever else we could find as a handhold or a foothold to help us get to the top.

When we finally scrambled onto the roof of the ruined ship, Lejuun was waiting for us at the bottom hatch of our own ship stationed above, his hand held down to help us.

"Here." he shouted, and Teum hoisted Ariance's limp body up for Lejuun to pull into the ship.

Jaan and Teum climbed up next, followed by the professor, and I jumped up as well, grabbing Lejuun's hand. As I did, the derelict ship I stepped off of gave way and I looked down to watch the huge wagon wheel collapse into the abyss underneath it, riding the oily mudslide into the drain before it disappeared entirely.

"They're in." Lejuun cried out to the cockpit.

236

As I stepped through the hatch, the ship took off, and I looked back out of the hatch as it closed to see at least two dozen teardrops drop and hit the ground across the landscape. The world sped away from us now, and in an instant, we were miles above the ground. The hatch sealed shut, and I raced to join the others in the cockpit.

Enough teardrops had fallen now that most of the planet was covered with black divots. The terrain appeared riddled with bullet holes. Across from us and above, many of the drips that had not fallen into the planet were now pulling away and drifting into space. Once we were a million or two miles away from the doomed planet, it slipped away.

"There it goes," said Jaan.

We all joined her at the side of the window closest to the carnage. The world crumbled, destroyed from the center as the Nuul ate away at its insides. The planet was gutted, and within moments, nothing was left but the telltale debris field made up of countless bits and pieces. We all looked out, horrified. I looked back at the hologram model of the planetary system hanging above us in the cockpit. The bountiful worlds that once made up a vital civilization were gone. The Nuul had eaten through it all, like hungry locusts, and left nothing but ring after ring of dead asteroids. After several excruciatingly heartbreaking moments, the destroyed remnants of the last world in the system disappeared.

"Our course is set for the gateway," the professor shared, and we all retired downstairs, knowing it would be many hours before we got anywhere close to the wormholes.

As I reached the top of the steps with Cooper at my side, I peered down into the central chamber and saw bright blue and silver light filling the room below. There was Ariance reclining on the large fragment of Payraydayzay, holding her baby, Ella, in her arms.

Ariance beamed with light and energy. Clearly, she had undergone her own transformation.

Juulez was sitting next to her with the Shaman, and they were chatting like old friends. When Ariance saw me step off the last stair and into the chamber with Cooper, she stopped talking and beckoned me to join her.

"You found my baby. I'm so thankful to you."

"Not me. We did it together. And she's beautiful," I responded. "But Axzum…"

"I know," she interrupted. "They already told me. But you completed your brother's mission, saved your niece, and brought her to me."

I watched the baby melt her body even deeper into her mother's arms.

"But that was only part of Axzum's mission, right? There's still more work to do."

She looked back down at her baby with pride, and my focus moved to Lejuun, who was standing on the other side of the room, examining the orbs, and talking with Jaan, Teum, and Professor Yuung. Cooper and I crossed the room and joined them.

I surveyed the alcoves. The one that had been holding Ella was now back in its home in the wall, as well as the orbs used for healing, communication, and transport. And there was the Shepherd and the knowledge orb that was given to us on Apotheon.

"We only need two more." I stated.

"No. Three." Lejuun said. "We will need the Ninth Orb in order to achieve our goal."

"So, where to now?" I asked.

"We may have an idea where we could find an orb, based on the words of an old poem."

"A poem?"

"I don't suppose you remember this."

Jaan recited:

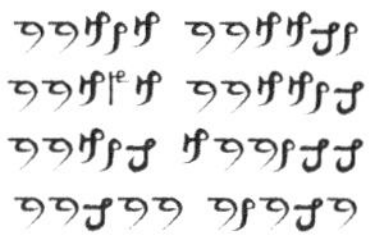

ꚇꚇ�96ꚇ ꚇꚇᛛᛛᏨ9
ꚇꚇᛛᛙᛛ9 ꚇꚇᛛᛛ9ᚫ
ꚇꚇᛛ99 ᛛꚇꚇ9ᚫᚫ
ꚇꚇᚫꚇꚇ ꚇ9ꚇᚫꚇ

And then she stopped and looked at me, waiting for the translation. I smiled at her and then responded,

Wild roses sing,
Their petals laugh,
Circle filled with life,
Always be, always last.

The room burst into applause and laughter.

"I think you may be returning to us, Oakruum." Jaan quipped. "Finally."

"I can remember singing that as a child. Where petals laugh?" I asked.

"They don't laugh exactly," Lejuun explained. "But I've been to a place where you could be fooled into thinking they do."

The ship was now filled with life. Professor Yuung and Lejuun returned to the cockpit to research the navigational system. Jaan and Teum wandered down to the tool room to tinker around. Ariance made a nest on the big rock and tended to her baby. Mira, Muurchia, the Crow, and the Shaman retreated to the library to relax, read, and talk philosophy. Juulez, Cooper, and I investigated the galley in search of a snack. We sat at a table, Cooper folded up, sleeping at our feet, and we shared with each other our experiences in the darkness.

"What was it like for you?" Juulez asked me after a time, "When you were reminded of your traumas?"

"I guess as I was reliving each experience, I kept thinking to myself, I can live through this, I can overcome. In the moment, don't we find the strength to face whatever comes? It's the memory. It's when we look back and we are reminded of the event that it grows in size and threatens to eat us, to consume us."

"ᗡᘀᗡᘓᗡ" Juulez said to me.

"Yes," I said, taking in the beauty of her eyes.

"We are not what happened to us. We are who we choose to become."

She reached across the table for my hand, which I gladly gave her, and we sat there for the rest of the trip, sharing our experiences through existence.

When the alarm bell rang out from the cockpit, announcing our arrival at the gateway, we joined the others clamoring up the staircase to witness the transition to a new system.

In the cockpit, Professor Yuung and Lejuun sifted through a handful of handwritten notes, and outside the gateway world loomed large, the swirling black eyes opening and closing in an intricate dance. The professor reached up and took the light blue beacon, showing our position, and placed it in orbit around the massive body.

From the window, we could see a swarm of wheels surrounding the gateway world, waiting for their wormhole to open. We imagined most ships were fleeing the same catastrophe we fled, but more disturbing was the horde of black teardrops that grouped around the terminal with us. Horrifyingly, instead of orbiting and waiting for a calculated gateway, these drops were randomly crossing into whatever swirling wormhole that opened. What systems they crossed into, and what destruction they would spread, was inconceivable.

"This is how it spreads," Muurchia remarked.

The gate that we needed opened. Professor Yuung placed the light blue dot into the gate in the hologram above us, and the ship rocketed through the wormhole and into a new system. Immediately, the translucent navigational chart switched above us in the cockpit, revealing a new array of captivating worlds. All were multicolored and absolutely massive, one planet bigger than the next, two so big their hologram didn't even fit completely into the cockpit. Before us, just outside the gate, was a tiny planet that looked like a jewel, glowing a bright fluorescent pink.

As we got closer, its size became more pronounced. It was no bigger than a moon, maybe even an asteroid. I went to the hologram planet circling above us, but could not find its model in the room.

"Where's its map?" I asked Lejuun.

"It doesn't have one," Lejuun responded.

"So, it's uncharted?"

"Not exactly."

"Are you sure we'll find an orb on such a small world?"

"Look again, Oakruum. The world you're looking at, that little planet…that is the orb."

CHAPTER THIRTEEN

THE CROW

Although my memories were returning to me, I could not recall time beyond my captivity in the flesh on Gaieos. Dreams were a valuable source of lost events and faces, but the process was slow, like putting together a million-piece puzzle, one agonizing piece at a time.

Memories of my life on Gaieos were clearer. Yet, all the new knowledge I received and continued to absorb was reframing those events. Growing up, constrained by limitations within my human body and mind, I believed in the supernatural, ghosts and spirits, and the voice of God. One life-changing experience formed my story, which I'd tell from time to time when someone asked me why I chose to go into the ministry.

There's a place in Death Valley, California, where the arid valley rises to a proud mesa covered with brush, cacti, and the kind of pines that can tolerate the heat. Camping there with a group of friends as a young adult, I had crawled out of my tent to pee in the darkest hour of the night. Once I had relieved myself, I took a moment to enjoy what was spread out before me: to the northwest, the jagged peaks of the Sierra Nevada Mountains, their black profile blocking the star-filled horizon, to the southeast, Badwater Basin, the lowest point in the forty-eight states.

As I gazed up into the Milky Way above, the space around me became electrified and I thought I heard a voice speak to me. It's hard to say exactly what the word was, but over the years, I would tell people that the word I heard was fire. I reached into my pocket and pulled out the marble I'd been given by the angel years before. I held it up to the light and peered through the glass, not realizing the actual wonder I was holding.

"Fire." God spoke.

For me, at the time, there was no other logical explanation for the voice in the wind. It gave me clarity and direction in life. Unfortunately, my interpretation of what was said and who was saying it was wrong, and the more I learned, my most excellent Theophilus, the more I realized how illogical my conclusions had been.

As the spaceship approached the rose and silver swirling orb hanging in space, the entire crew gathered at the window to take in the spectacle. Once we were close enough, maybe a few hundred thousand miles away, I could better estimate its size, maybe half the size of the Earth's moon. I scanned the surface as we drew near, trying to predict where we might land, but this globe had no solid surface, as it was with the other six orbs I had encountered. Its outer edges made up of streaking beams of light, giving the massive body a mystical appearance. So, I was only slightly surprised when, instead of landing on the surface, our ship rocketed directly into the orb, breaking the twinkling membrane without resistance.

Immediately, gravity released, and we were weightless in the cockpit. Our surroundings changed as the star-filled blackness of space gave way to a brilliant thicket of roses. The giant flowers, their petals ten times the size of the ship, seemed to emit light and energy. Their green thorny stems, tangled in every direction, did not seem to be rooted in soil.

As the pink flowers and the green leaves filled our window on all sides, I felt like a tiny insect, maybe a bee, which had flown into the branches of a rose tree. I looked over at Juulez, who was floating in the cockpit next to me. She turned and smiled.

"It's incredible."

In a matter of moments, we had navigated to what I estimated was the rose tree's center, filling the entire orb it lived in. The wheel came to a stop and rotated in place. The collected group of gawkers floated from one side of the cockpit to the other, trying to take in the botanical garden outside.

"I don't understand. What exactly is this place?"

Mira looked at me, but before she could answer, a voice from outside the ship spoke, a deep rumbling voice that seemed to come from all around.

"ꝺꞇꝺꞇꝺ," came the voice. It was the same word that was given to me in the desert years before.

"I know this," I whispered to Mira.

"ꝺꞇꝺꞇꝺ," the voice repeated.

"Fire."

"Not just fire, Oakruum." Mira said. "It means much more than that. ꝺꞇꝺꞇꝺ is an Originals word meaning fire, heart, sacrifice, and fruit—all at once."

Then, the Crow began to sing the old Payraydazian word with an almost operatic voice. Outside the ship, the roses echoed the Crow, singing the same line in a slightly different tone and color. Mira and Lejuun joined the choir, the harmony causing my eyes to fill with tears.

The powerful words of the hymn caused vines to burst forth from inside of the Crow. The branches, which sprang from his chest, shoulders, arms and legs, spread across the floor, and immediately ran to the rest of us, curling and climbing from our feet up to our heads.

As the vines wrapped around our bodies, new

branches sprang from the rest of us and tumbled to the ground. I wept, sang and sprouted, as the vines grew and merged with one another, intersecting with the old, dead vines embedded in the rock of the ship, instantly bringing them back to life.

A surge of life pumped through the dead vines like cleansing blood through the veins of a body and transformed the grey trunks into lush branches throughout the whole vessel, including the windows of the cockpit where the vines gave birth to bright flowers and watery fruits. The once cold, cavernous chambers and tubes of the wheel were now bursting with light and life from one end to the other, making the vessel feel less like a spaceship and more like a conservatory.

Transported, I found myself back on that hill in the California desert, overlooking Death Valley, wrapped in the same branches. The vine that curled down my arm to the palm of my hand opened and bore fruit, a cluster of juicy grapes.

Amazed, I plucked a grape from the cluster and ate it, expecting its succulence. But its tartness caused my mouth to pucker, and I thought I might spit it back out.

"ᗡᗡᎩᗡ ᎩᎩᗡᗡ ᗡᗡᗡᗡ ᎩᎩᎩ ᗡᎩᗡᗡ"
"Fruit is sweet when shared."

I looked back into the star filled sky that hung over the mountains in the distance and I held out my hands to receive the word once more.

"ᗡᎩᗡᎩᗡ," the word came again, but now I understood its deeper meaning. It wasn't a command to be obeyed, it was an invitation to live in beloved connection with everything, bearing fruit by giving and receiving.

Then I was back in the cockpit where music rose to the ceiling along with vines, leaves, flowers and fruit which adorned the windows all the way to the top of the dome.

The song reached a crescendo, with every voice holding a very long, sustained note while the vines continued to grow and shine across the cockpit.

The Crow held out his hand, palm up, and as he finished singing, the entire orb which surrounded us on all sides reduced to the size of a golf ball and rested an inch above his palm. The wheel had been inside the orb, now the orb was inside the wheel.

The rose trees that had taken up our view were gone, and a star-speckled cosmos returned to the window, our feet returned to the cockpit floor. I crossed the room to look into the Crow's palm, and to my utter amazement, I could see the now shrunken rose tree within the bright spinning orb.

"This is my mentor," the Crow said. "The Prophet."

I looked at the crow, and then to the orb, and then back at Mira.

"Do you mean to say that this is some sort of being?"

"Oolah," Teum grunted, and we all glanced over at Teum, shocked to hear him speak at all.

"Oolah is everything," Mira explained. "Even you and I."

I watched the spinning orb as it sang its soft lullaby, and I thought about all of my interactions with the orbs until that point. Certainly, they were more than mere inanimate objects. Each one seemed to have its own autonomy.

When the orb had finished its song, Mira put her hand on my shoulder, and while looking around at the other faces in the cockpit, she whispered to me.

"We need to show you something. Do you still have it?"

Mira referred to the marble she had given to me in my childhood. I carried it with me every day of my earthly life until we left Gaieos, when I put it in a small box and placed it on a shelf in the library for safekeeping. Prompted by Mira, I left the cockpit and went down to the library to retrieve it.

In the library, I found the Shaman, sitting cross-legged on the block in the middle of the room. His eyes closed—I assumed he was in deep meditation—so I moved to the bookshelf to retrieve the marble. As I pulled the box from the shelf, the tortoise spoke to me.

"You've been faithful," the Shaman said, his eyes still shut. "You have lived up to your call, but now it is time for you to be ꟾꟾꟾꟾꟾ."

"Fire?" I responded. "Or fruit?"

"Yes." The Shaman opened his eyes and looked at me. "The Crow's the key."

He closed his eyes once more and returned to his meditative state.

I left the library, more confused than enlightened. In the lightning room where the rest of the crew had assembled, white light from the electrical bolts ricocheted about the spherical chamber and flickered across their faces. Without a word, I moved to the rod and placed my marble upon it. It levitated there, inches above the top of the rod. Beams of light crossed above our heads, struck the marble and held their light stream, until a new scene from my ancient history played out before us.

The movie that unfolded before us took place in the Great Room of the wheel. In the projection, the chamber was empty. There seemed to be no movement at all except for what looked like shadows coming down the spiral staircase in the middle of the cavernous room. But as I took a step closer, I could see it was not shadows. It appeared to be a flowing river pouring down from the cockpit above, following the contour of the spiral staircase and draining out of the hatch below.

"This is the Wake," Lejuun explained. "A stream of Vortai at the tail end of a star system."

Taking a closer look, I could see the endless spinning Vortai washing through the chamber like water from a fountain. But this wasn't water, this was gravity. Oolah, as they called it. I pulled my hand out to touch it as it flowed down, but this was a vision, a mirage, and my hand went right through.

"This is the source of the orbs, where they are harvested," Lejuun continued. But the swirling Vortai that flowed by were dark—no silver or blue streaks of light.

"The Vortai must be captured in a vessel."

"A vessel?" I asked. "What kind of vessel?"

"Watch," Mira whispered to me, and she put her hand on my shoulder as if to say, "brace yourself."

Two beings entered the chamber in the vision. I recognized one of them as my brother Axzum. The other looked like the being in the painting that hung on the wall in my room on Apotheon.

"This is your brother, Axzum, and your father, Renstruum," Mira explained.

"My father?"

The man was tall and strong, and carried a being in his arms who looked seriously injured, possibly dead.

"You were sick. Your selfishness allowed you to be overcome by the shadows." Mira continued. "If he didn't do what he did, you would not be here."

Sure enough, the man who was being carried was me. The tall being, evidently my father, whom I was seeing for the first time, laid my limp body on the ground and stroked my forehead. Then he looked up toward the flowing river of Vortai, traveling effortlessly down the staircase and through the ship.

He walked toward the stream, his left hand reaching out toward the font. Axzum followed him, and grabbed his arm, as if to stop him from going any further. Before he could be stopped, he turned to Axzum, embraced him for what ended up being the last time, looked back at my motionless body, and then stepped completely into the cascading current.

Initially, the river flowed over his translucent body, but as Vortai penetrated into his skin, through his head, shoulders, arms, and chest, the space voyager became part of space.

"The Oolah is only contained by a worthy vessel," Muurchia remarked.

I stepped even closer and put my hand up to touch the face of this courageous man who was forming into something new.

Soon, the man was gone, melted into the stream as it consumed him, or perhaps he consumed the stream, for in the next heartbeat, a silver and blue glowing orb emerged from the spring. White light streaked across it as it spun violently in the middle of the room. I took a step back as I recognized the sphere as the very first orb I encountered in the woods upon Axzum's arrival. It was my father who had come for me.

In the vision, Axzum picked my broken body off the floor and placed it within the orb.

"Your father saved you that day," Mira said to me. "But that choice changed him forever."

I watched the vision in amazement as my body came alive within the orb.

"We are Oolah," I said, trying to understand. "We are the vessels."

"For those who are worthy and willing, yes," Muurchia answered.

As the vision faded, Mira removed the marble from its place over the rod. The lightning returned to its striking state above us, and I surveyed the flashing faces of my friends, each full of life and joy. The vision moved them as much as it did me. I turned and ran down the tunnel to the Great Room, Cooper at my heels, the rest following close behind. I found the alcove where the blue and silver orb spun, and took it from its home.

The golf ball-sized orb spun like a dervish just above my palm.

"This is him?"

"It is," Mira said. "And it isn't."

As I watched the globe, I understood what she meant. I could feel a familiar connection that I had not felt before, and not just with the orb in my hand, but with every single one spinning in their respective notches. These were not tools to perform what seemed like magic to me, these were souls, beings, who had become bridges for us to cross into the *now*, and there may not be a better gift, a better existence, than to give others direct access to the *now*, where there is perfect transformation.

As I slept that night, I dreamt of my father, events that had been blocked from me, my father's quest to save my life, which led him to step into the wake. As the memory of my father flooded back into my mind, my dreams that night became a kind of eulogy, and at one point, the emotions became so intense that I woke up to see the blue and silver orb floating just above my bunk. He continued to watch over me.

"ᗡᎧᗡᎧ"

The next morning at breakfast, Lejuun invited us to join him and Professor Yuung in the library for a meeting. Along with every other chamber of the wheel, the library was now filled with bright flowery vines that covered the walls, windows, and ceiling. The fragrant plants served as sources of beauty, fruit, and glowing light. The effect was magical.

As we trickled into the room, we could see the tortoise, the Shaman, still perched on the onyx block in the middle of the room, and one of the orbs was floating above his head. It was the green knowledge orb given to us by the Council on Apotheon, and it was open to about the size of a car. Inside the glowing orb was a single star the size of a pinhead.

We all found a comfortable place to be in the library. Juulez and I sat on the windowsill with Cooper at our feet, the stars traveling behind us as the wheel continued to rotate in space. The Crow came in last and stood at the doorway. We remained in silence until the tortoise finally spoke.

"To know fully and to be known fully, there is nothing greater."

The knowledge orb enlarged itself further, engulfing everyone in the room. Now we were within the orb, looking out upon a sky full of swirling galaxies of all shapes and sizes. In an instant, we were transported to the very beginning, or a three-dimensional projection of it, anyway.

"This is the center of all things," said Lejuun. "The place where the universe began and where it will end and where it will begin again."

"Everything revolves around this point," Professor Yuung followed. "As worlds move about their star, galaxies move about this sacred center."

We all looked out at the galaxies, which seemed to accelerate, traveling furiously around us. Then, amazingly, they all collapsed down into us, and expanded back out again. It was exhilarating.

"All of this happens in a breath," Lejuun said. "It is gravity, Oolah, which slows down our perception, creates time, and grants us moments to exist and create. Galaxies behave in much the same way. Billions of stars wrap around a sacred center."

Yuung pointed to a galaxy, which we traveled to in an instant. We witnessed in full speed the life of a galaxy as it spun like a top on a glass table, died out and then was born anew.

"This brings us to the star systems," Lejuun said. We suddenly stood on the sun, as an ocean of bright, hot gas tumbled just below us like an active volcano, a sun flare arching over our heads.

"We perceive a star system as flat and static, planets moving in a circle, horizontally around the sun. But this is not the case. In reality, the star is spinning and moving through space at an incredible rate of speed."

We now rode the star through the cosmos, all other objects a blur as we sped by, held on by gravity, the sun's planets speeding along as well, racing around the star like a corkscrew.

Suddenly, we jettisoned from the star and were left floating in space within the orb. We watched the whole system speed by, the careening star and its worlds flinging themselves toward the sun, trying to keep up.

"All of this movement creates a wake at the tail end of the spiraling system."

The tail of the system appeared before us, a wild river of swirling bubbles of gravity, large at first and then sputtering down to a pop.

"The Wake. This is where we can harvest the Ninth Orb."

With that, the orb we were in collapsed back down to its original size and floated back above the tortoise, and we were back in the library.

"That seems pretty straightforward," said Jaan, reclining in one of the white, plush chairs. "Which star system do you propose?"

"Our own," Lejuun replied.

"The Three Sisters?" Jaan shot back. "Are you crazy? We'll have to go through Gaddaraw."

"Gaddaraw?" I chimed in.

"On earth they call it the Oort Cloud, but Gaddaraw is less of a cloud, and more of a giant pinball machine filled with asteroids and deadly comets. We'll be annihilated."

"Well, that's our plan," said Lejuun flatly. "Unless you have a better one?"

Jaan was quiet. We all were. Professor Yuung broke the silence.

"Yes, this will be dangerous, but in order for there to be restoration, we must be [illegible]."

With the mission set before us, the meeting adjourned and the crew set out to other parts of the ship to execute the plan. Ariance, Muurchia, and Mira returned to the fragment in the Great Room. Jaan and Teum went to prep the hatches, and Lejuun and Yuung went back to the cockpit. It would not take them long to navigate the wheel back through the gateway, returning us to our system. The tortoise and the Crow remained behind, looking at each other mysteriously. It did not come as a surprise to me when they stopped Juulez and me as we were walking out.

"Oakruum, Juulez," the tortoise beckoned. "Please stay and talk with us."

The Crow sat down in one of the deep chairs, Juulez and I followed suit with Cooper nestling down between us. Once we were comfortable, the Shaman, wasting no time on small talk, asked me,

"Do you now realize who you are?"

I looked at Juulez and then back to the tortoise.

"I'm not sure exactly, but I suspect that I'm to be the one who will be the vessel."

"It is admirable that you would be ready to offer such a sacrifice. But no, it is as I told you: the Crow's the key. His real name is Bowee, and he is to be the Ninth Orb."

Upon hearing this news, I was relieved and disappointed at the same time. I looked at the Crow, Bowee, with a new sense of admiration.

"We each play our part to serve the whole," the tortoise continued. "Once we have the Ninth Orb, we will still be one short."

"The last orb is on Gaieos," Bowee said. "You'll need to retrieve it."

"Absolutely," I answered. "Anything."

"Do we know where it is?" Juulez asked.

"It was in my possession centuries ago," Bowee responded. "When I lived in the flesh in Florence, I placed it in a lock-box which I designed myself, and stored the box in a hidden chamber underneath my antique shop. I was an antiquarian named Anton. I had in my possession a finger bone that had once belonged to another great space voyager, Galileo Galilee. Find the finger, find the orb."

Juulez and I promised to retrieve it, embraced Bowee and the Shaman, and then joined the others.

In the cockpit, Lejuun and Professor Yuung had already engaged the ship, and we were approaching the swirling gateway world at the far end of the star system.

We orbited around the blossoming wormholes for a few minutes, awaiting the precise gate that would take us home. When it appeared, Professor Yuung reached up to the light blue dot marking our position, and placed it into the black hole. Instantly, the ship darted into the opening iris. We emerged into a star-filled expanse, and a new series of hologram planets appeared in the cockpit. Juulez and I walked across the room where the projection of the three sister planets orbited. Gaieos, Avesta, Payraydayzay, each one, a green, blue, and white jewel, dotted with settlements.

"Beautiful, aren't they?" Juulez said.

"The most beautiful."

We shared a bittersweet moment, knowing that in reality one world had been destroyed, another was lifeless, and the lone survivor's days were numbered.

"Ready?" Lejuun called to Yuung.

"Yes, I'm ready."

Professor Yuung reached up and grabbed the light blue dot, and Lejuun moved to the central control.

"What is it?" I asked. "What are you doing?"

"Switching to pilot control," Lejuun replied as he hit the bar, causing the navigational scheme above us to switch. The worlds disappeared, and a field of chaos appeared in their place.

"What is that?" Juulez pointed. "You're not taking us in there, are you?"

"It is Gaddaraw," Lejuun replied. "Now please, be quiet."

Gaddaraw, which was at the rear tip of the system, laid out in a navigational projection, and looked like the tail of a comet, except much larger. Large pieces of rock and ice reduced to a slender tip, which I deduced was our destination. To get there, Professor Yuung would have to pilot the wheel through a shooting gallery of swirling fragments. He levitated into place above us in the cockpit, right in the middle of the projection, and moved the light blue dot toward the hologram map. Outside, the wheel changed trajectory, bringing the bedlam into full view.

We rocketed toward the debris field at a dizzying speed, and before we could even take a breath, we were inside the tail, dodging rocks and evading ricocheting bits and pieces. Professor Yuung, hovering above us, moved the dot through the hologram map, like pushing a marble through a maze, sometimes threading dangerously between two or three massive chunks. At one point, Yuung had to duck underneath a roaring comet and then bounce above another as it shot past from the other direction.

We all jumped, and Juulez screamed, covering her mouth as to not distract the professor. Soon the larger pieces gave way to smaller chunks, and then, at the very tip, beyond the torrent, we entered the last remnants of the traveling star and its worlds, the Wake, a trickling stream of residual gravity swirling in tiny whirlpools as it tumbled into oblivion.

That challenge was over, and a new one was upon us. The professor brought the wheel to a resting position almost at the tail and descended back down to the floor. The stream of dark Vortai hit the top of the ship and poured over the sides. It was as if we had been caught in a heavy rainstorm, but instead of raindrops, millions of spinning balls of Oolah hit the roof.

A moment later, we gathered back in the Great Room. The hatches opened and a stream of Vortai tumbled down from the cockpit above. The river of gravity followed the contour of the staircase and emptied into the hatch below. The bubbles of spinning Vortai made the stream look like a thousand little hurricanes. It swirled and spun as it flowed through the middle of the ship. The waterfall of gravity had an attractive quality and one could feel the Vortai pulling energy in.

The Crow stepped forward and looked to each face as if to say goodbye. Mira met him as he moved toward the stream and embraced him, causing the light and colors within his body to brighten and spring about.

Mira released Bowee from her embrace and the Crow stepped into the rushing current. Immediately, the ferocious Vortai spilled over and into him, like a pitcher into a chalice, until his whole body dissolved into the flow. For a moment, there was nothing, and then the stream emitted a silver glow and a spinning white Vortai emerged from the deluge.

The hatches closed, the Vortai stopped flowing, and before us, spinning majestically, was the Ninth Orb. It was silver, with white streaks of light traveling across its face.

We all felt its force as it pulled everything in the room towards it like a magnet. Each of us grabbed whatever we could reach to keep from stumbling into its core, but there was nothing to stop the other orbs as each one was pulled from its place in the wall. The pink orb containing the rose tree sprang from its hole and set into orbit around the Ninth Orb. The yellow shepherd's orb and the green knowledge orb followed suit, and then the rest jumped across the room and into an orbital path around the newly formed sphere.

The result was an electrified object that looked like a life-size atom. The smaller seven electrons encircled the newcomer feverishly, causing its power and energy to magnify. Chaos ensued as every one of us fought the vacuum. Overwhelmed by its strength, I fell face first into the cobblestone floor and grabbed at the stones with my hands and feet to prevent being pulled in. Those who could retreated down the spokes to avoid the pull of the strengthening orb. Juulez held on to the railing of the spiral staircase. Her legs lifted off the floor as the orb tried to drag her in.

In the end, it was Ariance that saved us.

She was hiding behind the large fragment of Payraydayzay, hunched over in the fetal position, protecting her dear child, while she softly sang a lullaby. It was the same song that the Crow sang to the rose tree.

As she sang, the Ninth Orb responded, slowing its pace and faintly echoing the same tune. The other orbs joined the hymn, each one widening its orbit as it sang. Soon, every being and orb in the chamber had joined the choir and the gravitational pull of the giant atom weakened. As the music crescendoed, the orbs slowed to a crawl and returned to their nooks in the wall. This left the Ninth Orb rotating in the middle of the room, holding the final, euphoric note.

Juulez's feet returned to the ground, and she crossed the room to give Ariance a thankful embrace. Mira joined them and the Ninth Orb floated toward the women. When it came within reach, little Ella caught the orb out of mid-air and held it to her chest, between her chubby hands.

Ariance rose calmly with the babe in her arms, and took the Ninth Orb along with Ella to the cocoon room, where we had laid the child after we had found her.

Juulez crossed the room and helped me off the floor.

"There has to be an easier way for me to get my wings," I quipped.

"Let's go, old man," Juulez teased back, "Just one more to go."

We surveyed the Great Room as we climbed back into the cockpit, noting the single empty alcove that remained.

Once we were back in the cockpit, Lejuun magnified the hologram of Gaieos and touched the red dot, which sat in the middle of the boot of Italy. In an instant, the wheel exploded out of its grave underneath the rubble and out into space as we raced toward the inner solar system and the three sisters.

Knowing the trip would take many hours, most of the crew retreated to their bunk room to relax, but Juulez and I stayed up in the cockpit for a while and took in the stars. Cooper and Nigel joined us, as always. We stood at the window without a word, letting the universe speak for us. Juulez was the first to break the silence.

"I'm looking forward to putting my feet on solid ground."

"Oh yes, me too. And maybe jump into the closest body of water. It doesn't matter how cold. River, ocean, pond, or public fountain, I'm diving in."

"Let's sit in the grass and watch the sunset."

We continued like that for quite a long time, talking all about the things we wanted to do once we got to Earth.

Neither of us was concerned about how the changes we had experienced would affect those desires, or even how things may be different when we arrived. We assumed that things would be as they had always been. Change was not a consideration.

Twelve hours later, long enough for all of us to rest and eat breakfast, the alarm in the cockpit rang out, marking our arrival to Gaieos. The entire ship filled with excited energy as we anticipated completing our mission and enjoying the sweet fruits of the remaining sister. Most of us made our way to the cockpit to witness our reentry into the atmosphere of the big blue marble. But as we broke into the upper atmosphere and rocketed toward the surface, the changes revealed themselves.

The planet that once boasted large swaths of green and blue had only brown and tan to show us. As we got closer, the damage was easier to see. Buildings and homes, bridges and roads, torn up and in ruins. The land looked poisoned, the water lifeless. We walked around the window, searching for signs of life as the wheel came within a few hundred feet from the ground. As we skimmed the surface, we were given even more evidence of some sort of apocalyptic event: buildings and vehicles hollowed out and left for dead. Anything made of iron was almost completely disintegrated by rust. Vines of long-dead plants wrapped around houses that were melted to the ground.

"Oh no," I said, squeezing Juulez's hand. "What's happened here?"

"I think you might find," said Jaan, putting her hand on my shoulder, "That some time has passed."

"How much time?" I choked.

"I don't know, centuries, maybe."

CHAPTER FOURTEEN

THE CAVEMAN

We shot across the surface of the ocean, mere feet from the waves. It would only be a matter of minutes until we reached our destination halfway up the Italian peninsula to retrieve the last orb. It was Cooper who trotted up the spiral staircase into the cockpit and altered the plan entirely.

Cooper had a sack in his mouth, like the sacks that we had been given on Apotheon, which were full of seeds. The sack that Cooper carried was different.

The lab dropped the sack on the cockpit floor with a thump, clang, then sat down before it, letting out a bark. I don't know why exactly, but there was something about that bag hitting the ground that unlocked something inside me and fresh memories flooded my mind.

"Raykuum. His name is Raykuum."

The name sounded familiar, but distant, coming from my mouth.

"Raykuum?" Juulez leaned in. "Who's Raykuum? What are you talking about?"

"We've been here before. Mira and Muurchia, Jaan and Teum, the Shaman, the Crow, you and I, we all left Payraydayzay together, the day it was destroyed. I remember now."

Cooper barked at me again and nudged the bag with his nose.

"We didn't come to Gaieos together in my ship. We used another," I continued.

"We crashed," Juulez whispered, staring out the window at the approaching horizon.

"You remember too?"

"It's all distant and fuzzy, like fractured pieces of a fleeting dream."

"Raykuum. The ship belonged to Raykuum. I remember now."

A memory of our escape flashed across my mind: Juulez and I running toward the ship as black teardrops rained down from above, pulverizing the ground. Raykuum, my friend and co-pilot, stood at the hatch of his ship, waiting for us to board. Raykuum grabbed my hand as I arrived, his other hand on my back.

I glanced down once more at Cooper, sitting loyally at my feet and looking back up at me with focused intensity. People had always commented to me about how intelligent Cooper was, gifted and well trained. The truth was, I never had to train him. He had been a part of my life from the day I had gotten my marble from the angel in the basement. Afterwards, I returned upstairs and gone to the kitchen for a glass of water, and there he was at the back door. I never told anyone how old he was, and no one ever asked. Cooper was always there. Man's best friend.

I picked up the bag and opened it to find a handful of tools. Each looked more alien than the next, but they were no doubt the tools needed to repair a disabled ship.

"Where? How did you get these, Coop?"

Suddenly, something in the bag flashed a bright yellow, and the shepherd's orb leapt out, shooting around my body and head. I instinctively jumped back, lost my balance, and stumbled to the floor. Cooper barked at me once more, and the orb stopped just above my head and floated in place.

"Oakruum." Juulez shouted, and she moved to my side, but it was too late.

In the next moment, my conscious self was inside the orb, watching my body collapse on the floor as if I was knocked out cold. The last thing I saw was Juulez holding my head and trying to wake me.

In the blink of an eye, I traveled inside the orb to the other side of the world, traveling at what I believed to be at least the speed of light. I found myself in a place the orb wanted to take me, and I saw what the orb wanted me to see.

I was underground, in a deep pit, looking out from inside the orb. The light from the orb spread across the surface of a wheel, where another ship stood embedded in the bedrock, a piece of it hanging out over what looked like an underground lake. The gold light projected from the orb glistening on the foggy water.

On the edge of the lake, on the rocky shore, there was evidence of life, scattered tools, the half-burned logs of a fire, and a handful of dead animal carcasses. I scanned the cavern for movement, but nothing stirred.

A moment later, I noticed the tattered and ripped up remnants of a tan protective suit resting on the ground draped over a wet rock.

"Axzum," I whispered, and almost as if that were the cue, the orb shot back to the ship and deposited my conscious self back into my body.

There, I opened my eyes to see Juulez's face, her hand still on my head, as if no time had passed at all.

"Axzum," I said to her. I looked over at Mira. "Axzum, he's here, he's alive."

Jaan said, "What are you talking about?"

I got up, and I picked up the bag of tools again.

"And the ship, Raykuum's ship, I saw it. Axzum, he's there, I know it."

"Axzum?" Ariance said, as she crossed to me, holding her child. "Where is he?"

"I'm not exactly sure. He's somewhere underground. There was a lake."

Before anyone else could speak, a row of dark teardrops fell into view immediately outside of the ship. The whole cockpit responded with a gasp.

"Please," Ariance said. "Take me to him."

"There's no time for that." Jaan barked.

The entire sky filled with teardrops now, all the way to the horizon, and as we paced the window, we could see, it was to every horizon, in every direction.

"Juulez, please," Ariance whispered once more.

Juulez, our faithful leader, looked at Ariance and then to Jaan and to the rest of the crew, and then back to the descending blobs outside. She put her hand on Ariance's shoulder to comfort her.

"We will find him, but we know exactly where the orb is. Let's find it first, and then search for Axzum."

As Ariance gave a gracious nod, the yellow orb sprang to life once more and whirled around our bodies a dozen times, and then shot out of the window and sped into the blob-filled sky.

"Hey, wait." Lejuun shouted.

"Where's he going?" Jaan followed.

"Axzum," I said.

The orb rocketed back toward the ship, made a circuit around the wheel, and sped back out in the same direction.

"He wants us to follow."

There was no more debate about whether to search for Axzum now or later. The Professor reached up and took the light blue dot, and Lejuun disengaged the autopilot. The wheel switched course, and we followed the yellow ball across the sky. The orb zipped along, evading the falling teardrops like one of those Olympic downhill skiers doing the slalom. Yuung kept up impressively, piloting the ship back and forth in between the multiplying shadows.

The race jarred my memory and visions, an event from long ago bursting into my mind. We had all been in a similar situation before, but instead of teardrops, we were dodging fiery meteorites, pieces of our destroyed Payraydayzay raining on Gaieos.

And it wasn't Professor Yuung at the helm, it was Raykuum, my forgotten friend.

I looked over at the professor, who was expertly navigating the ship through the storm, and I could see Raykuum in my mind's eye. I closed my eyes to focus on the memory.

"I had forgotten you, Raykuum. I'm sorry."

Cooper, who had ventured over to me, rubbed his face on my leg. I looked over at the hologram projection of Gaieos rotating slowly in the room.

The light blue dot, now manipulated by Yuung, had been on course to reach southern Europe and was now traveling above northern Europe and into what had been the country of Russia. Outside, the terrain looked nothing like the Russia I knew. The ground was dry and rugged, vegetation long dead, the remnants sticking out of the earth like brown pipe cleaners.

We trailed the Shepherd as it led us over the towering Ural Mountains and into Siberia. The land below us, once covered with permafrost, now looked like Swiss cheese, with big craters littering the dry, lifeless ground.

Holes peppered the land and spread out in every direction, giving the world a pock-marked complexion. If it wasn't for the orb, we would have been searching for Axzum forever. As it was, the yellow dot shot across the valley, skimming just above the ground, and disappeared into an opening.

The professor steered the wheel into the crater, at least ten times its size of the ship. Descending into the darkness felt like dropping into a big coffee can. The walls of the crater were sheer cliffs shooting straight down to the floor, which I estimated to be nearly a half mile below the surface. The daylight beamed down from above like a dim flashlight, creating very little ambient light. How anyone or anything could survive more than a day in the dark tunnel we landed in was beyond me.

A part of me doubted that we'd find anything alive at all. The large hole opened up at the bottom to an even bigger chamber. Outside the window, we could see the towering walls and the high ceilings of an underground cavern, along with the gravelly shore of a subterranean lake, the water which was a foggy grey.

The light from above only illuminated a small area around us. We could not see extending passages or to the other side of the lake, if there was one. All we could see was the outline of a wrecked spacecraft, half embedded in the rock. The sight of the ancient shipwreck threw the cockpit into a stir and sent us scrambling down the stairs to prepare for an expedition.

We met back at the hatch, climbed out of the ship, and stepped onto solid ground. It was Juulez and I, Cooper, Yuung, Jaan, and Teum, and of course Ariance, who insisted on coming.

Having my two feet on the earth once more felt strange. While I was thankful to be held down by a familiar gravity, I could now feel something else, something strange, a cold and ominous presence. I wondered if this was new or if it had been there all along and I was simply unaware of it.

Gaieos had been a kind of prison, holding us for millennia. I could sense the overwhelming power of deception seep into my being as I walked hesitantly from the hatch out toward the underground lake.

Cooper ran ahead of us, sniffing around and scouring the shoreline for a recognizable scent. The rest of us scattered about, searching the rocky beach for signs of life. Teum, Ariance and I held our lanterns high. I went directly to the suit, holding it up to confirm that it was the same one worn by Axzum the last time I'd seen him, when we freed Ella from the sea.

The suit was worn and tattered; it had been there for a long time. I wandered up to the very edge of the lake and held the light out over the water. Although the water was foggy, no doubt clouded by a high mineral content, I could see to the sandy bed. I bent down to get a closer look and noticed an indentation in the sand. A footprint.

I turned to tell the others, but before I could speak, Juulez shouted, "Oakruum. Over here."

With Cooper's help, they had found the same tracks. I joined them, and upon further investigation, we found a worn path that led into a dark tunnel opposite the lake. We approached the cave slowly, led by Cooper and the lanterns. When we got to the mouth, we stopped to peer in.

A slight waft of air drifted past us from within. It smelled of old garbage and rancid meat. I looked over at the professor as if to ask, "who's going first?" He returned the same look, but Cooper was not as hesitant and nosed into the darkness, followed closely by Ariance, who held out her lantern like a sword. Strengthened by the dog's courage and Ariance's faith, the rest of us followed.

With every step, I could feel that part of me that had been freed returning to captivity, and the thought of being exiled on Gaieos again sent a shiver down my spine. We crept down the short tunnel, which emptied into a larger cavity, where we spread out to explore. It most definitely had all the signs of being someone's or something's habitat. The floor of the cave was muddy and strewn with bones, animal pelts, and debris. My eyes followed a trail of garbage that disappeared into an alcove on the far side of the cave where I could see the outline of a dark human shape hidden within.

"Someone's here," I whispered. "See? Right there."

As I pointed and held my lantern out to shed light on the corner, it jumped out at us with a shriek, swinging a stick the size of a tree branch. The heavy end of the club hit the side of my head and I stumbled to the ground, the lantern falling away. The shot did not knock me out, but I was quite stunned, and what happened during the struggle that followed was a chaotic blur.

The creature that was attacking me had long, dark, tangled hair, broad animal features around his nose and mouth, and his eyes were shut and almost non-existent. He continued to shriek like a banshee as he chopped at the ground next to me. I'm sure if he had been able to see, I would have been killed. Fortunately, he missed, but pulled the stick back over his head for a second shot. At that moment, Cooper, barking ferociously, rushed across the cave and jumped on the man's chest, knocking him down before he could bring the branch down upon me. The stick fell to the side as the troglodyte wrestled with Cooper.

I know it wasn't the dog's intention to kill or even injure. In all his years, Cooper hadn't even run down a mouse or a rabbit. But knowing Cooper's strength, I rose to my feet, expecting to pull him off the man, and surprised when Cooper let out a piercing yelp and fell to the ground. The man scrambled to his feet and fled back into the dark corner from which he came, and Cooper lay on his side on the wet rock, bleeding, a sharp head of a spear lodged in his neck.

"No. Cooper."

I went to him, pulling a shard of grey slate from his neck. I tried my best to hold back the blood, pressing with both hands into the wound, but with every heartbeat, the flow of blood spilled out around my hands and fingers and onto the ground.

In the meantime, the monster cowered in the corner, whimpering like a wounded animal himself.

Jaan, Teum, and the professor approached the beast slowly, their arms out, ready for another attack.

Juulez joined me at Cooper's side.

"Is he going to be okay?" she asked.

I felt him slip away, his heartbeat stilling. My efforts to stop the bleeding were failing. The beats of his heart were slowed until finally they stopped altogether.

"He's gone."

She put her hand on my shoulder.

The creature was breathing heavily in his hiding place, and as the crew got closer to him, he flailed his arms wildly like a toddler who didn't want to take a bath, shrieking and crying in terror.

"We don't want to hurt you," the professor said to him, but the caveman screamed all the more, batting their hands away and sliding down the wall until he was on the ground. The horrible sound he made echoed in the cave, amplifying its volume and intensity.

Juulez and I remained at Cooper's side as we watched Ariance slowly approach the savage. She got down on her knees before him and put both of his dirty hands in hers. To our amazement, the man did not resist. I thought back to that moment in the shack when Axzum did the same and shared Koinonae, his deepest desire, with me. The act of vulnerability set me on this journey to begin with. It had been a vision of Ariance, and now Ariance was sharing Koinonae with the wild beast.

I couldn't help but see myself in the man, and all the rest of us, who bury ourselves in dark holes.

I don't know what vision Ariance shared with the man, but when she was finished, they both opened their eyes and looked at one another. The man's eyes were slits, sensitive to the light from the lanterns. Ariance rose to her feet and pulled the man by his arms up to stand, and there they embraced, kissing each other like long-lost loves. I want to say that watching an alien kiss a caveman was the strangest thing I saw during our quest to find the orbs, but it probably wasn't.

A small flame flickered above them.

"It's Axzum," I said to Juulez. "We found him."

How many lives he had led since I lost him in the ocean, I did not know, and no one knew at that point what his mind was like, what he could remember and what he couldn't, but we found the body he was indwelling, and as my experience taught me, it would all return in time. Ariance and Teum both put their arms around Axzum and helped him across the cave toward the exit. I would have laughed at the absurdity of it all if I hadn't experienced firsthand what the man was going through. The first steps out of the deception are the most awkward.

We get so used to life in the prison that we hold on

to what is known when what is unknown beckons us to freedom.

I picked up Cooper's body, the grief of the loss only beginning to hit me. Juulez and I moved toward the exit as well, maneuvering around boulders, bones, and garbage. We had made it halfway through the tunnel connecting the small cave to the larger cavern when the shadows appeared at the opening, blocking our escape.

We stopped in our tracks.

"No, not now." Jaan gasped.

The menacing shadows poured down the corridor toward us. Both Professor Yuung and Jaan were grabbed by their wrists and ankles by multiple spirits and dragged out of the tunnel. The caveman was completely enveloped and disappeared into the darkness.

"No." Ariance screamed. "Axzum."

As she yelled after him, she was grabbed as well, and we were all pulled from the tunnel and into the larger chamber where the ship was also being overtaken by a massive arm of the teardrop that hovered just above us. The ooze draped over everything, and before we could act, we were completely engulfed. The last thing I saw was Juulez's shoulder and head disappearing into the shadow.

Inside the glob, I struggled to break loose, flailing, my limbs reaching in all directions to no avail. And then, despite the panic that wanted to control my body, I was able to collect myself, focusing on my internal energy. I had freed myself before from within; perhaps I could do it again. The result was a growing nexus of energy and light beginning in my core and moving down my limbs to my hands and feet. My hands, growing active with energy, were able to grab hold of the elusive goo that had me, and I pulled the shadow open like a curtain. I did it, I thought,

I'm out, and began mapping my way to rescue Juulez, but the shadow responded violently to being torn open and immediately slammed my back onto the wet, jagged rocks at the very bottom of the pit. There, I was pinned as the darkness poured over my body and disappeared underneath me.

When the last of the shadows sank beneath me, I was in the open air, free—or so I thought. I tried to move but could not; I watched as the globs holding the ship and the rest of the crew disappeared into the larger teardrop. Beyond the teardrop far above, I could see the opening of the pit and the ominous sky beyond that. The black waves of a dark ocean rippled into view.

I closed my eyes for a moment and when I reopened them; I was no longer in the pit. I found myself on my back in the snow outside the cabin, immediately after being pushed down the stairs. The never-ending stream of white snow covered my face.

Kisses from heaven.

My heart stopped. My body stiffened.

"Wait. Where am I? What is happening?"

I was cut in half.

The darkness beneath me, holding my body to the ground, cut me into two pieces, and then those two pieces were divided into two more pieces, and then those pieces were divided as well.

There is an ancient math problem which asks: how many times can something be divided in half? The answer is beyond our comprehension.

Infinity.

I was separated from myself, over and over and over again, each piece of me pulled away from the others until I was a table of scattered puzzle pieces, sinking into the ground.

"Oh God," I pleaded into the cosmos. "Help me."

I waited through a long silence. There was no answer. No response from without. The answer came from within.

The next moment, I was standing on the small shining world at my very core. The minuscule volcanoes spewing steam, my little red rose reaching its petals high. Dr. McLeister, my old mentor from the university, stood there with me, looking out into my personal cosmos.

"You see?" He spoke. "Your rescuer isn't out there. Your salvation is here."

"Atman is Brahman." I responded.

He nodded and put his arm around me.

"You are loved, and you are Love."

This was the spinach I needed.

I returned to the cavern floor, my person chopped into a million pieces. Way down the shattered veins of my arm, way down in my right index finger, two tiny pieces of me that had separated, drifting away from each other as they were dragged into the earth, suddenly changed direction. Instead of slipping into oblivion, the two reached for each other, made contact, and rejoined. The result was a blinding light, as if a new star had been born. Two other pieces reconnected halfway down my left leg, giving off another micro-explosion of light, and then two more in my chest, and so on, until an enormous wave of fusion reactions spread across my body as it reconnected.

The newly formed stars consumed each other, giving me more than enough energy to rise from the floor.

Light filled the pit as my body, emanating energy and heat, grew to such a size that I could hold the teardrop in my hand. I gripped the teardrop by its slender neck, holding it like a bag of potatoes, and reached into the bulbous belly and pulled my friends from the darkness within.

First was Juulez, then Jaan, Teum, Yuung, Ariance, the caveman, and finally Cooper's motionless body. I placed each one on the pit floor. Once I had pulled the ship out of the Nuul and returned it to solid ground, I smashed the teardrop in my glowing hands as if it were a paper bag. Then, I was returned to my normal size, standing next to Juulez at the lakeshore. Her eyes were big, her hands shaking.

"Breathe, Juulez. You're safe now."

I placed my still-glowing hand on her shoulder, and when I did, her body splashed with light from within.

I looked to the others, who were all in different stages of recovery, and noticed the caveman still lying on his back.

"Axzum," I said. "Is he okay?"

Ariance, who was already attending to him, responded, "Still alive, but unconscious."

"We can carry him," I instructed, and Teum joined Ariance to help.

"We need to get out of here," I said, pointing to the ominous shadow cloud rolling above.

I turned to pick up Cooper, but was stopped by a glowing light that was hovering a few inches above his dead body.

"Oh!" I said in surprise, which caught everyone's attention, and we all watched the speck of light grow. It grew into the shape of a being, filling out into legs, hands, and feet. Soon, what sat beside Cooper was a complete person of light who opened his eyes and greeted us.

"My god!" I said. "Raykuum."

Raykuum stood up and gave Cooper's head a gentle caress. Then he looked at me and then to Juulez.

"Hello, friends," he said. "Oakruum, Juulez."

He looked up at the wrecked ship that was stuck in the earth halfway up the wall. It was his ship.

"The tools from Apotheon, do we still have them?" he asked me.

"They're on board," I said, and I pointed to the wheel sitting at the lakeshore, my ship.

Then I approached Raykuum and embraced him.

"I missed you, my friend."

He returned the embrace. "I never left you," he said, looking up at the tumultuous ocean in the sky. "Now, we'd better get to work."

So, we returned to the ship.

I put Cooper's canine form on the table in the tool room; we decided we'd dispose of it properly once we had time to do it with honor.

Yuung and Ariance laid Axzum's human form on the large fragment of Payraydayzay in the Great Room. It would no doubt take a few days, or even longer, to heal him. We had hoped that parts of his true person would awaken after connecting with his home world, or at least a piece of it. Raykuum reunited with the rest of the crew on board, Lejuun, Mira, and Muurchia, before retrieving the bag of tools he had stolen as a dog from Apotheon.

We reconvened in the Great Room where Raykuum pulled the transport orb from its place in the wall. I stood back and watched with fascination this new member of the crew move about the ship like he owned it. I guess it shouldn't have been a surprise that Rakuum's personality was so similar to Cooper's. Nonetheless, I was enthralled.

"There's no time for this, Raykuum," Jaan barked. "We have to get off this planet right now."

"I'm not leaving here without my ship, Jaan. Leave me here if you must, but I'm going out there."

This time, it was Lejuun and I that joined Raykuum on the expedition. The three of us stepped into the glowing Vortai, which floated through the bottom of the hatch, back into the grand cavern. Now that I understood how the Vortai were created, I wondered who the being was that surrendered themselves to such a service. Traveling in the spinning orb, we rose from the floor of the pit up to the shipwreck site, halfway up the shaft. As we approached the side of the ancient wheel, the memory of the wreck opened into my mind. I shut my eyes to focus.

"I can remember now being together in the cockpit with you, Raykuum. With the others. Fire raining down all around us."

"That's right," Raykuum replied. "I tried to find a safe place for us to land, but we were hit."

"And we tumbled to the ground," I said, and I could see in my mind's eye the last terrible moments of our journey to earth.

"And she's been lying here ever since," Raykuum pointed to the vessel, its side hatch almost within reach.

I looked up and tried to measure the distance to the surface above, how much time it must have taken for the vessel to be buried so deep.

"The funny part is," said Raykuum. "It's a pretty easy fix, if you have the right tools."

He held up the cloth sack with a smile, which vanished as the sound of a ground-shaking explosion echoed through the chasm.

"It's starting,"

Another massive bomb burst splashed from above. The teardrops were dropping. We had to hurry.

It took all three of us to pry the side hatch of the ship open, but once it was ajar, we could squeeze our bodies through, something we probably could not have done if we were flesh and bone.

We left the orb in the ship's toolroom, engaged our lanterns, and rambled down the corridor to the center chamber. The Great Room was identical to the other ship's Great Rooms, with eight open portals and eight alcoves cut into the wall. I thought about how wonderful it would have been if the alcoves each had a twirling orb dancing within them, but no, they were dark and empty. We ascended the spiral staircase and stumbled into the wheel's cockpit. The only light came from our lanterns, for the windows were covered with layers of earth and rock from outside.

Raykuum pulled a tool from the sack and dropped the bag on the floor. Using the tool, he opened a hatch in the cockpit floor and climbed down into a maintenance box.

From there, he could call out orders to us, where to shine the lanterns and which tools to bring him from the bag. It wasn't lost on me that I had spent years as Cooper's master, and now he was mine.

In a matter of minutes, with a series of bright flashes from within the box, the ship was repaired. The wheel whirled to life and the navigational hologram flickered on above us, projecting the majestic worlds of our system.

As Raykuum pulled himself out of the box and re-secured the hatch door, I magnified the image of Gaieos and found the light blue dot marking our location on the planet. Northern Siberia, I noted, and suddenly caught movement out of the corner of my eye. I jumped, turning to see what was there.

What looked like a phantom ran by me to the other side of the cockpit, followed by another. They were barely perceptible and completely silent, although they looked as if they were screaming and shouting.

"What was that?!" I shouted. "What's happening?"

"Echoes," Lejuun replied. "Don't worry, they can't harm you. Just echoes from the past."

I stepped back as I realized what I was seeing. The ghosts, or echoes as Lejuun called them, were us. It was Juulez and Raykuum and me trying to save the ship as it faltered so long ago. I watched the ship's long-lost memory get played out in the cockpit, Jaan and Teum bracing for impact, Juulez folding into my embrace. The entire crew suddenly looked out in the same direction, presumably to the point of impact, and then the echoes disappeared.

"There's nothing we could have done, Oakruum."

"We can still undo this," I replied.

Three titanic explosions hit the surface above, rattling the ship and the earth around it like an earthquake.

Lejuun joined Raykuum at the helm, but our release came not from anything the two pilots did. It came from outside, with three more powerful teardrop impacts, each one closer than the next.

The first hit knocked us all off our feet and dislodged some of the rock just outside the ship, causing small pebbles and chunks to tumble down the glass outside. The second thunderous explosion came seconds later and loosened the earth around the wheel so that it slipped out of its place in the wall and tip toward the bottom of the pit.

As the rock and dirt fell away, the lake shore and

the ship next to it came into view. My ship was rotating and starting its ascent.

The wheel righted itself as it was pulled from its grave, and for a moment, it climbed toward the opening and the flashing lightning above. I exhaled as I realized we would all soon be safely away, both ships, and we would have to find a suitable place to rendezvous and plan the next steps. There was one more Vortai to retrieve, after all.

Then the third teardrop landed.

It was a direct hit, covering the entire crater and everything around it. The drop hit the ground and then cut into it like a power drill. The earth and the rock were shredded as it plowed into the ground. The teardrop had fallen from the black, oily ocean raging above and was headed to the core of Gaieos with all the other drops.

This one was going to take us with it.

The wheel tumbled end over end, down into the pit, with all the other rubble around it. Inside the cockpit, we all tried to hold on the best we could, but our bodies were thrown around the room violently.

The view from the window was chaos as we fell down the shaft. I got a glimpse of the other ship, also falling like a quarter that had been flipped in the air.

"Juulez." I shouted and watched as the water was completely drained from the lake. The ground underneath it collapsed, and the bottom of the pit broke into pieces and became a bottomless hole which we fell into and kept falling. The teardrop outside seemed to pull and push us at the same time. The balancing pressure caused the ship to stabilize and we could rise to our feet again.

We held on to whatever we could, as we burrowed deeper into the earth, riding the dark teardrop like a wave. The falling glob seemed to accelerate as it broke through the outer crust and into the Earth's mantle. It was now coursing by us as we sped to the bottom. It felt like riding a speeding elevator to hell. The mantle gave way to a liquid outer core, an ocean of hot metal. Pieces of boulder and rock that had been dragged down from the upper crust melted into the void. The teardrop took us to the solid inner core of the earth and then into an open space between the solid shell and a jagged, statuesque piece of stone.

The teardrops were gathering, encircling the vulnerable core like hungry sharks. Our ship was released from the belly of the blob, and we were free to navigate on our own. The other wheel had the same experience and there, at the center of Gaieos, we orbited the ornate statue.

"What is that?" I asked Lejuun.

"That is the planet's seed. Look at it. It's become rotten. It's sick."

I watched the seed, motionless, still like a statue displayed in a museum. I thought it was beautiful.

"It looks fine to me."

Lejuun looked at me with surprise. "It should be alive, bright, fiery, and fierce. It should shine like a thousand suns."

We orbited three or four times as the cavity around the seed filled with teardrops that burrowed in from the surface, and finally all the drops came together to form one large blob that consumed the lifeless seed as if it were a harmless insect.

"There it goes," Raykuum said.

And with that, the solid core surrounding us broke apart, filling the void with massive chunks of stone. Our two tiny ships could only weave in and out of the cracks that widened in between the broken pieces of Earth.

Gaieos was crumbling into bits from the inside out.

CHAPTER FIFTEEN

THE ORIGINALS

Abiogenesis. The idea that life arose from non-life three to four billion years ago earth-time. It theorized that the first life forms were generated out of some sort of inorganic material, a primordial ooze. There was a chemical reaction and maybe a bolt of lightning, and zap—out of the rock came life.

Religious folks saw it differently. They argued that life was created by the hand of God, pointing out the probability of abiogenesis being extremely low. And they would be right, there is virtually zero chance of abiogenesis occurring.

In fact, it was disproven in the 19th century. Thus, the ongoing debate on Earth of the origins of life had been two-sided between two impossibilities: that life came from a chemical fluke, unlikely, or by intelligent design, also unlikely.

In my years on Gaieos, it was easiest and most politically advantageous for me to side with the creationists. That is, until I had my own crisis of faith, which led to my renunciation and subsequent exile. After that, I wasn't sure what to believe, and like most people I would imagine, I didn't really think about it.

The origin of life was shrouded from me like so many other truths; what's one more mystery in an endless hall of mysteries? It never occurred to me that there could be another explanation, one more plausible than the mythical hand of God or the unlikely happenstance in the ooze.

At the very beginning of all things is life, not non-life. Life has always been and always will be. Even the particles that swirl into the collapsed singularity at the center of everything have the capability, the potential, to become anyone or anything. The universe didn't give birth to us; we gave birth to the universe.

The worlds, too, have a similar genesis. Planets don't form and then create an environment to host life. What a sacrilegious notion. No, it is life that creates and forms a world in which it can dwell.

The reason I know this is having witnessed it for myself, and now I pass this information on to you.

At the very center of the earth, as we witnessed its destruction from within, we realized we had little time to find Galileo's buried treasure, the final piece of the cosmic puzzle. Outside, massive chunks of rock peeled away from the hole and drifted into each other as the planet crumbled from the inside out.

I paced the window, trying to keep track of the other ship, but the wheel ducked into a sliver of space between two colossal slabs, and I lost her.

"Lejuun." I shouted. "Through there."

Lejuun, standing at the controls, didn't respond. He reached up to the hologram projection of the doomed planet and touched the red dot with his hand. It was the dot that marked our final destination. I hoped that the ancient Italian city would still be there when we arrived.

As the light blue dot moved from the center of the illuminated globe back toward the surface of the planet, the wheel we were in suddenly shifted course and shot in between two bouncing tectonic plates while dodging many smaller shards of tumbling debris.

We pierced towards the surface at a dizzying speed, zigzagging around every imaginable size of rock. As the fragments pulled farther apart and broke down into smaller pieces, the alley opened up and we could see the way before us.

I wondered if the ship would be destroyed by the piping hot mantle that the cold teardrop had shielded us from on our way down. Surprisingly, by the time our ship traveled through that layer of earth, the hot sea of magma was gone, extinguished by the darkness and the cold vacuum of space that was invading the gravity-less body.

It was as if the earth's blood turned to stone and its bones torn asunder. As we traveled toward the surface, the planet continued to pull apart, so much so that by the time we got to the surface, it was gone. All that was left were the remnants, an endless debris field containing every kind of conceivable object. Large planetary fragments remained, the terrain covered with derelict buildings and roads, were accompanied by boats, cars, dead trees, and telephone poles wrapped in wire, all floating in space, all at different speeds and in different directions.

The planet had almost completely disintegrated around us, yet the wheel continued to travel through space, undaunted by the changing topography or whatever random piece of earth it encountered. The destination still existed after all, even if it was detached from the whole and wandering adrift.

I scanned the skies, not only gawking at the incredible events occurring all around us, but searching for any signs of the other ship, hoping they were headed in the same direction as us.

"Heartbreaking," Raykuum said, watching the horror taking place outside. "First Payraydayzay, now

Gaieos. Avesta will be next, I'm sure. All three sisters, gone."

What remained of Gaieos was spread out before us. Its gravity was gone, which left its atmosphere and its only satellite pulverized by a hailstorm of fragments that dissipated into space, like a dying man taking his last gasping breath. Above us in the cockpit, the floating image of Gaieos stayed fixed, and we watched as the light-blue dot quickly approached the red one.

"Almost there," I shouted, and we tried to match the map with the chaos outside the ship.

Raykuum pointed at a larger asteroid that we were approaching. One side of it was solid granite, but the other side had a topography that may have once been part of the planet's surface.

As we got closer, ruined buildings with terracotta shingles appeared, confirming Raykuum's hunch. Florence had been ravaged by an earthquake of an unimaginable scale, leaving every other building, bridge, and road in heaps of rubble. The once beautiful Arno River was a bone-dry riverbed. Now, the village drifted in space, and so anything that was not attached to the ground was floating away: bricks, vehicles, old furniture.

We came to rest above an old stone building which was almost a perfect cube, with eight pillars for the ship's spokes to rest upon. The streets and alleys of Florence lay out before us.

As I stood at the window, scanning the cityscape, an ancient train car, rusted out and decayed, floated up from the ground and drifted out into space.

Forgoing any kind of preparation, we rushed to the transport orb. We traveled out of the hatch and down to the building below the wheel. We floated down the outside of the big cube to the sidewalk as bicycles and manhole covers rose past.

Once we reached street level, the streaking orb crashed right through the glass door entranceway, and we found ourselves inside a grand marble foyer of a history museum. Antique telescopes, floor globes and a white marble bust of Galileo were floating about in the exhibit hall.

As we floated through the room, past the countless displays of early astronomical instruments and tools, I marveled at their unique value and utter uselessness. In the world I'd grown up in, these antiques would have been priceless. Now, in the face of total destruction, they were all but worthless.

How much is a dollar worth in the *now*? I thought. Or the biggest diamond in the world, for that matter?

We entered the second exhibit hall to find a gold-plated display case in the middle of the room.

Floating weightlessly inside the case was a glass egg attached to a white marble base, and inside the egg, our prize, a sacred relic, a finger bone, the middle finger bone of Galileo Galilei.

The orb that held us butted up against the glass case, and I smashed my hand through the orb's membrane, through the glass, grabbed the gilded egg and pulled it into the Vortai. I broke the glass egg and pulled out the bone to get a closer look. I ran my finger over the bone, and I could feel where the notches had been carved.

Almost instantly, a long-lost memory awakened in my unconscious, and it drifted up out of the depths of me and into my consciousness. It came from long ago when I was trapped on Gaieos in the flesh.

In the memory, I stood on a balcony at the Palazzo

Ducale in Venice, Italy, overlooking St. Mark's Square and the Bacino di San Marco, the large marina that led into the Grand Canal. It must have been well past midnight, for the square was empty and not a single vessel moved upon the water. The night was still; the sky was clear, and I leaned over the banister with a brass spyglass held up to my eye. I made an observation of the moon, put down the instrument, picked up a quill pen, and jotted down some notes.

Pausing the memory in my mind, I noticed my withered old hand, my fingers straining to grasp the pen—the wrinkled skin sunken in between the thin bones and purplish veins.

There it was. The same middle finger.

"You've always had the eye, Oakruum; just ask the questions. They will lead you to solid ground."

I returned to the museum, still holding the ancient finger in my hand. Before I could even acknowledge this new memory, a loud grinding noise erupted to a roar, and when we looked to the window to find its source, we saw a building across the street ripped from its foundation and sent adrift into the sky. A moment later, the next building did the same thing. Everything on the fragment of earth, whether bolted down or not, was detached from its base and hurled into space.

The entire building we were in rumbled and lifted off of its foundation as if a giant picked up the building and threw it into the sky. The cube tumbled out above us, somersaulting away, our ship still hanging on to the landing pad on top.

I held on tightly to the bone as I watched the building we had just been standing in roll away from us. Our ship, still on the roof, appeared and disappeared as the building twirled around in the sky. Beyond that was the vast asteroid field that was once a most beautiful and vital world, expanding its length and breadth.

"We're too late," Lejuun said.

I looked over at him, his face tensed with fear. We had pulled him from a tomb in a graveyard similar to the one this asteroid was becoming. We all had the same morbid thoughts running through our heads, so when the marble floor beneath us came undone and joined everything else in the air, we each released a terrified scream; yet the flipped-away floor panels didn't open up to our graves, they opened to our salvation.

"There." I shouted. "Down there." I pointed to the dark cellar that had been exposed.

As dusty picture frames and old wooden crates rose from underneath, we ventured down into the basement, still traveling within the protective orb. The large, square cellar had stone walls like the ones on the ship in the Great Room. The floor was an ornate mosaic, a fantastic piece of art made of tiles of varying shapes and colors. The room had been jam-packed with wooden shelving, crates, and big steamer trunks filled with unique relics.

With the marble floor above now removed, these items were levitating out of the catacombs. Within minutes, the basement was empty except for some wire, the furnace in the far corner, and a small brass ring on the floor that had been hiding underneath a rather large trunk now ascending into the night.

We moved to the ring, and I reached down and put my finger through it and pulled. The ring was attached to a round wooden lid, maybe six inches in diameter. It had been covering a hole dug into the floor, within it an iron safe with a round metal door, and a latch with an oddly shaped keyhole.

I got down on my haunches to pull the safe out of the hole, but the iron box wouldn't move. After three more attempts, with Raykuum's help, it would not budge. I pulled the finger bone back out of my pouch, fit it into the keyhole, and with a clockwise turn, the latch opened. Inside the vault was the last Vortai. Like the others, this one was the size of a golf ball spinning ferociously, streaking beams of light. I reached in and pulled the orb from the box, stood as it floated inches above my palm, and presented it to the other two.

"Let's go."

What happened next was miraculous. We did go, but not in the way I'd meant. In a flash, all three of us were vacuumed up into the metallic-looking Vortai and we shot into space within it. It was like being sucked into a kaleidoscope.

As we sped away from the asteroid and the debris field, we watched as the fragments reversed course and began reconnecting with each other. Now, instead of breaking apart, the world started coming back together.

In mere seconds, the massive body clicked back together like Lego blocks and was wondrously whole once again. Mountains, hills, valleys, streams, and oceans returned as well. Clouds reformed as the atmosphere blanketed the reborn planet.

But how could it be reborn when only seconds ago it was sick, brown, and lifeless?

"I think we're traveling through time," Raykuum whispered. "Backwards."

He was right. As we rocketed around Gaieos maybe twenty or thirty times per second, we could see the planet's condition reversing. First the air cleared, the landscape greened, and the lights of civilization appeared, and then brightened.

In a brief moment, the planet's cities gleamed in the sun and sparkled in the night, and then faded. In just a few speeding orbits, the cities were gone, replaced by the flickering light from sporadic fires, then the fires disappeared. Human civilization came and went in a blink of an eye as we rolled back in time.

The orb seemed to accelerate, magnifying the spectacle. The movement of continental plates across the face of the planet, events that must have taken eons to occur, were now shooting by us vigorously in reverse. Continent-sized glaciers moved down the face of the Earth, and the atmosphere went dark. The planet raged with fire, tidal waves engulfed, and colossal storms washed over the world in a dizzying display.

Millions of years flashed by in seconds. In mere moments we arrived at the event, the asteroids and meteorites from the destruction of Payraydayzay exploded out of the Earth. The fiery shards sprang out of the ground and soared out of the Earth's atmosphere and back to where they came from.

"Ella," I whispered, as the rock that I had freed her from splashed out of the sea and rocketed by us on its way back home, along with a spray of other rocky fragments. What was left was a dazzling emerald of a planet, a world awash with wild vegetation and vitality.

The orb we traveled in zipped around the globe and then raced after the broken pieces of Payraydayzay to their place of origin. The cosmos had a fantastic quality as we moved through space. Instead of a black void, it was now through the lens of the sphere, a bright multicolored tapestry of geometric shapes and design, none still or stagnant.

The surrounding universe was ever moving, changing, spiraling, and spinning. We shot by the red planet, dusty Avesta, and watched as large chunks of Payraydayzay emerged from its crust as they reeled back into their source. The result of this time reversal was a world, green, blue, lush, and welcoming.

As we approached the graveyard, the meteorites previously spread across the solar system, unleashing untold carnage, harmonized and restored the planet to its original state.

In a heartbeat, the most beautiful world stood before us, bold and strong. She looked indestructible to any weapon or attack. The majestic Payraydayzay dazzled, boasting every imaginable hue, prompting the onlooker to explore every mountain, canyon, and crevasse.

The orb we were in swirled around the regal globe a dozen more times, and as it did, time continued to retreat, causing every natural occurrence from rain to wind to ocean tide to unnaturally go backwards, like sand going up in an hourglass.

Each of the Three Sisters spun backwards on their axis, and orbited the sun in the opposite direction, millions of times per second, until we had reached the very beginning, the birth of the worlds.

The surface of Payraydayzay gradually got redder with heat until the entire sphere raged with the ocean of hot magma. Then, the spinning ball intensified with heat and light until its mass collapsed into itself, culminating to a bright white point.

Finally, the celestial world reduced to a bright nucleus with seven or eight electrons feverishly orbiting its core. The seed looked like a Christmas angel, white with a haloed blue aura.

"You see," Lejuun said. "That is what a healthy seed should be."

The heat, energy, and life that should have been emanating from this mother were actually receding in the reversal of time. But even the retreating force was awe-inspiring. I gave Lejuun an understanding nod, wondering how such a powerful force could ever be stilled. Suddenly, the giant atom pulled apart and the electron balls shot off in various directions. The nucleus, now naked, sailed toward the sun as we continued to travel time all the way back to the beginning.

As the nucleus approached the sun, orbiting in a series of smaller and smaller circles, it was joined by its electrons and the ten other nuclei from the ten other worlds in the system and their corresponding electrons. The glowing seeds seemed to accelerate as they got closer and closer to the star, which was now itself beginning to break apart.

We were watching the birth of a star and its system, but in reverse.

When the seeds met the sun, the whole star disintegrated into a million tiny seeds, and for a moment it looked like a huge white dandelion, before it dissipated, as if blown by the wind. What remained was a beautiful, arching nebula spanning across the cosmos before us, revealing our origin.

We traveled into the blue, pink, and white space cloud, its dazzling architecture producing jaw-dropping shapes and curves spanning all directions. I had seen pictures of far-off nebula taken by high-powered telescopes, so I had assumed that they were objects fixed in space. This was not the case.

The cloud of light now shot through space just as

fast as the star had, if not faster, like a swarm of angry bees knifing toward an aggressor, and this was not a lifeless plume of dust and rock—the formation was radiantly alive. The nebula at the beginning, the pregnant mother that gives birth to us all, was a community of persons, infinite beings of light, spirit, and Oolah.

As we cut through the field, the orb we were in suddenly stopped, and we hovered still, with no movement in space or time, and we got to see the Originals. It felt like swimming in a bright, busy coral reef made up of tiny, spinning, multicolored orbs.

"Oolah," Lejuun whispered. "We are all made of Oolah."

The collective beings that made the worlds were light, gravity, and life.

The number was countless. I couldn't even guess how many. But one thing I can guarantee you, my most excellent Theophilus, is that you were there, right at the start.

You were there. I was, too. We all were.

Life doesn't spring from non-life, it's the other way around. We must have traveled as far as we needed to go, for the orb changed course and we started going back in the other direction. I remembered my experience in the pit, when I was divided into tiny pieces, and then those tiny pieces reunited, and when they did, the fusion reaction caused my body to come alive and burn brightly.

This same thing happened, but now inside the nebula. Oolah cannot help but join with the other Oolah.

We are essentially made of gravity, after all. But something extra-wonderful occurs when two become one. Within the intense pressure and energy of the nebula, fusion, hot, bright, blinding fusion. It was just a handful at first, a pop of light here, and another way over there, but the fusion reactions became contagious, and our field of vision began filling with the blinding dots of light.

Soon, not only was the nebula growing into one body as the Vortai connected with each other, but it coalesced into a spinning ball still rocketing across the cosmos.

"We just witnessed the birth of a star," I whispered to Raykuum.

Raykuum nodded in silence, taking in the sacred moment.

Through the lens of the orb carrying us through time and space, we saw more detail than even a high-powered telescope could see. We witnessed life, not just making up the now fiery ball, but orbiting, or even dancing, around it. It was hard to gauge where we were in time and space, but I surmised we were now flowing forward in time rather than backward, and we must have been moving fast, possibly millions of earth years per second, for what we witnessed next must have taken eons.

The spinning sun we were watching gave birth to a white orb, similar to the orb that the crow had transformed into when he stepped into the wake.

The white, dazzling ball orbited the star, streaking around it like a toddler who had just learned to run. Then the sun produced another orb, then another. In all, the fertile mother gave eleven eggs.

"Are they light, gravity, or an actual living being?" I asked Lejuun.

"Yes," he replied.

The cosmic children stretched out. With each orbit, they ventured a little deeper into space, until mother sun fertilized each orbiting egg with a handful of Vortai that surrounded each child in the same sort of pattern that electrons make around an atom. This caused each seed to burst with even more energy and light, and gave them the power and autonomy to widen their orbit, till the eleven were fixed in their place within the system, where they grew, receiving more life from the mother, until they had matured, and were ready to create.

Our orb shot across the system, returning to Payraydayzay, where we watched the world blossom and bear fruit. It was the first planet in the system to produce plants and animals, the first to host intelligent beings that gathered in community, the first to have settlements, and the first to colonize other worlds.

Orbiting Payraydayzay at a dizzying rate of speed, its entire history flashed before us, until it came to its tragic end, insides torn out and scattered to the cold void. Then, we jumped to Gaieos, where a few more turns gave way to its destruction, and then to Avesta, the red planet, where it also crumbled into pieces.

The orb had taken us to the beginning, and now, evidently, we were going to the end. Concerned what that might mean, the three of us pushed at the Vortai's membrane, searching for a way out.

"How do we stop this?" I wondered out loud.

Outside, the universe darkened as it dimmed to a cold, blue-purple color. Everything in the system, living or not, had been detached from the other. Every seed, the original eleven, each had been turned to stone, and now their mother was disintegrating. Soon, it would all grow dark, leaving nothing but fractured pieces.

"Is this really how it ends?" I said, turning to Raykuum. "What a waste of time. We should have stayed in the shack."

Raykuum stood for a long time, looking out at the chaos, deep in thought. And then he turned to me, put both of his hands out, an invitation I knew well. He wanted to share his deepest desires, his Koinonae with me. I'm uncertain why Raykuum chose that moment to share; perhaps he felt I needed the encouragement. Perhaps he thought we were about to die, and this was his way of giving his own eulogy.

I closed my eyes and put my hands into Raykuum's, and he shared with me a vision of his deepest desires.

In the vision, we were on Apotheon, at the great table where the city had its feasts. I was indwelling Cooper now, sitting quietly on the ground between two chairs. A hand reached down and scratched my head.

And then I was lying under the table in the galley on the wheel as Cooper, napping as I listened to all the warm conversations of the gathered friends.

And then, I found myself in the cabin, up in the mountains on earth. I was Cooper again, lying on the floor by the hearth. I could feel the warmth of the fire on my nose. I looked up to see myself, my old human form, complete with white beard, cooking at the stove, filling a plate with food, and sitting down at the table to eat.

As Cooper, I got up and wandered over, sat down politely, and set my nose on the table, looking for a handout.

Mira, the angel, Muurchia, Jaan and Teum, sat at the table, eating with me.

The ghosts.

The vision shifted, and we were at the big table on Payraydayzay, all seated together: countless faces, including Axzum and Ariance with their daughter, Ella, and my own face, next to Juulez. Then I saw what I think

Raykuum wanted me to see, the face of a being sitting at a place across the table, smiling and laughing.

"Her name is Edorra," Raykuum said, narrating the vision he was revealing to me. "I don't know where she is, or what happened to her. But this is what I thought would be at the very end. Me and Edorra, together at the table."

We separated, letting go of each other's hands, and opened our eyes.

"I cannot accept that this nothing is at the end."

But outside, through the lens of the orb, the once blinding star which we orbited was turning to dust. The closer we got, and the more time that sped by, the more the flame cooled until finally it was completely snuffed out and disappeared into smoke.

"At the end, there is but chaff," Lejuun grunted.

And we all stood there, at the very end of time, with our hearts in our throats.

The orb stopped, dead still. Stopped spinning, orbiting, and there was nothing left to orbit. We simply stared into the cold nothing. I could not tell if we were still traveling time.

And it really didn't matter. What is time in the nothing? I do not know if we stood there for hours, days, or centuries.

Friedrich Nietzsche once said, "Battle not with monsters, lest ye become a monster. And if you gaze into the abyss, the abyss gazes into you."

This is exactly what happened to the three of us as we stared into the nothing. The nothing stared back and burned its way into our being. The bright, colorful strings within us turned grey, and I felt as if I were turning to stone. A deep, paralyzing depression washed over me. Even breathing was a pointless task.

I had a fleeting thought: we needed to escape this place. But even this small expression of will was crushed by the fatal emptiness. I suppose I'd still be there right now, another victim of the nothing, if we had not been found.

An eye appeared through the lens of the orb of which we gazed out, a rather large eye that took up our entire field of vision. A beautiful brown eye, an eye I knew very well.

The next moment, Lejuun, Raykuum and I were expelled from the orb and we were back in the museum's basement. Juulez stood there alone with Galileo's orb in her hand.

"Put it back in the safe." Lejuun cried.

But Lejuun didn't wait for a response from the stunned Juulez, who started to get pulled into the brown orb herself. He grabbed the orb out of her hand and returned it to the vault on the floor, slamming it shut and closing the lock. He stood back up, holding the finger bone key.

"You don't want to see what that Vortai wants to show you," he told Juulez.

Juulez nodded and embraced all three of us in turn. However, each of us stood cold in her embrace, without returning the expression or emotion.

The world was still falling apart all around us, the ship in which Juulez had come hovered above us. I knew I should have felt gratitude for the rescue, and love for Juulez, and a sense of urgency to get away, but I didn't feel any of those emotions. All three of us stared out in silence as the transport orb rose out of the basement and into the wheel above.

"I'll send Jaan and Teum back down with some tools. They'll bring up the whole vault," said Juulez.

She could tell that we were not in our right minds.

She took the bone from Lejuun as we passed through the hatch and into the Great Room in the belly of the ship. Inside the ship, there was a stir of activity. Juulez barked out orders and Jaan and Teum raced to the tool room to retrieve tools to pull the safe from the basement floor. As they exited the chamber, they ran by two beings we did not recognize.

As I scanned the room, I saw a whole new cast of characters, at least ten to twenty new beings, resting against the walls or sitting on the floor. The caveman still lay sleeping on the fragment, but now was joined by a coyote, an otter, a goose, a fox, lizard, and a few other beasts. A barn owl was perched on the railing of the spiral staircase.

Muurchia stood before us, smiling ear to ear.

"We went back to the tavern to get the others," he said, arms spread wide.

They certainly had. It looked as if they had transferred everything from the back room of the tavern into the ship, plants and all. The Great Room, its vines now bursting with life, felt like the jungle room at the zoo.

"We got them. All of them."

I know I should have shared in Muurchia's excitement. It was no small feat in the midst of the apocalypse happening all around us to pull anyone from the flames, but I felt hollow. I tried to push a grin at Muurchia, and then turned and wandered down the tunnel toward the galley. Lejuun and Raykuum followed me. We must have looked like three angry teenagers lumbering down the halls of a high school.

The three of us dropped into three empty places at a random table in the dining hall, and there we looked at each other, speechless. Around us, others were engaged in lively conversation, which was understandable given the earth-shaking events that were occurring around us, yet we remained stoic.

After a few minutes, Mira came into the galley and over to our table. We looked up at her vacantly and then back down at the table. Mira took a breath and took a seat across from me and next to Raykuum. Wisely, she sat with us until one of us was ready to speak. It was Raykuum.

"We saw the end. There's nothing."

"Maybe," Mira replied.

"No," Lejuun said. "Not maybe. We saw it."

"Yes, maybe," Mira countered. "You may have witnessed an end, but that's all it is—an end. One of many possible endings. Existence isn't a single line, but infinite layers of lines wrapped together, wound like a rope. Yes, one strand may fray and lead to nothing, but another may lead somewhere else. I choose the table."

She placed both of her hands on the table, palms down.

"See," she continued. "Put your hands here."

We looked at her, refusing to move.

"Just do it."

Raykuum acquiesced, and placed his hands on the table first, followed by Lejuun. Then they all three looked at me.

"Okay," I said. "All right." I placed my hands on the table, palms down.

The tables in the galley, like everything else on the ship, were made of some exotic slab of crystallized rock, so at first, all I could feel was the cold stone of the table's surface. But then, we watched as energy, light, and ribbons of color gathered in Mira's hands and emptied onto the table's surface and spread to our colorless fingers. I had not noticed, but the experience with the nothing not only left us feeling empty and cynical, it had drained our bodies of all color and pulsing light.

Then, the table became the table from Raykuum's vision, his deep desire, the table on Payraydayzay, with his Edorra. A solid slab of white stone, possibly marble or granite, was majestically set for a royal banquet, with an endless string of lanterns hung from above. On the table were ornate vases, plates, jugs, and hands, millions of brilliant hands emitting ribbons of color and light which wove into each other, creating an elaborate tapestry so vast that you could not tell where the table's surface ended and where the beings began.

"There are many possible endings," Mira whispered. "Just as there are the many new beginnings that can follow. Now, if you three are done staring into the abyss, there is something I want you to see."

She stood up with the strength and fight of a valkyrie and moved with command to the portal. We slowly peeled our hands from the table and unenthusiastically followed her down the wagon spoke to the Great Room. The vision of the table had done nothing to quell the overwhelming sense of hopelessness we each carried.

The tableau that greeted us there was quite a scene: the entire crew and all the refugees crammed into the cavernous space to witness what was about to take place.

Around the circle, every alcove now had a small spinning orb, except for one empty altar in the wall where Jaan and Teum stood holding the iron safe they had pulled from the floor in the museum basement.

With every eye upon them, Teum held the box out for Jaan, who opened it with the finger bone, pulled the orb from within and quickly transferred it into its notch in the wall before anyone could get sucked in. The crowd exploded in celebration, cheering and hugging each other, as all eight orbs rotated in their proper designated places, filling the Great Room with the song of a thousand angels.

Raykuum, Lejuun and I remained apathetic.

Lejuun, who was next to me, put his hand on my shoulder. Then he turned business-like and headed up the staircase into the cockpit. Raykuum, Juulez and I followed. Professor Yuung was at the helm. The ship had traveled far enough away from the debris field that we could now see the totality of the destruction from end to end. The earth had crumbled into millions of tiny fragments, drifting away from each other. I didn't think my heart could sink to a sadder place, but seeing the dead world sent it there.

The five of us stood for a long time at the window, watching as the distance widened between the wheel and the ground-up remains of earth.

Once it had been quiet for several hours, and the debris field was a faint line in the distance, Ariance crept up the stairs and came to us, her baby sleeping in her arms.

"Oh, Oakruum, Juulez—Come and see."

She turned and danced right back down the stairs and we followed. We found the Great Room almost empty, besides a handful of napping mammals and the caveman still lying on the black rock. But as the man sat up to welcome us, it wasn't a caveman at all, but Axzum, his true self returning to the surface, the space voyager I had first met in the woods, up in the mountains that snowy night, tall and strong, straight and true.

"He may not recognize you yet," Ariance said to us. "He's still recovering."

"I understand more than you could ever know," I said, smiling at the sight of my beloved brother.

"I want you to have the honor," Ariance said to me, repositioning the baby in her arms.

"The honor?" I asked.

And she handed me the child, who I pulled into my chest and held tight. The experience of holding the child should have provided beautiful feelings of joy and wonder, but I felt as if I were still staring into the abyss.

I approached the fragment on which Axzum sat, rubbing his face and looking around. His eyes met mine, and he focused in and raised his hand to greet me as if he had a vague memory of my face. Then, he climbed down from the fragment and stood before me, looking me over like a scientist.

I held the baby out for him to hold.

Axzum looked down at the child and put his hands and arms beneath her, and I emptied her into his care and took a step back. The light that emitted from the ever-bright and glowing child increased its intensity and flooded into Axzum's body until he, too, was just as radiant.

"ꟼꟼꟼ ꟼꟼꟼ ꟼꟼꟼ," Axzum finally spoke, his eyes moving from the gift in his arms and into my eyes and into the depths of my being.

"The end is the beginning."

CHAPTER SIXTEEN

THE GOLDEN TREE

In the year 444 BC, earth time, a Greek thinker by the name of Empedocles posited that there is a force in this universe that is totally and completely dominant and unifies all things. Not knowing what else to call this force or exactly how to describe it, he labeled this force "love" and made a most provocative claim that this force is never still nor static, that it is always on the move, always changing, always growing, always transforming. Nothing in this universe ever comes to be or perishes, he said. Instead, all of this, everything, is suffering continual rearrangement.

Out of the remnants of a destroyed star comes the birth of a new one. From the dying collapse of an entire universe springs another, and beings for which the universe and systems originate also transfer their nature from one expression to the next. Stardust to seed, vineyard branch to crawling creature, to spinning Vortai of gravity and light.

One is never created or extinguished, our energy simply transfers from one thing to the other. The Nuul counterbalances this process by dividing, separating, and turning the most dynamic entities catatonic.

The very last time I saw the great planet of Gaieos, not one stone lay upon another. It had been completely torn apart, and its pieces scattered across a wide spray of space, each fragment a grave holding countless bodies, not dead, but hanging in suspended animation, in infinite darkness.

Axzum, still holding Ella, had ventured down the corridor to the library. Ariance, Juulez and I followed.

Raykuum joined us as well.

In the grand study, the Shaman sat on the large rock in the middle of the room, meditating, and several other beings, refugees who had escaped the apocalypse, sat in various places throughout the room, quietly watching the drama outside unfold from the window. All of us relieved to be reunited after our own dark slumber.

Raykuum shifted his weight, which caused us to share our tension with him. We fully understood his longing, and sought to provide as much compassion as we could. Suddenly, a voice echoed in the room.

"They say a shaman is one who knows, but in actuality, we know no more than anyone else."

We all turned and looked at the Shaman, who stared back at us.

"The knowledge is already within you. A Shaman is simply a guide to the knowledge buried deep within. Come, sit with me, and let me be your guide."

We moved away from the window as the debris field that had been Earth disappeared from sight and populated the seats around the Shaman.

"It's yet another great paradox," the Shaman said. "In order to truly tap into the knowledge within, one does not think. In fact, the more one thinks, the further away the knowledge gets. Do not think. Just be."

As he closed his eyes, the Shaman's face burst alive with ribbons of light and color and energy, and his body emitted an indigo blue aura. Axzum, Ariance, Raykuum, and Juulez had their eyes closed as well, and although their glow lacked the Shaman's intensity, they each had a glowing aura, magenta, blue, and green.

I looked over my own body, but no aura appeared. In fact, my body had turned a lifeless shade of grey since experiencing the nothing at the end and seemed to grow darker with every breath I took.

My mind jumped from one dark thought after another like a flat rock skipping across a pond until it was numb. The ripples faded, everything stilled, and my consciousness was released from the prison of my body. My mind's eye rose out and over my form, circling the library, traveling through the window and out into space, where I orbited the wheel, sometimes outside the ship looking in, and sometimes inside the ship looking out.

In the galley, space voyagers gathered at tables. In the bunkhouse, others rested. In the cocoon room, Mira stood, examining the Ninth Orb spinning in its notch. In the cockpit, Lejuun and Professor Yuung poured over their notes. Every inch of the ship was now covered with brilliant vines, flowers, and fruits. The once empty, lonely wheel transformed into a bustling village with a sprawling vineyard. My consciousness made its rounds, covering every part of the ship, then returned to the library, hovered over my body for a moment before descending back into it.

Was that it? I wondered. Was that the knowledge the Shaman wanted to reveal? If so, it wasn't profound and lacked illumination.

"And now," the Shaman interrupted my inner monologue. "Let us begin."

In an instant, I was no longer in the library, but standing upon my shining core with the three minuscule volcanoes and the red rose, looking out into the swirling universe within myself.

"Have you even begun to explore this place?" asked the Shaman, who was no longer sitting on the block, but standing next to me on my bursting heart.

"Explore? I didn't know that was possible."

"Too many spend their time looking out from here, just watching, stargazing. Instead of living out their true call as a space voyager."

I looked out into the wild chaos crashing out before me, swirling, shooting bodies of light, galaxies, stars, and planetary systems. The uncontrolled mayhem scared me, and my leg shook at the very thought of stepping out into it.

Without expression, the Shaman held his arms out as if opening an invisible door for me. I took a breath and stepped off the pinpoint and out into what I thought was empty space. But when my foot fell, it landed on a safe and solid path. Incredulous, the trail before me was translucent, almost invisible, but each step revealed a clearer path with new, intersecting trails verging off in all directions.

"How can this be? I thought this was the center."

The Shaman laughed. "There's no such thing. No one ever arrives. There's always another door to open, another path to take."

"How do I know which way to go?" I asked the Shaman as we walked together on the ribbon-like path within the cosmos of my own being.

"The way matters not. Think about where you are. There is no destination, really."

With every step I took, there was a distinct change, as geometric shapes and patterns danced, and rippled out from me as if my emergence was creating new things.

I walked on, trying to fully experience every step that was given to me. We hiked until we came to a grand staircase with see-through stairs that led down into a star with its worlds swirling around it.

We descended into the tiny planetary system, passing gas giants that were maybe the size of sports stadiums, and rocky worlds the size of a hot-air balloon. I wondered about Juulez, Axzum, and Ariance, whether they were having a similar experience within themselves—was the Shaman their guide as well?

The staircase emptied onto a small moon, so small that I thought one could walk all the way around its wooded and grassy surface in about twenty minutes. We walked in the tall grass, playing with the tops of the waving blades as we went, until the trail opened up into a familiar clearing, one with a cabin, surrounded by a patch of meadow, with sunflowers and wildflowers where the grass met the wood.

I stopped in my tracks as the shack door opened and a white ball rolled out, bounced down the steps, and barreled across the grass, as a small beam of light tore out of the cabin after it.

Astonished, I took a step back. This was not what I expected to find here, a small child playing with a ball in a flower filled meadow. The child ran after the ball with light and determination, and then kicked it with everything he had. The ball flew toward me, and I caught it, chest level, with both hands, and examined it for a moment.

"What are you doing?" the child said. "No hands!"

Embarrassed, I dropped the ball to my feet and kicked it back.

"Come on," he cried as he trapped the ball like a pro. "Let's play."

Without hesitation, I jumped, skipped, and ran after the boy, who cheered as if he had just scored a goal. We kicked the ball all around that meadow for what seemed like an entire afternoon, as if nothing else mattered. And in a genuine sense, nothing else does. And, the greatest treasure of all, I am there with him still, right now, kicking that ball around.

When we finally tired, we sat down at the steps of the shack, and the Shaman joined.

"That was fun," I smiled at the boy, and then at the Shaman. "But I don't understand. I thought you were going to show me some profound knowledge, some cosmic mystery revealed."

"This is all you ever need to know," the Shaman responded, and then he looked at the child. "You're getting big, Oakruum, you're looking good out there."

"I've been growing," the child responded.

"I know," the Shaman said. "Keep going."

"Oakruum," I whispered. "You're Oakruum?"

"Of course," the boy shrugged. "Who else would I be?" The child opened his arms wide. "See?"

The boy, like myself, was a being of light, and had within his center his own cosmos, with galaxies, planetary systems, and trails to hike.

Where do those paths lead? I wondered. Would they take me to another meadow, with another Oakruum with his own cosmos within containing even more trails to explore?

"Yes. Your Being is infinite," the Shaman said. "But that's not entirely what I wanted you to know."

"Then what?" I asked. "What more could there be?"

The boy reached out and touched my cheek with his hand. As he looked at me with his big, bright eyes, his face bursting with ribbons of color and light, he whispered,

"I love you, Oakruum."

I was caught without words. "I love you, too" sprang into my head, but never made it to my lips. It didn't need to.

"You've been growing," the boy said. "Keep going."

Then, he leaned into me, and gave me an embrace, the light and energy of our cores radiating like the sun.

The next moment I was back in the library at my seat, the Shaman was still seated on the block in the middle of the room, and the alarm was sounding from the cockpit down the corridor. As I looked around the circle, I watched the others awaken from their meditation.

Raykuum broke into laughter upon seeing me.

"What?"

"Oakruum. You have the look of a child."

"Check in the mirror," I countered.

It was true, we all looked like children now, sitting around the Shaman in the library, each of our auras glowing bright. The entire room couldn't help but break into laughter. I looked over at Juulez, now a giggling little girl, with big brown eyes and dimply cheeks. Axzum and Ariance, too, were miniature versions of themselves.

"There are many more paths to explore," the Shaman said. "This is just the beginning."

We nodded and smiled excitedly at the wise elder and at each other. I, for one, couldn't wait to go back and venture deeper within. I think we might have all returned right then and there, if the cockpit alarm hadn't signaled.

We all took one last deep breath in the chair, an attempt to save and preserve the transformative experience before we slowly rose to our feet.

As we stood up and made our way to the threshold, the connections we held with our core weakened and our auras faded. By the time we traveled down the corridor and joined the crew and the cockpit, we were no longer children, but grown adults, a disappointment to us all.

In the cockpit, the entire crew, and even some refugees, had gathered to witness our arrival to Payraydayzay. Most of the newcomers had not seen their home planet since it was shattered so long ago, or not so long ago, depending on whose watch you go by.

As we got closer to the asteroid belt, the gasps and whispers from the onlookers got louder and more frequent. The teardrops had come, and the black taffy-like ooze we had seen before draped from one rock to the other, creating a messy, greasy-looking spider web in space.

"Soon, every world in this system will look like this," Muurchia remarked, "If it doesn't already."

"And then mother star at the center will be put out," added Professor Yuung.

"Then, an endless nothing," Lejuun said.

A wave of fear traveled through the group as the web drew closer, almost taking up the entire window now.

"We don't have to do this," Lejuun said. "We can find another system."

A murmur spread through the crowd with comments such as, "There are plenty of worlds for us to live on, and there's nothing here for us now. We should move on."

The fear was taking root, so I stepped forward.

"Payraydayzay is our home. We can't leave now."

"Our home is gone," countered Lejuun. "We must preserve what is left. We must retreat."

"No." I said. "This is the moment we begin again."

"This is the end." Lejuun said. "You've seen it yourself. You know it."

Lejuun and I looked at each other for a tense moment. He was right. I had been there. I saw it with my own eyes. I knew how it all would end.

But then, I looked at Juulez, to Raykuum, and Mira.

"Lejuun, the end…" I tried to interrupt him, but at that very moment, the bulbous end of a long, black tentacle reached out from its snare and attached itself to the top of the domed window of the ship. There were shouts and screams, and everyone scrambled for cover. Some dove to the floor, hands over their heads, some ran for the stairs.

Outside, the tears dripped down the window on all sides; the streaks fell like a curtain closing. Juulez grabbed my hand and pulled me toward the staircase with everyone else, but my attention was focused on what was happening outside. The glob was covering the ship and pulling it into its lair. It would not be long until it had broken through the hatches and imprisoned everyone on board.

There was little time left to act. My heart was racing to the point of collapse. The crew trampled down the spiral staircase. Lejuun and Professor Yuung were the last to leave, followed by Juulez and me. As I stepped out of the cockpit, I looked up to see the top-glass hatch open up and the shadows empty into the chamber.

Everyone flared into a panic. Juulez began tugging on my hand, pulling me down the stairway toward the Great Room, but I didn't move.

"It'll be okay, Juulez."

I let go of her hand.

"Oakruum."

"Keep going," I told her. "I'll catch up."

Juulez gave me a trusting glance and continued down the stairs, joining the throng huddled together in the Great Room, finding refuge wherever it could be found. I stepped back out into the center of the cockpit where the hologram planets flickered off as the nothing replaced them. The flowers and fruit shriveled on the vines as the Nuul drained their life and vitality with a cold ooze, leaving dead branches in its wake. It spilled onto the floor like blood and crawled toward the center where I stood. Visions of the shadows ensnaring me and then cascading down the steps to enslave every occupant ran through my mind.

I closed my eyes, raised my arms in a V and made the now familiar journey down into the depths of me, across the bridge, through the gates, to the center of my mandala. Then down into the depths of the sea, through the great star-filled expanse, to the little beaming world, down the stairway to the grassy meadow where the little boy played. Then I stepped up onto the front porch of the cabin and through the door.

To my surprise, inside the shack, instead of a hearth, a cot, a table and a light, I found the golden tree, its branches reaching out in every direction and its leaves shivering with energy, making it look as if the tree was on fire. The golden tree wasn't rooted to the ground, rather floating in space. I orbited the magnificent tree a few times as if I was its moon and then absorbed into the noble tree's branches. I became the tree. ילילי. I was fire, heart, sacrifice and fruit.

I had a swell of thankfulness rush over me as I experienced every joyful moment I ever had all at once. I was kicking the ball and running through the field with the youngster within. I was caught in a rainstorm in a cornfield with Juulez, drenched, laughing and together. I was back in the old wooden shack, reading in my orange chair as Cooper lay sleeping by the hearth.

Every place I was, was *now*, right *now*, and the only expression, the only feeling I could possibly have, from kicking the ball, to caught in the rain, to reading in the chair, to standing in the cockpit as the shadows descended, and, yes, even staring into the scattered nothing at the end of time, was and is, thankfulness. They were all just little nows within an infinite existence. There is only *now*— nothing else matters.

I opened my eyes in the cockpit once again to see a dome of white light formed around me; the shadows pressed against it from every side. For the moment, they were abated.

I looked down into the Great Room below where everyone had grouped together. I put a hand of reassurance out to them, and there was a moment of calm, and then all attention shifted away from me to one of the tunnel openings where there was sound and movement.

There was a gasp as a figure appeared in the passageway entrance—Mira, who was holding with both hands the Ninth Orb. The bright spinning ball floated just above her hands.

The Ethiopian woman glowed like a celestial being, her shawl a sparkling silver garment. She walked to the spiral staircase in the center of the room, where she held out the orb like a holy offering. All the orbs in the wall, almost simultaneously, popped out of their notches and, like bullets, flew to the angel, where each zipped around the Ninth Orb in a synchronized dance. Mira looked like she was holding a giant atom with eight electrons orbiting a blazing nucleus. The exhilarating power of the collective orbs finally united, caused a storm of energy, light, and gravity to swirl through the room.

The air within the circular room began funneling into a hurricane. Every being in the room was bowled over, and those who had nothing to brace themselves with were dragged toward the Vortai.

The room melted into chaos as the orbs grew in size and intensity. If she didn't move soon, the swirling seed would consume the entire ship. The angel walked slowly up the steps, still holding the cosmic seed and the eight smaller spheres orbiting so fast they each transformed into a circular beam of continuous light.

As Mira stepped into the cockpit, I had to grip the control panel bar with both hands to keep from being pulled into the cyclone. She held the star up above her head, and with a swoosh, the shadows haunting the cockpit were sucked into the spinning orb and disappeared.

Then the angel locked eyes with me.

"Oakruum. My Koinonae—my desire."

"Yes. I remember."

"It's up to you now."

"I know."

"Restore the Three Sisters."

"I will not fail this time."

"I know," she said with a gentle smile. And then, with a burst of energy and light, she was consumed by the giant atom. She wasn't destroyed or killed or lost in any way. No. Mira, in that moment, became part of that seed, along with the other beings who offered themselves to the Oolah. The Crow, the Prophet, my father, very much alive and bound together for a larger purpose.

The growing ball of dancing energy and light rose within the cockpit toward the opening hatch above. Outside, the ooze still covered the windows and hovered at the entrance, threatening to drop in once again. But as the orb ascended, its power intensified, causing the darkness without to pull away from the ship.

Once it was free of the cockpit and the top hatch shut, the angel grew two or three times its size in just a few seconds. The inside of the glowing, spinning ball swarmed with all kinds of plant life, white, gold, and silver. A white vine with golden fruit and silver dandelions with glistening papas of feathery bristles. What I thought was a white moth turned out to be an elegant orchid that opened up to full bloom and then transformed into angel wings, completely covered with eyes.

The ball rose out, and into the dark web suspended between the asteroids. As it grew and moved into place, the ooze that blanketed the field was ripped away from the rocks and moved toward the growing seed. I wanted to defend the sprouting seed from the surrounding shadows, but the shadows were not attacking. Rather, the orb was willingly wrapping itself with the Nuul. The black ooze poured in from all directions and poured around the seed until it was entirely covered with a dark ocean of sludge.

When the last beam of light disappeared under the blanket of shadows, a herd of passengers scurried up the stairs to see the murky, black sea floating out in space, its waves cresting, creating light grey crowns. The mass before us began to shift and change, moving from a glistening liquid form into a thick, calcified, solid piece. Like batter being baked in an oven, the waves froze and turned cake-like. The result was a cracked and brittle ball of dirt. The menacing shadow had turned to soil.

It remained like that for just a few moments before the first mighty sprouts poked through the dirt in holy defiance. Seedlings sprang forth across and all around the surface of the crusted sphere and quickly grew up and out. They looked like tree saplings, but bright gold. Soon, these golden saplings reached into space, sprouting branches on all sides and twisting every which way. The trunks grew thick and sturdy and cut into the grey matter they had broken through, and eventually the ashen earth was gone and every golden trunk was connected to the others at their bases. The ball of sludge was gone and, in its place, grew a golden tree, stretching rapidly in every direction. I couldn't believe it. It was the same golden tree that dwelt within me.

How can this be? Is everything occurring simultaneously, inside and outside?

The glowing branches soon flowed around the ship and in front of the window. Professor Yuung tried his best to navigate the ship through the expanding branches that were curling at the ends like fiddlehead ferns. To avoid getting trapped in a dense thicket of overlapping branches, the professor followed one limb, growing faster than the others. Like riding a roller coaster, we hung on as we spiraled alongside the branch, dodging every other limb that shot by. The pointed end of the treetop we followed targeted one asteroid drifting alone in space. As the bough approached the rock, I thought it may avoid it, or maybe wrap around it like a vine. Instead, the branch stabbed it with its pointy head, and devoured it like a snake eating a mouse. All around us, the tree branches consumed asteroids. As the limbs engulfed the fragments, golden leaves sprang from their twigs, filling the sky with a most delightful explosion of life.

We could see the outline of the devoured rocks as they traveled down the inside of the tree, toward the thick trunk, which widened and strengthened with each digested meteor. Then, the tree curled, every limb and branch curled like a nautilus shell, and the entire newborn tree world set into its rotation, gravity intensifying, which caused even distant asteroids in the vast belt to drift toward it. The new world absorbed each asteroid as it approached. The center of the planet, fueled no doubt by the angel and the seed, grew brighter and larger with each added fragment.

Inside the cockpit, the great cloud of witnesses stood in awe, tears streaming, faces and bodies bursting with bright ribbons of color. I pulled Juulez so close that the celestial bodies dwelling within us passed effortlessly from one body to the other. A flame flickered above our heads, Axzum and Ariance standing next to us experienced the same gift. Raykuum alone stared longingly out the window at the enlarging world.

"Soon," I whispered to Raykuum, "Very soon."

Raykuum smiled at me with a hopeful grin, and then we were all knocked off of our feet as a wild branch speared the ship and swallowed us whole.

As we stumbled to our feet, I could see that we were now inside one of the golden tree branches, traveling toward the increasingly larger boughs and branches. If the outside of the golden tree was bursting with life, the inside was a hundred-fold as every kind of tree, vine, and flower sprang up and met our window as we sped by. The inside of the tree was a jungle of exotic orchids of all sizes and colors hanging off the inside of the branches. As we traveled deeper into the tree, the vegetation became much more varied, more dense and more colorful.

We flew into a larger bough, where we met a stream of water cascading over a ledge. It tumbled down into an even larger limb. Below us, a glistening river valley buzzed with light and life, lavish palm trees and tropical plants clamored for space with huge fruit trees and grapevines.

Muurchia pointed to a clearing full of grass, pussy willow and golden wheat.

"There. Set the ship down right there."

"Here?" I said, "We're going to land here? Do you think it's safe?"

Muurchia laughed. "You've never been safer. Welcome home, Oakruum."

With those words, the entire cockpit seemed to exhale as elation replaced our anxiety. As Yuung set us down in the grass, we could see a long, wide path of wild wheat stalks leading from the clearing and spreading out to the horizon. The ship landed softly in the grass and we filed down the stairs, through the Great Room and onto the receiving ground of Payraydayzay, which instantly poured new life and energy into each of us, rendering us all whole.

We wandered out into the meadow, each of us at their own pace, every eye gawking at the utopia before us. It felt like standing in a gigantic tube with the plant life hanging down from the roof above.

Lejuun stumbled into the golden field, fell to his knees, and wept. As his tears nourished the soil, his body and soul filled with light, making his resurrection complete. He had been trapped in the darkness for a long time; now he was free.

Jaan and Teum went into the woods to explore. Muurchia laid down in the grass, laughing, his arms and legs splayed out. Professor Yuung headed for the river, which flowed swiftly through a bed of large boulders.

Juulez took my hand and led me to the bank and into the stream, the water flowing over our toes and feet as we stepped from stone to stone. When we got to the middle of the river, Juulez sat down on a fully submerged rock and let the water flow over her back and shoulders. She looked up at me and slapped the water, inviting me to join her.

We sat together in the river for a long time, watching the stream go by, our fingertips playing with the current. Then, I laid back and let my whole body, from head to toe, become completely submerged in the river. One moment the river was flowing over me, under me, around me, and through me, and then in the next moment, I was the river, the whole river from one end to the other.

I was connected to every drop, and I melted out into the rest of the golden tree. I was every twig and leaf stretching into the cosmos, every branch flexing like a bicep, and I was the core, the thick trunk, and the deep roots of the massive oak. In the inner depths of my being, within my unconscious self, the same thing was happening.

I saw the big asteroids and the chunks of old Payraydayzay dissolving inside the tree limbs as they moved towards the center of the newly forming world. And as the fragments came apart, beings, Payraydayzians who hung in the darkness of suspended animation, were freed from their tombs.

As the shadows had spilled out of Lejuun, these beings experienced the same emancipation. The shadows, as soon as they were expelled from the bodies, were instantly eliminated, the darkness being overcome by the light. The newly freed beings were cradled by the tree, given a soft bough on which to awaken, and awaken they did. The long slumber ended as each being began to stir in their own time, hundreds upon one bough, thousands upon the trunk, millions within the whole tree.

The graveyard of cold stone where imprisoned souls had been held captive was gone, souls set free, the stones used to build a new home.

I rose out of the water, still next to Juulez, who sat up as well.

"I wonder if this is heaven," I said to her, looking over my translucent body once again swimming with colorful ribbons of light.

"Maybe," she replied with excitement. "I always thought of heaven as a mythical place, a flat cartoon where angels sit on clouds and play harps. But this is real."

We connected, palm to palm, the river still cascading over and around us.

Raykuum came to the river and then splashed across

the water in front of us, but with his eyes fixed on something beyond and behind us.

"Raykuum," Juulez said, "What is it?"

"Look for yourself," Raykuum replied, pointing toward the far horizon. Juulez and I climbed to our feet and turned to see what Raykuum was seeing. Way out in the distance, in the middle of the wide golden swath of wheat, a being was running toward us and waving. Soon, a large flock moved towards us, waving and crying out and connecting with one another, embracing each other like long-lost friends.

"They're alive," Raykuum said.

Raykuum stood with us on the rocks in the river, watching the oncoming throng increase tenfold. As the first of the newly freed citizens got to the river, Raykuum spotted who he was looking for.

"There she is." He waded out of the water and started running full sprint toward the parade. From within the jubilant crowd, a voice, a small voice, shouted above the others,

"Raykuum."

Raykuum raced to Edorra, and they slammed into each other with a grand embrace.

Other refugees from the ship, those who had been exiled on Gaieos with the rest of us for so long, also spotted old friends and family in the multitude of beings swarming into the valley and hurried to them.

Muurchia was reunited with his wife, Clairias.

Teum found his brother, Grinnell, a head and shoulders above the rest of the crowd.

Jaan and her father shared a tearful embrace.

And when Juulez finally saw the face in the crowd that she had been searching for, she bellowed: "Momma!"

Juulez ran to her mother, Miretta, where they shared in a long, emotional reunion. Nigel, the old grey cat, ran a figure eight between their legs as they embraced.

Raykuum brought Edorra over to us for a joyous introduction. The laughter lasted for many hours as the community grew by the thousands every minute.

Amid this long celebration, I noticed Jaan and Teum reemerge from the woods and stand at the edge of the forest. I nudged Axzum and gestured towards the duo. Amazingly, they each had a glowing orb in their hand. Both orbs were gold, which took turns zipping around and through the two space voyagers' bodies.

"I think you want to see this," Jaan hollered to us, and turned back into the woods, Teum close behind.

Axzum, Ariance holding Ella, Juulez and I, Raykuum and Edorra, followed them. We walked along the side of a small brook, a tributary of the larger river, through the tall trees and clusters of spiraled, stemmed fiddlehead ferns at the forest floor. The hike took us to the base of a grassy hill where a glistening object sparkled at the top.

When we got to the crest of the hill, we stood underneath a grand tree; its limbs and branches held leaves which were translucent, allowing bright ribbons of color to be seen within. The leaves spread above us like a canopy with hanging clusters of fruit. But the fruit wasn't grapes, nor apples nor pears. The clusters were made of glowing spiral spheres.

"Not just gold," Jaan pointed out. "Every kind."

Sure enough, the clusters hung down in every imaginable color. The grand choir of a thousand voices blended in perfect harmony. Axzum pulled a blue orb from the cluster and held it out so it hovered over his palm.

"This is just the beginning."

We spent the rest of the evening celebrating, reconnecting with old friends, and exploring our new home. We all sat in the grass on that hill underneath the orb tree, enjoying its sweet cantata, and watching the ongoing celebration in the wheat-covered valley below.

Later that night, I laid down with Juulez on that hill, under the golden tree and I made the long journey back, out of the tree limb, down the front steps of the cabin, into the meadow with the little boy, up the grand staircase, past the little planet with the red rose, through the mandala, to the drawbridge at the castle gate.

I found myself, once again, outside of the cabin, on my back in the snow after falling down the stairs. My face caught a flurry of flakes as they came down from the night sky. I felt as if I were traveling time.

Kisses from heaven.

There, on the cold ground, I took my final breath, my body turned to stone, and my soul was set free.

Our stories are eternal, part of the winding wheel of infinity, which is circular, sometimes fraying to the end and other times bringing us back to the start. As I've said, these events may have not yet taken place. Or they may have occurred a long time ago. It matters not. These events are constantly happening *now*.

I met the space voyager on my one hundred and second birthday, or so I thought.

As it turns out, I have no birthday, and neither do you. None of us are ever created or destroyed, but we are simply changed.

All of this, everything, including you and I, is suffering continual rearrangement.

EPILOGUE

THE FINAL WORD

Many moons have passed since that celebration underneath the golden tree, and the first days of the restoration of Payraydayzay.

The core of the planet grew and expanded as it matured. The limb was flooded by magma, and the golden tree gave way to bedrock, mountains, valleys, deep oceans, and dry ground.

In the meantime, our new crew, the Esregg, caretakers of the Three Sisters, set to work preparing for the journeys ahead. Many trips were taken to Apotheon, where partnerships were forged and resources shared. In the Wake, noble sacrifices were made and new seeds created.

Raykuum and Edorra, with help from Jaan and Teum, were able to recover Raykuum's ship from the fragment on Gaieos where we had abandoned it.

Payraydayzay became inhabitable once again, and settlements were established on the new world. Seeds were sown, forests and fields grown, and a new table built for gathering feasts.

On the one hundredth millennial anniversary of the rebirth of Payraydayzay, we gathered in the newly constructed temple to celebrate. We ate, sang, danced, and held a commemorative ceremony using gold pollen. As I stood next to Juulez on the elevated platform with Axzum and Ariance, and watched the gold dust escape the round opening atop the glass dome, I knew the mother of our world, Mira, was smiling upon us.

"The angel's dream is made real today," Juulez

whispered.

I watched the dust drift into the night sky, turn to light, and beam out in every direction into the cosmos. After a long moment, an old, familiar feeling rose up. I turned to Juulez.

"Juulez."

"What is it? What's the matter?"

"I don't know. Suddenly, I'm afraid."

"Afraid? Of what?"

"That, somehow, Mira's dream is *not* made real today. That you, me, all of this—its not real at all. Is this just another delusion?"

She grabbed my hand and held it tight.

"Don't be silly. Not only is this really happening. This is really happening, now and always."

She kissed my cheek.

"Oakruum, you found me." She whispered in my ear. "And, on the way, you found you."

Only hope lies ahead now. I hope this manuscript is delivered to you in time and that these words bring you illumination. I hope for a new seed to bring rebirth to Gaieos and release to all those entombed within its scattered fragments. I hope to see you again, my most excellent Theophilus, my dear child, Christian. You've always had the eye—just ask the questions.

And now, here is the final word of this manuscript. It is a Payraydayzian word. No one is sure of its origin, but it is believed to be as old as the universe itself and may go back beyond that to the universe before this one. A word that, when spoken, sharpens the eye, enhancing the questioner's vision:

ꙮꙮꙮꙮꙮꙮ

There is no easy translation; it means both unchanging and ever-changing at the same time—a great paradox in one word.

The great river ꙮꙮꙮꙮꙮꙮ
While constant
It is dynamic
As a world, star, or soul

As everything
It is with me
It is with You
You are now

You've always been
Always will be
With every breath
A new Being born

Whether indwelling
A crow, snake, mouse, or tree
You do not dwell in this universe
The universe dwells in You

Discover that piece of You
That was never born,
You will find that part of You
That will never die

ꙮꙮꙮꙮꙮꙮ

Printed in Dunstable, United Kingdom